Winner of the coveted Golden Heart Award, Patricia Gaffney garnered rave reviews for her first Historical Romance, *Sweet Treason:*

"A stunning debut. I foresee a shining future for this bright new star."

—*Romantic Times*

"The action is non-stop, the writing at times reminiscent of Kathleen Woodiwiss. One of the better historicals to come out recently."

—*Rendezvous*

Now Patricia Gaffney has fulfilled the promise of her first novel with *FORTUNE'S LADY:*

"Patricia Gaffney is a sparkling new talent destined to win readers' hearts!"

—*Romantic Times*

PASSIONATE ENEMIES

"Get out of here right now and don't ever come back!" she yelled.

"Why so angry, Cass?" he asked softly. Because of what we did? Or what we didn't have time to do?" His hand on the soft nape of her neck silenced whatever reply she was going to make. He watched her lovely gray eyes darken to pewter, then kissed her as gently as he'd ever kissed a woman. He felt her breath on his cheek, warm and sweet. Heard her soft sigh. Stepped back as if he'd been burned.

Belatedly, Cass brought up a clenched fist and scrubbed furiously at her lips. "You're vile." He only smiled. She looked around for something to throw.

"You'd better go," she said boldly to his retreating back. "If you ever touch me again, I'll blacken your eye as well as your jaw!"

He turned at the door. "I'll remember that. Will it be before or after I take you to bed, do you think? Just so I'll know when to duck."

Fortune's Lady

Patricia Gaffney

A LEISURE BOOK®

April 2000

Published by
Dorchester Publishing Co., Inc.
276 Fifth Avenue
New York, NY 10001

ISBN 0-8439-4801-9

The name "Leisure Books" and the stylized "L" with design are trademarks of Dorchester Publishing Co., Inc.

Printed in the United States of America.

I

"RECEIVE, ALMIGHTY LORD, THY UNWORTHY SON, PATrick Flynn Merlin, into Thy care. In Thy boundless mercy, forgive his most grievous sins and grant that he may reside with Thee in the kingdom of heaven forever. Amen."

"Amen."

The Reverend Juvenal Ormsby closed his prayerbook with a snap, uttered a few more pious generalities and sailed out of the churchyard, black robes billowing. Six hired pallbearers soon followed. The mourners who were left mumbled hasty, embarrassed respects and drifted away, leaving the family alone.

Misery settled a little more heavily on Cassandra Merlin's shoulders as she watched the last of them go. She pulled off the veil her aunt had made her wear over her heavy black hair and let the night breeze cool her face. She had no tears left, but there was a hollow core of loneliness inside her.

I should be grateful, she chided herself tiredly, lifting her gaze from the crude coffin to the clouds gliding across the moon. True, the funeral service had been conducted in scandalous haste, her father's so-called friends had absented themselves in droves, he was being buried on the north side of the church in unconsecrated ground—and yet, it was no more than she'd expected and more than she might have hoped. Felons, after all, weren't usually permitted to be buried in cemeteries at all; instead they were interred at crossroads or in plain open fields, without markers or crosses. Reverend Ormsby had granted to Patrick Merlin's earthly remains this narrow gash of Southwark clay, within sight of Blackfriars Bridge and the Thames sliding unctuously beneath it, for what amounted to a ten-pound bribe—money her aunt could ill afford now, and with which she'd parted with a pointed lack of grace.

"This damp air is unhealthy, Cassandra; Freddy and I are going to the carriage. Besides, he wants his snuff. Don't linger, will you? I've sent the torchbearers away—the moon is bright enough, and after nine o'clock it's another sixpence apiece."

"Yes, Aunt."

"I thought it went as well as it could, everything considered. Thank God it's over! I wonder if I shall ever get the mud out of the hem of this gown? Now remember, Cass, we've only hired the carriage till ten, and after all there's nothing more to do here, is there?"

The Dowager Lady Sinclair slanted her eyes in the direction of the muddy hole at her feet and then looked quickly away, her mouth turning down in a little moue of displeasure. How careless, how tactless, it seemed to say, of her brother to allow things to come to such a pass. She put a manicured hand on her niece's elbow and gave it a sharp squeeze.

"As soon as we're home, Cassandra, we'll have that little talk." Lady Sinclair gathered up her skirts and rustled away.

"Is that she?" Philip Riordan murmured, peering through the peeling branches of a plane tree at the receding figure thirty yards away.

"No. That's the aunt."

Riordan brought his dark-blue gaze back to the woman beside the grave at the bottom of the bumpy, tombstone-dotted hill. All he could make out from this distance was that she was tall and slender, with glossy black hair tied in a heavy knot on top of her head. He brushed leaves from the flat peak of a nearby headstone and perched on it uncomfortably, long legs stretched out. "I don't like it, Oliver. She's even got his hair."

"What's that got to do with anything? She saw him once or twice a year at most; they were never close."

"I don't care. She was his daughter. She's not going to feel kindly disposed toward the men who helped hang him."

Oliver Quinn frowned down at his companion's dark, silver-streaked head. "You may be right, but there's no one else. We have no choice but to approach her."

"I don't like it," Riordan repeated.

"You haven't seen her. She's perfect. Attractive, alluring—exactly the kind of woman Wade pursues. And fortunately for us, she has no bothersome moral scruples to stand in the way of an intimate relationship with him."

Riordan smiled without humor. "I'm familiar with the type."

"I imagine you are," Quinn returned dryly.

"Damn it, Oliver, for all we know she could've been in on the plot *with* Merlin."

"That's absurd."

"Is it?" Riordan stared intently at the silent, utterly still figure in the distance. "We can't afford to take any chances." When he looked up, opal moonlight shone palely on the clean, patrician lines of his face. Suddenly he smiled. "I've got an idea."

Cassandra watched her aunt's retreating back, then closed her eyes briefly, anticipating their "little talk." She turned back to the unfilled grave and rested her chin on her folded hands, but it was impossible to pray. She found herself repeating the minister's platitudes because no words would come from her own heart. But what could she say that would help her father now? He'd died an atheist; the crime for which he'd hanged was heinous indeed. Was even God merciful enough to forgive him?

"Oh, Papa, how could you do it?" she burst out softly. "How could you betray your own country?" She felt swamped by a mixture of anger, shame, and grief. She pictured his flashing black eyes and coal-black hair, the reckless grin. It seemed impossible that he was dead, his restless, exuberant energy extinguished forever. What would make sense of her life now? What could she hope for?

Unbidden, an old memory surfaced. She was in boarding school in Paris, where her aunt lived, and where he'd sent her after her mother's death. He was coming to visit for the first time in more than a year. They were to spend the whole day together, and her eight-year-old heart was bursting with excitement. All morning she waited at the gate in front of the school, until at last Mademoiselle called her to dinner. She waited again all afternoon, jumping up to peer through the black iron bars at every passing horse or carriage. When it grew too dark to see, the headmistress came and took her inside. That night a messenger brought a china doll, with real hair and arms that moved. The scribbled note said that important business had forced him to leave for London a day early. He would see her on his next trip, which he was sure would be soon. He loved his princess very much and was counting on her to be a good little girl.

How much, she asked herself now, had she really changed since that day ten years ago? She'd long since stopped being a good little girl in order to make her father love her—lately, in fact, she'd tried hard to be exactly the opposite—but she'd never given up hope that someday he would love her. Now it was too late.

Her throat ached. "Goodbye, Papa. I love you! Please, God, please forgive him." She carried a sprig of rosemary, for remembrance. Before the tears could start again, she kissed it, threw it into the grave, and turned away.

The two men watched her go. One smiled in grim anticipation as she disappeared among the low-hanging boughs of a weeping willow.

Ely Place was in a section of Holborn that might with kindness be described as "shabby genteel," although one could be forgiven for not readily spotting much evidence of gentility in its sagging townhouses and weedy gardens. Number 47 was no better or worse than its neighbors. Inside, there was too much furniture and not enough heat, and the servants were surly. Lady Sinclair, a dowager baroness used to a life of comparative opulence in Paris, found it all so appallingly squalid that for three weeks she had not even unpacked most of her trunks and persisted in referring to her new quarters as "temporary." How this could be, given the precise nature of their financial condition, her niece was at a loss to understand; but as was her habit, she did not challenge her aunt or encourage in her a more realistic view of things. It would not have done any good.

"Freddy, take your foot off the tea cart this instant. Look at the mud you've gotten on the wheel."

Sir Frederick Sinclair shifted his ponderous buttocks and crossed the offending boot over his knee. A smile of apology lumbered across his somewhat vacant face. His thinning, sandy hair was covered by a white periwig; torn between vanity and fashion, he worried constantly that wigs were going out of style and that the day was fast approaching when he would have to expose his balding head to the *haut monde*. He sneezed boisterously into his handkerchief, put his snuff box away, and brought out his pocket watch.

"Ten-fifteen," he announced genially. "What are you ladies doing tonight?" Cassandra, his cousin, looked at him wonderingly in the mirror above the fireplace mantel. "Eh?" he prodded. "Jack Wilmott wants me to meet him at his club at eleven; then we're going on to supper at Herrick's. I say, Cassie, tomorrow night there's a masked ball at Vauxhall. I was thinking, you know, that since we'd go incognito, you wouldn't have to wear mourning. No one would know it was *you*, d'y'see, so you could wear anything you liked. It's only nine shillings, Mother, so don't fly into a pucker." Freddy was picking up popular London slang at an admirable rate.

Cassandra turned around slowly. Her face momentarily reflected disbelief. She glanced at her aunt, who was imperturbably sipping a glass of ratafia. But Cass had long ago stopped seeking guidance, moral or otherwise, from that quarter, and was not really surprised now by the absence of censure.

"Freddy—" She stopped. She was too tired to

explain why she wouldn't go with him to a masked ball at Vauxhall two nights after her father had been publicly hanged for treason. Not even incognito. "No, I don't think so," she told him quietly.

"Oh, Cassie, do go. Ellen Van Rijn is going, she's a smashing girl, and if you were there it would be so much easier—"

"Freddy, run along, will you?" Lady Sinclair interrupted peremptorily. "I want to speak to Cassandra alone."

"Eh? Oh, right-o." His muddy boot dropped with a thud to the floor and he surged to his feet. Tall, raw-boned, fleshy, he was the image of his father, the long-dead Sir Clarence. He'd spent almost the whole of his twenty-five years in Paris, yet he had a hearty, uncomplicated bluffness that stamped him surely and unmistakably an Englishman. "I'll go and have a smoke at Weston's, then, shall I?" He picked up his hat and cane and opened the drawing room door to go out. The maid, Clara, came through with a dish of cheese-cakes. Freddy took two without stopping. "Ta!" he called from the stairs, his mouth full.

"Will yer be wantin' anything else, merlady, afore I locks up ther larder?" queried the girl.

Lady Sinclair flinched visibly. "I think not."

"Right you are, merlady." Clara dropped a sort of curtsy and retired.

Cass smiled, catching her aunt's look. "It's only temporary," she said consolingly.

Lady Sinclair waved this away. "Come here, Cassandra; sit beside me. Heavens, you look thin in that dress. I won't be able to keep you in mourning for very long, child, but we'll speak of that later. At least you've stopped crying; Freddy and I were becoming concerned. You weren't looking at all well, you know, and at your time of life a girl needs her looks more than she ever will again. Which brings us to the point, doesn't it?" She smiled, but only with her lips. "Clara tells me you sent Edward Frane away this morning without seeing him."

Cassandra blinked. "Aunt Beth, today was—my father—"

"Yes, and I'm sure Mr. Frane quite understood. It's been a difficult time. It's over now, though, and we must begin to think about the future. I'm not a wealthy woman, as you know. My brother provided for you over the years as best he could—which isn't to say there weren't times when I had to supplement his support out of the very modest legacy Sir Clarence left me. Not that I begrudge one penny of it, Cassandra; you know me too well ever to think that, I hope. But now that his support is at an end, and the circumstances of his death have made an inheritance for you out of the question. . . ."

"You mean his fortune's been confiscated by the Crown and you haven't enough money to keep me." She kept her voice light and suppressed the little jolt of anger that spurted through her.

Aunt Beth laughed her silvery laugh. "Ah, Cass. Always the little realist. But the truth is, Freddy's inheritance is not large, and it's imperative that he marry well. In order to do so, he must turn himself out as best he can and be seen in only the best places. That will be expensive." She laid a hand on Cass's arm; the younger woman was surprised, but not moved, by the uncharacteristic familiarity. "I, of course, want nothing for myself. The happiness of my children means everything to me, and I couldn't love you more if you were my own daughter."

Cass reflected that this was probably quite true, and that it didn't reflect well on her aunt's maternal instinct.

"Now," Lady Sinclair went on, "although Mr.

Frane, I would venture to say, is not a *handsome* man—"

"Ha!" It came out without volition—her first genuine laugh in days.

Her aunt narrowed her eyes in irritation. "No, not a handsome man, perhaps, but a gentleman, and more to the point, a gentleman in possession of above three thousand pounds a year. I have this on excellent authority. You tell me you don't want to marry him; naturally I would never force you to do so. But let's look at the alternatives. If you're not to be a wife, Cass, then perhaps you could be . . . oh, let me see . . . a governess?" She arched her brow in a questioning glance. Cassandra stared back stonily. "Hmm? No? No, I didn't think so, either. You were a charming child, but not really what one would call bookish, alas."

Cass didn't return the falsely kind smile, but she was honest enough to admit the accuracy of the assessment. In truth, it was a wonder she could read and write, she thought moodily as she stared into the fireplace. Studying had always given her a headache. And with no one who cared enough to compel her to attend to her studies, it had been the easiest thing in the world to shirk them. Then too, the schools to which her aunt had sent her valued dancing and deportment far above mathematics or spelling or geography. Thus she knew nothing whatever about history or politics, but she could draw, paint, and sing, play the harpsichord and the guitar, sew and embroider, pour tea and move about a room like a duchess. And once her "formal" education had ceased, a new set of instructors had taught her how to flirt, that most useful of social skills, as well as to ride and fence, sing bawdy songs, and drink young men under the table. But about this aspect of her education, presumably, her aunt was ignorant.

She thought of her cousin's invitation tonight. It hurt to think that he or anyone else believed her flighty or callous or stupid enough to behave after her father's death with such insensitivity, and yet she couldn't really blame Freddy for doing so. For the last two or three years she'd immersed herself in a circle of acquaintance whose credo was that the purpose of life is to experience sensual pleasure; and although there were moments when her existence among them had seemed hollow, when the shallowness of their pastimes had made her want to scream with frustration, she'd never once tried to extricate herself. They were, after all, the only friends she had. And it had amused and secretly pleased her that among them she'd been considered almost a bluestocking.

She dragged her attention back to her aunt, who was explaining with brittle, insincere sympathy why it would be impossible for Cass to become a lady-in-waiting in a respectable household. "I'm afraid genteel people won't want to employ the daughter of a man who's just been executed for trying to assassinate the king. The scandal is too fresh now, at any rate; and for all we know, it may never wear off. Society is more rigid here than in Paris, Cassandra. And speaking of that, I was chatting last week with Mrs. Rutherford, whose mother-in-law is Lady Helen Spencer, and whose great-nephew by marriage is a viscount, and she mentioned to me—in confidence, and in a spirit of genuine caring, I assure you—that there were certain—*rumors* that seem to have followed you from Paris."

"Followed *me*?" Cass winced, hoping her aunt had missed the inference of her emphasis. Lady Sinclair's love affairs, which were numerous and always conducted with discretion, were not a subject that had ever been broached between them.

"I'm afraid so," she confirmed, unheeding. "Oh, you needn't tell me your behavior was always perfectly innocent! As your guardian, I've tried to make certain that not the slightest hint of impropriety ever attached to your name."

At this Cassandra had to look away, it was so absurd. For twelve years Lady Sinclair had made a staunch practice of ignoring her niece as thoroughly as she possibly could.

"But as you'll learn as you get older, once a scandal like this starts there's almost nothing that can stop it, no matter how false or unfair it may be."

"*What* scandal?"

"Well, my dear, there's talk of an improper liaison between you and the Comte de Beauvois, for one thing."

Cass put her head back against the sofa and closed her eyes.

"And then there was that unfortunate episode of the fountain in the Tuileries."

Her eyes opened and she stared incredulously. "Can you possibly be serious?"

"I am in deadly earnest. What may have been youthful high spirits or a tiny, indiscreet moment in Paris will not be viewed in such a liberal light over here. Especially when you're already laboring under the handicap of your father's notoriety. The unpalatable truth is that, apart from marriage, there really are no respectable alternatives for you."

You mean for *you*, Cass thought with helpless, ice-cold anger, carefully unclenching her hands. That's what this "little talk" was about, after all. Cass's continued presence in her household was a social embarrassment Lady Sinclair couldn't endure, especially now that there was no longer any financial incentive to mitigate the shame. The blatant hypocrisy galled her, made her want to shout denunciations into Aunt Beth's haughty face. Instead she closed her eyes and said nothing.

She heard the watchman pass in the street below. "Past eleven o'clock, a fine night, and all's well!"

Her head had started to ache; she massaged her temples tiredly, watching the quick, nervous tapping of her aunt's toe beneath the hem of her skirt. So more was coming.

"Of course, if you truly despise Mr. Frane and are determined not to have him . . ." Aunt Beth cleared her throat. "We're women, we can discuss these things freely, I hope. It would be silly to pretend another choice doesn't exist, that of becoming a man's . . . less legitimate companion and receiving, in return, sufficient remuneration to allow one to live a comfortable if not sumptuous—"

"A mistress, you mean, Aunt? A courtesan?"

She laughed lightly. "Some might call it that."

Cass shook her head, smiling faintly. She spoke without thinking. "I'll leave the taking of lovers to you."

The vicious slap across her cheek stunned her, but not as much as the look of pure hate that flashed in her aunt's eyes and was gone almost instantly. Then they were both apologizing profusely and with every evidence of heartfelt sincerity, but in that split second Cass was able to confirm what she'd long suspected—her aunt despised her. A deep weariness settled over her with the knowledge; she could not even bring herself to feel resentment. She had a swift and unwelcome insight that Lady Sinclair's dislike was rooted in jealousy, and that it had started when men began to pay more attention to her niece than to her. With an odd sort of detachment she contemplated her aunt's smooth white skin and voluptuous figure, the reddish-blonde hair that was still luxuriant but now enhanced by art. Her beauty was fading as a vague but unmistakable look of willfulness encroached on the once delicate features. Her tragedy, Cass saw clearly, was that her only identity was her beauty—a quality necessarily fated to abandon her.

The two women were standing, holding each other's hands.

"I only want what's best for you, Cassandra, truly I do. What will make you happy."

"I know, Aunt Beth." She was too tired to contest this transparent piece of humbuggery.

"If I didn't think marrying Edward Frane would make you happy, I'd never urge you to do it. He'll come again tomorrow, I've no doubt, and what you tell him will be your own decision. Will you see him?"

"Yes, of course."

"And will you think about what we've said tonight?"

"I'm sure I'll think of little else!"

"Good girl." She gave her a quick embrace and kissed her forehead.

On her way upstairs to bed, Cass reflected that Aunt Beth's tolerance of her presence seemed to rise as the time neared for her to leave. In fact, if one overlooked the little matter of a slap in the face, she'd lavished more physical affection on her niece tonight than she had in years.

"Is my aunt up yet, Clara?"

"Yes, miss, up an' out, makin' 'er mornin' calls. An' Sir Freddy's still abed, so you can have a nice, quiet sit-down here with yer tea."

Cass smiled appreciatively. Clara drove Aunt Beth wild, but she found the little maid quite

charming—perhaps for that reason. "I'm expecting a visitor, Clara, probably this morning. Bring
him right up and take him into the sitting room."

"Yes, miss. That'll be that Mr. Frane, I expect?"
Her thick brows lifted and her mouth pulled to the
side in an expression of disapproval.

Cassandra raised her own brows back. "I expect
it will, not that it's any business of yours. Now go
away so I can read the paper."

Clara sniffed and left the room.

Cass took a sip of tea and tried to concentrate on
the *Daily Advertizer*. She'd slept badly again and
her head was throbbing dully. The room was cold,
though it was already high summer.

Still, Cass wouldn't have traded all the mild June
days of Paris for a single damp, foggy English
morning. The years in France had always seemed
like a banishment, but now they were over and she
was home. Her childhood in Surrey, before her
mother died, had been the happiest six years of her
life. Later, when loneliness was her closest companion and she'd given up trying to understand what
she'd done to deserve such an abandonment, it had
seemed as if happiness might still be possible if she
could only be in England again. What she'd never
foreseen was that the public trial and execution of
her father would be the occasion of her homecoming.

She stood up and took her tea to the window. It
still hurt that he hadn't let her visit him in Newgate
in the final weeks, no matter how she pleaded with
him in her letters. It seemed he was pushing her out
of what remained of his life, as he had kept her out
of the past twelve years. She wrote to him every
day, pages and pages filled with love and sadness
and terror. He never wrote back. Anger and a sense
of injustice wrestled with her fear as the long days
dragged past, days so full of anguish she couldn't

even remember them now except as a blur of suffering.

Then, on the very last day, a note had come. The sight of the familiar scrawl had wrung her heart.

"My dear Cassandra,

"So. The gamble did not pay off, and now I must forfeit everything to satisfy the wager. Forgive this conceit, my dear, but gaming metaphors come easily to me nowadays. They say a man dies the way he's lived. I shall try to take to the scaffold what's passed for forty-four years as a sort of reckless bravery, though there are many who would call it cheap bravado. But it no longer matters what it was.

"I wish I were leaving you in better hands than Elizabeth's, but that's only one of my innumerable regrets. She's a vain and selfish woman, and yet she has a knowledge of the world which may prove useful to you. Heed her advice sparingly. Try to be happy. Forgive me for leaving you with nothing, not even memories. All that consoles me now is that I did truly believe in the Revolution. I die for the one honest act of my life.

"I trust your threat to attend the hanging was only that—a threat. Don't come, Cassie. If I believed in the immortal soul, I would tell you ours will one day be together—but alas, I never could. Good-bye, my beautiful child."

"Well, fer the lord's sake, she's startin' in again. Here, now, dry 'em up, yer caller's in the sittin' room. There, there, it ain't so bad."

Cassandra stared down at the filthy handkerchief Clara had thrust into her hand. Through the tears, she couldn't help laughing. "I'll use my own, thanks," she snuffled, wiping her eyes.

"Suit yerself, Miss Priss. An' by the way, it ain't Mr. Frane a'tall, it's a bloke named Quinn."

"Quinn?" frowned Cass.

"Quinn. Said as how he wanted ter speak with you about yer father. Yer want me ter bring in some food? Biscuits er wine, like?"

"That would be nice, Clara. Then go away, and no listening at the door."

"Hmpf," answered the maid, flouncing off.

A man was peering at the framed portraits of Cassandra's parents on the fireplace mantel. He straightened at her quiet "Mr. Quinn?" and turned to greet her. They studied each other during this formality, and Cass saw a tall, thin man of about forty-five, with lank black hair combed straight back from a high forehead. He struck her as a mixture of schoolmaster and priest, with glowing black eyes that seemed to see everything. His face was bony and intelligent, the face of an ascetic, or a fanatic. He had a high, reedy tenor voice and a bulbous Adam's apple that bobbed when he spoke. There was nothing foolish or laughable about him, though; if he were a schoolmaster, there would be no tricks played while his back was turned.

"You're younger than I thought," he said.

"I'm—"

"No, not younger." He raised a finger as if testing the wind. "Fresher. May I sit down?"

"Of course." She gestured toward the sofa and took the wing chair beside it for herself. "Were you a friend of my father's, Mr. Quinn?" Before he could reply, there was a knock at the door and Clara entered.

"Have you any plain barley water?" asked the visitor, declining the offered tray.

"I'm afraid not."

"Ah. No matter." He watched the maid leave.

"No, Miss Merlin, I wasn't a friend of your father's. You've very little French accent, have you? Hardly even noticeable. How long did you live in Paris?"

"Twelve years."

"Tell me a little about yourself."

Cass hesitated. "Mr. Quinn, I don't mean to be rude, but why should I? I don't know you at all; I have no idea why you've come."

He stared at her out of his strange, searching eyes. She had an impression he was re-evaluating, changing an opinion he'd had of her. His hand went to the inside pocket of his coat and brought out a folded piece of paper. "This document will introduce me. I'm an agent of His Majesty the King." He stood up and handed it to her. "I've come to ask for your help."

In growing perplexity she opened the stiff paper, staring at the regal-looking seal at the bottom. The document identified Oliver Martin Quinn in legalistic but vague terms as a member of His Royal Highness's personal ministry, empowered to act in furtherance and on behalf of the security and safety of the realm. Cassandra raised her eyes to the man who stood quietly watching her. "Mr. Quinn, how could I possibly help you?"

"Have you heard of the Constitution Club, Miss Merlin?"

"No, I haven't."

"The Revolution Society?"

"No."

"The Friends of the People?"

She spread her hands helplessly.

He smiled, but he was watching her carefully. "These are organizations in England of men who sympathize with the revolution in France and would like to see its anarchic principles take hold here."

"I see. Was my father a member of one of them?"

"Of all of them, I should think, at one time or another. You weren't aware of his sympathies?"

"No. That is, I knew he sympathized with the Revolution and that, as a journalist, he often wrote in support of it."

"Indeed. Many supported it, especially in the early days. But your father's support went a bit further, didn't it?"

Cassandra felt herself grow warm. "He did what he believed was right," she said stiffly.

His brows lowered; his eyes burned into her. "Do you defend him?"

She felt ensnared by his eyes; she couldn't look away, couldn't even blink. "No, I don't defend him. I'm ashamed of him," she admitted weakly. It was as if he were drawing the truth from her without her permission. She stood and went to the window, putting the wing chair between them. "But whatever he may have done, Mr. Quinn, he was my father. If you're expecting me to revile him, you'll be disappointed."

She half-expected him to pursue her, but instead he walked over to the mantel and picked up one of the miniature portraits. "Your mother?" Cass nodded. "A beautiful woman. You're even more beautiful."

"Thank you," she said lightly. Compliments sounded odd coming from him, she thought.

"Men are attracted to you." It was a statement, not a question, and it didn't sound like a compliment at all. "In a vain and foolish world, that's a useful skill to possess, Miss Merlin. A very useful skill."

She made no answer. She couldn't imagine what he was leading up to. She finally identified the odor that emanated from him ever so faintly. It was incense.

He put his hands behind his back and began to

pace before the cold hearth. "Your father belonged to another group besides the ones I mentioned, Miss Merlin. A much more dangerous group, one whose name we don't know, if it even has a name. It meets clandestinely, unlike the others, and its purpose isn't just to drink toasts to the Revolution and talk of a Jacobin utopia. Its purpose is to create chaos in this country by any means available, so that a republic modeled after the one across the Channel can supplant our constitutional monarchy."

He stopped pacing. "We believe we know the name of their leader, but we have no proof. And because the man is the son of an earl, we must move carefully. The earl in question is a trusted and, as far as we know, devoted friend of the royal family, so there's a need for extreme delicacy. Do you understand me?"

"I think so. Who is the man?"

"I will tell you his name after you've agreed to help us."

"Help you in what way?" Cass burst out, exasperated. "Forgive my ignorance, but I still don't know what you would have me do!"

Quinn put his fingertips together and pressed them against his lips, studying her. "I would have you befriend him."

"Befriend him," she repeated stupidly. But even as he spoke again, the light was beginning to dawn.

"Make his acquaintance, win his confidence. Your father's just been executed, you've spent most of your life in France—it shouldn't take much to convince the man you're as devout an enemy of England as he is. Make him believe you want revenge. Let him talk of *fraternité* and *égalité* until you seem as fervent a believer in the Revolution as any Jacobin. In the meantime, keep us informed of his activities, the names of his friends, whom he meets with in secret." He spread his hands. "Simple."

Cassandra came around from behind the chair and sat down. "Simple," she breathed, massaging her forehead. She tried to gather her wits. "You want me to be a spy."

"Not—"

"You want me to befriend a man who leads a group trying to overthrow the monarchy."

"In—"

"And the manner in which you want me to gain this man's *confidence*, as you put it, is very likely to mean taking him for a lover. Isn't that true, Mr. Quinn? Isn't that what you have in mind?"

For once he was at a loss for words, but only momentarily. "Miss Merlin, it's perfectly immaterial to me how you engage the man's confidence. I would leave that entirely up to you."

"How magnanimous!"

"It may be the quickest approach, then again it may not. May I speak frankly?"

She stifled a giddy laugh. "Do you mean you haven't been?"

"I meant, may I speak my mind without fear of giving offense?"

"That depends on what you have to say." But she thought she already knew.

He hesitated, and she gave him credit for at least attempting to be delicate. "Contemporary morality means nothing to me, Miss Merlin; it's too apt to be different tomorrow from what it was yesterday. But unfortunately, we live in a society governed by rather strict rules of conduct, rules that are no less binding for their being often capricious or unfair, especially as they apply to women, and—"

"Mr. Quinn, I thought you wanted to speak frankly."

He stopped and clasped his hands behind his

back, bobbing a bit on his toes. "Quite so. It's only this. I would never have suggested or implied that you become our traitor's mistress if I hadn't been in possession of information to the effect that such a relationship would not be a—a novel one for you, if I make myself clear. And that you would fit easily into the style of life in which our man is known to indulge."

"The style of life—ah, I see. He must be a terrible libertine." She was laughing softly, leaning back in her chair. "Mr. Quinn, I'm sure I should jump up and slap your face, but I fear it would do no good. My tattered reputation is beyond repair, I perceive." She laughed again, but there was a bitter sound to it. "I suppose it wouldn't help to tell you that my reputation for decadence is a bit exaggerated? No, I thought not. It doesn't matter to me what you think, but I feel bound to tell you that if you're looking for a truly wicked woman for this role,—a *femme fatale*—you would really do better to look elsewhere."

"I thank you for the warning, but I'm satisfied with my choice."

"I wonder why I don't feel complimented," she said dryly, bringing the first smile to Quinn's thin lips.

He pulled a straight chair away from the wall, placed it near her, and sat down. "You're wondering, naturally, what I'm offering in return for your cooperation," he said in his oddly boyish tenor. "The possibility of physical danger to you is extremely remote, I assure you, but I won't say it doesn't exist; thus I wouldn't ask you to begin such an undertaking on the strength of mere . . . patriotism."

The emphasis he gave the word struck her as almost sneering. "Actually, Mr. Quinn—"

"If I may be blunt again, I have information that

your financial circumstances are unfortunate, your prospects for improving them not good. Plainly speaking, you're incapable of making an advantageous marriage, and the combined circumstances of your father's death, the reputation you inherited from him, and the one you've made for yourself make the possibility of any other course of action equally bleak."

Cass couldn't speak. Mr. Quinn's words were like an echo of Aunt Beth's last night, only somehow much worse. How had this happened? When had it begun? A feeling of helplessness settled over her as she watched him rub his hands together almost with relish.

"I can rescue you from this situation," he was saying softly, leaning forward and fixing her with his unnerving stare. "I'm prepared to give you five hundred pounds right now, this moment. When you finish your work—that is, when the situation is resolved one way or another—you'll receive an identical amount, as well as passage to America."

"America!"

"Or Italy, the Netherlands—wherever you like." He waved a dismissive hand. "Someplace where you'll have a chance to begin again, unencumbered by the past. There's little for you here in England now; I daresay when this is over, there'll be even less."

She rose from her chair slowly and went to the fireplace. She found she had to lean against the mantel to steady herself. "Let me be sure I understand you," she said in a low, controlled voice, without turning around. "You're asking me to prostitute myself to a traitor in return for a thousand pounds and exile from my own country forever. Do I have that right, Mr. Quinn?"

She heard him clear his throat and get up from

his chair. He started speaking again, but she stopped listening, stopped thinking about anything at all. She picked up her mother's picture and stared into the clear gray eyes, so like her own. There was an ache deep in the center of her chest; pressing her hand against it brought no relief. Carefully she replaced the picture frame on the mantel and turned. Quinn stopped talking when he saw her face. "Please go away now."

He opened his mouth in astonishment. "You refuse?"

She looked down. "No, though with all my heart I wish I could. But I must think about your offer."

"If the money isn't enough—"

Her head snapped up. "It isn't the money! I wish I could hurl your filthy money into the Thames!"

"But that would be impractical, wouldn't it?" he said quietly, noting the clenched jaw and flashing eyes. "You'll need clothes, jewelry, the things women buy."

"But I'm in mourning for my father!"

"I understand. Black weeds aren't very flirtatious, though, are they? They don't send quite the right message. I'm afraid they would have to go."

Cassandra swallowed and clutched her hands together. "Mr. Quinn, you may find this hard to believe, but there is someone who I have reason to think wants to marry me. A gentleman." Her chin lifted defiantly. "I haven't decided yet whether to accept his offer. When I've made up my mind what to do, I will let you know. And now if you'll excuse me, I'm not feeling very well." It was true; her head throbbed as if twin hammers were beating at her temples.

Quinn rubbed his chin and watched her through narrowed eyes. "Of course. I'll say no more, except that we believe the men who failed to murder the king this time will try again, perhaps soon, and the need to infiltrate their numbers is urgent. This is the simple truth." He walked to the door.

"One other thing," he said offhandedly, as if as an afterthought. "This man, the one we would like you to . . . come to know. He secretly betrayed your father and his friends to us the day before their scheme was to be carried out. We don't know why, but it appears he meant for them to hang." Impassively he watched her face turn ashen. "I must have your answer early tomorrow; if you agree to help us, send a message to this address. I'll arrange for you to meet our would-be assassin tomorrow night." He laid a card on the small table by the door. "Oh, and Miss Merlin—I wouldn't expect too much from Edward Frane. As to his being a gentleman, I'd venture to say you've been misinformed."

"Well, miss, it's him this time."

Cassandra removed her gaze from the view of dreary, unkempt gardens outside her bedroom window and pressed the bridge of her nose between her fingers. "Who, Clara? What are you talking about?"

"That Mr. Frane. This time it's him. I put him in the sittin' room and give him the newspaper and told him ter wait. Said you'd be down when it suited you."

Cass closed her eyes and leaned her forehead against the glass for a second, feeling as if she were floating in a viscous mixture of dread and inertia. She was no closer now to deciding what to say to Mr. Frane than ever, but here he was. Presumably she would say *something* to him when—or rather, if—he asked her to marry him, and it seemed they were both going to learn what it was at the same moment. Ah, well: That wouldn't be very far from the way she'd made most of the major decisions in her life. With a weary sigh, she crossed to the bureau and peered into the glass.

"Do I look all right?" she asked the maid, not really caring but patting her hair into place and smoothing the bodice of her dress.

Clara gave an unladylike snort. "A witch on a broomstick would look like a flamin' beauty next ter that one. Aye, yer look fine, but peaked as usual. Didn't eat yer tea, I see."

Ignoring this, Cass shook out her skirts, straightened her spine, and moved toward the bedroom door.

"Figured out what he looks like," Clara tossed after her.

She rolled her eyes but couldn't help pausing with her hand on the knob. "What, Clara?" she asked, with exaggerated patience.

"A mouse wearin' breeches."

"That's very unkind." But she had to turn away to hide a trace of a smile. It was also unoriginal— the same thought had already occurred to her days ago. She opened the door and went out.

Unkind, unoriginal—but true, she couldn't help thinking as she met Edward Frane in the sitting room and gave him the tips of her fingers in greeting.

"I vow, Miss Merlin, you look more beautiful today than ever. It seems misfortune becomes you," he told her, his tiny dark eyes gleaming with excitement.

She murmured something appreciative, astonished by his tactlessness, then went back to staring with a kind of veiled chagrin at the man she was contemplating marrying. Mr. Frane's chief, though not his sole, physical defect was that his swarthy, mole-flecked face was too small for the rest of him—which would not have been so daunting if

only his body had been larger. He looked more like
an ill-formed child than a man, although she knew
him to be forty if he was a day. She was ready, even
eager, to overlook this as well as his myriad other
shortcomings if only he would show her some
compensating fineness in his character—superior
intelligence, a playful wit, spiritual depth. But up to
now Mr. Frane had been content to keep his nobler
qualities to himself.

She offered him a chair but he declined, and she
was too keyed up herself to sit down. She stood by
the window, debating whether to ring and ask Clara
for tea, or swallow her medicine now and let him
have his say. She could see from his agitated
manner that he wanted to tell her something, and
she was dreadfully afraid she knew what it was.

"I've brought you a gift," he announced importantly, reaching into his inside coat pocket and
removing a thin, tissue-wrapped object some four
inches square.

Instantly she guessed what it was. Years of finishing school training enabled her to smile courteously
with her hand extended when it would have felt
more natural, and infinitely more satisfying, to
clutch at her hair and cry "Oh *God*!" "Why, it's a
playing card," she declared after she'd unwrapped
it. "My, isn't it pretty?"

He laughed indulgently. "Not just *any* playing
card, my dear girl. It's over a hundred years old.
Flemish, you know. Notice the real gold leaf on the
sides. And best of all"—he rubbed his hands
together with suppressed glee—"the middle pip is
asymmetrical!"

Cassandra's lips quivered, but she hummed politely. She was so very tired of Mr. Frane's antique
playing cards—a life-long hobby and, apart from
herself, apparently his only interest. But his gift
told her he meant business; although he'd shown

her dozens of cards during their brief acquaintance, never until now had he favored her with one for her very own. What did he see in her? she wondered desperately. They hardly knew each other. She'd never encouraged him, had had to struggle to be civil to him. Perhaps if she knew what it was about her that drew him, she might like him better.

"A rare card for a rare lady," he was saying in his fatuous way, coming closer and taking her hand in both of his. It was a liberty she hadn't allowed him before now, and his heightened color testified to his appreciation of it. They were much the same height, she noticed distractedly; for that matter they were much the same weight. It was shallow of her, she knew, but somehow she'd always thought her husband would be bigger than she was. She gazed back into his bright brown eyes, trying to imagine waking up beside him each morning, day after day, year after year, for the rest of her life. Her spirit cringed. How vain of her, how frivolous—and yet she couldn't, really she just couldn't—

"My dear," he cried, holding tighter as she started to draw her hand away, "what a difficult time you've had! I thought of you all day yesterday. I felt such helplessness, such sympathy."

But not enough to attend my father's funeral, she thought, and had to press her lips together to keep from saying it out loud.

"But for now, enough of sadness—you and I must speak of other things. I'm sorry to intrude on your grief in this way, but I assure you my purpose is to ease your mind, not burden it."

"You're very kind." She tugged again to release her hand, now slippery with his sweat, but his grip didn't slacken. "Won't you—sit down?" she tried again.

"Have you given any thought to what you'll do now?" he asked, oblivious. "You must forgive me for this unseemly haste, but I have reason to know that your father's death has occasioned a need for some changes in your life in the very near future. I pray I don't flatter myself when I venture to hope those changes might include me."

His breath smelled like cheese. Beyond that, it irritated her to think that his "reason to know" anything at all about her must surely have come from Aunt Beth. The thought of the two of them discussing her in any way whatsoever annoyed her out of all proportion. "Mr. Frane—" she began.

But he was working himself up to it and there was no stopping him. "You must know the high regard in which I hold you, Miss Merlin," he said feelingly, "you couldn't possibly not know. Although we haven't known each other long, I feel a very deep, very strong attachment to you. I know I'm not much of a man for words, but—I think you're splendid! And I can provide for you handsomely, I do assure you, for I'm quite a wealthy man."

She stiffened her arm, endeavoring to maintain the gap of space she'd put between them and which he was doing his best to close. "Oh, Mr. Frane—"

"And generous as well, if you've not already noticed. No woman has ever had cause to complain of Edward Frane's openhandedness, you can be certain of that."

"I'm sure. It's just—"

"You'd have everything you've ever wanted—beautiful clothes, jewelry, even your own carriage. And you could live anywhere you liked in all of London. But of course, my house is in Aldersgate, so you'd want to be in that general vicinity for the sake of convenience."

Cass blinked. "What?"

"As for availability and all that sort of thing, we can work out the details later, but I tell you I'm prepared to be flexible. My only absolute requirement is Sundays—you would have to be at my disposal on Sundays. It's my day off."

Fighting a strong temptation to laugh—not at him but at herself—Cass used her left hand to pry the fingers of her right out of his wet, spidery grasp and took a step back. "You're asking me to be your mistress," she said, enunciating carefully.

"You'd never regret it, I promise you. Cassandra —Miss Merlin—do say yes. I'd give you everything you ever wanted, I swear it. My dear, you're so lovely—" He reached for her and she took another hasty step back.

"You won't marry me?"

"Marry you!" He was astounded. His eyes widened to the size of sixpences. "My dear girl—"

"Why not?"

"Why not! Well!" At least he had the grace to blush. "It's nothing against you personally, but it—it's just not possible."

"Why isn't it?"

"You must know I *couldn't*. It would be—"

"It would be what? Tell me!" Why was she tormenting him? She knew the answer as well as he. In truth, she wanted to see him squirm.

"It's out of the question. You—you're—No, no, it's impossible. Besides, my father's a clergyman."

"Your—" Her jaw dropped. "You're saying he'd be upset if you married me, but not if you only— fornicated with me?" This time she did laugh, though without a particle of humor. "What sort of clergyman is he, Mr. Frane?" His small face went a mottled shade of red, but before he could answer she pointed to the door. "I want you to leave now, sir. You are not welcome in this house."

"Here, now! Here, now, there's no need to take that tone! We're adults. We can discuss this calmly, I hope. I'm asking very little of you, Miss Merlin.

Discretion, really, that's all I'm asking of you, in return for quite a comfortable living. And what else can you do? Be realistic, I implore you. Who else would ask you? There's no one but me and you know it!"

Only the realization that he was speaking the truth kept her from losing her temper completely. "I told you to go," she got out through stiff lips. "If you don't leave this minute, I'll have you thrown out." By whom, she wondered, Clara? Perhaps between them—

"Look here, you can't talk to me that way!" he cried, angry himself now. But he took a defensive step back. "Who do you think you are? I came here to offer you a decent living with a generous allowance—"

"Decent!"

"—which is a damn sight more than any other man would do for you now. I know all about you, girl, so this lily-white act is a waste of time with me."

"How dare you!"

"Your aunt can't keep you! Now that they've hung your old man, you'll be lucky to find work in a bawdy-house!"

She advanced on him furiously. "Get out! You *toad*!"

He retreated, thin legs churning, until he was half in, half out the door. He called her a short, ugly name, one she'd never heard before. She seized an umbrella from the stand by the door. But all she had now was her dignity, and she chose not to squander it on a rat. Instead of pummeling him, she tore his antique Flemish five of hearts into pieces, threw them at him, and slammed the door in his face.

II

CASSANDRA STARED DOWN AT THE SOFT, FLUID FOLDS OF her pretty white muslin gown and worried that it wasn't suitable. She'd seen none like it in the three weeks she'd been here, though in Paris the new Grecian style was swiftly becoming the *dernier cri*. She guessed it was a bit provocative, worn without stays or a "false rump." The old style of dress had enclosed women in a kind of fortress. Now, she reflected, there was nothing to prevent a girl from giving way to any passing caprice. Or as her friend Angelique put it, "It doesn't show afterwards."

She shrugged at her reflection. Provocative or not, it was the only white dress she owned, and Mr. Quinn wanted white.

She went to the bureau and pulled out a red and blue scarf. Should she wear it? The tricolor was worn with such patriotic fervor in France these days—would it send the traitorous Mr. Wade the correct signal? Impulsively, she tied it around her waist as a sash.

She stepped back to see herself. She'd rejected the classical headdress she usually wore with the gown; instead she'd pulled her hair back rather severely from her forehead, secured it in back with pins, and let it fall freely past her shoulders in its usual curly, often unruly, mass. Surely *that* wouldn't be thought provocative. She couldn't see her lower half in the mirror over the bureau and so could only guess at the effect of her thin-soled buskins laced over the ankles. It occurred to her she'd seen none of them in London, either. Apparently the passion for dressing up as a Greek goddess hadn't taken hold of Englishwomen yet. She made a wry face in the mirror. Perhaps she would set the style.

She went back to the high bureau and folded her arms across the top. Was there something in her face that others could see and she could not? She studied her large gray eyes in the mirror, the black lashes and arched brows. Her nose was straight, her lips seemed all right. She smiled, then grinned. Straight teeth, none missing. Black hair, clean if not always tidy. Her skin was healthy, not blotched; men, and less often women, had even complimented her on it.

She could see nothing extraordinary. She had to wonder about the adequacy of Mr. Quinn's intelligence-gathering if his information regarding her so-called decadent style of life in Paris was no more reliable than her aunt's. Oughtn't spies to be able to ferret out the truth, not settle for gossip? Why was everyone so ready to believe the worst— Aunt Beth, Mr. Quinn, Edward Frane?

She watched a slow flush color her cheeks at the thought of Mr. Frane and ground her teeth in fury. That—*bastard*! The unfamiliar curse gave her a thrill of satisfaction. She said it aloud, enjoying the coarse syllables. But it was exactly what he was and she wasn't sorry for saying it. Since yesterday she'd been regretting she hadn't beaten him with the umbrella after all. But anger at this point was a useless luxury she couldn't afford to indulge. With characteristic resolution, she put it aside.

Her hand went to Mr. Quinn's letter on the bureau and she automatically unfolded it. His handwriting was small, obsessively neat, somehow depressing.

"Dear Miss Merlin," she read again. "Your decision, though difficult, is the right one. I doubt you will regret it in the end, although it must seem frightening now. You say you will accept the money only as a loan. That, of course, is up to you; but as far as I'm concerned it's yours, all of it, to use at your discretion. As for where you will live afterward, I would only urge you not to make a hasty decision now, as things may look quite different when our project is finished. In any case, the offer remains open.

"And now to business. Our quarry is a man named Colin Wade. He is the third son of the Earl of Stainesbury; he possesses no title, but receives an allowance from his father which permits him to enjoy a life of considerable luxury. His wife is unwell and usually resides at their country home in Bath. They are childless.

"I will tell you more about him in time, but for now I think it best that you make his acquaintance without preconceptions.

"His one known vice is gambling; fortunately for him, he wins more often than he loses. Tonight he will gamble at the Clarion Club, as he does almost every Monday, usually after midnight. You will have no trouble recognizing him—he's considered an exceptionally handsome man, so I'm told, and is a great favorite with the ladies. Meet him; attract him. His marriage will be no obstacle, as he's known to take mistresses. Be discreet. Let him be the first to refer to your father, then speak of him reluctantly. Your role is to be that of a rather silly *ingénue*, without too many scruples. At the same time, you would do well to show enthusiasm for the so-called ideals of the Revolution, as well as a basic knowledge of current events. If possible, go unchaperoned. If that proves impracticable, go with someone who will allow you as much freedom as possible to cultivate Mr. Wade.

"Another man will be at Clarion's tonight. If all goes well, he will act as liaison between you and me once our scheme is afoot. Wear white; over the course of the evening he will make himself known to you.

"Good luck, Miss Merlin. Only be yourself, and you cannot fail. I will be in contact with you at the appropriate time."

The letter was unsigned, presumably to protect Mr. Quinn's identity.

Tight-lipped, Cass folded it and tore it into shreds. Was he being deliberately insulting? "Be yourself," he advised, directly after telling her to be a foolish *ingénue* without scruples. She knew she should laugh, but somehow she couldn't manage it.

There was a rap at the door. "Cassie, the hackney's come! I'll wait for you in the hall, shall I?"

"Thank you, Freddy, I'll be right there."

She carried the shredded letter to the wastebasket, picked up her reticule with all the money she was prepared to gamble—three pounds and seven pence, a pitiful stake—and went out.

Freddy was wearing a taffeta frock coat in the fashionable *boue de Paris*, or Paris mud, shade. He whistled when he saw her. "Lord, Cassie, you're a game one, ain't you? Lucky it's a warm night or you'd catch your death in that, I'm bound. You look as pretty as a pheasant from a brush blind."

Heartened by this tribute, Cass put her head in the sitting room door to wish her aunt good night.

Lady Sinclair looked up from her fashion magazine. "Come in, Cassandra, let me see you." She regarded her niece for a long moment in silence.

Cass found her expression of knowing satisfaction almost too much to bear. "Will it *serve*?" she asked, with more impudence in her tone than she'd ever used before.

Lady Sinclair's brows went up, but she chose to ignore the question's unpleasant implication. "You look lovely, as always. Enjoy your evening, my dear."

"I'm sure I shall," she shot back, anger spoiling the cool exit she'd meant to make.

As Freddy handed her into the coach and settled himself heavily beside her, she thought of Aunt Beth's words yesterday, after Edward Frane had gone.

"You refused him?" she'd asked calmly, when Cass had informed her of the precise nature of his offer.

Her mouth had dropped, then she'd recovered herself. "Yes, Aunt, I refused him."

"I see." A long fingernail tapped against her lips. "What will you do now, do you think?"

The question had chilled her; it was so patently her aunt's way of washing her hands of her. Would she actually go so far as to put her out of the house? Cass thought it entirely possible. "I'll think of something," she'd promised.

Then she'd written her letter to Oliver Quinn.

Damn Edward Frane, she thought again, shutting out Freddy's amiable chatter as the carriage moved west, away from Holborn toward Piccadilly. But no—that was in the past; she wouldn't think about it again. She had to concentrate on the here and now. She had to concentrate on Colin Wade.

What would he be like? she wondered for the tenth time. Cruel and villainous, or only a dedicated revolutionary who believed any means justified his end? Either way, would she be able to win his trust and discover the secrets Quinn wanted her to learn? It seemed an impossible task even if she became the man's lover—and she had no idea whether she could or would do that. How *could* she, apart from any other considerations, if he had really betrayed her father and caused his execution? Was she making a bargain with Quinn under false pretenses? If she admitted her reservations, would he find someone else for the job? And if he did, would she be glad or sorry?

"Hullo, we're here! I feel lucky tonight, Cassie; I'll lay you five-to-one odds I break even or better."

Freddy threw open the carriage door with a flourish. They had arrived at the Clarion Club.

Riordan stopped massaging the pair of dice in his fingers long enough to check his pocket watch for the third time in ten minutes. Half-past twelve. The chit was late. He pushed away from the wall he'd been lounging against and moved nonchalantly into a dimmer area of the crowded gaming room, where he would be less conspicuous. He'd chosen Clarion's because he never gambled there and his well-known face was less likely to be recognized, but even more because Colin Wade never gambled here and wouldn't come strolling in at any moment to scotch his little plan.

There was nothing actually wrong with the club; its clientele was a reasonable mix of the respectable and the debauched, the play was passably fair, the wines good—or so he'd been told. It just wasn't fashionable. And Philip Riordan, the newest and, some said, most dissolute Member of the House of Commons never went anywhere that wasn't in the vanguard of fashion. It might be a cock fight, a fancy masked ball, or a brothel—but by God it would be fashionable.

Grimacing, Riordan took a miniscule sip from his glass of claret and rubbed the back of his neck. Lord, he was tired. What he wouldn't give to be at home with a good book, or better, sleeping. Even better, sleeping with Claudia. Slim chance of *that*, he thought with a faint, self-mocking smile; the woman was a walking suit of chain mail. He stifled a yawn. He had an early meeting tomorrow with a committee drafting the enclosure bill he would sponsor next term. He'd grown adept at impersonating a man with a blinding hangover, and he supposed he would reenact the role tomorrow with his usual aplomb. But what a blasted bore it all was. If he never saw another dawn through the smoky haze of a gaming hall or pretended a lewd interest in another silly, brainless *demimondaine* intent on showering him with her oft-sampled favors, it would be too soon for Riordan. What the masquerade was accomplishing was beyond him. Oliver said to be patient, but his patience was wearing wafer-thin.

For God's sake, wouldn't he serve the government far better by being the best Commons man he could be, rather than by posing as a drunken wastrel with a taste for light women? Oliver thought not, so he had no choice. He'd promised his old tutor two years of his life, and there were still fifteen months left of his sentence, or penance, or whatever the bloody hell it was.

But he had to agree with Quinn that the unexpected appearance of Cassandra Merlin offered the opportunity they'd been waiting for. Oliver, having met her, claimed she was exactly what she seemed—a foolish girl without a protector, whose indiscreet past made her ripe for their purposes. Riordan wasn't so sure. And since it was he who stood to lose the most if she proved as treacherous as her father, it fell to him to discover a few things about her before he allowed her entry into the tiny circle of persons who knew his secret.

He looked up from contemplating the buckles on his shoes, his attention nudged by a subtle change in the room's atmosphere. A woman was standing in the arched entrance to the gaming room, quietly surveying the restive crowd of gamblers, drinkers, and idlers. Riordan set his glass down with unusual care and clasped his hands behind his back. He took a deep breath, willing his face to abandon the stunned look he could feel on it. Gradually he became aware that he wasn't the only one observing the girl with more than passing interest. Gentlemen and ladies stared, openly and covertly, at Cassandra Merlin—for surely it could be no one but she. *Black hair and a white dress*, Quinn had told him. Riordan's appreciation for his friend's gift of understatement deepened. He moved closer.

Attractive, he'd called her. The old mossback was as blind to women as Riordan had always suspected. Calling her "attractive" was like—he shook his head, unable to think of a sufficiently preposterous analogy. But Lord God, what was she wearing? Fragments of conversation began to penetrate his strangely fogged-in brain. "Who is she?" was the question most often asked at first, but soon the speculation took a more personal, less respectful turn. A man playing whist expressed, crudely and succinctly, a desire to know her better. For no reason he could fathom, the vulgarity made Riordan angry. He was frowning when the girl's seemingly idle gaze came to rest on his, and for a moment their eyes locked. He saw color of the

palest pink stain the impossible whiteness of her
neck, her cheeks. She didn't seem to be breathing;
he knew he wasn't. Then her gaze swiveled away,
her expression unchanging, so that he found it
impossible to put a name to what had just passed.
He unclenched his hands and reached for his drink.

A portly, somewhat vacant-looking fellow joined
her then. Spotting friends across the way, he waved
and nodded, took the girl by the arm, and moved
with her toward the hazard table. Riordan followed
automatically, until he was standing among a circle
of onlookers whose attention was unequally di-
vided between the game and the woman in the
astonishing white dress. "How I should love to play
Adonis to her Aphrodite," sighed someone at his
elbow. Riordan scowled down at a foppish fellow
in a black wig. "Imagine her rising from her
bath. . . ."

The analogy irritated him, though he couldn't
deny its aptness. She did look like a goddess in
that—dress, he supposed it was, though it really
seemed more of an arrangement of draperies. Her
arms were bare, her shoulders almost so, and her
bosom was more than generously displayed above
an artful twisting of white muslin worn in a sort of
tunic fashion. The question of the moment, it
appeared from the searing scrutiny of the bystand-
ers, was whether she was wearing anything under it.
Riordan's annoyance increased when he realized
he'd have given a good deal to know the answer
himself. He had a sudden vision of her jumping naked into a fountain, drunk and laughing,
surrounded by cheering young men. When Quinn
had told him the story, he'd only laughed cynically,
already weary at the thought of having to conduct
business with a jaded Parisienne who was practically a whore at eighteen. Now he was ready to revise
his opinion, and he wasn't sure why. Perhaps it was

because, despite all he'd heard, she didn't look particularly decadent. She looked young, and a little sad. If she were to strip and jump into a fountain tonight, he could imagine himself leaping in after her and wrapping her up in his coat.

She was laughing at something some puce-coated roué was muttering in her ear when once again her gaze chanced to meet his. Her eyes were gray, he saw, the lashes long and black. He watched the humor leave them, her smile slowly fade, before she looked away and started to fiddle with her purse. He glanced around for an empty chair, grabbed one, and ruthlessly pushed his way through the tight knot of gawkers until he was standing at Cassandra Merlin's elbow. Rather pointedly, he thought, she didn't look up. He stationed his chair behind her and a little to the side, and sat down.

"Bets, please."

"Are you playing, Cassie?" Freddy's normally pasty face was rosy with anticipation. "I'll stake you if you like."

With difficulty Cass concentrated on what her cousin was saying. She'd already forgotten the names of the people he'd introduced her to less than a minute ago. "No, thank you," she said softly, almost whispering. But she knew the man could hear, he was sitting so close. She opened and closed the clasp of her reticule, keeping her eyes on the dice in the little wicker hamper the banker overturned with each new bet. She didn't have to look, though, to know that he was leaning forward, wrists crossed over one black-clad knee, long-fingered hands cradling a full glass of wine, and that he was staring at her.

He spoke, and she nearly jumped out of her seat. Belatedly, she realized he was answering a question of Freddy's. "They say the Chambertin is drinkable. At six shillings a bottle, I suppose it ought to be."

"All right with you, Cassie?"

What? Oh, the wine. "Fine. Perfect."

Freddy turned away to speak to the waiter and Cassandra devoted her attention to the game, or pretended to. The man in the puce coat was saying something vaguely obscene in her ear; his lavender scent was so strong she had to will herself not to wrinkle her nose at him. But she heard none of what he said because the man on her other side was speaking to Freddy again. His words were commonplace, ordinary—how had they started such a vibrating in her chest? She felt like a harp or a lute, some stringed instrument his voice could play on at will. When the waiter placed a glass by her hand, she drank half of it down without a pause. She heard the man chuckle. As she inhaled, she turned to look at him.

Her frown and his smile evaporated and it was happening again, the same wordless, breathless exchange. Impossibly, it was even stronger now because he was so close. So close she could reach her hand out and touch the harsh, elegant bones of his face, or smooth her thumbs over his straight black brows. Or push her fingers, like a comb, through his extraordinary black-and-silver hair. . . .

"D'you think it's a love of antiquity or old-fashioned Christian charity that makes her show so much skin?"

The words, uttered by some wag behind her, might have passed Cass by unheard if she hadn't been looking into the man's eyes. She reacted with a start to the violence that leapt into their dark-blue depths and then was gone, leaving her wondering if she'd imagined it. The sense of the overheard words assaulted her all at once and she felt herself flush, overcome with embarrassment. In the swift, humiliating space of an instant, she understood perfectly what was wrong with her gown and how she must look to these people.

The impulse to bolt was strong, but she suppressed it. Instead she turned back to the gaming table, elaborately casual. Her fingers on her glass shook ever so slightly as she took a steadying sip of wine. She removed a pound note from her purse. "Even," she said to the banker when next he called for bets.

"Three. Five. Five."

She watched her note disappear and replaced it with another. "Five."

"One. Three. And four."

The second note went the way of the first. Cass took another sip of wine, fingering her last note.

"I propose a private wager."

She thought she'd shut out every sound except the clack of the dice, but the low, rumbling intimacy of the man's voice penetrated her defenses effortlessly. She stared straight ahead, waiting.

"Bet this on the next throw. If you win, the money's yours. If you lose, you must contrive to get away from the amiable booby you came here with and go with me into the garden." He nodded toward open French doors across the way. "There you must favor me with the pleasure of your company for—let's say thirty minutes. Not a second less." Very slowly he moved a hundred-pound note across the table until it lay in front of her. Over the noise Cass thought she could hear it, the light rubbing of flesh on paper, paper on green baize. "Do we have a bet?"

Wonderingly, she watched her hand go out and capture the note, her fingers just missing his. "Six," she told the banker. She had to repeat it before he

heard her. She said a silent prayer of thanks that
Freddy wasn't watching this outrageous transaction.

"Two. Three. And five."

Her breath came out in a long sigh. That surprised her; she hadn't known she was holding it.

"Freddy." She touched his shoulder.

"Eh? What?"

"I'm going outside now, into the garden. This gentleman is coming with me."

"Oh, right-o." He was hardly listening; he nodded and smiled jovially, then turned back to the betting.

Cass stood. "Shall we, Mr.—?"

"Wade. Colin Wade."

The garden of the Clarion Club was small, but laid out in such a way that its one winding path seemed to traverse a much larger area. Each turn in the flagstone trail was lit with rush-lights, an unnecessary accommodation tonight since the moon was nearly full. The principal diversion here, after drinking, was seeing and being seen, although resourceful couples always contrived to find a bit of privacy among the verdant yews and hollies. The scattered benches were all occupied when Riordan guided Cass along the path toward a small fountain in the center of the garden. They stood for a moment and silently regarded the kneeling, all-but-naked figure of a nymph, perpetually pouring water from a stone ewer.

"Are you cold?" asked Riordan suddenly.

Cass searched his face for a leer, a swiftly hidden glimmer of lechery or amusement, but could see nothing except innocent concern. Still, the similarity between her gown and the kneeling nymph's was not lost on her—nor, she believed, on him. She shook her head and they continued their slow stroll. She was glad to be outside where it was dark, away from all the searching eyes. It made her feel slightly more in control, which was a good thing. Fortunately, Mr. Wade had been the aggressor and contrived their *tête-à-tête*, because up to now, mysteriously and unaccountably, she'd hardly been able to utter a word to him. She supposed it was because he was so handsome—"an exceptionally handsome man," Quinn had written. And yet handsome men were common in the circles she frequented, and she was never tongue-tied among them. Her cheeks burned when she thought of the way she'd stared at him. Her conversation now was scarcely more eloquent than it had been inside, she realized suddenly, and cast about in her mind for a suitable topic.

They had come to the bottom of the garden, where a solitary iron stool was situated against a profusion of shrubbery. Riordan seated Cass and then stepped a few paces away, telling himself he didn't need his wits muddled now by the naked expanse of bosom her much-maligned gown exposed. There had been a moment by the fountain when he was sure she was remembering another fountain, one in the Tuileries a year or so ago. An image of her came to him, wet and naked, head thrown back, water running down her throat and her breasts. . . .

He mentally shook himself. He was much too aware of this woman physically. Following her out of the club, his enjoyment of the unfettered view of her from behind had been tempered in an odd, sobering way by the knowledge that there wasn't a man in the house who wasn't entertaining the same lecherous thoughts about her that he was.

Enough. This was business. He was here to discover whether or not she could be trusted. To do that, he had to stop thinking like a randy schoolboy and start thinking like Colin Wade.

"You have a very slight, very charming hint of a French accent, mademoiselle," he opened casually. "Have you spent time in that country?"

"Most of my life, although we spoke English at home. My family is English."

"Ah. Allow me to say you wear the new French fashion most beautifully."

Her chin came up. "Thank you." She suspected he was baiting her.

"The English, of course, are quite backward in such things. They see these French styles as harbingers of atheism and social collapse. You mustn't pay them any mind. In a year's time, I daresay every woman in London will be wearing a Galatea gown or Diana dress."

Cass felt absurdly comforted. "You're very kind. But if I've been embarrassed tonight, the fault is my own. I've only been in England a short time, not long enough to gauge the national tolerance for nudity, it would seem. I assure you, in Paris this dress is thought quite modest."

"Indeed?"

His tone was friendly, but the frank, admiring glance he swept across her seated figure was anything but brotherly. "Oh, yes," she rushed on. "Ever since Marie Antoinette was painted in her *robe du matin*, without evidence of stays or even a corset, Parisiennes have been disrobing with great enthusiasm." She frowned; that hadn't come out quite right.

"I suppose it's amusing to enter into the skin of the ancients by showing as much as possible of one's own," Riordan drawled, enjoying himself.

She let that pass. "It raised quite a furor, of course; people were shocked that the queen had let herself be painted in her chemise. Still, it set a style for liberating, egalitarian garments." There, she thought with satisfaction. He could pursue that or not, but she'd made a beginning in the portrayal of herself as a woman of the people.

"Was it the violence in Paris that brought you to England, Miss—"

"Merlin. Cassandra Merlin." She watched his face for a sign of recognition, but at that moment a waiter came out of the shadows with two glasses of wine on a tray. Riordan took them and handed one to Cass. This time their fingers made contact. She'd read in a dozen cheap novels about the stupefying effect a casual touch of hands could have, and had always dismissed the phenomenon as absurd, exaggerated. Until now. She took a hasty sip of claret and nearly choked. Eyes watering, cheeks blazing, she set the glass down on the grass beside her and folded her hands in her lap. A moment passed before she remembered his question. "No, Mr. Wade, it wasn't the violence that brought me. It was the arrest and execution of my father for treason."

There was no sound but the distant din of gambling from inside the club. Riordan looked into the wide, guileless, slightly challenging gaze of the woman seated before him and gave her high marks for boldness. "I knew him," he said slowly. "Slightly." The last thing he'd expected to feel was a reluctance to lie. The next words he spoke from the heart, surprising himself. "I'm deeply sorry for your father's death. It must have been terrible for you."

Cass heard genuine sympathy, and felt like a fool when tears sprang to her eyes. She blinked them back briskly. "Thank you. But he died in the service of a cause he believed in, as many others are doing today in France, sir. I expect there are worse ways to meet one's end."

Riordan congratulated her again on her directness, and decided it was time for some of his own.

"And do you share your father's . . . enthusiasms, Miss Merlin?"

She let a noticeable pause fall before she answered. "If I did, I would be very foolish to say so, wouldn't I, Mr. Wade?"

"I expect that depends on to whom you said it."

Cass stared up at him, trying to think of a suitable response. Things were moving too fast. Mr. Wade was disconcertingly tall and broad, and his wide shoulders blocked the moon, making it difficult to see his face. His dress was conservative, yet the tailoring of his black breeches and rust-colored coat was immaculate and obviously expensive. He gave the impression of a man who paid tailors and valets a fortune to insure he made a proper turnout in society, then forgot all about it himself. She remembered with a queer feeling that he had a wife. An invalid, Quinn had said, living in Bath. Was that why he took mistresses? Did he have one now? She looked away, then started when she saw he was holding out a hand to her.

"Do you care to walk?"

She rose. He tucked her hand under his arm and they began to amble along a thin, hard-packed path beside a thorn hedge. There were no rush-lights here, but the moon illuminated the way sufficiently to see. Beyond some shrubbery to their right a woman's shrill laugh sounded, and the moment of apprehension Cass had felt at their seeming isolation vanished. They moved well together, she couldn't help noticing, in spite of the fact that he was probably six stone heavier and a foot taller. It was strange, she reflected, that she could think of him as an adversary, but not yet as an enemy. But Quinn said he'd betrayed her father and sent him to his death. For the first time, it occurred to her to wonder if Quinn was telling the whole truth.

"Why didn't your father send for you when living in Paris began to be dangerous?" Riordan wondered aloud. It wasn't a calculated question; it was something he was curious about.

Cass stared straight ahead. That still hurt, but it wouldn't do to let Mr. Wade know. "Because he knew I sympathized with his ideas and that I would want to join in whatever plans he was making in England," she fabricated. "He did it to protect me."

A bold stroke, thought Riordan; probably too bold. "And how do you like living here?"

"I hate it! I find the class system repulsive. You saw how I was treated tonight because I don't fit into their *bourgeois* mold. I tell you, Mr. Wade, they may have hanged my father, but they can never kill the ideals of *liberté* and *fraternité*!"

He admired the proud tilt of her chin, and especially the way the thrusting back of her shoulders made her breasts stand out against the material of her dress. But he had to hide a smile at her patriotic outburst. It was too melodramatic, and she'd gotten her terms mixed up. Revolutionaries glorified the *bourgeoisie*; it was the nobility who scorned it.

But he was ready to acquit her of being Patrick Merlin's henchwoman. After all, if she'd wanted to help Wade, she'd have told him by now of the plot against him—"Mr. Wade, you're in terrible danger!" or some such thing. Instead she had made skillful overtures and conversed carefully but naturally, exactly as he would coach her to do when the real time came. Now the question was whether she had the wit to pull off the long-term, elaborate masquerade he had in mind. If not, she could be in danger. It was important to him that she not be in danger.

They stopped walking under the low-hanging

boughs of a beech tree. Cass leaned against the trunk, and Riordan reached both hands up to grasp a thick limb. "Were you among the women who marched to Versailles for the king's head, Miss Merlin?" he asked mildly, enjoying the stretch in his shoulder muscles.

"No. That was"—she calculated swiftly—"three years ago, Mr. Wade. I was only fifteen."

"But I thought many in the crowd were children. With their mothers."

"Y-es. I recollect now my aunt was ill at the time. Else I'm certain we'd have gone." Her lips quivered as she tried to imagine Lady Sinclair marching to Versailles with the mob to demand bread. "'We have the Baker, the Baker's wife, and the Baker's boy!'" she recalled the slogan for his benefit. "It must have been a glorious day."

"What *quartier* did you live in?"

"The Palais Royale."

"Ah, you've lived through exciting times, then. Besides being the center of café life, I recall the Palais Royale being the meeting ground for all manner of political agitators and amateur orators. It must have been quite stimulating."

Actually, Cass had found it quite tiresome. She hadn't a political bone in her body. From her narrow vantage point, all the Revolution had accomplished so far was an end to outdoor concerts, the necessity to pay twenty francs for a simple frock, and a tendency in her favorite cafés to water the wine. She murmured vaguely.

"You wear the tricolor, I see," he went on after a moment. She hadn't pursued his last lead; he would try again with this one. "What was the mood of the city after the invasion of the Tuileries?"

She stared blankly. She'd heard of it—but what had she heard? It had happened in June, just before she'd left for England. Something about the mob

holding the king and queen prisoner, but the rest of
it eluded her. "Tense," she hazarded, tensely.
"Nothing like that had ever happened before." She
hoped. "But everything is back to normal now."
Was it? She hadn't the slightest idea. Oh, she was
botching this! She sounded as much like a revolutionary as Freddy!

"Do you feel more politically compatible with
the Jacobins or the Girondins, Miss Merlin? Or
perhaps the Feuillants?"

Cass raised her eyes to heaven, but no divine
intervention was forthcoming. "Oh, the Jacobins,"
she answered positively. Why was he smiling?
"And you?"

"Oh, the Jacobins."

Was he mimicking her? He looked huge, hanging
by his hands from a limb and swaying slowly back
and forth. She still couldn't think of him as a
villain, but there were moments when it seemed as
if he were playing with her.

"Do you like Rousseau?" he was asking now.

Rousseau, Rousseau. Some French writer.
"Above all men," she answered sincerely.

"Then you must admire Edmund Burke as well."

"A genius. *Par excellence.*"

Riordan dropped his arms and straightened his
waistcoat. The interrogation was over. Cassandra
Merlin couldn't convince a grammar school dunce
she supported the Revolution, or indeed, that she'd
even heard of it. They would either have to take
another tack with Wade, or Miss Merlin would
have to undergo a fast course in political reality.

Question two was answered. That left question
three—his favorite. How far with Wade would she
be willing to go?

He heard murmured voices and watched a young
couple pass, arm-in-arm, along the path twelve feet

away. There was no real privacy here, but at least their spot under the beech tree was dark and out of the way. The girl's white dress might even be an advantage: lovers seeking seclusion would see it and search elsewhere.

A twinge of conscience surfaced momentarily, but he scuttled it without difficulty. This was no innocent maid he was sparring with, after all. She might look like an angel, but she was no different from all the empty-headed lightskirts he'd been trifling with for years. Until he'd met Claudia. Tonight's bit of business, it occurred to him, was destined to be added to his lengthening list of unsavory doings about which Claudia was better off not knowing.

Anyway, he only wanted to test this girl's willingness. A kiss or two and he would have her measure. To go beyond that would be—well, unsportsmanlike. That she'd come out here with him at all, alone, on the strength of a cast at hazard, said much for the quality of her moral discretion.

When he leaned his hands against the tree on either side of her face, Cass knew he was going to kiss her. Her first emotion was relief—at least he would have to stop asking questions! Apprehension followed quickly. But then, what could he do with her in a garden that she hadn't already allowed half-a-dozen suitors to do with her in a closed carriage or Aunt Beth's drawing room? That was a singularly uncomforting thought. Then she remembered that Quinn's "liaison" was supposed to be lurking about somewhere. Some mole-like person with huge ears from listening at keyholes, she didn't doubt, probably spying on them right now. Good. If things went too far, she would start screaming and he could rescue her.

Riordan watched as Cass wet her lips and tilted

her head back. Desire spurted through him unexpectedly and he slid his hands down to her waist. "Good lord," he murmured without thinking.

"What?" Her eyes were shining with a silver radiance in the leaf-filtered moonlight. "What's wrong?"

Should he tell her? What the hell. "It's only that I've never touched a clothed lady around the middle before and been able to feel her real body under my hands. No stays or corset or whalebone whatchamacallits."

"Oh." She looked away, embarrassed again.

He pulled her chin back to face him. "It feels like heaven." He stroked her slowly, back to front, enjoying the feel of soft muslin rubbing against softer skin. A fragrance he couldn't quite name came to him from the place between her breasts; he wanted to bury his face there and inhale the sweetness. "And I've never seen anyone with gray eyes so clear and perfect, no other color but gray. Like a slate roof after a rain." He was in complete earnest, so the amused twinkle in the very eyes he was extolling took him aback. "Do you doubt my sincerity, woman?" he demanded gruffly. He rubbed his thumbs along her ribcage and felt her shiver.

"No, indeed," she answered breathily. "It's only that I've never heard my eyes compared to a slate roof."

"After a rain, don't forget that." He brought his hand to her throat and touched it softly, feeling the pulse quicken under his fingers. "I won't even tell you what your skin is like," he said in a husky whisper, "for fear you'd mock me unmercifully."

"I wouldn't—" She broke off with a little gasp when he bent his head and put his lips in the hollow of her throat. A moment later she felt his tongue there, warm and teasing and dangerous. She reached back blindly for the tree and he followed, pressing lightly against her with the full length of his body. What was he doing with his mouth? she wondered disconnectedly. What *could* he be doing to make her feel this way, as if her bones were melting, her skin catching fire where his lips were—

And then he was straightening, and the air was cold and wet on her throat, and he was running his palms up and down her bare arms in a distracted way. "You make a man lose his wits, Cass Merlin," he murmured, trying for a light smile.

Her voice came out too high. "You make a woman lose hers, Colin Wade."

Riordan tensed at the name. He dropped her arms and stepped away. Confused, Cass hugged herself, watching him. "Who did you come here with, Miss Merlin?"

"My cousin," she answered, bewildered by his cool tone. "Frederick Sinclair."

"Cousin, eh? Not much of a chaperone, is he?"

She spun around. Below the beech tree the ground sloped gently to a low brick wall; she could see an alley beyond it, the moon silvering the cobblestones. A tabby cat on top of the wall seemed to be staring directly at her. From the club came a man's muffled shout of triumph. Cass took a deep breath of night air, the better to comprehend what had just happened. Had she done something to offend him? She couldn't think what. Always it was she who broke away from an embrace, never the man. He seemed almost angry with her. What could be the matter? Why did she feel so stricken?

Her hands tightened on the rough bark when she felt him touch her again. She stood rock-still while he stroked her shoulders, then delivered a light massage down her back with his thumbs. What was his game? she wondered almost desperately, feeling herself starting to respond. Was he toying with her on purpose? If so, she didn't like it; it was childish and silly. Oh, but now he was pulling the dark, heavy hair away from the back of her neck and teasing her there with light, playful nibbles, and then hot, open-mouthed kisses.

"Miss Merlin, you taste as sweet as wine," she thought he murmured. The sound of his voice set off the uncanny vibrating in her chest again, but now it was happening to her whole body. She felt his lips, then his teeth, pull lightly at her earlobe, and the weakness in her knees became a helpless trembling. She knew where his hands, clasped over her midriff, would wander next unless she did something. She did nothing. *Touch me*, she pleaded silently; *please, please touch me*.

But at the moment when he would have, she lost her courage and twisted around to face him. His eyes were glowing blue fires. Moonlight on his strange silvery hair made her think of a predatory lion. "Cass," he growled in his throat. He took her shoulders and slammed her gently back against the tree. Holding her face, he ran his thumbs along her lips until they parted. He nodded, satisfied, and brought his mouth down. Her hands went to his chest, as much to steady herself as to touch the hard smoothness of muscle under cool silk. His kiss was gentle, reined in, introductory. He sucked softly at her lips, nudging them farther apart. She didn't know whether he was saying her name or only sighing. His tongue flicked across her lips, then across his, before thrusting sleekly into her mouth.

Lights exploded before Cass's tightly closed eyes. She flung her arms around his neck and arched her body against him. Never, never had she been kissed like this. "Oh!" she breathed, and the intoxicated sound of her own voice thrilled her even more.

Riordan's breath hissed through his teeth and he pressed closer. When he began to stroke the roof of her mouth with slow, sensual laps, her knees gave way. She might have slid to the grass if he hadn't tightened his arms around her waist and ground his hips against her.

He pushed higher, wanting her to feel his hardness between her thighs. "I want to touch you everywhere," he whispered against her mouth. He put both hands on her buttocks and pulled her hard against him. "I want you under me. I want to see you lose all control, Cass, all restraint." He saw a tear shining on her lashes and immediately gentled his hold. He took her mouth again, and her long moan of helpless pleasure was like music until he remembered where they were.

"Hush, love, hush," he murmured, pressing light kisses on her cheeks, her eyelids. This couldn't go on, but it couldn't stop. "Come home with me, Cass. Come now. Say you will."

"I can't!" She could barely speak. Her answer was automatic, unconsidered, the one she'd been giving in situations like this—but not really at all like this!—for years. Then all at once the shocking thought struck that she *could* go with him—she was *supposed* to go with him! Her breath caught and her hands tightened on his arms. She had *permission* to go home with this man and to finish the splendid, terrifying thing they'd started!

But it's wrong, a soft voice reminded her in her other ear; it's a sin, and if there's a God he'll punish you. Yes, but—but he's a spy, an assassin, and I've pledged myself to try to stop him! Sophistry, the voice whispered scornfully; it's hardly patriotism that makes you feel this way, and you know it. It's lust.

That was when Riordan unknowingly interrupted the inner debate and took unfair advantage. Holding her neck, he kissed her again, savagely this time, while cupping his hand over one full, muslin-covered breast. The soft voice in Cass's ear was heard no more, and she slumped bonelessly back against the tree.

"Say yes. Cass, say yes." He stroked the taut peak through her gown with his fingertips, rasping it lightly with his nails, and a jagged dart of liquid lightning jetted through her.

"Yes. Yes. Oh, please."

Riordan took a long, shuddering breath and stepped back an inch. This was absolute madness. He knew it, but he wouldn't think about it. If he gave three seconds of rational thought to what he was doing, he would have to stop. That was unthinkable.

"Come on." He took her hand and pulled her down to the path the way they'd come. She had to run to keep up with him. The proof of his desire for her was still evident, but he didn't care. All he wanted was to get her out of here, into his house and into his bed.

The interior of the gaming establishment seemed harshly and unnaturally bright. Would she come to her senses now? Would he? He kept her hand in a tight grip and steered her quickly through the staring crowd toward the front door.

"Wait. Colin, wait!"

Grinding his teeth at the name, he stopped and turned back to her.

"My cousin—I have to tell him something."

The cousin! He'd forgotten all about the bleeding goddamn cousin! "I'll go," he told her. "Wait for me here." He jostled her toward an empty space of wall by the door and gave her hand a quick squeeze. "Don't worry." He saw the door open, but turned away before the new arrival entered. It was not until he was halfway between Cassandra and her cousin that he heard three dreadful words.

"Hullo! Colin Wade!"

Riordan halted in his tracks and turned around very slowly, like a Christian martyr about to be stoned to death. It was easy to locate the speaker, a young man in a white wig sitting at the loo table between him and the door. He knew before he looked at him that the fellow wasn't speaking to him, but to the handsomely dressed, yellow-haired gentleman who stood in the doorway, smiling and rubbing his hands, nodding genially to his acquaintance across the way. The next thing he saw was Cass coming towards him, stopping midway, then turning back to Wade and holding her arm out in a baffled, beseeching gesture. Her lips were moving, but by some great good fortune her words were so far inaudible. He reached her in four long strides.

"You—Colin—"

"Shut up!" he told her in an intense whisper. "My name is Philip Riordan. I'm with Quinn."

"Quinn!"

"Lower your voice, damn it." His hold tightened on her arm as she tried to pull away. From the corner of his eye he could see Wade watching them. She spun around and took a purposeful step toward Wade. Not knowing her intent, Riordan grabbed her with both hands.

"Let go!"

He had to shut her up. He did it the way that seemed most natural, by kissing her. He held her in a breath-robbing bear hug and kissed her soundly and thoroughly. Part of him wanted to keep it up until she responded, softened against him and kissed him back, but another part told him that wasn't likely to happen this time. He let her go reluctantly.

Cass caught a shaky breath, brought her fist back, and struck Riordan in the face with every ounce of strength she possessed. While he swore and clutched at his jaw, she darted past him and ran out the door.

III

THE COBBLESTONED STREET WAS TORTURE; SHE MIGHT as well have been barefooted for all the protection her thin-soled sandals provided. "Damn, damn, damn," she panted, almost weeping, exhausted but afraid to stop. She'd heard no sounds of pursuit, yet she was sure he would come after her. She had no idea what ill-lit street she was on, but a long stone wall bordered it on the left and beyond the wall was a park. Hyde Park? Green Park? St. James's? She knew the city hardly at all, only from brief and infrequent visits over the years, but she knew it well enough to recognize that she was nowhere near Holborn. How would she get home? It must be after two o'clock. She still had a pound and seven pence, more than enough to hire a hackney, but she'd seen no carriages at all in this darkened, residential section of Piccadilly. And she couldn't venture closer to the clubs and alehouses she'd run away from for fear of molestation. Or worse—of Philip Riordan.

If only Freddy would come for her! But she had small hope of that. If Riordan couldn't find her, there was little chance Freddy could. Limping now, she came to a halt by a bench beside the stone wall and sank down on it gratefully. It was dark here; she would rest for a minute and decide what to do.

There was a light on upstairs in the house directly across from her. She imagined herself going to the front door and knocking. Dogs would bark, neighbors might look out their windows. After a long wait she would hear footsteps inside. The door would open. A servant, probably, in nightshirt and cap, holding a candle. "What do you want?"

The fantasy ended there because she couldn't conceive of a suitable answer. "Sanctuary!" she thought wryly, then sobered—a church! No, no, she didn't want sanctuary, she wanted a ride home. There weren't even any chairmen about at this hour, at least not here. She braced a heel against the edge of the bench and massaged a sore foot. Behind her a night bird bleated a monotonous two-note chant. She shivered, wishing she had a shawl. The moon had set behind the roofs of the houses; there was nothing left of it but a milky blotch among the occasional drifting clouds.

She had two choices. She could stay where she was all night, and at dawn she could set out to find a carriage. Or she could go west now toward lights and noise and people, and find a carriage. A third alternative suggested itself: she could return to the Clarion Club and see if by some miraculous chance Freddy was still there. This idea seemed so unlikely that she abandoned it and went back to the first two. Neither appealed to her. But staying here all night struck her as cowardly, so she chose the second. She dusted off her hands and stood up.

Glory be to God, a carriage! It was clattering toward her at top speed, but elation turned to alarm when it occurred to her Riordan might be inside. It was too late to run now. Her white dress was like a signal beacon; the driver began reining in the horses as soon as he saw her. The hackney had barely stopped when the door opened and a man jumped down. She relaxed slightly. It wasn't Riordan, it was an older man. Tall and very thin, with stooped shoulders and a—all at once she recognized Oliver Quinn. She stood stock-still and waited for him.

"Miss Merlin, please get in the carriage."

No "Thank God you're safe!" or "I'm so sorry this happened," just a sharp, ungracious order. If her shoes had had heels, she'd have dug them in. "I prefer to walk," she told him icily.

"Walk! Don't be absurd, it's not safe. You could be attacked."

"You should have thought of that before you set your hired rapist on me."

Some emotion swept across his stern, priest-like visage, but she couldn't tell in the dimness whether it was anger, embarrassment, or amusement. After a pause he said stiffly, "I apologize for what happened tonight. It was not planned that way."

She shook her head in disgust, then stared without seeing down the black street. An inadequate apology if she'd ever heard one, but it would have to do. She'd never had any real intention of refusing to go with him. "Very well, you may take me home."

He took her arm in a civil grasp and helped her into the coach. They set off, and after a few minutes of stony silence Cassandra decided she would wait for him to speak first no matter how long it took; they could ride all the way to Holborn before she'd give him the satisfaction of opening the subject that was so patently on their minds. After a full five minutes, her patience was rewarded.

"I tell you again, I sincerely regret the events of this evening," he said after clearing his throat a time or two. "Things weren't supposed to go so far. Mr. Riordan ought to have revealed his identity sooner, there's no question about that. I can't excuse his—"

"Mr. Quinn, our bargain is over."

His mouth dropped open in surprise. "What?"

"Well, what did you expect?" she demanded angrily. "You lied to me and played a despicable trick on me, for reasons I can't begin to fathom."

"I can explain."

"I'm not interested in your explanation. I only want to be rid of you and your—colleague." She spat the word venomously.

"Please listen. It was necessary to do what we did in order to test your loyalty. We had no idea whether—"

"Test my loyalty!"

"—you could be trusted to—"

"My *loyalty*!" Her fists clenched in impotent fury. "How dare you? There's no one more loyal to this country than I! I was born here. Every drop of my blood is English. I've come home after twelve miserable years in a country I could never call mine, and nothing and no one will ever force me to leave again!"

"I beg your pardon, but—"

"And anyway," she added furiously, "it wasn't my *loyalty* Mr. Riordan was testing!"

"I've already apologized for Philip's behavior. It was inappropriate."

She made an angry, inarticulate sound. Inappropriate!

"But I confess, I don't quite understand your agitation. After all, nothing really happened."

Cass opened her mouth, then closed it and sat back in seething exasperation. It was pointless to tell him no man had ever taken such liberties with her before. Or, if that wasn't quite true, at least not in the same *way* Mr. Riordan had taken them—and never with such devastating results. "We appear to have different views on what constitutes 'nothing,' Mr. Quinn," she said with frosty dignity. "But never mind; as I said before, our bargain's over."

He put his fingers together and pressed them against his lips in the prayer-like way he had. "I'm afraid it's not that simple."

"What do you mean?"

"You can't break our agreement now; it's too late."

She laughed without humor. "Nevertheless, I do break it. You'll have to carry out your devious little scheme without me."

"You don't understand. You *can't* break it."

"What do you mean?" she said again, frowning.

"Very simply, you know too much. You know me, you know Riordan, and you know who we're after. You have no choice now but to help us."

"But I refuse."

"Then you'll be arrested."

She forced a laugh. Quinn stared back owlishly, and she realized he was serious. "You can't do that," she scoffed.

"Of course I can, with the greatest ease. I can instruct the driver of this carriage to take us to Newgate right now, where you can be imprisoned for as long as I like, on any grounds I like. I most certainly have the power, Miss Merlin, and I promise you I'm not bluffing."

For the second time in the same day, Cassandra called a man a bastard.

"I would do it in a minute," he continued as

though she hadn't spoken, "though certainly with great regret. Now, listen to me. You're angry and you feel insulted, perhaps even ashamed. For the third time, I'll tell you I'm sorry it happened. But it's over. It's time to get on with our business, which is a little more important than your hurt feelings. I'm prepared to double the money we agreed on before; you can consider it payment for services rendered, shall we say, beyond the call of duty."

His cold-bloodedness appalled her. She was preparing to tell him precisely what he could do with his money when the carriage came to such an abrupt stop that she was almost thrown into his lap. In the next moment the door was yanked open and the enormous torso of Philip Riordan filled the portal. "Where the bloody hell did you find her?" was his gracious greeting.

How could she ever have found his angry, arrogant face handsome? wondered Cass, willing herself to sit still and not shrink away from his intimidating presence. She noticed with a mixture of horror and satisfaction the faint bluish bruise on the left side of his jaw—not, it was true, as noticeable as the one on the knuckles of her right hand, but definitely visible. She couldn't recall ever having struck anyone before, not even a childhood playmate.

"In Piccadilly," Quinn snapped. "Miss Merlin has just been telling me she doesn't wish to continue in our employ."

"Oh, she doesn't, eh?" He turned to her; their eyes clashed. In that instant Cass remembered every detail of what had passed between them, and there was a glimmer in the depths of his dark-blue scowl that made her afraid he was remembering, too. "In that case, I'll have to take her dolt of a cousin up on his offer to shoot me in the morning."

Her hands flew to her mouth. "Oh God! Freddy called you out?"

He made her a low bow. "Freddy called me out," he confirmed with an unpleasant smile. "On Hampstead Heath, no less. My choice of weapons. I suppose I'll choose pistols; I haven't fenced in weeks."

"You can't!"

"Ah, my sweet, your concern moves me deeply. Don't worry, though; I'm quite a good shot."

"Not you, you blackguard!"

He put his hand over his heart. "I'm wounded to the quick."

"Damn and blast!" This was Cass's day for cursing. "You mustn't meet him! Oh, please, you'll kill him. He's no good at shooting—he's no good at anything!"

"Then he ought to be shot, the bleeding rotter."

"*Will you listen to me?*"

"Philip, shut up. Miss Merlin, get hold of yourself. No one's going to shoot anyone."

"Not true, Oliver. The man's challenged me in public. My honor's at stake. Indeed, my *honor*," he insisted when Cass snorted in disgust. "Nothing could prevent me from meeting him. Nothing, that is, except . . ."

"What?" she cried in exasperation when he paused interminably.

"Except your solemn promise that you'll finish what we started tonight." He grinned at her indrawn breath and hot rush of color. "You misunderstand," he purred in a soft, intimate voice, as if they were alone. "I meant, of course, our business with Wade."

"Blackmail!" she choked. She longed to hit him again.

"Do you agree? Yes or no, Cass, and be quick. It's

nearly dawn; if it's no, I must go home and get my dueling pistols."

She stared at him incredulously. She turned to Quinn, but his watchful silence told her he would offer no assistance. Her helplessness infuriated her. "I despise both of you," she said in a high but steady tone. "You have my promise."

Riordan studied her a moment longer, then jumped down from the carriage step into the street. "So be it. I'm off to declare my cowardice. Good night to you both." He slammed the door and disappeared.

The hackney started up again. The driver must be one of Quinn's men, Cass speculated dully; he seemed to stop and go without orders. The rest of the way she was silent, her thoughts a chaotic swirl, and Quinn did not interrupt them with small talk. At the door to her aunt's lodgings he told her a coach would come for her tomorrow at four o'clock. She could tell her aunt and cousin she was taking tea at the home of the Honorable Mr. Philip Riordan. Then he tipped his hat and bade her good night.

There were no lights at Number 47. Cass made her way up the two narrow flights of stairs to her bedroom in pitch blackness. It came as no surprise to her that Aunt Beth hadn't waited up and that no one was about, not even Clara. She kicked off her shoes in the darkness and wondered dispiritedly what her life might have been like if her aunt or cousin or father or anyone at all had exercised a little control over her during the last few years. Perhaps her reputation would be intact today, not the shambles it indisputably was; an honorable man might even want to marry her. She sighed wearily as she stripped off the infamous white dress and crawled naked into bed. It was pointless to think about that now, and profitless to blame others for the circumstances she found herself in. She sandwiched her head between two pillows and prayed for sleep.

It came quickly, but didn't last. An hour later she was wide awake, staring at the ceiling, obsessively recalling the most humiliating moments of the evening. She saw Riordan hanging by his hands from a tree limb, innocently asking question after question about France, about the Revolution. And laughing at her all the time, she didn't doubt, delighting in her ignorance. She saw it so clearly now and cringed when she thought of it, but she couldn't stop thinking of it. Of course that wasn't the worst. She pulled the sheet up to her neck and tensed every muscle in an agony of mortification. She remembered with hellish clarity every caress, each murmured word, until the feelings they'd evoked before threatened to return and consume her again. Oh God! How could she have let him touch her that way? She made an anguished sound and rolled over on her stomach.

I loathe you, Philip Riordan, she raged silently. You're a manipulator, an abuser of women—I wish Freddy had shot you!

I want to see you lose all control, Cass, all restraint. . . . She groaned and put her hands over her ears, grinding her teeth. How horrible to think she'd have gone with him gladly, freely given her long-defended innocence to a common seducer! A man who didn't care anything at all for her, who saw in her nothing but a willing body on which to vent his lust.

She turned onto her side and curled into a ball, forcing herself to turn the indictment around. What had she seen in him? A willing body. A devastatingly skillful lover on whom she would gladly have vented her own lust. Perhaps she'd used

him as much as he'd used her. After all, her
ultimate goal had been to trick him. Never mind
that she'd completely lost sight of the goal
everytime he'd put his hands on her.

Very well. She was as ashamed of herself as she
was angry with Riordan. It didn't excuse what he'd
done, though, not at all. And now she was supposed
to *work* with him somehow, as if nothing had
happened, while she met and cultivated the real
Colin Wade. Her deepest wish was that the earth
would open up and swallow either Riordan or her,
it didn't matter which, as long as she need never see
him again. But that wasn't going to happen; she'd
given her promise to continue the ludicrous charade. The thought of meeting him tomorrow—
today—made her wince with embarrassment. He
was loathesome, despicable, a liar, the worst kind
of—

A muffled crash from somewhere in the house
made her sit up. She listened intently to the pre-
dawn silence. A burglar? Another crash, then a
thud, and now a low, agonized moan. Oh heavens,
it was Freddy! She leapt out of bed and made a grab
for her robe, hastily tying it while she threw open
the door and raced down the darkened stairs. If
that monster had shot him after all—!

She found him in the drawing room. "Freddy!"
she cried, rushing to the sofa where he lay, face
down. Snoring. Reeking of gin. "Oh, Freddy," she
sighed ruefully. She bent and gently straightened
his wig.

"Touching."

She jumped as if a gun had gone off in her ear.
Riordan was standing in near-darkness by the door.
He came toward her and she clutched at her robe in
a purely instinctive gesture of self-defense.

He stopped when he was four feet away, the
tea-table between them, and studied the clear out-

line of her breasts under the worn silk dressing gown she was pulling so tightly around her. Her hair hung about her shoulders in a glorious tangle; her thin white feet were bare. She was naked under the robe and he already knew what it was like to touch her. . . .

Bloody hell! He wasn't going to let her do this to him again, the damned witch. He glowered at her, unwillingly beguiled by the set of her small, determined jaw.

"What are you doing here?" Cass asked in a quaking but low voice. Now that she knew her cousin was only drunk, not dead, she wasn't anxious to rouse the rest of the house.

"Why, I'm bringing young Freddy home," Riordan explained amiably. "We've been drinking."

Cass glanced from the motionless dead weight of her cousin on the couch to the alert, upright posture of Riordan. Freddy might have been drinking, but this man definitely had not.

"Why?"

"Because we're old friends, are Fred and I. Ever since I explained to him that the little contretemps he witnessed between us at the Clarion Club was only a passionate lovers' quarrel. And that if he shot me it would break your heart."

She stared, open-mouthed. "You—you—" Words failed her.

Riordan smiled; there was nothing he liked better than rendering Cass Merlin speechless. "Shall I leave him here, do you think, or shall we put him to bed together?"

"Just go!" she hissed furiously. She badly wanted to yell at him. "Get out of here right now and don't ever come back!"

He came around the side of the table and stood in front of her. She held her ground, primarily because if she'd taken a step back she'd have fallen on top of Freddy. "Why so angry, Cass?" he asked softly. "Because of what we did? Or what we didn't have time to do?" His hand on the soft nape of her neck silenced whatever reply she was going to make. He watched her lovely gray eyes darken to pewter, then kissed her as gently as he'd ever kissed a woman. He felt her breath on his cheek, warm and sweet. Heard her soft sigh. Stepped back as if he'd been burned.

Belatedly, Cass brought up a clenched fist and scrubbed furiously at her lips. "You're vile." He only smiled. She looked around for something to throw. "You'd *better* go," she said boldly to his retreating back. "If you ever touch me again, I'll blacken your eye as well as your jaw!"

He turned at the door. "I'll remember that. Will it be before or after I take you to bed, do you think? Just so I'll know when to duck." Cass bent and picked up one of Freddy's shoes from the floor. Riordan chuckled. "See you this afternoon, sweet. Wear another one of those goddess dresses, will you? I love the way you feel in them."

He was through the door before she could bring her arm back.

John Walker poked his head in the bedroom door. His employer was shaving himself, as he preferred to do when he had time, wearing nothing but a towel knotted around his waist. "Excuse me, sir."

"What is it, John?"

"Mr. Quinn is downstairs. Shall I tell him you'll be down shortly?"

Riordan drew his lips in to shave under his nose. "No," he answered after a moment, "tell him to come up. Oh, and John."

"Yes, sir?" The secretary opened the door wider.

"Get Beal in here and tell him to find me something to wear."

"Yes, sir."

"Also, I'm hungry."

"Very good, sir."

The door closed and Riordan went back to shaving. He squinted at his face in the mirror. Three hours sleep in the middle of the day; this decadent life was sure to kill him. Was his hair getting grayer? He ran his fingers through it, peering at his reflection critically. After last night, it was a wonder he wasn't bald. Women were always saying they liked the silver streaks, but he wasn't sure anymore. He was always quick to tell them it had started coming in this way when he was twenty. Now that he was nearing thirty, the explanation wasn't as consoling as it used to be. Well, he guessed he could always take to wearing a wig.

Somebody's flat palm pushed the door open on a rush of air. He didn't have to look around to know it was Oliver, mad as a hornet.

"So. You're awake."

He turned, razor in hand. "Have I been sleeping too long?" he asked with deep sarcasm. Quinn made an erasing gesture with his hand. "I was occupied with a drunken baronet until dawn; my meeting with the committee went on till noon. I didn't realize a few hours rest in the afternoon would discompose you so, Oliver."

"Never mind that. I just have one question, Philip: What in the name of God were you thinking of?"

Riordan turned back to the mirror, avoiding the older man's eyes. "At what particular time?"

"Don't play games with me."

He laid his razor down and picked up a towel, still not answering, trying to shake the feeling of being a naughty boy who has angered his schoolmaster. After twenty years, he marveled, Oliver still had that effect on him.

"A dozen people saw you with her," Quinn persisted. "Didn't you realize it?"

"I thought no one would recognize me."

"No one would have if you hadn't made such a spectacle of yourself! Did you think you could"— he sputtered, then got it out—"have *intercourse* with her in a public garden?"

In spite of himself, Riordan laughed. "The thought crossed my mind," he admitted.

"Idiot! Even Wade saw you mauling her! If you were trying to test her, why not do it in private?"

There was a knock and the door opened. It was Walker again.

"Go on, Oliver. You can speak in front of John."

"I asked you a question."

The door opened again; to Riordan's relief it was Beal, his valet, in front of whom they couldn't speak. Behind him was a yellow-haired chambermaid with a tray. She set it down on a table by the bed, blushing prettily at the intimidating sight of the master's all but naked body, and went away.

"Anyone care to join me?" asked Riordan, indicating the tray. No one responded.

"I've already laid your clothes out in the dressing room, sir," said the valet in an aggrieved tone.

"Oh, have you, Beal? All right, then. Go away."

"Yes, sir." He left.

"I'm still waiting," Quinn reminded him.

Riordan went to the tray, picked up a meat pie, whole, and took a tremendous bite out of it. He stared at Quinn, chewing slowly. Walker stood a short distance away, hands behind his back, quiet and unobtrusive as always. Finally Riordan swallowed. "What was the question?"

Quinn let out an angry breath. "The whole plan is ruined, thanks to you! How is she supposed to begin an affair with Wade when everyone thinks she's having one with you?"

"That is a bit sticky, I can see that," he returned, unrepentant. "I guess it wasn't such a good idea to use Miss Merlin after all."

Quinn turned sharply to the secretary. "Walker, would you mind leaving us for a few minutes?"

Riordan protested; Quinn insisted. The secretary excused himself.

"Now," said Quinn.

Riordan spun on his heel and went into the dressing room, unfinished pie in hand, but it was no use. Quinn was right behind him. He threw off his towel and reached for the white cambric shirt Beal had put out.

"I'd hoped the kind of behavior you exhibited last night was something you'd safely relegated to the past." Quinn's voice was heavy with disapproval. "What happened?"

Riordan pulled on his breeches, avoiding the other man's eyes. "Nothing happened," he said sullenly. "She was there. She was willing. That's all. For Christ's sake, Oliver, I'm only human."

Quinn shook his head. "I'm disappointed, Philip. I was sure that kind of woman no longer appealed to you."

"What kind of woman is that?" he asked very softly, his hands suddenly still over the buttons of his shirt.

Quinn looked at him in surprise. "You know what kind of woman I mean. The sort I thought you'd given up by now. You weren't drinking, were you?"

"No!" he denied hotly.

"Thank God for that, at least."

Riordan turned around and tied his cravat in silence, then sat down to pull on his stockings. "It wouldn't have worked anyway," he muttered defensively. "The girl is hopelessly naive about politics. She'd never have been able to convince Wade she gave a damn about the Revolution."

"That could have been remedied. She's not stupid, after all."

Riordan shrugged. "Wade would've seen through her in a minute," he insisted.

"What was your impression of her? Aside from politics, I mean. Would she have been shrewd enough to pull it off?"

He took a long time answering. He put on his shoes, shrugged into his waistcoat and coat. He ran his hands through his hair to comb it, peering into the wardrobe mirror. Finally he turned around. "I'm not sure."

Quinn frowned. "You're not sure? Philip, this is what you were supposed to be finding out last night, remember?" He sighed in irritation. "Do you agree that she's passably intelligent?"

"Yes, yes."

"Could she convince Wade she feels angry and resentful over her father's death?"

He hesitated. "Perhaps. Yes, probably," he conceded unwillingly.

"Could she seduce him?"

Riordan's scowl blackened. A number of answers came to mind, but in the end he only laughed harshly and said, "Oh, most definitely."

"Fine. And we already know she'd be willing to seduce him, after her performance last night with you. At least you were successful at finding out one thing." He stared at his friend speculatively. "You seem upset, Philip. Is something wrong?"

"No."

"Good. What time is it?"

Riordan patted his empty pocket, then went to the mahogany bureau and opened a jewelry case. "Four-fifteen," he answered, pocketing his watch.

"She's late. She was late last night as well. Oliver, I just don't think she'll do."

"Because she's not punctual?"

"No, of course not. She's too—" He paused, unable to think of the word. "Young," he said finally, although that wasn't quite it. Quinn sent him a long, measuring look. He was relieved when Walker appeared again in the open door.

"Miss Merlin is here, sir. I've put her in the library."

"Thanks." He looked back at Quinn. "Well?" The older man went first. Riordan followed him out of the room and down the stairs.

Cass was too nervous to stay seated in the chair the man named Walker had guided her to. Almost before the door closed behind him she jumped up and began pacing the large, sunny, dark-paneled library. Turkish carpets on the shiny wood floor were thick and richly colored; the windows were old-fashioned casements overlooking a small but charming garden. The high ceiling was carved and decorated with what she supposed were scenes from classical antiquity; there were busts in niches along the wall, no doubt representing great thinkers, though none looked familiar to her. The faint smell of leather reminded her of the library at Madame Clement's, her most recent finishing school, and made her feel slightly nauseated.

She moved restlessly about the room, stroking a huge globe and sending it spinning in its stand, staring without seeing at the enormous framed maps on the wall. She wandered back to the windows. What did Riordan do for a living? she wondered for the first time. Probably nothing; people with homes as large and grand as this one didn't need to work. Everything was very quiet, though the house was in the heart of fashionable

Mayfair. A curved velvet seat below the bay window looked inviting. On it sat a viola in an open case; Cass bent down and ran the backs of her fingers across the strings once, wondering who played.

Footsteps sounded in the hall. She patted the sedate knot she'd tied her hair into and smoothed the skirt of her deliberately sober, dove-gray silk dress. It took courage to leave the quiet seclusion of the window and venture into the center of the room, there to greet three rather grim-looking gentlemen.

"Ah, Miss Merlin," Quinn said with somber cordiality. "Did you meet Philip's secretary, John Walker?"

She said she had, nodding again to the fair-haired, serious-looking young man, and wondering why Riordan needed a secretary. She also wondered why Quinn was taking the lead with greetings and introductions. Wasn't this Riordan's house?

She took a breath, for the first time allowing her eyes to flick across him. She had a hasty impression of a tan coat and brown breeches, and a wary expression on his much-too-handsome face. Quinn invited her to have a seat; she took the same high-backed velvet-covered chair she'd had before, and he took an identical one beside her. Mr. Walker asked if he should take notes. Riordan shook his head and sat on the edge of the large desk nearby, facing her. She was intensely aware of him as he leaned back on his hands, one long leg outstretched. She looked away, but at the edge of her vision she took note of the muscles in his stockinged calves, the smooth power of his thighs. Quinn was speaking. She tried to attend to his words, but instead caught herself remembering the extraordinary sweetness of Riordan's kiss a few hours ago. Against her will, her gaze moved slowly away from

Quinn to Riordan, until she was held by the intent blue stare—not mocking now, but searching her face as if for the answer to a question. His cheeks had a faint pinkish glow. She imagined him shaving or being shaved, and was inexplicably stirred by the image, the thrilling intimacy of such an everyday act. She realized he was staring at her mouth. An erotic rush flooded through her. She tried to look away, but it was impossible. A sound like falling water filled her ears and everything blurred except his face, which stayed in sharp, uncanny focus. Finally it was Quinn's voice, loud and almost peevish, that brought her back to reality.

"Did you hear me, Philip?"

"Every word, Oliver," Riordan answered, less than truthfully. In the light of day, Cass Merlin was as beautiful as he'd remembered, perhaps more so. His actions last night began to seem much less irrational. In fact, he began to feel considerably better about everything. "And I agree with you completely—I do owe Miss Merlin an apology." He stood up and made a small bow. "My conduct last night was inexcusable. I beg your forgiveness. Regrettably, it will never happen again."

"Philip," said Quinn in a warning tone.

"I meant, of course, such a regrettable thing will never happen again," he amended, straight-faced.

Cass was speechless. An apology was the very last thing she'd expected. She struggled for a response. She didn't believe he was particularly sincere, but she was as eager to put the embarrassing incident behind them as Quinn was. One way to accomplish that was to appear to accept his contrition at face value. But there was a mischievous blue glint in his eye that held her back.

"Well?" urged Quinn impatiently.

She looked between the two men. She wondered fleetingly what Mr. Walker, sitting quietly in the corner, was making of all this. "It seems to me it doesn't matter whether I accept your apology or not. I've been threatened with imprisonment as well as the murder of my cousin unless I continue to cooperate with you." She looked down, missing the surprised, half-angry glance Riordan threw Quinn. "About one thing I do wholeheartedly agree—it certainly will never happen again." She looked up sharply. "I've said I will help you in your scheme against Mr. Wade, but now I attach a condition: that the subject of what happened last night will never, ever be mentioned again by any of us."

"Agreed," said Quinn swiftly.

"Agreed," Riordan replied more slowly. "As long as you place no condition on remembering it." He wondered why he persisted in teasing her. It wasn't really like him. But she turned such a lovely shade of pink when she blushed, he couldn't help himself.

"Enough, Philip," Quinn chided, standing up. "We have much to discuss."

"Have we?" he asked, puzzled. "I thought we'd all but decided Miss Merlin's usefulness was at an end."

"Did you?" Quinn sent him a measuring look. "I don't recall deciding that. It's true, her usefulness in the original role may be over, but that only means we'll have to be more resourceful. Flexibility, that's the key. A shift of focus. The goal isn't to establish a relationship between Wade and Miss Merlin anymore, at least not immediately. It's to establish one between *you* and Miss Merlin, one which Wade will believe he can infiltrate and compromise."

There was a silence. Cass's wits were slow today; she couldn't immediately comprehend what Quinn was saying.

Riordan's were quicker. Almost before Quinn had finished speaking, he was grinning and slapping the top of the desk with his palm. "Of course! Oliver, you're a genius. This is even better than the original plan. This way we not only learn things about Wade from Cass, we can pass selected information to him through her. It's perfect!"

"Yes, I thought you'd like it," Quinn smiled thinly.

Besides feeling a mounting sense of alarm, Cass was growing tired of being spoken of as if she weren't in the room. "I'm afraid I don't understand," she interjected sharply. "Why would Mr. Wade want to infiltrate a relationship between Mr. Riordan and me?"

Riordan glanced at Quinn. "You didn't tell her?"

"No, there wasn't time."

"Tell me what?" She looked back and forth between them.

"Mr. Riordan is a Member of the House of Commons," the older man explained.

Cass looked at Riordan for half a second before bursting out with a spontaneous laugh. An answering chortle sounded from the direction of Mr. Walker, although at a hard look from Quinn, it turned into a choking cough. "You're joking, of course," Cass stated with certainty, still smiling.

"Odd, a lot of my new constituents had the same reaction," Riordan smiled back amiably. "But I'm afraid it's true. You see before you the distinguished junior Member for St. Chawes."

"St. Chawes?" It had to be a joke.

"In Cornwall. A small borough, it's true—only twelve voting burgesses. It helped at election time that my father's wool business employed all twelve of them. My father is the Earl of Raine, by the way. He was a Member of the House of Lords until a few years ago, when drink and syphilis finally incapacitated him. Now he stays at home, peacefully counting my mother's lovers. No easy feat even for a man in good health."

Cass could only stare. His tone was jocular, but there was a tightness around his mouth that made his smile seem forced.

"It's really true?" she asked after a full minute. "You are truly a member of the Parliament?"

"My dear, this continued skepticism is beginning to hurt my feelings. Believe it. It's true."

"Then . . ." She put a hand to her forehead; this was getting too complicated. "How do you expect to make people believe we're involved?" She directed the question to Quinn. "I mean, why would we be? Mr. Riordan is the son of an earl, he holds a high position in the government, he's obviously wealthy." Unconsciously her chin rose a fraction. "On the other hand, you've had the goodness to point out a number of times that any hopes I might have had for a respectable position in society are unrealistic." She held out her hands in honest perplexity. "Why do you expect Wade or anyone else to believe he would want me?" she asked baldly. She threw a glance at Riordan, who was looking at her with an expression she'd never seen before and couldn't name. She turned back to Quinn, who was standing behind his chair, his thin arms folded across the back.

"Because you won't be the only one playing a role," he told her matter-of-factly. "Philip has been playing one for months. For reasons that don't immediately concern you, we've gone to a great deal of trouble to establish a reputation for him in fashionable society as a drunkard, a gambler, and an indiscriminate womanizer."

"Oh, I see," she said softly, sitting back. "No wonder, then."

"Oliver, for God's sake," Riordan muttered.

Now she understood the look in his eyes. Pity. "The profligate peer and the gay grisette," she mused with a tight smile. "Very clever. And very believable."

"Yes, I think so," Quinn nodded seriously. "I agree with you, Philip—in some ways this will be more to our advantage than the first scheme. Wade won't have any trouble believing Miss Merlin would enjoy the attentions of two men at once." He began to pace back and forth across the Turkish carpet, oblivious to the taut quality of the silence in the wake of his words. "And when she confides to him that she misses France and feels bitterness toward England because of her father's execution, with any luck the idea of using you will come from him first. But if not, we'll pass some innocuous bit of intelligence to him through Miss Merlin in an offhand way, and that will give him the idea."

Cass thought she'd insulated herself against Quinn's insults; it must be because she wasn't alone this time, that other people were hearing them too, that made the barbs seem so piercing. She carefully unclenched her hands. "One thing puzzles me," she said when she could speak in a normal tone. "If I'm such an enemy of the English, why would I associate with a man who represents the very government I profess to despise?"

"Because he's rich," Quinn answered promptly. "You'll have to make Wade believe your desire for a wealthy protector is even stronger than your hatred of England."

"Ah, of course. Greed over patriotism."

"Precisely. Greed and revenge, Miss Merlin, those are your two motivations. In that order."

"Yes, I think I've got it. It should be easy, shouldn't it, Mr. Quinn? In the theatre I believe it's called type-casting." She stood up. "If you don't mind, I'd like to leave now." Riordan stood too, but she didn't look at him. "I expect I'll be hearing from you quite soon."

"Not from me anymore," said Quinn, "at least not publicly. Philip is your contact from now on. He'll contrive your first meeting with Wade. I'll go back to my role as merely an old friend of Philip's, a drab government drone with some vague, unimportant job in the ministry."

Cass took his outstretched hand stiffly, absorbing this news with mixed feelings. She turned away, anxious to be gone.

Riordan's voice stopped her. "Wait, Cass. Before you go." He crossed the room to a wide shelf of books on the far wall and ran his hand slowly along the top row. He halted at a thin volume and extracted it. "Here," he said, coming back and handing it to her. "Read it."

She looked down at the title and felt her face grow warm. *Contrat Social*, by Jean-Jacques Rousseau.

"I've lent my English copy to a friend. Can you read it in French?"

"Of course," she muttered, embarrassed and angry at the same time.

"Good. I'll just see Miss Merlin to the carriage," he said over his shoulder, taking her elbow. Walker hastened to open the library door and bowed politely as they went through; Cass nodded to him, wondering again what he must be thinking.

Riordan walked slowly but didn't speak as they crossed the wide, elegant foyer to the front door. The carriage was still by the curb, the coachman engaged in grooming one of the matching gray geldings while he waited. They stood on the shallow flagstone stoop, two steps up from the sidewalk; after a moment Riordan dropped her arm, as if just realizing he still held it.

"Goodbye," said Cass. He was frowning; she had the impression he wanted to say something.

"Cass, you mustn't mind Oliver. Tact isn't his strong suit."

"I had noticed that," she said coolly. "It doesn't matter in the least." She turned away; for some reason his attempt at an apology on Quinn's behalf deeply embarrassed her. She went down the steps, then stopped, remembering. "Would you do me the favor of reminding Mr. Quinn that I've not yet received any of the payment he and I agreed on?"

At her words, his eyes narrowed and his lips twisted in a cynical smile. "Of course," he said, bowing.

She stiffened. "Surely you can appreciate that my new role necessitates certain expenses. Clothes, for one thing. And my aunt—" She broke off in anger, watching his eyes take on a sardonic gleam.

"I'm sure it does," he agreed smoothly. "A girl has to look out for herself, after all. Strike while the iron is hot, eh? And I expect you'll want to set something by for a rainy day."

She spoke through clenched teeth. "I declare, Mr. Riordan, you're more edifying than a wallful of samplers. But now if you have no more clichéd advice, I'll bid you good day."

To her dismay, he descended the two steps in one stride and took hold of her arm again. Surely there was no need for him to clasp her waist so tightly as he helped her into the carriage, nor settle her skirts around her with such lingering solicitousness that it was all she could do not to slap his hands away.

"I'll come to see you tomorrow, Cass," he said with one hand on the door, leaning in toward her. "Around four again, I should think. Have the book read by then so we can discuss it." He smiled at her expression. "But you'll be *rereading* it, won't you?

I'd forgotten that you admire Rousseau 'above all men.' "

She felt like sticking her tongue out at him.

"And Cass, do something about your attitude, will you? You're soon going to have to convince people we're having a liaison, you know. You might start by calling me by my first name."

She glared down at him with all the haughtiness she could summon. "I'm a very good actress; I think I proved that last night rather spectacularly. Although it's the hardest role I'll ever have to play, when the time comes I'm sure I'll be able to convince people I can bear to be in the same room with you. But in the meantime, I see no reason to hide my dislike. In fact, I feel quite incapable of it. Good day, *Mister* Riordan."

So quickly she had no time to react, he swung up into the carriage and sat down, facing her, on the little bit of seat left between her and the door. Her skirt was pinned under his thigh, making it impossible to move over. She had no desire to enter into a physical struggle with him. For one thing, it would be vulgar; for another, he would win. She could scream, but on the whole it didn't seem worth it. She tried to freeze him with an icy-cold look of disdain, but its only effect was to make his smug smile widen.

"Acting, Cass?" he asked softly. He was watching her mouth again. "Are you sure that's all it was?"

She felt a treacherous tremor in the pit of her stomach. "Acting," she insisted. "That's all it was for *both* of us. Please get out of the carriage now and let me—"

"Would you like to make a small, private wager? Because if it was only acting, I could touch you now, like this, and you would feel nothing. Absolutely nothing. How does this make you feel, Cass?"

"Stop it. Take your hands off me."

"I only have one hand on you," he corrected, a little hoarsely. He moved his fingers from the side of her jaw to her throat, confirming what he'd hoped—her pulse was racing. "*Now* I have both hands on you." And he put his other hand on her stomach.

Her lips parted in shock, but she didn't move. "I'm not afraid of you, Philip Riordan." She didn't even try to steady her voice.

"I'm glad, Cass," he whispered. "I never want you to be afraid of me. Now let me see how well you *act* while I'm kissing you."

"Don't! Don't—"

"It's for the wager. Show me how you don't feel anything. Open your mouth, love. Yes." His palm was pressed against her heart. He caught the back of her head in his other hand and held her like a fragile treasure while his mouth made love to her. Hazily, Cass decided her most dignified defense was to be still and let him kiss her until her unresponsiveness chilled him. By the time the defects in this plan were clear to her, it was too late to institute another. She made a faint-hearted attempt to push him away, but the touch of her small hand on his chest made her think of rolling a boulder uphill. Her name on his lips was the most seductive sound she'd ever heard. She had enough presence of mind left not to moan out loud, but not enough to keep herself from giving him her tongue when he demanded it, nor from quivering with pleasure when he sucked it between his lips and gently bit it.

"You don't like it, do you? This is torture, right, Cass?" he muttered thickly, before his impatient mouth found hers again and delved into its warmth and wetness without waiting for an answer. He could feel his control slipping away, just as it had last night. He hadn't been going to touch her like this, but his hand was sliding slowly up and down between her breasts, the fingers splayed. When she didn't resist, his excitement flared hotter. He would stop in a minute, as soon as she . . . as soon as they . . .

"Philip!"

He froze.

Cass squeezed her eyes shut and jerked her head away, clutching both hands to her chest.

There was something he wanted to tell her, but at that moment the words eluded him. Shielding her with his body from Quinn's furious glare, he turned to face his old tutor. "Don't say anything, Oliver. The blame is entirely mine. Miss Merlin was just . . . there." In a voice loud enough only for her to hear, he added, "And more than I could resist." He did her the kindness of not looking at her as he lowered himself from the carriage to the ground.

Quinn's bony, clever face was bright red with anger. "Then apologize to her, damn you, and let her go," he grated through clenched jaws.

"Indeed I will. Miss—"

"It's not necessary," said Cass in a shaky murmur that stopped him cold. "Mr. Riordan and I were—settling a wager." Her chin went a little higher, her voice a little lower. "I lost." She looked directly at him, unblinking. Riordan could only guess at what the effort cost her. Her face was grim and defeated, and he felt no sense of exultation at her admission.

Quinn's eyes shifted between them as a glimmer of alarm began to supplant his anger. He reached around Riordan and closed the carriage door with a slam. "Take her home, Tripp!" he called to the patient coachman. The vehicle jerked forward, and the thread holding Cass and Riordan's gazes finally snapped.

Unmoving, Riordan watched the coach disappear around the corner, heard the clatter of hooves and wheels die away. The taste of her was still on his tongue, the imprint of her delicate throat on his palm. She'd said she wasn't afraid of him, and he was glad. But by God, she terrified him.

IV

"VERY WELL, GRANDMOTHER, I'LL PLAY IF YOU ABSO-
lutely insist." Lady Claudia Harvellyn laughed in
mock defeat and sat down gracefully at the piano-
forte. She threw Riordan an amused glance and
began to play, her long-fingered hands sliding over
the keys with perfect confidence.

Riordan relaxed against a satin-covered loveseat
in the Harvellyns' best drawing room and sighed
contentedly. There was nothing he enjoyed more
than sitting quietly for an hour or so, listening to
soothing music expertly played and feasting his
eyes on the lovely Claudia. In the past months these
occasional family evenings had been a godsend, a
blessed respite from the pointless round of frivolity
he had to endure every day. Here he could be
himself, he thought comfortably, taking a sip of tea
from a cup so delicate he could almost see through
it. Ah, this was what he needed. Peace, quiet.
Civility. Association with people who loved music,

who read books and talked about ideas. What an ironic joke that, just as he was beginning to understand himself, he was forced to waste precious time impersonating a wastrel to satisfy the debt he owed Quinn. But he'd given his promise, so there was no way out. The thought of going back on his word never occurred to him.

He set his cup down on a rococo side table and sat back, eyes half-closed, and contemplated Claudia Harvellyn's chestnut hair and flawless complexion, her ripe, womanly figure. At twenty-four, she was skating dangerously close to the thin ice of spinsterhood, but the awful prospect didn't seem to alarm her overmuch. She liked to say she was waiting for the right man, and Riordan liked to think he was that man. But no promises had been exchanged; in fact the subject of marriage hadn't even been raised between them. They had met at a house party in Norfolk nearly a year ago, on one of the rare weekends when Riordan had been sober, and he'd been attracted to her immediately. She was beautiful, of course, but what had drawn him even more was the aura of quiet self-confidence she projected. Here was a woman who knew and was satisfied with who she was. It was a quality he hadn't found in many people, and it had had a curiously soothing effect on him. In combination with her keen intelligence and a dry, subtle sense of humor, it had made her irresistible; he'd decided then and there that she was the woman for him.

So far the progress of his pursuit had been somewhat halting, he reflected wryly, lacing his fingers together and watching her over clasped hands. The dissolute life he'd lived for a dozen years had ended abruptly on a night ten months ago, and since then his debauchery had been only a well-acted charade. Claudia was one of a bare handful of people who knew of the reformed status of his character, yet she had shown no inclination so far to deepen their friendly, virtually platonic relationship. Riordan was frustrated by her detachment because he saw in her the perfect woman—beautiful, brilliant, accomplished, poised. The ideal wife for an ambitious young statesman. Once his obligation to Quinn was paid, he'd decided, he would court her publicly, and then he had no doubt that she would capitulate. She was strong-willed, but so was he. He intended to wear her down, pursue her without mercy until she simply gave up and married him.

His gaze wandered lazily around the handsome, well-appointed room, where Claudia's quiet good taste was so much in evidence. Her grandmother, Lady Alice, dozed peacefully in her chair. Her back was still arrow-straight, however, and she would happily have eaten worms before doing anything as vulgar as snoring. One only had to examine the elderly lady's aristocratic features and papery, blue-veined skin to see what her granddaughter would look like in fifty years, Riordan thought idly. A proud, cultured face, elegant and slightly haughty. Claudia's father, seated nearby on the sofa, had the same regal bearing, though in him it was softer, almost other-worldly, probably due to the delicacy of his health. Lord Winston had had a bad heart since boyhood; yet he'd outlived his younger, immeasurably healthier wife by a good ten years so far. Riordan theorized that he'd kept himself alive by developing a life of the mind, diverting all the energy others might expend physically into the fierce cultivation of the intellect. Claudia wasn't so doggedly cerebral, thank God, but she had unquestionably inherited her father's rational turn of mind.

For no reason, he rubbed his still-sore jaw and thought of Cassandra Merlin. What a contrast the two women made! He tried to imagine Claudia angry enough to strike him—or anyone—and found it impossible. Laughable. Claudia was a lady to the marrow of her bones, and he very much wanted to cast his lot with her. He'd known enough women like Cass Merlin to last a lifetime, beginning with the ones in his own family. Flighty, empty-headed females whose sole end was the pursuit of pleasure. He wanted nothing more to do with them, and looked forward to the day when his forced "relationship" with Miss Merlin was at an end.

And yet he hadn't been able to get her out of his mind all afternoon. Even while Oliver had lectured him on the evils of giving way to his fleshly impulses, he'd thought of her, of her face just before the carriage door slammed. She was precisely the kind of woman he wanted to avoid, and yet she had some quality—apart from the obvious—that drew him, a sort of fragile, battered dignity he didn't want to see injured. Wanted, in fact, to protect. Which was absurd; from all he'd heard, there was precious little left to protect. And anyway, she seemed perfectly capable of taking care of herself. She was young, that was all, and at his and Quinn's urging she was about to begin playing a very serious game. It was natural for him to feel a little responsible for her.

He thought of the way she'd looked in his library that afternoon, sitting bolt upright and fighting for control while Oliver's thoughtlessly callous words echoed in the room. He realized now that he'd wanted to go to her, to console her. What would she have done if he had? Flinched, or at least stared reproachfully back at him out of those extraordinary gray eyes. But what might have happened if Quinn hadn't interrupted them in the carriage at the moment he had? He imagined himself pulling

the coach door closed, insuring their privacy. She
would let him touch her, he knew it, but he would
ask her first before taking each pleasure. *May I
touch you here, Cass? Ah, sweet, let me kiss you
there.* . . . He'd pull the pins from her hair and feel
its slippery coolness, watch it fall down around her
shoulders and create that stunning contrast of black
hair and white, white skin. Then he'd brush her
swollen lips with his fingertips, and she would sigh
his name as she had last night. She would say yes to
everything he wanted, and when he kissed her,
she'd—

"I said Grandmother's going to bed, Philip. Did
you want to tell her good night?"

Riordan shot to his feet with guilty haste and
cleared his throat. "Yes, of course. A pleasure as
always, Lady Alice." He took the dry, shriveled
hand and kissed it. Inwardly he was wondering how
long he'd been sitting there, unaware that the music
had stopped and people were talking to him.

"I'm a bit tired; I believe I'll go up myself," Lord
Winston decided, reaching for the cane he kept by
his side. "Come again soon, Philip. I always like
talking to you. Next time, remind me to give you
that monograph on penal reform, will you?"

"I will. Good night, sir." They shook hands, and
Lord Winston followed his mother slowly out of
the drawing room. In the hall, the butler would
meet him and help him upstairs to his room.
Riordan reflected, not for the first time, that it was
fortunate the elder Harvellyns got out into the
world so infrequently; otherwise they would be sure
to become acquainted with the precise nature of his
reputation and feel compelled to restrict Claudia's
contact with him. As it was, they only knew him as
a young, wealthy, and well-connected M.P. who
had thus far shown no bothersome inclination to

break with the Whigs, and thus he was a welcome visitor in their home.

"That reminds me. I have a book for you, too, Philip. It's here in my sewing basket, I think. I've been meaning to return it for ages."

"Give it to me later. I want to talk to you, Claudia."

She looked up, and her face became serious. "You look tired. I noticed it earlier. You seemed so distracted."

"No, I'm fine."

She walked to where he was standing and reached a hand up to touch his cheek. The unusual endearment surprised him. Never one to pass up an opportunity, he seized her hand and kissed it, then held it while he spoke. "I wanted to tell you before you heard it from some damned gossip. I'm going to be—linked, as they say, with a woman. A woman with a rather unsavory reputation. I'm sorry."

"Oh, poor Philip, not again. What a bother for you." She smiled sympathetically.

Her total absence of jealousy provoked him. "Yes, well, this time our supposed liaison will probably have to be a bit more blatant." He realized with a touch of shame that he was trying to raise at least a hint of jealousy from her.

"I suppose she's very beautiful."

He smiled. "Ugly as a hedgehog."

"That's what you said about the French opera singer Mr. Quinn thought was a spy."

"But she *was* ugly."

"Philip, I saw her."

"Oh." He kissed her hand again. "You really don't care, do you? There isn't a particle of jealousy in your hard shell of a heart."

Claudia narrowed her eyes in thought. "No," she

agreed after a moment, "I don't suppose there is. Well, it wouldn't make much sense, would it? I don't suppose you could help yourself if you were attracted to another woman. And it would be foolish of me to worry about it before it's even happened."

"Your logic is as unassailable as always, my darling. And you are just as exasperating."

"Silly." She removed her hand. "It's late. Let me give you your book, and then you'll have to go."

He sighed in defeat. She went to her sewing basket and rummaged through it until she found a small volume bound in red leather. He recognized it, and smiled. His English copy of the *Social Contract*. "What did you think?" he asked, superfluously; Claudia always told, asked or not, what she thought of books.

"Stimulating, but more on an emotional than an intellectual level."

"Coming from you, that's the kiss of death."

"The first sentence sets the tone," she went on, ignoring him. " 'Man is born free, and everywhere he is in chains.' I deplore that kind of sensationalism. And I can't agree with his premise that man in his natural state is gentle and even timid. I'm much more inclined to believe, with Hobbes, that men are by nature selfish and amoral. Which renders the concept of a social contract absurd. The revolution in France is certainly proof that the mob can't be trusted to govern itself."

She continued to speak while Riordan listened carefully, nodding when he agreed, frowning when he didn't. After a while he lost track of the words, though, and began to concentrate on the way her lips moved. She had a nice mouth. She'd let him kiss her on a few occasions, but he knew he couldn't push his luck. She never told him to stop;

she just froze, and then it was like embracing a snowball.

"To believe that," she was saying, "one would have to agree with Rousseau that man consults his reason before listening to his inclinations, and what could be further from the truth? One can't— Philip, you're not even listening. I knew you were tired. Now you must go home. Shall I tell Robert to bring the carriage round?" She'd taken his arm and was leading him down the hall to the front door.

"Sorry, I was thinking of something else. No, it's too late, don't bother Robert. I'll walk."

They argued for a minute before she gave in. "Shall I see you on Thursday? It's the Chiltons' card party."

"I doubt it."

"No, I suppose you'll be engaged with your new *protégée*," she said archly. "What's her name? Just so that if I hear of you in connection with yet another lady, I *shall* have something to feel jealous about."

"I'll look forward to that," he smiled tiredly. "Her name's Cassandra Merlin."

"Merlin? Wasn't that the name of the man who was hanged?"

"Yes, and this girl's his daughter. But don't ask me anything else, Claudia. I'm likely to tell you, and then Oliver will have my head."

"Very well, I won't. But you do know that nothing you tell me ever goes any farther, don't you, Philip?"

"Of course I know it." He touched her hand. He considered kissing her, but decided it wasn't worth risking that look of grave surprise she always turned on him afterward. "Good night, my dear." And he opened the door and went out.

* * *

Cass sat on the edge of the bed, pressing her fingers hard against both temples. *All men are born free and equal. No man has a natural authority over his fellows. To renounce liberty is* . . . She pushed the heel of her hand against her throbbing forehead and gritted her teeth. *To renounce liberty is to renounce being a man.*

She fell back on the bed with a groan and stared dismally at the ceiling. Fifty pages, the blasted book had, with two columns per page, and print so tiny a flea would need glasses to read it. How galling it was going to be to admit to Riordan that she'd only finished half of it.

What would Papa say if he knew she was reading Rousseau? she wondered. Why, he'd be proud, and surprised, and—she caught herself up with a familiar start. It was going to be a hard habit to break. All her life she'd imagined what her father's reaction would be to whatever she might be doing or thinking; she'd done it so often it had become automatic, as unconscious as a reflex. Every decision she'd made had been based on his imaginary approval or disapproval, at first with things she'd done to please him, later with things she'd done to shock him—anything for a morsel of his attention. And of course the irony was that he'd never cared, and he couldn't care now. Then as now, she had no one to live for but herself. The insight was new, if not the condition, and it occurred to her she had no idea how to begin.

There was a knock at the door. "Come in," she called, sitting up.

It was Aunt Beth. She didn't immediately speak, but stood in the doorway for a moment with an enigmatic expression on her rice-powdered countenance. "You're a deep one," she announced finally, folding her arms.

"Pardon me?" Cass made her voice innocent, but felt her face begin to flush.

" 'I'll leave the taking of lovers to you,' " she mimicked with an unpleasant smirk. "God, what a hypocrite you are."

Cass came off the bed abruptly and went to the mirror. "Do I take it my visitor's arrived, Aunt?" she said stiffly, smoothing her skirts and tugging at her bodice.

"Philip Riordan." Lady Sinclair shook her head, unable to keep a trace of admiration from her tone. "I believe I may have underestimated you, Cassandra. May I ask how long you've known him?"

"Not long." She chided herself for not having thought of a story by now to account for her acquaintance with the Honorable Mr. Riordan. She saw she looked pale and drawn in the glass, and pinched her cheeks for color. "We met in church," she lied smoothly, not particularly caring what her aunt believed. "Now if you'll excuse me—"

"Wait just a minute, Cass. I think it's my duty to warn you, on the slim chance you weren't already aware of it, that Philip Riordan is not a gentleman. His reputation is deplorable, in fact."

That almost made her laugh. It was on the tip of her tongue to inquire who was being a hypocrite now. "Then we're a perfect match, aren't we?" she said instead. Aunt Beth's eyes narrowed. Not caring to continue the conversation, Cass went past her quickly and down the stairs.

She could hear masculine voices in the sitting room. She stood in the doorway for a moment before he noticed her; he was saying something to Freddy to make her cousin shake with laughter, but he broke off when he saw her. She greeted him self-consciously, relieved when Freddy interrupted her stilted little speech with a stream of genial chatter. Where were they off to? A stroll in St. James's Park, eh? Well, they certainly had the day for it. Oh, say, he'd heard Vauxhall wasn't at all fashionable anymore, that Ranelagh was the thing; what did Philip think? And by the way, who made his shirts? Cass stood quietly while Riordan responded to the rambling interrogation with surprising good grace. Then it was time to go, and he was guiding her out the door with a light and perfectly proper hand on her elbow, and handing her into a closed carriage with all the respect a gentleman might show to his elderly aunt.

She was sure he would revert to his usual tormenting self once they were alone, but to her relief he did not. He settled himself beside her at a polite distance and sent her a bland smile, devoid of connotation. "I'm glad to see you looking better than you did a few minutes ago, Cass," he said with genuine-seeming concern. "You haven't been ill, have you?"

"Thank you, no, I'm perfectly well." It was almost true; her headache was nearly gone and it was a beautiful afternoon. "It's fortunate the rain stopped this morning," she added, hoping she didn't sound as inane as she was feeling.

"Yes, indeed," he agreed, and went on to make a number of mundane observations of his own, until gradually Cass began to relax and even enjoy herself. For reasons of his own it seemed he was going to be on his best behavior, she realized with gratitude, and she made up her mind to respond in kind. She was conscious of a tiny feeling of disappointment, but attributed it to nerves and foolishness. Their last meeting had been so turbulent, at least for her, that she'd hardly been able to think of anything else in the last twenty-four hours. She'd lost the wager, proving spectacularly that her performance at the Clarion had had nothing to do with acting. She'd known it all along; the only thing standing between her and total humiliation was her hope that *he* hadn't known it, and now that was gone. That he'd thought her the kind of woman who would go home with a man she'd known for an hour had shamed her dreadfully. As long as it was Wade he thought she'd have gone with, she'd been able to bear it, but now he knew otherwise. It was he, Philip Riordan, she couldn't resist.

That he seemed today to have forgotten all about the incident filled her with confusion. She'd expected him to make smug, victorious references to her capitulation in the carriage, but his behavior was impeccable. Through her bewilderment and regret, she saw clearly enough that his reaction was healthier, and surely much wiser. She determined she would emulate him.

The neighborhood they were passing through reminded her of one in Paris where she'd gone to school as a girl; she told him so, and he began asking questions about what it had been like to grow up in France. She was hesitant at first, and kept her answers brief and factual. Yes, she'd always gone to boarding schools, even though Aunt Beth lived in the city. No, Freddy had never bullied her; if anything, she'd bullied him. Lonely? Oh, no. Not really. Well, at times, perhaps; but after all, what child isn't? Then, gradually, as the questions continued and she began to accept the possibility that he might really be as interested as he seemed in the answers, her reserve melted and she found herself telling him things she'd only told friends before—and a few things she'd never told anyone.

"What was your father like?" he asked, resting one arm on top of the seat between them. "Or does it bother you to talk about him?"

"I miss him, of course, but I don't mind talking about him. I loved him very much, although I didn't see him often. He was handsome and intense and exciting. I used to daydream about him all the time when I was a child."

"What would you dream about?"

"Oh, that he'd come and take me away from this or that boarding school, and then we'd live together in our old house in Surrey."

"You were six when your mother died?"

"Six, yes. He kept me with him for about a year afterward, but then I think he started to drink too much and—things. So he sent me to Paris to live with Aunt Beth."

"Ah, the charming Lady Sinclair. We met. Tell me, does she always flirt with your suitors?"

"Yes, always," she admitted candidly. "That is, when she's not accusing me of flirting with hers!"

He laughed. "So your father was the knight in shining armor who was one day going to rescue his princess?"

"So I thought. He even called me that, his 'princess.' But I was a perceptive child; at around fifteen or sixteen I realized that was never going to happen. I also realized neither my father nor my aunt wanted me around very much."

"Why not, do you think?"

His tone was matter-of-fact, his face and manner empty of pity, prompting her to answer with the simple truth. "I never understood why," she confessed softly, pleating a fold of skirt between her fingers. "I'd spent a lifetime trying to be a good girl, pliant and obedient, the kind of child they seemed to want. But it never worked, never made them love me. So I stopped trying." She gave a little Gallic shrug and smiled to leaven the words. "And then I found a group of friends who liked me, and finally I was happy."

A large, changing group of friends, she thought to herself, who seemed always to be just on the other side of respectability—the couple whose baby was born seven months after the wedding, the young men whose only means of support appeared to be gambling, the ladies who went off on dubious escapades unchaperoned and were rumored to allow their beaus unconscionable liberties. It was a crowd best termed "fast," but not truly wild, and very far from decadent. They were light-hearted and tolerant, and had welcomed her into their number at a time when she'd badly needed companionship. None had become a close friend, yet at that moment she missed them all.

"Are you happy now, Cass?" Riordan asked gently.

"Perfectly." Her answer was automatic, but the question shook her; it demonstrated how unguarded she'd grown with her confidences. "And what about you, Mr. Riordan? How does it happen that a rich, respectable M.P. is playing the part of a rake?" she countered, knowing full well her diversionary tactic was transparent.

He stared at her a moment, then answered in the same light tone. "Oh, Oliver saved my life once, in a manner of speaking. When I entered Parliament, he asked me to repay him in this way. It's only for two years, and it's almost half over."

"Mr. Quinn saved your life?" He nodded, but seemed unwilling to elaborate. "You must find it very tiring at times, the decadent life; very boring. At least I should find it so."

"Would you, Cass?"

She bristled slightly. "Yes, I *would.*"

"But not if there were a fountain around; then I expect your spirits would lighten considerably."

She flushed. "Do you always believe what you hear?" she demanded heatedly, scowling at his ill-concealed relish. "If so, you're no better than Mr. Quinn. I'd have thought you of all people would be more careful in what you took for the truth about others, being such an innocent target of gossip yourself."

"*Touché*! But it's only recently that I've been 'innocent,' you know. My reputation for depravity was richly deserved for a very long time."

"I'm not in the least surprised," she retorted, turning away from him to look out the window. She should have known he couldn't remain civil for long. Yet he intrigued her. She wanted to know more about his family, his syphilitic father and promiscuous mother. And his relationship with Quinn, and how it had come about that the older man had saved his life.

"We're in Pall Mall, Cass. Would you like to get out and walk from here?" She agreed with a cool nod, and he called for his driver to stop. "Take the carriage round to the south entrance, Tripp, and wait for us there," he told him when they'd alighted. "About an hour, I should think."

The carriage started off and he offered Cass a polite arm, evidently ready to resume his good manners. She thought again that they moved well together, comfortably, more like an established couple than the chary, on-guard strangers they were. They might even have collaborated on their dress today, so perfectly did her gray-blue muslin frock complement his waistcoat of lavender silk. They chatted easily and naturally about everyday things. He pointed out one of his clubs to her, a hoary-looking edifice fairly reeking with privilege, as well as a number of other well-known gentlemen's establishments lining the street. When they came to the park, he told her they would quite likely be meeting friends of his, and that when they did he might put his arm around her waist or a familiar hand on her shoulder. "Merely to foster the illusion of *tendresse* between us, Cass. I didn't want to take you by surprise."

She searched his face for a sign of facetiousness, but he kept it poker-straight. "I'll do my best not to shrink away in tell-tale horror," she returned in the same manner. After that they walked along the Mall in silence, thinking their private thoughts.

"It occurs to me we might even meet Colin Wade," Riordan said suddenly. "If that happens, I'll nod to him and we'll keep walking. I'm not ready for you to meet him yet."

Cass didn't think she was ready, either. "You're acquainted with him, then?"

"Acquainted, yes. Not friends."

"What's he like? Mr. Quinn told me very little."

"Wade? Blond and beautiful, or so the ladies tell me. You can almost picture him in a toga, wearing sandals. He affects slow, languid movements, and he likes to put his thumbs and forefingers together in a saintly way when he talks." He demonstrated, causing her to laugh at his conspicuously unsuccessful attempt to look effete. "Since the gesture is always unrelated to the point he's making, it's safe to say he only uses it to draw attention to his hands—which are, of course, long and white and beautiful. It's very effective."

"I shall remember to be impressed."

"He's partial to pastel colors in his dress, which is always immaculate. The other night at Walbridge's he had on a pink waistcoat. Pink!" He shook his head in wonder. "Women swoon over him for some reason, but he holds them at a distance, picking and choosing like a rajah. I'd say the best way to attract his notice is to flatter him."

"And his wife? What's she like?"

"She used to live in Lancashire on his estate, but now she stays in Bath. The official line is that she's an invalid, but the rumor is she's as mad as a March hare."

"Good heavens." She walked along, trying to absorb it all. "From the way you describe him, he doesn't sound like the kind of man who would bother himself about revolutions and anarchy and assassination."

"No, I agree. But then, they say Guy Fawkes was thought a very cheery, temperate sort of fellow by all who knew him. Anarchists don't always look like slavering madmen, unfortunately."

Cass murmured in agreement, wondering who Guy Fawkes was.

They stopped to watch the pelicans in the canal. He took her hand without thinking. "Wade's a very secretive man and not much is known of his private life. He has dozens of acquaintances but no close friends. The political side of his life is not public knowledge; what we know of it has only come from slow and painstaking intelligence work. He lived in Paris for a few years before his marriage, and we think that's where he fell in with a radical element. It probably began innocently enough—young hotheads talking revolution in fashionable cafés—but now it's quite serious. He really does want to overthrow the English monarchy, and he learned his anarchic principles from the Paris revolutionaries in the '80s."

"Why do you think he betrayed my father and his friends to the government?"

"Is that what Quinn told you?"

Cass whirled on him. "Do you mean to say it's not true?"

He held up his hands placatingly. "I didn't say that. In fact, it probably is true. It's only that no one's been able to prove it. Your father and his cronies refused to implicate Wade when they were arrested, even after they were told he'd sacrificed them. I'm a little surprised Oliver said it, that's all. I know he can be a bit single-minded, but at heart he's an honorable man. Cass? What's wrong?"

She'd gone a sickly shade of gray. After Riordan said "refused," a horrible, unspeakable thought occurred to her and she went deaf to everything else. She felt frozen inside and wanted to stay that way, but forced herself to speak. Knowing the truth would be better than fearing it the rest of her life.

"Will you tell me something honestly?" she said in a low, shaky voice.

He watched her stricken face in perplexity. "Yes, if I can. Cass, for God's sake, what is it?"

She swallowed hard and drew a painful breath. "Was my father beaten when he was in prison?"

He swore under his breath and reached for her. She tried to pull away, but he held her arms firmly. "Listen to me, love."

"He was, wasn't he?" To her dismay, tears began to streak down her face in a helpless flood. She let him lead her away from the path to a private place by a little copse of trees; when he pulled her into his arms, she felt too devastated to resist. "Oh God," she sobbed against his shirt. "I thought he didn't want to see me because he didn't care for me. My God, my God."

He let her cry. Her words were so thick with grief, he could hardly understand her. She's so young, he thought as he held her and stroked her back in slow, soothing circles. Her hair tickled his lips as he crooned meaningless comfort against it, and her slim hands pressing against his chest reminded him of another time she'd done that. He wasn't aroused, but every part of him that touched her was acutely aware of her womanliness.

"I'm all right now," she whispered, pushing back.

She wasn't; he gave her his handkerchief and held

on. "Listen to me, sweet. I don't know it for certain; it's possible he wasn't. But—"

"Don't say anything else. Please." She thrust him away and turned around.

He stared bleakly at her back, struggling for the right words. "I never met your father, Cass, and I won't pretend to admire him for what he did. But I know he believed in the course he chose and obeyed the rules he made for himself. No one could deny that what he did took courage. And dying for one's principles isn't such a tragic way to go, is it?"

After a long moment she turned back. Her face was ravaged from weeping, but she held her chin high and her voice was steady. "No, it's not a tragic way to die. Perhaps it's an enviable one. I beg your pardon for behaving as I did. It was naive of me not to have seen the truth before now. My excuse is that I didn't want to see it. I'm ready now if you'd like to go on our way."

It took all his willpower not to reach out for her again. But she thought all he felt was pity, and he didn't want to make her feel shame now on top of her grief. So he clasped his hands behind his back and stepped aside, bowing as she preceded him back to the path.

He began to speak of ordinary things—the loveliness of the late afternoon, the blight that seemed to be ruining all the dogwood trees this year—and after a little while he was rewarded by a ghost of a smile and a few quiet words in return. Emboldened, he told her a joke. It was a long, complicated, and very silly joke, and when she laughed at the end he suspected it was as much at him as at the point of the story. But the sound of her laughter warmed him like sunlight on a frozen pond, and at that moment he'd have stood on his head for a chance to hear it again.

"Philip! Philip Riordan!"

"Oh, bloody hell," he cursed under his breath. Cass stiffened and he casually slid his arm around her, pulling her against him. "You're about to have the pleasure of meeting a few of the people I'm obliged to call friends," he muttered grimly. The call came again; he stopped and turned around. Two couples were bearing down on them. "Hullo, Wally, Tom," he called in a voice that made Cass look up at him in surprise.

"I knew you'd heard me, you old sod," complained one of the gentlemen when he reached them. The fast walk seemed to have winded him; he wiped his corpulent face with a scented handkerchief and breathed through his mouth. "Ain't you going to introduce us to your charming friend, Philip?"

"No."

"Ha! Then I'll do it myself." He bowed to Cass as deeply as his paunch would allow. "Your humble servant, madam, Wallace Digby-Holmes. And this is Tom Seymour, a scurvy youth not worth your notice. And these three ladies are our friends."

"Two," corrected Tom. "These *two* ladies."

"Damn me, that's what I said. This one's Gracie —wasn't it? And this one's Jane; I'm sure it was Jane. Now, where were you two bound for? We'll go with you. Or if you've got to run off, Philip, I'll be happy to see the lady home myself. It's Miss Merlin, ain't it? I vow, you Commons fellows don't care a damn for manners anymore—begging your pardon, ma'am." He tipped an imaginary hat.

"Oh, bugger off, Wally," Riordan snarled, slurring his words a little.

"Tut tut! A trifle foxed, eh? I say, you wouldn't have a drop on you at the present moment, would you? Eh? God's truth, you're a good man!" He accepted the silver flask Riordan removed from his pocket, took a long pull, and handed it to Tom. The two ladies giggled and tsked. They were coarse-featured and colorfully dressed; Cass thought that if they weren't whores she was a parrot's pinafore.

"We won't keep you," Riordan muttered with a scowl, taking his flask back and swaying slightly.

"Whoa, what's your blinkin' hurry? The lady looks like she wants to go with us instead of you, Philip. I've a sixth sense about these things, y'see," he winked at Cass, tapping his forehead and moving closer.

Tom had an idea. "Why don't we let *her* decide?"

Wally grinned and clapped his friend on the shoulder. "Faith, why not? Eh, Philip?" Riordan continued to glare and sway. "Well, Missy, who's it to be? This drunken, bloody-minded lout you're attached to around the middle, or a couple of light-hearted, free-spending, good-looking bounders such as ourselves?"

The ladies were snickering again behind their hands; Cass had an urge to join them. "I believe I'll stay with the lout," she said demurely. While Wally and Tom roared their disappointment, she stole a glance at Riordan's face. He was still scowling down at her, but there was a decidedly humorous quirk at the side of his mouth.

"Women," Wally grumbled. "If it wasn't for—oops, beg pardon. Faith, we're off, then. Are you coming to Flaherty's tonight, Philip? If you do, I'll show you my new pistols. Come on, Tom. Hullo—June, ain't it? Take my arm, there's a good girl. Joan, you say? Well, make up your mind, woman. . . ." His words trailed off as the gay foursome moved away down the path.

As soon as they were out of earshot, Cass started to laugh. She'd found Riordan's friends harmless and amusing, although she could see how they might soon grow tiresome; in fact, albeit older, they reminded her a good deal of some of her old set in Paris.

Riordan smiled down at her, savoring the rare sound of her laughter and hoping she'd keep holding his arm like that. She didn't. Something in his eyes must have given him away, because her laughter died in her throat and she stepped away self-consciously. "We'd better go. It's almost dark."

It wasn't, but the sun was setting and their hour was up; Tripp would be waiting. He nodded sedately and they moved together toward the southern end of the park.

The carriage was there, waiting. Riding back to Holborn, Cass was astonished to hear that Wally was in fact Viscount Digby-Holmes, Lord Thomas Seymour was a baron, and they both sat in the House of Lords. "Good heavens!" she marveled. "That's shocking."

"Isn't it? Almost as scandalous as my being in the Commons. It's horrible accidents like these that give revolution a good name, Cass. Which reminds me—what did you think of the Rousseau?"

Her heart sank. She'd hoped he'd forgotten. "I adored it," she said on a note of finality. "That's Westminster Hall, isn't it? Aren't your chambers or whatever they're called inside?"

"Why, you lazy cow, you haven't read it."

"I have!" she cried indignantly. "'*L'homme est ne libre, et partout il est dans les fers.*' There, you see?"

"I see you've read the first sentence," he said, laughing.

"No, much more!"

"Indeed. And what did you make of it?"

"How do you mean?"

"What did you think?"

"About which particular part?"

He sighed patiently. "In general."

"I liked it, truly I did. But I didn't finish it," she confessed, shame-faced.

"Never mind. What do you think about the idea of a republic?"

She thought. "Well . . . I think people should have the right to have good leaders. If the leaders are incompetent or insane or evil or dangerous, then we ought to be able to expel them and elect new ones. And I think a king ought to rule because we've chosen him, not because God ordained him."

"Spoken like a true revolutionary."

"Certainly not!" she denied, shocked.

"What's your opinion of man in his natural state?"

"I beg your pardon?" Did he mean a naked man?

"In a state of nature, before society corrupts him, is he a simple, unaggressive sort of fellow or a greedy, amoral beast?"

It was a question she'd never considered. "I suppose it depends on his circumstances," she said slowly. "If he were warm enough and had plenty to eat, he'd probably be gentle and loving. But if his very existence was a constant struggle, I should think he'd be violent, even cruel." Her face cleared. "Is that right?"

Riordan laughed. "There's no right answer, Cass; it's all theory."

Then what good is it? she wanted to ask, but held her tongue.

He continued to worry her with questions about the origins of society and the social contract; after she realized that he wasn't going to make fun of her, she was able to concentrate on the notion and make connections that had never occurred to her before. He didn't patronize her, but listened carefully, interrupting to add an occasional thought of his own or to prod her out of a blind alley. It was a completely new experience for Cass—a conversation not about a person or a thing but about an idea—and she was amazed to discover that she enjoyed it immensely. When she looked out the window and saw her own house, she had no idea how long the carriage had been standing there.

"Goodness, I'd better go in."

"Yes, I suppose."

But neither of them moved. She watched him under cover of the gathering dusk, and thought that for all his able acting he really didn't look dissolute, unlike his friends in the park. His face wasn't puffy but taut, the lines of his jaw clean and hard. And his body was too muscular, his shoulders too straight. He had no belly at all and his thighs were so hard. . . . She swallowed and found her mouth had gone dry. "Well, I'd better go," she repeated.

"Cass, wait." He handed her something white. "This is for you."

"What is it?" Then she saw. Inside the envelope were ten hundred-pound notes. Her fingers tightened around them and her skin felt suddenly cold. She couldn't look at him. "It's a loan," she heard herself saying. "Did Quinn tell you it's a loan?"

"A loan? No, he didn't mention that."

The polite, uninflected tone of his voice told her more clearly than words that he didn't believe her. Anger flared quickly—at him, and at herself for wanting him to. It was a business transaction, wasn't it, loan or not? Payment for services rendered, Mr. Quinn had called it. And after it was all over, they expected her to leave England. Then why did she feel such hot, prickly humiliation as she sat holding the envelope, massaging its thick, weighty contents through the crisp paper? With a jerky motion she shoved it into her purse and pushed forward to the edge of the seat. "When will I be meeting Mr. Wade?" she asked tightly, staring straight ahead.

"Soon."

"Good. I want to start earning my fee as quickly as possible. Let me out now, please."

"I'll come again tomorrow."

"Fine. Please let me out."

Still she wouldn't look at him. He waited a moment longer, understanding only partly what had her so upset, then threw open the door and jumped to the pavement. He took her hand to help her down; she pulled away immediately and walked alone to her door. He thought she'd wait for him, let him open it for her, but before he could reach her she had disappeared inside.

V

CASS LEANED FORWARD AND PATTED HER HORSE BE-
tween the ears, wishing Riordan would talk to her.
She glanced at him, astride the fine bay stallion
beside her, and wondered what he was thinking. It
was impossible to tell from his blank, closed profile. Actually, neither of them had had much to say
this morning, or last night either, which was unusual. They had walked, ridden, dined, gambled and
danced every day and nearly every evening for
almost a week—but most of all they'd talked. Cass
hadn't even known there were so many subjects two
people could discuss. She had opinions now—not
deep ones, but respectable and reasonably well-
founded—on issues such as whether a Member of
Parliament ought to vote as his conscience advised
or his constituents demanded, and whether people
had a moral responsibility to overthrow a despot.
And the astonishing thing was that her new opinions weren't just mirror images of Riordan's, but

her very own. She wasn't even sure what his real beliefs were because his way of discussing them was to take the opposite of whatever view she took, argue until she either won or gave up, then take the other side and begin all over again. He never made her feel stupid, even when she stumbled into ridiculous *faux pas* that revealed how truly ignorant she was. He'd even paid her a compliment of sorts when he'd wondered once how she could be so bright, yet have had such a disgracefully poor education. She'd basked in the glow of that dubious praise for days. She still had difficulty with Rousseau and the other books he lent her to read, but had learned that if he summarized them for her she could grasp the fundamentals easily and accurately. She felt proud and exhilarated; for the first time learning was an enjoyable rather than a painful experience.

When they weren't discussing books and pamphlets and newspaper articles, they were abroad in high and low society, pretending to be lovers. They went to dances and routs, intimate supper parties, respectable and disreputable gaming houses, the theater, the opera; within days it was widely known that the Honorable Philip Riordan's new companion was the daughter of Patrick Merlin, that traitor they'd hanged at Newgate scarcely two weeks ago, and the chit wasn't even in mourning. But what could you expect of a damned Frenchwoman? Or as good as a Frenchwoman since she'd lived her whole life there and probably sympathized with the frogs just as much as her turncoat father. No one asked what the illustrious M.P. saw in her; they knew his reputation and they'd heard what she looked like. The only mystery was why he didn't move her out of her aunt's shabby digs in Holborn and set her up properly someplace in Mayfair.

Cass's appreciation of Riordan's acting ability deepened as she began to understand the real depth of the chasm between what he was and what he seemed to be. They developed a complex system of relating to each other in public as the days passed, until by week's end their teamwork was flawless. He drank alcohol in minute sips, and then only when he was being watched; Cass, who had always held her wine well, learned to drink most of her own glass of wine or claret quickly and then exchange it for his while no one was looking. She became adept at staying upright when he lurched drunkenly against her or stumbled while holding onto her. She grew used to his belligerence when he lost at cards, and acquired the ability to laugh heartily at his and his friends' ribald jokes.

The only thing she couldn't get used to was the intimate way he touched her in public—or more accurately, the way such intimacies had no meaning for him except to further the charade. When they were out, it seemed his hands were always on her, pressing, stroking, holding, and for the life of her Cass couldn't help but respond. Once at a pantomime in Vauxhall, he'd caressed her neck and shoulders for what seemed like hours, standing behind her in a crowd of his boisterous cronies. At last, blind to everything in front of her, knees trembling, she'd pulled his hand away and kissed the knuckles casually, just as though her bones weren't melting, her stomach knotted with warm, forbidden sensations. When they were alone later and he treated her with the same friendly politeness as always, she'd felt used, almost dirty—and oddly bleak.

She liked him too much. She knew it, but couldn't think what to do about it. He was the nicest friend she'd ever had. It didn't matter that their friendship was a purely contrived affair or that it had a finite end—he was warm and funny and exciting, and when they were together she was happy. She knew no good could come of it, but she lacked the sophistication or the cynicism it would have taken to hold herself away from him.

"What time is it?" she asked now, more to break the silence than to know the answer; it couldn't be very many minutes later than the last time she'd asked.

Riordan drew out his watch and flipped open the silver top. "Half-past eleven. He'll be along soon." He glanced across at her, taking in her new rose linen riding habit with what she could swear was disapproval before returning his stony gaze to the path.

"Do I look all right?" she asked anxiously, fidgeting at the pin that held her perky new riding hat securely to her upswept hair. Her palms were perspiring inside her leather gloves. She didn't understand his silence, his coolness, just now when she was finally about to meet Wade. She was as skittish as a colt, knowing that everything they'd worked for, that Mr. Quinn had paid for, was riding on her personal credibility for the next thirty minutes or so. But at the moment when she needed his support most, the free flow of words between them seemed to have dwindled to a trickle, and now came in infrequent drops.

He looked at her again, this time with a cold, assessing expression that came bewilderingly close to an insult. "Like a ripe plum, Cass, ready for plucking."

The words and his sneering tone were like a slap in the face. She turned her head away and bit her lip in dismay. What was wrong? What had she done?

"If you feel out of control even for a second, stop

your own horse, is that clear? We'll find another way to get his attention. I hate to see women galloping sidesaddle, anyway. Did you hear me, Cass?"

"I heard you perfectly," she returned tightly. "I'm an excellent horsewoman, Mr. Riordan. I'm hardly likely to lose control of this gentle hack, I assure you."

"Fine. Then you can concentrate on smiling and batting your eyelashes. Just don't say anything so stupid that you give the game away."

She stared. What was the matter with him? The contrast between this angry, unpleasant man and the generous, laughing friend he'd been was incomprehensible. It had started last night, she realized, when they'd begun to plan for Wade in earnest. She looked straight ahead, hands clenched on the reins, and willed herself to relax, not to cry, to think only of what she had to do. She jumped when a man's voice behind them called good morning, but it was only one of Riordan's friends and he rode on without stopping.

The day was overcast, the air oppressively warm. Hyde Park was emptier than usual for a Sunday morning because of the threat of rain. Colin Wade rode here every Sunday, and Cass alternately feared and hoped he would cancel his ride today. Nervously, she adjusted the maroon ascot at her throat and pushed back the sleeves of her jacket to reveal the snow-white lace cuffs underneath. She'd purchased the new riding habit, ready-made, with Quinn's money. Was that what was bothering Riordan? The idea made her angry. What business was it of his how she spent her money? Besides, what else was she supposed to do? Everybody expected her to seduce Mr. Wade. How was she to accomplish that unless she made herself attractive to him? She breathed a troubled sigh, then went rigid when she heard Riordan say softly, "There he is."

Up ahead, riding toward them, was a young man on a white mare. As he drew closer Cass saw, under cover of her lashes, that he was indeed, as Riordan had said, blond and beautiful. His waistcoat today was powder-blue instead of pink, his coat a striking damson. His pale yellow hair was combed straight back from a high forehead. Eyes set deep in a bony, perfectly modeled face wore a look of intense boredom. When he saw them, his brows rose slightly, accenting the haughtiness of his expression. He nodded distantly to Riordan and started to ride past when his cinnamon-colored eyes flicked across, then came to rest on Cass. He reined his horse to a stop.

"Wade," said Riordan.

"Riordan," said Wade.

Both men were watching Cass, whose wide eyes were fixed on the yellow-haired man as if he were a long-lost pot of gold. Wade waited expectantly; after a pointed delay, Riordan performed a graceless, grudging introduction.

"Miss Merlin," he intoned silkily, bowing from the waist, his eyes sweeping her from boot tip to hat top.

"How do you do?" Cass took off her right glove and put her hand out to him across a distance of six feet. Without dropping his gaze, he kneed his horse closer until the two animals were touching and his glossy riding boot nudged at her skirts. He took her bare hand, held it, smoothed the top with his thumb as if to make a place for his lips, and kissed it. Cass drew an audible breath, squeezing his fingers lightly, lingeringly, before letting go. She wet her lips with the tip of her tongue and threw her head back a little. Wade's thin, arrogant nostrils flared.

Riordan, who had been holding his breath, grabbed Cass's bridle and pulled her horse away from Wade's with an impatient tug. "We're in a hurry, Wade. Good morning to you."

"A hurry?" the yellow-haired man repeated, in a voice like honey flowing over velvet. "I thought the great House was in recess. A well-deserved one, I'm sure, after all the wise, far-seeing laws the honorable gentlemen passed this term. Statesmanship must be ever so exhausting." His smirk turned to a smile when Cass smothered a giggle against her palm.

"No, it's talking to maggoty, tarted-up coxcombs that's exhausting," Riordan snapped in an angry, too-loud voice. This time he spurred his horse to a walk, dragging Cass's mount with him. The mellifluous sound of Wade's laughter followed them until she twisted around in her saddle and sent him a heart-stopping smile. He raised his hand in a gesture of mingled promise and farewell; she returned it silently with her eyes, before Riordan's muttered oath made her turn to face forward again.

They rounded a turn in the path and stopped. Neither spoke for a moment. Now that it was over, Cass felt herself beginning to tremble in reaction. "It worked, didn't it? I think he liked me, don't you?" She took off her other glove and massaged the soft leather with nervous fingers. "Don't you think it went well?"

"I think if it had gone any better, the son of a bitch would've humped you right there in the bridal path." His lips thinned spitefully at the choking sound she made and the sudden rush of purple to her cheeks. "There's hardly any need for the second phase of the assault now, you were so successful at the first. I confess, Cass, I didn't sufficiently appreciate your talents in the art of seduction. I see I underestimated the vast diversity of your experience."

She swallowed with difficulty. "So it would seem," she said with icy, hard-won control. Bastard! she thought. Her chest ached and the sting of unshed tears was excruciating. He still had her bridle; she twitched it out of his hand and turned her horse around.

"Wait! You're going after him?"

"I always finish what I start, Mr. Riordan. Get out of my way."

"Remember what I said—end it immediately if you feel the horse running away or there's the least—"

"I said move!" The hard slap of the reins made her horse jump, shoving Riordan's mount aside as they jerked away. She heard him call something after her but shut her ears, concentrating instead on urging the well-bred hack to simulate a wild, out-of-control gallop. She could see Wade now, trotting away from her some thirty yards ahead.

"Faster, horse!" she called softly, swatting his hindquarters with the reins. "Faster!" But it was no use; she couldn't prod him out of his sedate canter. In desperation she took her foot from the stirrup and dropped the reins, hugging the horse's neck and seizing a handful of mane. If she couldn't make him look out of control, at least she could make herself look imperiled.

Wade heard them and turned around. As they flew by, Cass let out a terrorized scream. She was clutching the horse in earnest now as his choppy, frightened gait threatened to unseat her. A backward glance told her Wade was riding hard after, and she prayed she wouldn't fall off before he could

save her. Now he was beside her; she saw his hand
snake out and jerk the sagging reins. Her horse
pulled up sharply, so sharply she lost her seat,
rolled over his head, and landed in a loose heap on
the side of the path.

She sat up shakily, trying not to wince from the
shooting pain in her ankle. Wade was beside her in
seconds, touching her, asking if she was all right.
She became aware that her skirts were up to her
knees, dusty petticoats askew, her stockinged
calves fully visible to his interested gaze. She
wanted to jerk her gown down, but forced herself
instead to lie back against his snowy shirtfront with
half-closed eyes and moan a little.

"Oh, Mr. Wade, you saved me! I shall be forever
grateful to you." Riordan was right, she thought
swiftly; I *am* good at this.

"Thank God you're all right. Do you think you
can stand?"

"If you'll help me."

He grasped her around the middle in what would
otherwise have been an embrace and easily lifted
her to her feet. Afterward he kept his hands on her
for a little longer than was necessary. She put her
weight on her good foot and sent him a dizzying
smile of gratitude. Close up, he was older than
she'd thought, much older. His face was at the stage
in which one could simultaneously see the youth
he'd been and the middle-aged man he was becoming. The skin around his eyes looked dry and not
quite healthy; an early hint of jowl had begun to
show beneath his classically shaped jaw.

He took both her hands and turned the palms up,
examining the scraped skin. "You're hurt," he said,
frowning down in concern.

"It's nothing." She pretended to lose herself in
his cinnamon gaze, her lips slightly parted, breath

coming shallowly. She thought for a second he was going to kiss her, and something inside rose up to rebel, but instead he took her by the arm and led her a few steps away to a fallen tree trunk. Biting back a groan, she made herself walk without limping, and sank down on the log gratefully.

"Where's Riordan?" He sat beside her and took her hands again.

"He got down from his horse to—take care of a private matter," she said softly, blushing prettily. "I was annoyed and started to ride away. Then a rabbit dashed through my horse's legs, and before I knew it I was lying on the ground! Thank heavens you were here, Mr. Wade, or I don't know what might have happened."

"Call me Colin," he told her in his silky, languid voice. "Tell me, is it true that he's always drunk?"

She bristled at his impudence, but turned her face away as if in confusion. "Very nearly," she admitted. "But not today. At least, I don't think so."

"Then why do you—I beg your pardon. Forgive me for intruding on your private business."

She turned back. She opened her mouth and then closed it. She searched his face for a long, intimate moment, then spoke quietly. "A woman in my position can't always choose with whom she associates, Mr. Wade." She took a breath. "Colin." Their eyes held, and this time she was certain he would kiss her. But at that moment she heard a rider approaching and snatched her hands away. "It's Philip!" she said in dismay.

"Are you afraid of him? Shall I send him away?"

"Oh, no! Oh, please, you mustn't!" She let an edge of panic into her tone.

"Very well, but I must see you again. Tell me I may call on you."

Riordan was almost upon them. "Yes, yes," she

said distractedly. "I should like that ever so much. But you don't know where I live!"

"I'll find you." He took her hands again and touched his lips to the injured palms in a feather-light kiss. Cass sighed blissfully.

"Now, there's a sight to make a fellow want to puke." Riordan climbed off his horse clumsily; in the process his silver flask fell to the ground with a clatter. "Balls!" he roared, watching the brownish liquid seep into the ground. He advanced on the seated pair menacingly. "Why don't you get your prissy arse out of here, Wade, before I lodge my boot in it?"

Wade came off the log slowly. "Riordan, you're a drunken pig."

Cass caught his sleeve in alarm. "Please!" she implored softly. "Thank you for helping me, but truly, it's better if you go."

Wade turned to her uncertainly. "Are you sure? I don't like leaving you with him."

Riordan observed the touching exchange in mounting frustration. Everything was going well, better than he'd hoped, but all he wanted to do was knock their heads together like a couple of pumpkins.

"Very well, then, if you're sure you'll be all right." Wade straightened. "But I'd better not hear that this lady's been abused in any way, Riordan. If I do, I promise you'll regret it."

"This *lady* is none of your business, you pastel fop. Take yourself off."

"Just remember what I said," Wade warned, curling his lip with distaste. He went to his white mare and mounted. "*Au revoir*, Miss Merlin," he said with a bow and a melting smile that made Riordan want to spit. He gave her a slow, somehow suggestive little salute and rode away.

Cass leaned back on her hands and frowned.

"You came too soon. And you were much too harsh with him. What if you've scared him away for good?"

"Not bloody likely. The bastard knows a sure thing when he sees it. He'll come sniffing around tomorrow or the next day, like a hound after a bitch in heat," he snarled, glaring down at her. He felt like wiping the feel of Wade's lips from her hands. And then kissing her until she couldn't stand up.

"You're disgusting," she flared, red-faced. "You don't even need to act this part, do you? Because Wade was right—you *are* a pig!"

Growling, he grabbed her hand and yanked her to her feet. She yelped in pain and clutched at his lapels for balance, lurching against him. "What the hell is wrong with you?" he demanded, alarm causing his voice to sound even angrier.

"My ankle, damn you!"

"You fell off your horse?"

She refused to answer. She pushed at him and started to hobble away.

"You idiot!" He grabbed her in mid-limp and picked her up. "How could you be so bleeding clumsy? I told you not to let the horse—"

"Stop shouting at me and put me down! I don't want your help."

Their loud voices had spooked her horse; every time he got near enough to put her up, it skittered sideways, ears back. When he finally stopped swearing, the animal quieted. He stood beside it, Cass in his arms, their irate faces inches apart.

"Take your hands off me, Riordan. You make my skin crawl."

He smiled evilly. "That's good, Cass, because you'll need the practice. Pretty soon Wade's going to put his soft white hands all over you, and then your skin will really crawl."

"I'd a thousand times rather he touched me than you!"

"Really? Let's see."

She pushed backward as far as she could, but he had her against her horse; her head touched the saddle and went no farther. He kissed her thoroughly, expertly, using all the skills he'd acquired over a lifetime of kissing women. Her anger was her shield, but if he'd kept it up half a second longer, it would have crumbled. She knew it. When he drew away, she wiped her lips with the back of her hand, turned her head, and spat on the ground.

Riordan's face went as still as a stone carving and Cass felt a flutter of fear. For a moment his anger consumed him, and he was glad; the bright flames burned hotter than the sick, dangerous disappointment he felt inside. "Which ankle?" he ground out.

"Right." His eyes were blazing blue pools of enmity; for an insane moment she imagined him throwing her to the ground and stamping on her hurt foot.

"Can you ride?" She nodded. He sensed her fear with satisfaction—then shame, realizing that on some level he'd wanted to frighten her if he couldn't seduce her.

Cass gathered her courage. "I don't want you to touch me again, do you understand? Ever. If you do, I'm through helping you and Quinn." Her neck and shoulders were trembling from the effort to hold herself upright without hanging onto him.

He wanted to tell her that was fine with him, that was perfect. His lips curled in a sneer. "I'll touch you any damn time I want, Cass. Do you know why?" His eyes moved over her insultingly. "Because that's what you're being paid for."

The blood drained from her face. Her body was like a tight sack of sticks and stones in his arms, not flesh and blood. He felt a wave of contrition, knowing full well he was only taunting her because she'd committed the unforgivable sin of rejecting him.

Speechless, tears only a blink away, Cass let him seat her on her horse, left foot in the stirrup, right knee cocked around the pommel. She felt nothing now but numbness and fatigue. In a flat voice he asked if she was in pain, and she said no. He mounted his stallion and they began to walk, slowly and sedately, out of the park. Neither spoke, both thinking what it would be like if he never touched her again.

Cassandra watched the fog-shrouded street lamps drift past the window with diminishing frequency as the carriage rolled eastward, until they were driving in almost total darkness. Wade's arm pressed against hers with an intimacy she didn't welcome, and she had to will her body to relax, not tense away from him.

The evening had gone well. They'd dined at his club, then strolled in Oxford Street for an hour before he'd hailed a hackney to take her home. She'd done a convincing job, she knew, of conveying to him her antipathy to the English and her bitterness over her father's execution. She'd also managed to persuade him that she found him irresistibly attractive and that she despised Philip Riordan—the double lie that had always seemed to Cass the most incredible of all the lies she would have to tell him. But to her relief, the notion that she would endure the intimate company of a wealthy gentleman for whom she felt nothing but contempt hadn't seemed peculiar to Wade at all; in fact, he'd taken it as a matter of course. She'd feared he would offer, then and there, to become her new protector, and she hadn't known how she would respond if he did. What excuse could she make after sounding so eager to give up Riordan? That he was richer? But he had not offered, so she was safe for now. Her relief was enormous.

"Cassandra," he murmured, breaking the short silence. "What are you thinking about?"

She understood now what Riordan meant about the man's slow, languid movements; they'd begun to get on her nerves. Sometimes his voice was so honeyed and unhurried, she wanted to shake him. "I was thinking of my father," she improvised, making her tone wistful. "And how much I miss him."

He seemed to hesitate. "I knew him." At her look, he added hurriedly, "Only slightly. He was a good man, Cassandra. You have nothing to feel ashamed of, you know."

"Oh, Colin, I know that."

"As a matter of fact," he went on after a moment, "I was one of the small number of people who supported him after he was arrested."

"Publicly?" she couldn't resist asking.

"No, no. That was impossible. Try to understand, my dear, these are dangerous times; to admit that one favors a revolution in Britain could be disastrous."

"And do you?" When he didn't answer, she finished the question. "Favor a revolution in Britain?" She held her breath. The carriage came to a stop in front of her house, but neither of them moved.

"Do you?" he countered.

She too seemed to hesitate. "With all my heart!" she exclaimed finally, as if unable to control herself. "I wish my father had succeeded, Colin! How I should love to see this monarchy toppled, and men

like Philip Riordan brought down with it. And then
forced to struggle for their very existence like
everyone else!"

She was afraid that she had sounded too dramat-
ic, but her intensity had called up an answering
glitter in Wade's reddish-brown eyes. He seized her
hand and opened his mouth to say something, then
appeared to think better of it. He kissed her fingers
fervently instead. "I think you and I will do well
together, Cassandra Merlin," he whispered fiercely.
Then he opened the carriage door and jumped
down.

In the dim glow cast by the lamp near her front
door, he asked when they would see each other
again.

"I'm not sure," she answered slowly. "I want to
see you, Colin, but I must be cautious."

"Of course. I understand."

"It's not that I'm afraid of him. I can see anyone I
want. He doesn't own me. . . ." But she let a silent
"yet" sound between them. She knew it was wrong;
she was supposed to be encouraging him, not using
Riordan as a shield. But something about Wade
frightened her and she couldn't help it. She wanted
to go slowly.

"If you really mean that, then come out with me
tomorrow night."

Her heart sank; she forced a smile. "Yes, all right.
I will." Instead of smiling back or looking pleased,
he stared at her with an odd, unreadable expression. Now he's going to kiss me, she thought,
bracing herself. Relax, or he'll know.

Then something happened that she'd never foreseen. He made a clumsy grab for her shoulders and
kissed her hard, without preliminaries. Her head
struck the brick wall behind her with a thud and
she gave a little muffled cry. Instead of releasing
her, he only pressed harder. She tried to make her

lips soften, but he was mashing his mouth against her so hurtfully it was impossible. He didn't use his tongue, but his teeth clashed against hers repeatedly, until she thought she could taste her own blood. When he pulled back to look at her, she didn't have time to disguise her distress at his rough treatment. "This is how I like it, Cassandra," he told her in a curiously detached voice. "Like this."

He kissed her again in the same manner, but this time he reached both hands around and began to knead her buttocks with cruel, biting fingers, squeezing and pinching until she almost cried out from the pain. She endured it without moving, her mind a dark blur of shame and confusion.

Finally, he drew away. He put his hands around her neck and flexed his fingers lightly. "You like it that way, too. Don't you, Cassandra?"

She nodded mutely, shuddering.

His thin lips, red from mauling her, widened in a pleased smile. When he reached behind her she almost leapt away, but he was only opening the door. "Good night, my dear. I'll count the hours until tomorrow." He guided her inside solicitously and pulled the door closed in her white, stricken face.

Inside, Cass rested her back against the door in pitch darkness and listened to the carriage drive away. Tears rolled down her cheeks. "I can't, I can't," she whispered, fumbling for her handkerchief. All at once three violent knocks exploded in her ears, and she came away from the door as if she'd been knifed in the back. Her hand went to her throat and her breath caught painfully. Oh God, don't let it be him, please, please. Three more knocks, like a clenched fist smashing against the wood. She dashed at her eyes and put her hand on the knob. "Who is it?" Her voice sounded ludicrously casual.

"Open the door, damn it!"

Riordan! She threw open the door and would have flung herself against him in relief, but his face, and then his words, stopped her cold.

"You couldn't wait, could you, Cass? I told you not to see him without telling me first, but you couldn't stand it."

"Yes, but he—"

"It must've been hard for you all these weeks without a man. Why didn't you tell me? I'd have been glad to be of service, and I wouldn't have charged a thing."

She gasped. "What are you—"

"But don't go to him again without telling me, do you understand? No matter how hard it gets for you. Because the man's a killer, Cass, and you could get hurt."

She stopped trying to talk and stood still, waiting for him to finish.

"Or is that what you like about him, his killer instinct? That's fine with me, I don't give a damn, but I need you to stay healthy until this is over. After that you can do whatever you bloody please." He put his face close to hers and snarled. "But if you go with him again without telling me, I'll make you sorry."

She could hardly breathe. "You son of a—" she got out before he took her arm and forced her backward.

"Go inside and lock the door. Don't see Wade again until we talk." He pulled the door closed in her face, and she heard his fast, angry footsteps on the cobblestones. Too furious to weep, she pulled her foot back and kicked the door as hard as she could.

A chilly mist curled around Riordan's legs as he strode along. He turned up his collar and wrapped his arms around his middle, shivering. He wondered how he could feel cold when inside he was burning up. He'd come here tonight to apologize. He'd been feeling ashamed for days. He'd treated Cass badly and he'd wanted to put things right between them. Now he just wanted to murder her.

Jealous. He was jealous. It wasn't a completely new experience; he'd felt it a few times before with women. But he'd never felt jealousy like this before, never been burned up by it, as if in white-hot flames that left nothing but anger and ugly, spiteful words. He knew what Cass Merlin was; he'd always known it. Then why, when she merely fulfilled his sordid expectations, did he want to strangle her?

No, that wasn't quite it. What he wanted to do with Cass was seduce her. Take off her clothes, slowly, riding in a closed carriage. Or in his bed, quickly and desperately, both of them naked in seconds. Or slyly, secretly, in her aunt's sitting room, listening to her nervous, muffled moans as he undid the buttons. . . .

He stared up at the invisible sky. He'd thought at first that he wanted to avoid her because she was too much like too many other women he'd known, but there was more to it. It wasn't only that she embodied everything he'd rejected, called on all the carnal, unregenerate impulses he'd foresworn. It was that, but in combination with some other quality she possessed, one he didn't care to think about or give a name to, that made her so dangerous. She was a threat to his ambitions, as insane as that sounded. He wanted to make a difference in the world, use the undeserved power he'd been handed and leave things better than the way he'd found them. He wanted to marry Claudia. He wanted to work hard, earn the respect and admiration of his peers, and prove to them and to himself that he wasn't like his father or anyone else in his whole blighted family. His instincts told him the woman he'd just seen in Wade's arms could ruin all that and turn the useful, orderly life he wanted upside down.

He walked on, feeling strong and resolute. Crossing a dark intersection, he was struck by a brilliant mental image of Cass naked, lying across his lap, smiling with drowsy pleasure while he caressed her. He shut his eyes but only saw the picture more clearly. Saw himself stroking her between her legs, watching her face. . . .

He walked faster, whistling to distract himself. The next image was even more seductive, and more horrifying. He saw himself and Cass in his library, sitting in separate chairs before a crackling fire, reading aloud to each other from the books on their laps. She had a blanket over her knees, and he was resting his slippered feet on a little stool.

He slammed his open palm against a lamp post and kicked it with his boot. He muttered a string of foul oaths and walked on. He had a long way to go.

VI

"MISS MERLIN, IT'S ALWAYS A PLEASURE TO SEE YOU. Won't you come in? I'll take your shawl if you like."

"Thank you, John." Cass smiled at John Walker and handed him her wrap. He seemed to function as Riordan's housekeeper as well as his secretary, she'd noticed in the weeks she had been coming here. "Would you tell Mr. Riordan I'm here, please?"

Walker cleared his throat a little uncomfortably and his fair complexion pinkened. "Oh, dear, I'm so sorry, but he isn't here."

"No? But he sent a note saying he wanted to see me." A rude, cryptic note, the tone of which had annoyed her out of all proportion.

"Yes, I know. I had it delivered myself," he said apologetically. "But then he was called out—some trouble with a constituent—and I'm not quite sure when he'll return."

"I see." She weighed her alternatives. "In that case, I believe I'll go home."

He cleared his throat again. "Actually, he . . . wondered if you'd be good enough to wait. In the library. He gave me a book he said you were to—that is, if you wanted to, a book you might like to read."

Cass cocked a skeptical brow. She could well imagine what Riordan's actual words to his secretary had been, and congratulated the young man on the tactfulness of his interpretation. She decided she would stay so that he wouldn't incur his employer's unreasonable irritation, but for no other reason. "Very well, John, lead on."

The secretary sent her a grateful look and preceded her down the hall to the library, ushering her inside with a polite hand on her elbow. She smiled at him again. She liked John Walker. Sometimes she suspected he had a tiny crush on her.

She went directly to the windowseat, as was her habit. He brought her, not a book, but a collection of printed pages bound together at the edges with string. The tiny print and the length of the document made her quail, but she took it on her lap, plumped a pillow at the small of her back, and prepared to give it her best try.

"May I bring you something? Some tea, or a glass of sherry?"

"Not sherry—then I should fall asleep even faster," she laughed. "Nothing right now, John, thanks."

"Are you sure? If you'll pardon me for saying so, you're not—that is, I've seen you looking better. Are you quite well?"

"Yes, I'm perfectly fine. Thank you very much."

He hesitated a moment longer, then made a polite bow and left the room.

Cass put her head back against the window and

closed her eyes. No, she wasn't quite well, but she thought the rice powder she'd rubbed into the purple circles under her eyes had disguised the fact. There was nothing really wrong; it was only that her life was in such turmoil. She never knew what sort of mood Riordan would be in when they met, publicly or privately. Usually he was vile, but sometimes he surprised her by being extraordinarily gentle, almost as if he didn't despise her after all. And like a child, or a puppy, she would invariably drop her guard and respond warmly to him on those occasions, only to regret it the next time he was vile again.

As for Wade, she met him as infrequently as she could without raising his suspicions—or Mr. Quinn's ire. He'd never hurt her again the way he had that first night, but her fear that he would kept her constantly on edge. She'd been too angry at first, then too ashamed, to mention the incident to Riordan, but she'd made a secret vow that if Wade tried to touch her like that again, she would not allow it, even if it meant aborting her role in the plot against him.

Her decadent new life had caused her to reverse day and night; she was seldom in bed before dawn, and usually slept until afternoon—or more precisely, lay there until afternoon, fretting and brooding, trying to understand what she'd gotten herself into and wondering how much longer she could endure it. When she did sleep, she had bad dreams. She'd lost her appetite. And today was her birthday and no one cared.

Other than that, she thought dryly, everything was perfectly fine.

Now what did Riordan want her to read? she wondered on a tired sigh, settling herself more comfortably. Talking about books was almost the only way they communicated anymore without quarreling—a circumstance she would not have thought possible a month ago. She, Cass Merlin, a reader! She shook her head in weary wonder and read the title page. *Reflections on the Revolution in France,* by Edmund Burke. Burke, Burke. The name sounded familiar, but she couldn't quite place it. She smoothed the pages on her lap and started to read.

Two hours later Riordan walked into the library and went straight to his desk. He rummaged through the piles of papers and letters littering the top, looking for a speech he wanted to show his friend Spencer. A sound drew his attention to the windowseat.

Cass. He hadn't thought she'd wait for him this long; he felt a ridiculous lightness in his chest at the sight of her. She was asleep, still sitting up but slumped sideways, one shoulder pressed against the wall in an uncomfortable-looking position. He went closer, quietly, and stood before her with his hands in his pockets. She was breathing softly through parted lips; the white of her eyelids looked naked and unguarded. She mumbled something and he went very still, hardly breathing, hoping she wouldn't wake. A long, silky strand of black hair had fallen from the loose knot on top of her head; moving closer, he took it between his fingers and massaged the cool sleekness, remembering.

He sat beside her, his speech and the man in the drawing room waiting for it forgotten. "Sweet Cass," he murmured. He put a warm hand behind her neck and tugged gently; she hummed something in her sleep and obligingly shifted herself toward him. Now she was slumped against him instead of the wall, and he put both arms around her securely. She was wearing white again, but this time with perfect propriety—a light, summery frock trimmed with pale blue ribbons. Even asleep, she looked cool and elegant. It was the first time he'd held her since the day she'd said he mustn't touch her again. Such rules were made for breaking, he decided; they were almost like dares. He let his lips wander along her hairline as he breathed in her scent, that faint, flowery sweetness he still couldn't identify. Her hands lay open on top of the pages in her lap; the sight of the vulnerable, upturned palms stirred him.

"Cass," he said again, stroking the exquisite softness of her cheek, her neck. He tipped her head back on his shoulder and touched her lips with light fingertips.

She opened her eyes. "Riordan," she said on a long, soft sigh.

"Philip," he corrected, whispering.

Her gaze was dreamy, relaxed. He could feel his self-control slipping away as he abandoned himself to the warm, bottomless gray of her eyes. She had the longest lashes he'd ever seen. Her skin was like the petal of some exotic white flower. His mouth moved toward hers as if a strong magnet pulled him there. While he watched, the look in her eyes changed. Now she was very much awake, waiting, not breathing. Her hushed expectancy made him self-conscious at last; with his lips a scant two inches from hers, he asked her, "What is the effect of liberty on individuals?"

Her slow, confused blink made him smile. He gave her a tiny shake and repeated the question.

She frowned, thinking. "It makes them do what they please."

"So what ought we to do?"

"We ought to . . . see what it will please them to do before we risk congratulations, which . . . which may soon turn into complaints."

He nodded. "And do you agree with that, Miss Merlin?"

She couldn't think with him holding her like this. How had she gotten into this posture, anyway? "Yes, I think so. Excuse me, would you—"

"Oh, of course. Beg pardon." He unwrapped his arms and pushed away to give her more room. "How are you finding Burke in comparison to Rousseau?" he asked briskly, before she could ask him any questions about the position she'd woken up in.

She blushed, recalling the time she'd professed to admire them both equally. "They haven't much in common, have they?" she said, straightening her gown and smoothing back her hair.

"No," he agreed, tactfully not rubbing it in.

"Mr. Burke has a strong veneration for the past, I would say. And since the French Assembly is new and has no traditions of its own, he thinks it a worthless usurper."

"'A worthless usurper,'" Riordan repeated wonderingly. Cass flushed, but he was impressed as well as amused.

"And he's much more conservative, isn't he?" she rushed on. "Much less trusting of the people's ability to govern themselves."

"Does that surprise you? You've lived in Paris. You know what the mob is capable of, Cass."

She hesitated. "It's odd—everyone here speaks of the *mob*, the *mob*, as if they were all savages dressed in bloody rags. But do you know, Philip, the people in the mob are really only ordinary working men and women—bakers and soap-makers and drapers. The kind of people we buy the things we need from, people we'd be lost without." Riordan nodded thoughtfully. "And yet this man Burke writes so convincingly about the folly of leaving the government in their hands, I can't help but agree with him."

"It's his persuasive power. He's famous for it in the House. That pamphlet you're reading has had more to do with dampening English enthusiasm for the Revolution than anything else. It's already sold thirty thousand copies."

"Do you know him?"

"Very slightly. Men of his brilliance don't usually befriend youthful upstarts with bad reputations." His smile was tinged with irony, even bitterness.

"You admire him, don't you?"

"Very much."

"Perhaps—perhaps one day he'll know the sort of man you really are, and understand that what you've been doing has only been an act. And then he'll admire you, too."

A slow smile changed his face. "Ah, Cass." He reached for her hand. "How very nice you are." He kissed her fingers, but it wasn't enough. Before she could protest, he kissed her startled lips, tasting them, listening to the shallow sound of her breathing. That wasn't enough either, but things had a way of getting out of hand with Cass. He forced himself to stop while it was still possible.

He stood. Her eyes were huge, their expression either accusing or beseeching, he couldn't tell which. "I have to go, someone's waiting for me." She nodded. "I'll be back." She nodded again. "Keep reading," he ordered gruffly, and walked out.

Cass stared at the closed library door for a long moment, fingertips pressed to her lips. Finally she remembered the unread pages in her lap and Riordan's last command. With a weary sigh, she propped the pamphlet on a pillow in the corner of the window seat and scooted back a few feet; she could see the small print better that way.

The king of England is the king by a fixed rule of

succession, she read; *he holds his crown in contempt of the Revolution Society, who haven't a single vote for a king among them, individually or collectively. . . .*

Her mind drifted. She found herself recalling every word and gesture and nuance in what had just passed between her and Riordan, beginning at the moment she'd woken up in his arms. She remembered the day she'd told him he must never touch her again; until now—except in public, and then only casually—he'd obliged. What had changed? Was it possible he missed the closeness they'd once shared as much as she did? Had he also found it sweet, and irresistible?

Oh, what an idiot she was. She could hardly believe she was asking herself such stupid questions. Men were different—she'd known that for years. They liked touching for its own sake, and they had a strange and altogether unique way of leaving their emotions out of it. It was women who were cursed with this need to read deep meaning into any casual caress, and she was no different from the silliest of them. That was how hearts got broken. Hers, she vowed grimly, was going to stay intact. She would abandon foolish speculation on Riordan's motives forever. She would be cynical and sophisticated and always assume the worst. It wasn't an approach she'd ever employed with men before, but where Philip Riordan was concerned she suspected such measures were warranted.

She straightened her shoulders, scowling at the blurred pages in front of her, and made a ferocious effort to concentrate on royal authority against the needs of the state. The door opened again. She recognized Riordan's tread but didn't look up.

"I thought you were reading."

"I am reading."

"From six feet away?"

She ignored him. *The Revolution has degraded the king, the ministry, the judiciary—*

"Cass!" She jumped. "You need glasses!" He came toward her, his expression that of someone who had just made a shattering scientific discovery.

"No, I don't."

"Of course! The headaches, the slowness—everything pointed to it. Why didn't I see it earlier?"

"I do not need glasses."

"The hell you don't. Come on."

"What are you doing?"

"John! The carriage!" He was bundling her out of the room and down the hall. The secretary met them in the foyer. "On second thought, never mind the carriage. We'll walk. I know just the place. Does she have a cloak or something?"

"Yes, a shawl—"

"Get it! We're in a rush, John."

Mr. Walker hurried away.

"Riordan!" Cass cried, vexed. "I do not need glasses! I can see perfectly well. I'm looking at you right now, and I see you quite clearly."

"Don't be idiotic. Here, put this on." He took the shawl Walker held out and wrapped it around her shoulders. "Come on, we haven't got all day."

She threw the secretary a look of exasperation and let Riordan usher her outside. "Where are we going? Or would it be too much trouble to tell me?" He was walking swiftly, and since he held her hand she had to step lively to keep up.

"To get glasses. I thought you'd have figured that out, Cass."

She ground her teeth. "But I don't—"

"What makes you think you don't need glasses? Apart from the fact that you're not blind?"

"Once I mentioned it to Aunt Beth. She said I didn't need them."

He slowed down enough to look at her. "Oh, Aunt Beth said so!" he exclaimed with sarcastic wonder. "Well, why didn't you tell me sooner?"

She flushed and didn't answer.

"What if you broke your leg and Aunt Beth said you didn't need crutches? Would you drag yourself around on your hands and knees?" When she remained silent, he slowed down still more and put his arm around her shoulders. "Listen, love," he said kindly. "Ask yourself why your aunt doesn't want you to wear glasses."

"Why?"

"Well, think about it. We're going to get you some nice ones, but generally speaking spectacles don't enhance a girl's looks. Why would Aunt Beth want you to look your best, even if it meant you were hurting your eyes?"

She looked down. She knew the answer. "So she could marry me off sooner," she mumbled, embarrassed both by her aunt's pettiness and her own failure to recognize it.

"Precisely. The selfish old bitch."

"Yes," Cass agreed fiercely. "Selfish old—"

"Go ahead. Say it."

"Bitch!" She clapped her hand to her mouth, first in shock and then to muffle the giggles bubbling up irrepressibly.

"Good girl," said Riordan, proudly.

"Hypermetropia," Mr. Wopping pronounced, laying down his examining lens. "Your retina's in front of the main focus of your eye. You can't see divergent rays from a near object, my dear. You're farsighted."

"Oh no," breathed Cass, twisting her hands. "Is that—will I—"

"Oh, it's not fatal," the balding, elderly gentleman chuckled. "Pick out the frames you want and

I'll make you some convex lenses in a week or two. Here, these three styles are for ladies. Which do you want?"

Cass looked at the three pairs of spectacles on the velvet mat and tried to hide her dismay. She hoped she wasn't a vain person, but—oh, she was going to look so plain! "You say it's only for reading?" she asked hopefully.

"Until you're an old lady," he assured her. "Then I'll make you some Franklin glasses to wear all the time."

"Franklin?"

"American fellow, Cass. I'll give you some of his books, and then you'll know all about him." Riordan laughed, returning from his errand and entering the shop on a rush of warm air. "Are you all set? What was the verdict?"

"Hyperm-metropia," she said carefully. "I can see far away but not close up."

"Just what I thought. Where are your glasses?"

"It takes a week or two."

"What? No, that won't do, we need 'em right away. The end of this week at the latest. Is this all you have, these three? We want something lighter, more feminine. And with her coloring, we want silver frames, not gold, don't you think? Here, Cass, try these."

She slipped on the pair he handed her and blushed deeply under his scrutiny. "Ugly, yes?" He didn't say anything, only stared at her with a trace of a smile. "Well?"

"I was thinking how enjoyable taking them off would be," he said softly. She frowned, not understanding. He turned to Mr. Wopping briskly. "The shape of this pair is fine, but we want them in silver frames, and much thinner. And by Friday. Can you manage that?"

The two men argued while Cass stared at herself

in a small hand mirror, fascinated. They weren't really ugly, she saw, and they changed the whole aspect of her face in the most remarkable way. She looked older, more serious. She raised her eyebrows and pursed her lips. She looked *intelligent*! Like a schoolmistress, she thought—like Mademoiselle Dupuis at the school in the Rue de St. Clair! She laughed delightedly, then stopped—that spoiled the whole effect. She went back to the pursed lips and raised brows, turning her head and viewing herself from the side. She heard the shop door open and close.

"It's Philip, isn't it?" said a tall, fruity-voiced matron in an old-fashioned gown of maroon silk. She was peering at Riordan through an ivory-handled lorgnette with a haughtier version of the pursed lips and raised brows Cass had just been practicing.

"Lady Helena," he greeted her, smiling only faintly as he took the limp hand she held out to him. "How are you? Allow me to introduce Miss Merlin. Cassandra, this is Lady Helena Strong, a long-time friend of my family."

"How do you do?" said Cass with a polite curtsy.

Instead of responding, Lady Helena stared at her through the lorgnette as if she were some loathsome insect on the wall. The rude perusal went on and on; it became clear that she had no intention of speaking to Cass, but was going to stare for as long as it took to satisfy her ill-mannered curiosity. The absurdity of the situation intrigued Cass. If the woman's impertinence hadn't been so blatant, so outrageous, she wouldn't have done it, but she took off the spectacles she was still wearing. Folding them, she held one edge affectedly between thumb and forefinger, and peered back at her ladyship in a perfect parody of her insolent scrutiny. For heavy, interminable seconds the women stared at each other through their lenses. Cass made up her mind that no matter how long it took, she wouldn't look away first. Riordan's nervous throat-clearing almost undid her, but somehow she kept her face straight.

After a lifetime, Lady Helena lowered her lorgnette. She looked winded. "How do you do?" she got out, sounding as if a fish hook were caught in her cheek.

Cass glanced at Riordan, then looked away before his beet-red face could set her off.

"How's Walter, Lady Helena?" he asked in a strangled voice.

"Splendid! My son is doing splendidly, thank you very much," she assured him in rather strident tones. "I had a letter from your dear sister, Philip," she went on hurriedly, as if she couldn't get off the subject of Walter fast enough. "I mean Agatha, of course; Clarice wouldn't write a letter if the world were ending. She says she and the family are coming up to London next month. How many children have they now, Philip? Eleven?"

"Ten," said Riordan. "One died." He couldn't believe it when he heard an explosive snort of laughter, quickly muffled, from Cass, who was examining the men's glasses behind him. Even more incredible was his own sudden, uncontrollable guffaw. Lady Helena's pale blue eyes widened in shock. He knew he had to get out of there immediately.

"Always a joy to see you," he told her ladyship in a high, tight voice, then grabbed Cass by the arm. "Come, my dear, we're late."

Outside, they had scarcely reached the next shopfront before collapsing against it, shaking with silent laughter. Cass clasped her arms over her stomach and bent double, hooting, tears rolling down her cheeks. "One died!" she choked, clapped her hand to her mouth, and went into another spasm. Passersby were chuckling in sympathy. "I'm sorry," she moaned, snuffling and still holding her middle. "It's not funny." But that only set her off again. Riordan was laughing now more at Cass than at the situation. He gave her his handkerchief. She blew her nose and finally managed to get herself under control. She decided that if she tried to apologize now for laughing at his deceased nephew or niece, she would only have a relapse.

They started to walk, holding hands, feeling loose and affectionate. Every once in a while Cass giggled and had to wipe her eyes again. Riordan nodded and spoke to acquaintances along the way, and she nodded with him. She had a lovely, relaxed sense of belonging. Out of curiosity she asked him who Walter was; the mention of him had made Lady Helena nervous, and she wondered why.

"Lord Walter Strong, the Earl of Rotham, and the apple of his mother's eye," he told her. "A year ago he was a step away from felon's prison for embezzling a hundred thousand pounds from the family shipping company. Whenever Lady Helena waxes too insufferable, I like to ask how he's doing."

"What happened?"

"It was hushed up. The money was paid back covertly, and no one was the wiser."

"Then how do you know about it?"

"They needed a great deal of money in a hurry. Walter's not really a bad sort, and I'm an old friend of the family." He shrugged dismissively, then winked. "And they offered a very attractive rate of interest."

Cass smiled; she liked the idea of Lady Helena being in Riordan's debt.

She thought about her new glasses. She could

hardly wait for them to be finished. What would it be like to read for hours and hours and never have a headache or tired, watering eyes? What if she actually became more intelligent? What would Riordan think if she learned to discuss subjects with him on his own level? Well—no, perhaps not on his level, but at least with a modicum of intelligence, enough not to embarrass herself or— she pulled herself up. She was doing it again. Only this time she'd substituted Riordan for her father. Would she ever learn? Neither of them cared a whit what she thought or felt or accomplished, and it was high time she mastered that simple, painful lesson. She was on her own. At least she had some money now. She'd bought some clothes—and now some glasses—and she'd given Aunt Beth something for her room and board, but the rest she was carefully saving. When her involvement with Colin Wade was finished, Quinn and Riordan expected her to leave the country. The thought was so painful that she shunted it aside. But whether or not she left England, she would have to find a place for herself somewhere. No one would do it for her.

"What's wrong?"

She looked up with a mechanical smile. "Nothing. I was thinking about the glasses. It was so silly of me not to have realized what the problem was. Thank you. It's the nicest present anyone's ever given me."

"I hope not. Here, try this." He stopped walking and reached into his coat pocket. "Happy birthday, Cass."

She was too stunned to take the package he was holding out to her. "How on earth—? No one knows, how could you—? Aunt Beth, Freddy, they've never—"

"Open it, why don't you?"

She continued to stare at him, open-mouthed. People had to walk around them on both sides. He took her elbow and led her from the center of the sidewalk to a quieter spot near the brick facade of a draper's shop. "Go ahead."

She held it in her hands, weighing it. It seemed to be a rather heavy box. "I can't accept it. It was so kind of you to know it's my birthday and to—"

He interrupted with an impatient sound. "Of course you can accept it. It's not the Crown Jewels, for heaven's sake. Would you just open it?"

She did, warily. "Oh! Books!" She laughed with delight and hugged it to herself. "How *perfect*."

"Don't you want to read what it is?"

There was a soft light in his eyes and a look on his face she hadn't seen before. "What? Oh—" She saw that it was a novel in three volumes and read the title with a blush. "*Evelina, or a Young Lady's Entrance into the World*."

"The title struck me, though I wouldn't be surprised if Evelina's entrance into the world was a bit different from yours."

"Yes," she agreed, "I shouldn't wonder. I'll let you know. You haven't read it, then?" They started walking again, Cass holding her novel in one hand, Riordan's arm in the other.

"No, I'm afraid I don't have time for that sort of thing these days."

She worried her bottom lip with her teeth. "It's not a serious book, then?"

"God, I hope not. You've been reading so many serious books lately, I thought you could do with a little frivolity."

Her face cleared. If he didn't mind her reading something light, why should she? She'd already forgotten that his opinion didn't matter to her. "That was extremely thoughtful of you. But you must tell me—how did you know today is my birthday?"

"Doesn't your family celebrate it, Cass? A present from your aunt or—"

She burst out laughing, the idea sounded so ridiculous. "No," she said simply. "So tell me how *you* knew."

"Oliver told me. He must have found out during the investigation he and his men made before approaching you about Wade. They're pretty thorough."

A heavy silence fell. Riordan attributed it to the usual tension that came between them whenever Wade's name was mentioned, and he was sorry he'd uttered it.

But Cass's reticence came from another source this time. "They're not always that thorough," she said after a long moment, staring straight ahead.

"Who aren't?" He'd forgotten his last words. "Quinn's people, you mean?"

"Yes. They . . . make mistakes. They made one about me." Why was she saying this? She'd thought she had too much pride ever to say this to him, knowing he wouldn't believe her anyway. His loyalty was to his old friend, the man who'd saved his life. What could be more natural or inevitable? But now that she'd started, she couldn't stop. "My life in Paris was full of frivolity and harmless pleasure, but it was not decadent. It wasn't. I know what you've heard—I've heard the stories now myself." She kept staring straight ahead; if she looked at him she would lose her courage. "I never jumped naked into a fountain. I never had an affair with the Comte de Beauvois, nor with Jean-Claude Marisot or Fabien Bichet. In fact, I never had an affair with anyone. I—used to drink quite a lot, and then sometimes men would—"

"Cass."

"What?" She stole a glance at him and her heart withered. He looked embarrassed.

"Stop it. Please. There's no need for this."

She saw that he couldn't look at her, either. A slow flush of humiliation spread across her cheeks and a lump settled painfully in her throat. She wanted to let go of his arm—his touch was hateful to her now—but to do so would give too much away. "It doesn't matter. I don't care what you believe," she said without inflection. He didn't reply. She walked on blindly, speechless and miserable, cursing herself for being such a fool.

Neither of them spoke again until they arrived at his house. Riordan sent a footman for the carriage and told Cass to come inside to wait. She refused.

"I can report to you on Mr. Wade here," she said tightly.

"All right. Go ahead."

"Last night I told him about your meeting with Pitt and the other ministers. He asked if you thought they were leaning toward war with France."

"What did you say?"

"I said yes."

"Good. What else?"

"He began talking about going away in August, and who would stay in town and who wouldn't. He named a few names, all lords and ladies, and then mentioned he'd heard the queen would go to Koblenz. He wondered if the king would accompany her."

"Did he? Do you think he wanted you to understand the implications of that question?"

"I'm not sure. I've felt sometimes that he was about to take me into his confidence, but so far he hasn't. The arrangement is still that I'm to provide —mostly to spite you—as much information as I safely can for acquaintances of his who share my father's revolutionary goals. He's never admitted to being one of them, much less their leader."

Riordan grunted. "Anything else?"

"We met a man named Thorn. They spoke for a while in private."

"Ian Thorn. We know about him; he's one of them. Anything else?"

His impatient tone irritated her. "Yes. He said you were a turncoat Whig, a yes-man for the king, bound to the ministry by nothing but material interest. He said you didn't care a straw for public opinion, and that you stood in contempt of your own constituents, whom you'd bought like a parcel of serfs from the previous borough owner."

It came as a huge satisfaction to Cass to see Riordan lose his temper. He didn't rant or curse; in fact he didn't say anything at all. But the skin around his lips went very white just before the rest of his face turned a deep shade of purple. His dark-blue eyes glittered with a dangerous light; if she hadn't known him so well she might have felt frightened for a moment or two. But when he finally spoke, his voice was perfectly calm.

"Thank you for the report, Cass. When will you see him again?"

"Tonight."

His hand tightened fractionally on her arm as he put her into the waiting carriage. "Tonight. Another peep show, I wonder? How did you enjoy the Wicket Club, by the way?"

"Rather dull, we both thought," she said airily. She couldn't look at him.

"So I would imagine. Nothing like Paris, I'm sure. Why don't you try Conrad's? They have couples there who fornicate right on the stage."

She colored and didn't speak. She detested him. Damn, damn, damn! How did he even know she'd gone to the Wicket Club? Did he have spies? Had he followed her himself? That possibility shook her. What if he'd seen her there, pretending nonchalance while watching a tableau of naked women —"posture girls," they were called—some bent backwards and balancing wine glasses on their breasts? She and Wade had left early, to her unspeakable relief; he'd said the entertainment was too tame. They'd gone gambling instead, and then he'd taken her home. He hadn't kissed her. Sometimes she wondered if he even liked her. She wondered if her only appeal to him now was the information she gave him about plans for the upcoming term in the House of Commons or the other tidbits Riordan furnished.

Riordan still held the door open, scowling up at her. All she wanted was to get away. She flinched when he jumped up on the step and leaned in toward her. "Good-bye, Cass." His kiss was brusque, a farewell peck she had no trouble resisting. But then it changed. He caught her shoulders and pressed her lightly back against the seat while his lips opened hers and his warm, wet tongue came inside. She went from rigid resistance to helpless longing in the space of time it took him to pull her arms around his neck.

"We have to find a better place than this damn carriage," he mumbled against her mouth as he kissed her and kissed her. She was about to agree when the reality of what they were doing finally struck her.

She drew away, trying to disguise her trembling, knowing it was useless. "I appreciate your help with Burke and all the other books, Mr. Riordan," she said shakily. "But I'm already so good at kissing, you know, I don't even need to practice." She watched his eyes twinkle appreciatively. Then the devil took her. "At least, that's what Colin says."

She'd known that would darken the mood. But she wasn't prepared for the sinking feeling in the pit of her stomach when Riordan's face went still as a statue's and he jumped to the pavement as if there was a bad smell in the carriage.

"Happy birthday, Cass," he snapped, slamming the door. The carriage started off.

Halfway to the corner, she remembered. "Thank you for the book!" she shouted with her head out the window.

But the rumble of a coal cart coming the other way smothered her words and he didn't hear.

VII

"THIS IS WORTHLESS, PHILIP, UTTERLY WORTHLESS. SHE hasn't brought us one useful piece of information in all the time she's been seeing him."

"I know it."

"We're giving him a great deal more than we're getting, in fact, which wasn't the arrangement I had in mind."

"It's only been a couple of weeks, Oliver."

"It's been over a month."

"She has to go slowly. Otherwise he'll suspect what she's after."

"Granted. But I assume they're intimate by now, so why haven't we seen any results? Not even one name?"

Blank-faced, Riordan unfolded his long legs and levered himself up from the uncomfortable chair which, except for its mate, now occupied by Quinn, was the only seating accommodation the austere cubicle of a room afforded. He went to the window and gazed out at the tiny courtyard two stories below, surrounded by stone buildings identical to this one. Quinn rented this small sitting room in Lincoln's Inn Fields, along with an even smaller bedroom through a curtain in the wall, and made do with one all-purpose servant. It wasn't that he couldn't afford better; the tiny, uncluttered apartment suited his monk-like temperament perfectly.

Riordan turned away from the uneventful vista and leaned against the casement, hands shoved deeply into his pockets. The silence lengthened. He forced the words out, though he had no wish to hear the answer. "How do you know they're intimate?"

Quinn sat up straighter. "Do you mean to say they're *not*?"

Relief rushed through him like water from a burst dam. Oliver didn't know any more than he did—so it was still possible they weren't! She'd *said* they weren't when he'd asked her a few days ago, but he'd thought she was lying. He'd been so foul about it, he wouldn't have blamed her if she had been. "I don't know whether they're *intimate* or not," he told Quinn, curling his lip in distaste over the word.

"Well, for God's sake, man, find out! She's being paid too well to drag her feet now. *Deal* with her, Philip. I won't tolerate faintheartedness at this stage of the game."

Riordan rubbed his top lip with three fingers, then sanded the stubble on his jaw with his palm. He ran both hands through his hair and stared up at the ceiling.

"Well? You agree with me, don't you?"

After a long minute, he shifted his gaze to his friend. "Oliver . . ."

"Well?"

How could he say that the idea of ordering Cass to sleep with Wade was abhorrent to him? Unthinkable? It was what they'd hired her for, he knew, but. . . . His mind grasped at a straw. "Have you heard any rumors about Wade?"

"Rumors?" frowned Quinn. "What kind?" He rested his pointed elbows on his crossed knees, and Riordan was reminded of a grasshopper.

"That he's not quite right where women are concerned. That he doesn't treat them well."

"No, never. Nothing of the kind. Why?"

"Ah." He was relieved, of course, but Quinn's answer eliminated his only legitimate reservation. "It was just some tavern talk I heard."

Quinn uncrossed his thin shanks and pressed his folded hands against his lips. "Philip."

He winced inwardly, recognizing the stern, schoolmasterish tone even after twenty years; it usually meant a reprimand was coming. "What?" And now he sounded like a sulky schoolboy.

"Do you have *feelings* for this girl?" His inflection gave the word an odd, foreign sound, as if he were saying it for the first time, or as if he found it faintly distasteful.

Riordan went back to staring at the ceiling. What was there to say? He tried to answer truthfully. "She's young, Oliver, and she's involved in something that might be dangerous. She's helping us because her circumstances left her no other choice. I feel responsible for her."

"Is that all you feel?"

He pushed himself away from the window and flopped down again in the hard chair. "Yes," he said positively, knowing it was a lie. He wanted Cass, but that was none of Oliver's business. And it had no bearing on their situation, none at all.

"And your relationship with her remains purely on a professional level?"

"Absolutely. Purely."

"I'm very glad to hear it. Because we've set

something in motion that can't be stopped now. It's too late to replace either one of you. Beyond that, to become involved with someone like this Merlin woman would be ruinous, Philip. Ruinous. Everything you've worked for—"

"Damn it, I know it! I've told you there's nothing between us. Why do you say her name like that? 'This Merlin woman.' As if she weren't quite human."

"I have no idea what you mean."

He did it with *all* women, now that Riordan came to think of it. It was peculiar.

But as if reading his thoughts, Quinn asked next, "By the way, how is Lady Claudia?" His expression betrayed nothing but innocent interest.

"She's fine," he answered shortly.

"Good, good. A lovely girl. Excellent family."

Riordan didn't respond.

"I was speaking to Sir Lawrence Trilby about you not long ago, Philip. He's pleased with what you've been doing. Very pleased. I should think his gratitude would be substantial when this is all over."

Trilby was one of the king's deputies and closest advisors, a man of sizeable influence in Whitehall. Riordan grunted. "I wonder what it will take to keep his gratitude afterward," he said sourly. "Will I be expected to toe the royal line for the rest of my life?"

"Nonsense," Quinn scoffed. "Independence of mind is always a welcome quality in a statesman." He ignored Riordan's derisive snort. "So you'll speak to Miss Merlin about Wade soon, will you?"

Riordan's face went still. "Yes, I'll speak to her."

"When?"

He expelled a breath, rubbing the bridge of his nose. "Tonight. We're going to the opera."

* * *

"He's in the library, miss, if you'll—"

"Oh, it's all right, John, you needn't show me. I know my way by now."

"Of course. Miss Merlin, if I may say so, you're looking particularly beautiful this evening."

"Why, thank you, John. That's very kind of you."

She smiled and he bowed, and then she started down the dim, paneled hallway toward the library. Halfway there, the soft, muted strains of string music reached her ears, growing more distinct with each step. She reached the doorway and stopped. The room was unlit except for the pearl-gray remnants of dusk glowing palely in the open French doors to the garden, and it was a moment before she made out the figure of Riordan in the gloom. He was standing by the windows in profile, coatless, waistcoat unbuttoned, playing the viola. She held her breath, hoping he wouldn't stop. There was a scent of roses on the air, faint and sweet; it mingled with the low, lovely notes in a dreamy counterpoint. She watched his face, so serious, his eyes almost closed. His bearing was tall and graceful; twilight illuminated the silver in his hair and made her think of the snow-covered branches of some strong, straight tree. His fingers pressing the strings were supple and sure, his stroking of the bow delicate, even dainty. She thought she'd never seen anyone so beautiful. The knowledge that she loved him came slowly, like the notes of the song, and like the song, made her inexpressibly sad.

The last bittersweet notes died away. Riordan saw her when he turned to lay down the instrument. She was standing in the doorway, tall, still, elegant. He remembered the first time he'd seen her, far away in a churchyard, beside her father's muddy grave. He moved toward her.

"Cass." Her gray eyes rested on him so gravely. "Is anything wrong?" She shook her head. She was lovely. In the dimness he couldn't make out what color her dress was, some pastel shade that enhanced the mystery of her dark, lush hair. She wore it pulled back from her face in front, long and free in back—the way she'd worn it the night they'd met. He took her hands and kissed them. "You're so beautiful."

He stroked her palms with his thumbs, and a well of longing opened up in Cass. "So are you." She was afraid she would weep if he kept touching her, kept looking at her that way.

He smiled at her words. It would be so easy to kiss her now. Her mouth was exquisite. Her eyes were shining as if with tears. "Are you all right?" he murmured. He wanted to see her lips move.

She stood perfectly still, scarcely breathing. His white shirt glowed almost violet in the dusk, the lacy sleeves pushed back from his lean, strong wrists. She wet her lips, not knowing where to look. She wanted to tell him—she wanted to say—

"Cass?"

From somewhere she found the strength to pull her hands away. "I'm fine. Fine. You said to come early because you wanted to tell me something." She felt grateful for the support the doorpost provided; she'd almost done something irrevocable just now, and she was trembling in reaction.

He let his hands fall to his sides. "Did I say that?"

"Yes. You sent a note."

"Did I?" She nodded. She was staring over his shoulder, not looking at him. He touched her face, unable to help himself. "That's odd," he whispered. "I can't remember what I wanted to tell you." It wasn't true. But he could not say the words

Quinn wanted him to say. They would not come out of his mouth.

She sighed. She wanted to turn her face and kiss the open palm cupping her cheek. Instead she stepped out of his reach. "Then we'd better go."

In the dark hallway she was just a dim, shadowy form. The spell should break now, he thought; I can't even see her. But it didn't. "Cass . . ."

"Your coat—don't forget—I'll wait in the hall."

He watched her walk away fast, almost running. The sound of her footsteps died away and he thought, Now, *now* the spell is broken.

But it wasn't. He wondered if it ever would be.

Cass's nails bit uncomfortably into Riordan's wrist. "What does he say now?" she whispered tensely.

He pried the rigid fingers away and held her hand firmly. "He says, 'Eurydice, Eurydice, answer me! It's your faithful husband. Silence of death, vain hope. What suffering, what torment wrings my heart.'"

"Oh!" Tears rolled unchecked down her cheeks. She let the unearthly beauty of the music sweep her away, forgetting everything but the sadness and the pathos. "Now what is he saying?"

"He's going to kill himself. His grief is unspeakable."

She buried her face in her handkerchief and blew her nose.

"Wait, here's the goddess of Love to talk him out of it. She says, 'Hold, Orpheus!' She's reviving Eurydice. She lives!"

"Oh! Oh!" cried Cass, overcome, smiling with relief through her tears.

"'My Eurydice,'" translated Riordan.

"'My Orpheus,'" guessed Cass, sighing with contentment.

The music swelled as the lovers embraced for the last time, and the curtain fell.

Cass sat back in her seat, drained. "Oh, it was so beautiful, so beautiful. I want to see it again!" He laughed and she smiled back dazedly, her lashes still spiky from crying. "Didn't you like it?"

"Yes," he answered immediately, though he wasn't sure which he'd enjoyed more, the opera or her reaction to it. "Are you ready to go?"

"Yes, I suppose. It's hard to come back to reality, though, isn't it? Do I look all right?" She pressed her hands against her hot cheeks.

"You look magnificent." It was true, he thought; she was one of those rare women whose looks actually improved with weeping.

She smiled tolerantly as he put a gossamer-thin shawl around her shoulders and led her out of the box. His arm felt warm and solid under her hand. The press of people forced them to move closely, intimately, down the brightly lit hall to the stairs; to stay together, they put their arms around each other and took small, shuffling steps toward the exit. "We should have waited," Cass said loudly, standing on tiptoe to speak into his ear..

He nodded, but he was thinking he preferred it this way, all in all.

Finally they reached the lobby. Using the advantage of his height, Riordan surveyed the milling crowd. Immediately he spotted a familiar chestnut head. Claudia. She saw him at almost the same moment and waved gaily. He waved back, his smile not quite in place.

"Who is it?" asked Cass. They had several friends in common now.

"No one you know." He would have kept going, but Claudia was gesturing for them to join her and whomever she was with—Marchmaine, it looked like. He didn't have time to sort out his feelings; he only knew this was an introduction he'd hoped never to have to make. Slowly they made their way through the crowd to the waiting couple.

"Lady Claudia Harvellyn, allow me to introduce Miss Cassandra Merlin."

The name caused a glimmer of recognition, swiftly hidden, to flare in her ladyship's large brown eyes before she smiled graciously and offered her hand. "How do you do, Miss Merlin? And this is Mr. Marchmaine. You know Gregory, don't you, Philip?"

He should have known Claudia would take control and ensure that things went smoothly. As soon as the introductions were over, she began to chat easily and naturally about the evening's entertainment. "The music is lovely, of course, but what I can never understand is why the poor man doesn't just *tell* Eurydice, straight out, that if he looks at her she'll die. Think of all the trouble it would save!" She laughed charmingly. "Such glorious bombast, what sublime histrionics! Don't you think so, Miss Merlin?"

Cass hesitated. "No," she said with a diffident smile, "I thought it was very moving. I wept," she confessed.

Claudia raised her perfectly shaped brows in surprise, or perhaps amusement, but maintained her gracious smile.

"Did you, now?" declared Marchmaine, screwing his monacle in tighter to look at her.

Riordan remembered the scene in the eyeglass shop between Cass and Lady Helena, and spoke up hastily. "I confess, I felt a little dampness in the eyes myself. Besides, Claudia, if he simply *tells* her, we'd miss all that lovely music at the end. '*Che faro senza Euridice*!'" he sang robustly, making them all laugh. Claudia's laugh was a little stiff.

Marchmaine excused himself to go find a carriage. Riordan was thinking he ought to invite them to share his, but he had no enthusiasm for prolonging this odd encounter, however well it was going so far. The trio chatted politely and inconsequentially a little longer, then began to stroll toward the front doors.

Claudia inquired of Cass how she was finding her new life in London, conspicuously avoiding any mention of the circumstances that had obliged her to return. Riordan had the uncomfortable impression—for the first time ever—that Claudia's graciousness bordered on condescension. He watched Cass. She was tense, but her answers were open and direct and perfectly correct. A few minutes later Claudia pressed him to say whether he was coming to her house on Tuesday— Grandmother had asked about him in particular— and her insistence in front of Cass surprised him. Was it possible that she was jealous at last? The idea confounded him, but not as much as the realization that the very thing he'd been hoping for didn't bring him nearly the satisfaction he'd expected.

Their carriages arrived simultaneously. Claudia gave him her hand to kiss before the idea even occurred to him, and afterward she held his fingers for much longer than was her habit. With a bemused expression he watched Marchmaine hand her in and the hackney rattle away.

Cass watched his face for a moment longer and then looked away. She waited for him to remember where he was and that his own carriage was standing in readiness before them. He helped her into it absently, and they rode much of the way in silence.

Presently she noticed he was looking at her, and forced herself to say something. "Lady Claudia is very attractive," she murmured, without enthusiasm.

"Oh, yes."

"And very intelligent."

"Very."

She took a breath. "She's your special friend, isn't she?"

"What makes you say that?" he hedged, frowning.

What, indeed? What had possessed her to bring up a subject that could only cause her pain? "Because of the way you treat her," she plunged in stoically. "You don't pretend with her, you let her see who you are. And because she's obviously in love with you."

He laughed somewhat harshly. If Claudia was in love with him, it was for tonight only. "You're mistaken."

His tone indicated that the subject was closed, and Cass suddenly lost heart in pursuing it. He hadn't denied the woman was his "special friend." She stared out the window as a crushing feeling of aloneness settled over her. Her unhappiness was entirely self-made, for all the comfort that brought. She was falling in love with a man she could never have, and she had no idea how to stop. She saw with perfect clarity how far above her he was in every way—social position, respectability, education, accomplishments—and now she'd also seen the lady he would someday marry, or at least the sort of woman he would choose. An honest comparison between herself and Claudia Harvellyn made her ache with wretchedness and inadequacy.

If only she could get away! She was frightened of the pain seeing him every day was already bringing. To stop a heartache, one ought to avoid the person who was causing it. But in her case that wasn't possible. Not only had she to endure Riordan's company, she had to bear the agony of pretending in public that they were lovers. It wasn't fair! For as long as she could remember she'd dreamt of falling in love, of giving her heart to a kind, gentle man who would rescue her from her loneliness and treasure her for the rest of her life. Instead she'd chosen the very man most capable of hurting her. Was there something wrong with her? Did she *enjoy* suffering, or was she just a fool?

She swallowed down the lump of misery in her throat and squared her shoulders. She would persevere. She always had. Besides, what else could she do? She had no choice but to continue to save her money and wait for the day when she would be free to start a new life somewhere—alone. Meanwhile, she would protect her heart as best she could.

The carriage stopped. It wasn't until he'd handed her down from it that she realized they were in front of his house, not hers. "I remembered what I wanted to tell you earlier," he said by way of explanation, and led her inside.

They found his secretary writing letters in the library. "Good lord, John, are you still here? Don't you ever go home?"

Walker smiled, abashed. "I was finishing some work, sir. I can leave now, if you—"

"No, finish whatever you're doing. We'll go in the drawing room. And John—we don't want to be disturbed."

"Yes, sir," called Walker to their retreating backs.

Cass let him pull her back down the hall toward the drawing room, wondering what he could have to say to her. He seemed so energetic all of a sudden, so intense, that she couldn't comprehend his new mood.

The crystal wall lamps on either side of the door were burning. He lit a taper from one and carried it around to every candle, until the handsome, high-ceilinged room glowed as if for a festive party. Then he took off his coat, threw it on the sofa, and went to stand before the long front windows, unbuttoning his waistcoat. She expected him to draw the curtains over the huge black squares, but he didn't. He turned around and faced her. "Come here, Cass. I want you to kiss me."

Her eyes widened to saucers and she stared speechlessly. After a moment, her arm made a vague, hesitating gesture to the windows.

"Yes, I know—we can be seen from the street. That's the point. Wade has spies, and I don't want them to think we only touch each other when we're out in the world."

She gave a short, nervous laugh. "You're joking."

"Not in the least. Come, love, it's all for the plot. Purely professional and all that. Don't leave me standing here like an idiot."

"I don't believe you," she told him, even as her legs began to propel her toward him. She stopped when she was still four feet shy of him, and he made a lunge for her hand, pulling her the rest of the way.

"Would I lie?" he asked softly, resting his hands on her waist.

"Most certainly." She was already stirred by the frank wanting in his dark-blue gaze. Alarms sounded in the back of her head, but she refused to heed them. It was only a kiss; so much hurt was in store for her—couldn't she take a moment's pleasure? His face filled her vision before her eyes closed and their lips met in the lightest of touches. She tried not to move, to savor the subtle sweetness of their mingled breath and the soft, intoxicating texture of his lips, but already she wanted more. Her arms came up and she ran her hands through his hair, as she'd wanted to do for so long. "I love your hair," she almost said, but she was too shy.

He began kissing her face, her eyelids, murmuring in her ear. He slid his wet tongue along her jaw and delicately bit her chin, then moved down to nuzzle her throat. "I've been waiting for this all night." She wanted to tell him she'd been waiting too, that she was falling in love, that she wanted him so much she was bursting. But she only whispered his name. He found her mouth and kissed her deeply. She was shaking. Holding her head, he entered her, tasting the sweetness, wanting more, more. "God, Cass, I'm weary of pretending I don't want you!"

She felt lit up inside. "Touch me, Philip." Was she saying it or only thinking it? No matter—his hand went to her breast and she gasped in gratitude. They remembered the windows at the same moment and stepped backwards in tandem, like lovers dancing.

"I lied about Wade's spies."

"I know. I don't care."

Watching her face, he caressed her with both hands, feeling her breasts spring to life under his palms. She stumbled backwards until her shoulders were against the wall. "We mustn't do this," she whispered in a weak, temporary burst of sanity. "Why are you doing this?"

"Because I can't help it. Neither can you." He began to unbutton the back of her gown, kissing her all the while and murmuring lovely, absurd endearments.

"Oh, don't—" But she knew she didn't mean it, knew if he stopped now she couldn't stand it.

He tugged the top of her dress down, exposing the lacy shift underneath. No corset—thank God for Marie Antoinette, he prayed irreverently, before bending his head and putting his lips on her. He kissed her through the silky material until he felt her knees giving way. Then he gripped her around the middle and took her mouth in a frenzy of wanting.

"Quinn wants you to be Wade's mistress, Cass, but I won't allow it! Come and live with me. I'll take care of you." Her eyes were closed, her lips parted; she moved her head from side to side. "Does that mean yes?"

"Yes. *No.*" She pushed back, trying to think, suddenly embarrassed because the front of her shift was wet.

"Yes!" he insisted. "Move in with me, Cass. Your aunt treats you like some poor relation. We'll—"

"I *am* a poor relation," she said on a quavery laugh, trying to hold his hands still.

"You know you want to."

"I can't."

"Why?"

"Because. It's wrong." Finally she caught his hands and made him stop touching her. Her voice came out high and light. "If you want me, Riordan, you'll have to marry me!"

A spontaneous laugh burst from his throat before he could control it. Cass wrenched free and would have escaped if she hadn't stopped to cover herself. He grabbed her back and pressed her hard against the wall, holding her face in his hands. Knowing an apology would be useless, he kissed her instead, sinking his fingers into the silky web of her hair, inhaling her fragrance.

"God, you're so lovely," he murmured, touching her everywhere, making her kiss him back. He slipped her shift over one shoulder and softly stroked her bare breast until he could feel the tender flesh around her taut peak crinkle under his fingertips. She was trembling from the effort not to give in, and he was seized by a nearly violent need to make her surrender. When her mouth opened to him he kissed her ruthlessly, using his hands to mold her thighs, her buttocks, pressing himself against her.

A soft knock sounded at the door.

Incredulous, shielding her with his body, Riordan turned his head to see the door opening slowly. Before he could roar out his fury, Walker spoke in a voice quivering with embarrassment. "I'm most terribly sorry, sir—an urgent message just now—"

"Get out!" His rage made Cass jump and Walker blanch.

"Very good, sir. It's from Lady Claudia. I'll leave it here." He set an envelope on the table and pulled the door closed in haste.

Cass crossed her arms over her breasts and tried to stop shaking. She squeezed her eyes shut when he rested his forehead against hers, knowing exactly what was coming.

"I have to see what it says."

She pushed him away; trembling uncontrollably, she met his eyes. "Do you?"

He knew from her voice what it cost her to speak the words. He tried to bring her close, but she held herself back, curving her neck away from him. "Cass," he said, "I have to."

When he let her go, she turned around to face the wall. After a moment she heard him cross the room to the table, heard the ripping open of the envelope. A pause while he read. The sound of paper crumpling and then of him coming back to her. The touch of his hands on her bare shoulders.

"I have to go. I'm so sorry. It's her father—she says he's dying."

She started to pull her dress up. He helped her. "Wait for me, Cass," he whispered, buttoning the buttons. "Will you wait for me?"

She despised his comfort, the kindness of his hands on her skin. He was leaving, going to Claudia. Other than shame, she felt nothing but a black, bottomless despair. She turned around, dry-eyed. "No," she said, on a note of finality that chilled them both. "I won't wait."

Riordan smiled down at the stick-thin figure lying so still under the satin coverlet. "How are you feeling, sir?"

Lord Winston Harvellyn blinked in the dim candlelight and tried to smile. "Had no business bothering you this late, Philip. Women get wrought up. Nothing wrong with me a sound night's sleep won't put right."

"We'll see about that," Claudia chided gently. She sat on the other side of the bed, stroking her father's high, pale forehead.

"Touch of indigestion is all it was—I'll be sitting up at my desk in the morning, you see if I'm not."

"I'm sure of it." Riordan squeezed the bony hand lying open on the pillow and stood up. "We'll let you rest now, so you can be up all the earlier."

Claudia rose with him. "Good night, Father." She leaned over to kiss the aristocratic old cheeks. "I'm so happy you're better. If anything happened to you—"

"I'm good for a long time yet, my dear," he said with a weak smile, patting her hand. His heavy eyelids dropped closed then, and he was asleep almost instantly.

Claudia spoke in a quiet voice to Lord Winston's manservant, who would sit up with him during the night, before she and Riordan tiptoed from the room. "Father was right," she said ruefully, taking his arm as they went down the wide staircase to the hall. "I really shouldn't have bothered you."

"Nonsense, I wanted to come." He hurried on before the sheer enormity of this lie could discompose him. "You must have been terribly frightened."

"I was, Philip. I sent for you almost before I sent for the doctor."

"And the doctor said it wasn't his heart?"

"Yes, thank God. But he's been having these attacks more frequently lately, and they always send me into a panic."

"He looks frail, but sometimes I think he's as strong as we are."

"That's exactly what he says." They were standing in the entrance hall under a massive crystal chandelier, unlit. "Thank you, Charles, I'll see Mr. Riordan out," she said, dismissing the hovering butler.

"Are you all right now, Claudia? I can stay if you like."

"I should like it very much," she answered, startling him. "But it isn't at all necessary and you've been so kind already. Besides, it's very late; it wouldn't look quite right, would it?"

"I hadn't thought of that," he admitted. He was uncomfortably aware of a feeling of relief. "Well, then, if—" He broke off when she ran a hand up his arm to his shoulder and looked at him with wide, searching eyes.

"But hold me before you go, Philip, will you?"

He couldn't have been more surprised if she'd asked him to carry her up to her bedroom. He had the wit to answer, "Delighted," as he put his arms around her and drew her close. She smelled of the expensive perfume he'd once given her, and all at once he realized he was comparing her fragrance to Cass's fainter, more elusive scent. Guilt assaulted him. Why was it that when he was with Cass he never thought of Claudia, but when he was with Claudia—he put the bothersome question out of his mind and drew back to look at her.

Her eyes were closed and she seemed completely

relaxed in his arms, for once. She really was a beautiful woman—perfect skin, classic features. He tilted her chin up. No resistance. He kissed her gently. She sighed and put her arms around him. Without thinking, he parted her lips with his. He felt her stiffen slightly and went back to light, soft kisses on her lips and cheeks. She relaxed again and tightened her arms around his neck. More as an experiment than from any real desire, he slipped his tongue into her mouth.

She jumped away as if he'd bitten her.

"Claudia—God, I'm sorry—"

"No, no, my fault—" She made frantic erasing movements with her hands and turned around so he wouldn't see her wiping her mouth.

Riordan ran a hand through her hair and stared at her rigid spine, feeling a mixture of dismay, pity, and disillusionment—but curiously, no surprise. "You don't really like it, do you, love?" he said gently.

"I'm so embarrassed. I don't know what to say."

"Never mind." He moved around to face her and folded her in his arms again, careful to keep his touch impersonal. "It's all right," he told her, patting her shoulder. "It doesn't matter in the least."

"It *does* matter," she snuffled against his shirt. "I've heard the stories, I know you've had lots of women. That Merlin woman tonight, so beautiful, so—" She shook her head and wiped her eyes, fighting for composure. "Oh, Philip, how can you still want me if I'm cold?"

"You're *not* cold. You're not." He wondered which of them he was trying to convince. "You just need time, that's all, and I can be very patient."

"I don't know, I don't know."

"*I* know. It's all right, Claudia. Everything's going to be all right."

But as he held her stiff, unyielding frame against him, he was filled with misgiving. What was he promising? What was he giving up? A coldness began somewhere in his midsection and rapidly spread through his whole body. His eyes were bleak as he stared over Claudia's head, knowing she couldn't warm him.

The next morning, before dawn, Riordan got out of bed and reached for his robe. Barefoot, he padded out of the room and went downstairs. There was a carafe of tepid water on his desk in the library. He poured a glass and carried it to the windowseat. Cass's windowseat. He thought of her as he'd seen her here a few days ago, hunched over some book, completely engrossed, her hair falling down in wisps around her face. Pausing occasionally to take off her new glasses and rub the bridge of her nose.

He took a swallow of water and made a face. He'd come down here to *stop* thinking about Cass, stop obsessively comparing her and Claudia. It was insane, it was disloyal—Claudia was incomparable and she was going to be his wife. That was that. Cass was the kind of woman a man slept with, took for a lover, but never, never married. Why couldn't she see that? Why couldn't she be reasonable and become his mistress? Her talk of marriage was ridiculous, a joke—no wonder he'd laughed! Who did she think she was? And who did she think she was fooling, telling him that making love with him would be "wrong"? She was only nineteen, and for all he knew she'd had as many men as he'd had women, deny it all she would. But whatever her game was, it wouldn't work, because he was marrying Claudia.

He put down the glass and picked up his viola; he'd dropped it in the windowseat last night after he'd seen Cass standing in the doorway, watching him. He plucked the strings absently with his thumb, remembering. She'd wanted to tell him something. What? He'd had something to tell her, too, but couldn't force the words out. She would go to Wade over his dead body, he vowed, his hand surrounding the delicate neck of the instrument in a suddenly violent grip.

What would Oliver say if he knew he'd not only neglected to pass on the message about Wade, but had actually asked Cass to live with him? He shuddered inwardly, shrinking from a vivid mental picture of Quinn's wrath. But worse than his wrath would be his disappointment. Nothing pierced him more deeply than Quinn's disapproval. The power he held over him was very strong and very real, and it had been that way since he was nine years old. On top of that, he owed Oliver an enormous debt, and part of it involved handing Cass over to Wade.

He stood up, watching the sky lighten through the branches of the locust tree. The choice wasn't difficult. He wouldn't do it, not even for Quinn. The consequences of the choice didn't matter. Cass was his.

Two days later, he knocked loudly at the door to Number 47 Ely Place.

"Well, if it ain't Mr. Riordan. Good afternoon ter you," grinned Clara, dropping her version of a curtsy. "Come up, why don't yer? The young miss ain't home, but you could speak to 'er ladyship instead, if yer like."

"Where is she? Miss Merlin, I mean," asked Riordan, following the maid up the unlit staircase. The place was gloomy and damp and depressing, and he felt his usual frustrated annoyance at the thought of Cass living here.

"Mayhap yer'd best ask 'er ladyship about that,"

Clara advised after a pause, rolling her eyes mysteriously. She said no more until she had led him into the small, overcrowded sitting room where Lady Sinclair was seated at her desk, writing a letter. "Here's Mr. Riordan, merlady," she announced briefly, and retired.

They regarded each other across the width of the room with mutual dislike—he because of the way she treated Cass, she because her attempt to seduce him one night while he waited for her niece had been a humiliating failure.

"I understand Cass isn't at home," Riordan said coldly, forgoing a greeting. "Would you be good enough to tell me when you expect her back?"

Lady Sinclair laughed lightly and leaned an elbow on the back of her chair so that her breasts were more prominently displayed beneath her amber silk gown. "I'm sure I couldn't say, Mr. Riordan. I long ago gave up trying to keep track of my niece's whereabouts."

"Yes, I know," he agreed stonily. "I sent her a message. She was to meet me this morning in Green Park."

"Green Park! How *outré*."

"Do you know if she got my note?" he persisted, determined to keep his temper.

"I think it highly unlikely." She tapped her teeth with the tip of her pen. "Indeed, highly unlikely."

"And why would that be?"

"Why would that be? Because she wasn't here this morning."

His fists clenched at his sides. "Where was she?"

"This morning? At what time?"

He counted to ten. "At the time she would otherwise have been here to receive my message," he enunciated slowly.

"Ah! Well, I expect that would have been sometime around eleven. Now, let me see. If they stopped overnight, and I'm not at all sure they did, they might possibly have reached Stratford-upon-Avon by eleven this morning, I should think. He'd hired a post-chaise, though, and I believe they drive them straight through the night nowadays. Isn't it marvelous? Now, if that were the case, I expect they'll have nearly reached Manchester by now. But it's difficult to say, isn't it? It all depends—"

"Wade!" His face was livid and his voice shook. He took two steps toward her and Lady Sinclair's satisfied smile wavered. "It was Wade, wasn't it?"

"Why"—she laughed falsely—"I can see there's no use trying to keep a secret from you! Indeed, Mr. Wade came for her yesterday morning, very early. She was taken quite by surprise—or so she *said*," she amended with a little malicious sneer. "They spoke privately for a few minutes, and the next thing I knew she was packing a bag and bidding me a fond adieu."

"And you let her go?" He held his hands behind his back to prevent himself from shaking her.

Her ladyship shook her head sorrowfully. "In all honesty, sir, Cassandra has always been a wild, ungovernable child. And unfortunately, where men are concerned, completely lacking in discretion."

"If that's true, it's because she had an excellent teacher," he snarled. "Where are they bound for?"

She rose from her chair with an admirable imitation of affronted dignity. "I refuse to be insulted in my own home. Please leave."

She let out a little shriek when he sprang at her and pressed her back down in the chair. "I asked you where they were going. If you don't tell me, I'll break your arm."

She believed him. "Lancaster. He has a house there." She spat the words out, her eyes glittering with hatred. "Now get out. If you ever come back, I'll have you arrested."

He released her shoulders and smiled pleasantly. "You can't. I'm immune from prosecution for anything except treason." He bowed formally and went to the door. He thought he could hear Clara scuttling away on the other side. With his hand on the knob, he turned back. He regarded Lady Sinclair's tightly corseted figure, her reddish-blonde hair, the generous expanse of white bosom. She reminded him of a Rubens nude, fleshy and voluptuous, alluring, corrupt. "I'm going to find Cass and bring her back to London," he told her. "After that, madam, if it's in my power, I promise you you'll never see her again." He waited, but she didn't speak, and he closed the door in her spiteful face.

VIII

"WILL THAT BE ALL, MISS?"

"Yes, Ellen, thanks."

"Have a good night's sleep, then, miss. I'm sure you can use it."

Cass smiled at the pretty lady's maid and watched her go. She was more efficient and infinitely more polished than her maid at home, but somehow she missed Clara—missed her humor, which wasn't always intentional, and her blunt way of speaking. And Clara would have enjoyed the long, raucous journey much more than Cass had. She'd hinted as much to Wade on the morning he'd proposed this outlandish outing. But he'd derided her tentative scruple that a chaperone might be desirable, saying there would be so many people crowded into his hired post-chaise that they could all chaperone each other—which rather missed the point, she'd thought—and that when they arrived at Ladymere she could have as many maids as she wanted.

She settled back in the comfortable overstuffed armchair and took a bite of biscuit. She pushed her bare feet closer to the small fire Ellen had made in the grate to drive out the dampness. It had rained the whole last day of the journey, dousing the mood of the travelers along with the roads. But spirits had revived this evening among the six ladies and gentlemen riding in her coach when they'd won the impromptu race, arriving at Wade's palatial Lancashire estate well ahead of the other two chaises they'd set out with from London. There was a rumor that one had gotten stuck in the mud at Stoke-on-Trent, and the fate of the third was still a mystery. The charm of riding for thirty-six hours without stopping except for meals and tolls was lost on Cass; for her the best part of the journey was this moment. She was finally alone, finally comfortable, and finally able to think.

She hoped she'd done the right thing in coming on this wild ride. There had been no time to consult Riordan or Quinn about it; she'd had to rely on her instincts. But this was what she was being paid for, she reasoned, to learn as much as she could about the private life of Colin Wade. And she could hardly refuse an opportunity to discover if some of the guests this weekend were not only friends of his but members of his secret organization of assassins as well.

She looked around at the large, comfortable bedroom, expensively decorated in blue and yellow and lime green. As Wade's special friend, she'd been given the best guest room, and yet all the rooms she'd seen on her brief and incomplete tour this evening had been large and grand and opulently furnished. It made her wonder about the conflict between Wade's style of life and his supposed revolutionary goals. He was nearly as rich as

Riordan, whose wealth he ridiculed. How did he
rationalize the contradiction? Like Riordan, he too
was playing a role, living a life of luxury and even
decadence while hiding his true ideals. She suspected that, unlike Riordan, he relished the decadence, and his ideals allowed him to embrace
violence and political murder. If he ever took her
into his confidence, she supposed she could ask him
how he justified the difference between his way of
life and his principles, but until then she could only
speculate.

It was very late, and she was exhausted. She took
a final sip of tea and stood up, stretching. The bed
looked lovely. She blew out the candle, pulled back
the soft counterpane, and crept between the sheets.
Presently she could make out the shapes of tree
branches cast on the ceiling by the moonlight.
Where was Riordan right now? she wondered on a
tired sigh. It wasn't a new thought—she'd wondered it a dozen times over the course of the
journey. Had he gotten her note yet from Aunt
Beth? And if he had, would he care that she'd gone
off with Wade? Probably not.

It had been four days since she'd seen him—the
longest they'd been apart in over a month. He
probably welcomed the separation; it would give
him more time to be with Claudia. Were they
together now? Perhaps they were dancing, or walking arm-in-arm in a moonlit garden. Or listening to
music together. Yes, that was more likely—they
were both musical. In her mind's eye she saw
Claudia's glossy chestnut hair, her calm, superior
smile and perfect poise. "Such glorious bombast,
what sublime histrionics!" she remembered her
saying in her oh-so-refined accent. If Cass lived to
be a hundred, she knew she would never achieve
that airy, effortless sophistication. With a groan,

she turned on her side and drew up her knees.

It was all very well to say she'd come here to spy on Wade, but she knew in her heart that the true reason had been to get out of London, away from Riordan. She felt again, as she often had in the last four days, the scathing humiliation of his last abandonment—made all the more awful by the awareness of how close she'd come that night to giving in to him. God, how she'd wanted him! She hadn't known it was possible to want a man that way. No one had ever told her. Had her parents loved each other like that? She hoped so. Then a thought struck: was it possible Aunt Beth felt this same helpless, uncontrollable yearning for each of her lovers? Was it? No. A sure instinct told her that couldn't be true, that what she felt for Riordan was completely unlike her aunt's furtive, short-lived encounters with men.

And yet she didn't feel particularly loving or passionate at the moment. She felt angry and hurt and jealous, and she hoped whatever fatal disease Claudia's father had was contagious.

She rolled into a tighter ball, realizing what she'd just wished. *I'm sorry, I'm sorry, I'm sorry*, she chanted to her hazy, somewhat superstitious version of God, *I didn't mean it*! Oh, she was such a child. When was she going to grow up? She'd had some idea that wearing glasses and reading lots of books would turn her into an adult, but evidently it was going to take more than that. She had an urge to do something brave and wonderful so that Riordan would love her. That was even more childish, she knew, but the fantasy was too compelling to relinquish. She wanted to do something glorious and tragic, like—like dying for her principles. She saw herself walking toward the guillotine,

her head held high, shoulders thrust back bravely.
Rather than betray him, she was going to sacrifice
herself for Riordan. The taunting crowd would fall
silent, awed by her courage. And he would be
standing somewhere among them, watching her,
overcome with his terrible grief and fear. At the last
minute he would shout out his love for her and she
would be saved. Somehow. After that they would
be together forever, and he would adore her. She
fell asleep imagining herself riding before him on a
white stallion, his arms around her, both of them
staring straight ahead into the future . . . .

She slept late the next day, but so did the rest of
the household. A maid brought her tea and toast in
bed, and later she had a bath. She was dressed and
seated before the dressing table mirror, letting
Ellen style her hair, when a knock came at the door.

"Colin, good morning—or good afternoon, I
should say. Come in. It's all right; Ellen's doing my
hair." It occurred to her that she had Aunt Beth to
thank for one thing, at least—teaching her the
proper, or improper, way to greet a man in her
boudoir. She was relieved when he didn't send the
maid away, but leaned against one of the bedposts
and watched her in the mirror. He looked immaculate in a bottle-green coat and buff breeches.

"Good morning, my dear. There's no need to ask
if you slept well; I can see it in your face. You look
radiant. Ah, how I envy the resilience of youth."

She made a face. "Oh, indeed, you're such an *old
man*, it's a wonder you didn't expire along the
journey! Give me another minute and I'll help you
down the stairs."

He laughed appreciatively and reached into his
waistcoat pocket. "Here," he said, placing a small
box in front of her on the table, "this is for you.
Open it."

She did, with a pleased smile, while Ellen stood

back respectfully and waited. "Why, it's—it's—" She had no idea what it was. It looked like a piece of wood.

He laughed again, amused at her confusion. He leaned over and spoke softly in her ear. "I'll tell you what it is later, perhaps tonight. There are so many things we have to talk about, Cassandra." He put his lips against her cheek and then straightened. "Now, hurry down, my love. There's a light meal in the dining room, and then we're all going shooting."

She watched him go, wondering what he could want to talk to her about. She and Ellen examined the sharp sliver of wood on the bed of crushed white velvet but try as they might, they couldn't guess what it was.

An hour later she was walking among a group of ladies and gentlemen over a rough, stubbly field toward a wooded area in a far corner of Wade's estate. One of the errant chaises had arrived in the night, swelling their number to fourteen. They were an interesting assortment, Cass reflected as she tried to remember all their names. Most of them seemed to be capable representatives of the bored and idle rich—a viscount and his lady friend, a newly married and embarrassingly amorous couple, three giddy sisters named Lloyd whose first names all began with L, and a corresponding number of unattached young men. The two exceptions were Mr. Sherwood, a man in his late forties who rarely spoke and had spent most of the trip with his nose in a book, and Mr. Sloan, a young, impoverished law clerk who seemed devoted to Wade and hung on his every word. Walking beside her now was Mr. Everton, or Teddy as he insisted she call him, one of the unattached young men, who evidently found her better company than any of the Lloyd sisters and had hardly left her alone in two days. A gaggle of servants trailed behind, carrying guns and chairs and umbrellas and hampers of food and anything else one could think of for the comfort and convenience of the gentry.

"What are we going to shoot?" asked Cass, to make conversation.

"Anything that moves," answered Teddy with a smile. He was good-looking and smooth-talking, and Cass had known a hundred men exactly like him. "Do you shoot?" he asked.

"No, there wasn't much opportunity for it in the Palais Royale," she said, straight-faced. She felt comfortable with Teddy.

Perhaps too comfortable, she thought a few minutes later when they arrived at the park. "Anything that moves" meant rabbits, squirrels, and birds, she discovered. The ladies quickly grew bored and sat down on blankets away from the shooting. When Teddy offered to teach her to shoot, she readily agreed, already tired of the women's idle conversation. He led her away with a hand on her waist and pointed to a tree stump about twenty feet distant. "We'll try that first." He put his arms around her, ostensibly to show her how to hold the rifle, then stole a kiss on the cheek. She was used to such freedoms and admonished him good-naturedly. She took aim at the stump and fired, missing, and the unexpected recoil sent her back into his arms, where he promptly kissed her on the mouth.

"Don't, Teddy," she said, with considerably more force. "Colin would be furious," she added when he still didn't let her go.

"I've already asked him," he whispered, trying to nuzzle the nape of her neck. "He said it was all right."

She went very still. "You already asked him what?"

"You know."

"No. Tell me."

He had the grace to look a little embarrassed. "If he'd mind if you and I . . . became friends." He grinned engagingly. "Colin's a very generous man."

She regarded him steadily. "Indeed he is, but sometimes he's forgetful. He forgot to ask *me*." And she pushed him away and strode off to rejoin the ladies, where she remained for the rest of the afternoon.

She wondered why the incident surprised her. She'd known Wade had no real feelings for her, but usually a man's pride, if nothing else, made him want the woman he was with at least to simulate fidelity. Colin Wade was a puzzle to her, and the longer she knew him the more pieces he revealed; but she got no closer to solving it.

Dinner was a crowded, sumptuous affair. Cass saw more food brought out than she'd have thought any regiment of hungry soldiers could devour, but almost every tray was sent back empty. Shooting at small animals built prodigious appetites, she decided, watching as course after course covered the huge table. There was also wine with every course, and by meal's end they were a very merry group indeed.

She sat at Wade's right, with Teddy Everton on her other side. Her earlier rebuff had left him unfazed; he flirted outrageously as if nothing had happened. She paid only token attention to him, and instead concentrated on studying the other guests. Were any of them Wade's cohorts in treason? She discounted the ladies, and the silly young men who attended them. Certainly not Mr. and Mrs. Gonne; they were too wrapped up in each other to spare a thought for the overthrow of the monarchy. The Viscount St. Aubyn? She doubted it. He epitomized upper-class English hauteur, and

Cass couldn't imagine him taking steps to tear down the very social structure on whose pinnacle he proudly stood. Mr. Sloan, the fresh-faced law clerk? Possible, but not likely; too puppyish, too young, too . . . conservative. That left the silent Mr. Sherwood. He was about her father's age, she guessed, or a little older. Had they known each other? Could it as easily have been he as Patrick Merlin at the end of the hangman's noose? If so, did that make him her enemy? Or her friend? He looked up from his plate at that moment, catching her in her intently focused stare. She flushed and smiled, then quickly looked away.

After dinner, the ladies rose to leave. Hateful custom, thought Cass, trooping out with them. Doubtless the men would discuss politics now; if she could stay, she might learn something important. But no, she had to retire to the drawing room, where the conversation was insipid beyond belief, while the women waited for the men to rejoin them and life to begin again. She recalled a dozen stimulating conversations she'd had with Riordan. He enjoyed her company and had genuine respect for her ideas—she wagered *he* wouldn't send her out of the room after dinner like a child.

At last the men arrived, and the servants began setting up tables in the drawing room for gambling. Cass won eighteen pounds at loo from a two-pound stake, then quit despite all the urgings to continue. Gambling, she was thankful, was not one of her vices.

The Lloyd sisters complained that there was no music, and thus no dancing. Wade gallantly promised to send for some musicians tomorrow, and in the evening they would have a ball. To this there was enthusiastic applause. Cass noticed that he was drinking more than usual tonight; he was loud and talkative, and his eyes glittered with an excited light. When he invited her to go with him, alone, to the billiard room so that they could talk, she had trouble hiding her nervousness.

The billiard room was on the second floor. Servants brought refreshments and lit branches of candles at Wade's request, then scurried away, leaving them alone.

"Do you play?" he asked, chalking one of the cues and setting out the three balls, two white and one red. When she said no, he shrugged and took a sip of his claret, set the glass on the mahogany edge of the table, and began to play by himself. Cass had watched men play billiards before and the object of the game had always eluded her, even when it was explained. She watched with no more comprehension now than ever, waiting for Wade to introduce the subject that was on his mind.

"Did you solve the mystery of my little gift yet?" he inquired presently, banking the red ball off the cushion and into the spotted white.

"No, Colin, I didn't, and I'm dying of curiosity. You *must* tell me."

He smiled. "Very well. I've given you something that means a great deal to me, and I hope you'll treasure it as I have."

"If it means a lot to you, then it does to me, too," she responded dutifully, wondering if he was pulling her leg. "What is it?"

"It's a piece of the Bastille."

"A piece of the Bastille?" She conquered a swift, horrible urge to laugh and composed her features to reflect the right amount of awe. "Really? Truly? Oh, Colin."

"A close friend of mine took it out of the rubble in '89 and sent it to me. I wanted you to have it."

"Colin, I'm so moved. I don't know what to say." This was quite true.

"I've been watching you these past few weeks,

Cassandra. I've wanted so much to confide in you, but I haven't been sure I could trust you. Now I believe I can."

"You can!" she assured him fervently, resting a hand on his arm.

A quick spasm passed over his face, but he turned back to the table before she could read it. "Once I told you I knew your father slightly," he said, examining the tip of his cue. "That wasn't true. I knew him much more than slightly. We worked together, wanted the same things." He laid the stick down and faced her. "What I'm trying to say is, it was only through a quirk of fate that Patrick was arrested last May. It could just as easily have been I."

Cass's astonishment was real—she'd never thought he would say this to her. "You—you mean you're one of them?" she gasped, "one of my father's group of friends who tried to—"

"I'm not only one of them. I'm their leader."

Her hands flew to her mouth. "Colin!"

"What do you think of me now?" he asked curiously. "How do you feel?"

"I feel . . . frightened and excited, and—and glad! Oh, Colin, it's wonderful! Here I've been trying to be a little bit of help to my father's cause *through* you, and all along it's really been *you* I've been helping. If I'd only known, I could have done so much more!"

"That's precisely what I was hoping." He went to her and took her hand. "I hope you know I'd rather die than put you in any danger, but time is growing short. If England declares war on France, our cause here is lost. Besides that, I have reason to think the authorities are beginning to suspect me."

She widened her eyes in alarm.

"There's nothing to fear yet, but it means we have to move much more quickly."

She spoke hesitantly, praying she wasn't going too fast but unable to keep herself from asking. "And—is the goal still—the same as my father's was?"

"Yes," he confirmed readily.

Cass was filled with an almost unbearable excitement. This was the very thing Riordan and Quinn had needed to know—if Wade's target was still the king or if by now it was someone else—Pitt, or one of the more virulent anti-France ministers. It was the first really vital piece of intelligence she'd been able to glean in almost two months. She could hardly wait to get back to London and tell Riordan. "What can I do to help?" she asked sincerely.

"Exactly what you've been doing—stay close to Philip Riordan and pump him for information about the next term in the House."

"Yes, of course. You have a plan, then?"

"Yes, we have a plan. I can't tell you what it is now, but to put it into effect we have need for the kind of information that can only come from a Member of Parliament."

She had to bite her tongue to keep from badgering him for more. "Colin, I feel honored to help you, and so grateful for the chance to strike back with one little blow against the men who murdered my father."

"Not so little, I hope," he said, taking her other hand and smiling grimly. "If we succeed, my dear, you'll have helped topple a vicious, despotic regime." For one moment a gleam of pure fanaticism shone in his cinnamon-colored eyes. Then it was gone and he took a step away from her, all business. "Now, I have to ask you something, and I hope it won't alarm you. Are you absolutely sure that our friend Riordan is as reckless and apolitical as he seems?"

"Why, what do you mean?" She stifled a flutter of panic.

"I may be wrong, but sometimes I've had the feeling that some of his excesses are an act."

"Really?" She looked away as if she were thinking, then shook her head positively. "No, Colin, I don't think so. I would know. It *couldn't* be an act."

"How can you be so sure?"

"Because I've seen him any number of times when he's had so much to drink it's taken three servants to carry him home. No one could pretend to that extent." Wade looked thoughtful. "No, I'm sure you're wrong. He even drinks in the morning, Colin, before he's gotten out of bed." She kept talking, aware of the implications of that piece of information. "Can you imagine? It's the most extraordinary thing—he says it helps clear his head from the night before."

Wade raised skeptical brows. "Perhaps you're right, but it bears watching."

"And I shall, I assure you." She was practically hopping with frustration. She knew she should stop now, but she couldn't help herself. "Isn't there anything you can tell me about your plan? I can't help feeling if I knew what it was, I could help you so much more. For one thing, I'd know what to try to get out of Riordan."

He came toward her again; his eyes were gleaming with excitement. "I want to tell you," he admitted, "and someday I will. But for now it's too dangerous." She pouted prettily. He smiled and put his arms around her. "One thing I can tell you."

"What?"

"It's going to happen in November."

"November!"

He nodded and then pulled her up against him in a tight embrace. He was much stronger than he looked, she had time to think before he kissed her, hard. In a rush, all her fear of him returned. He backed her up against the edge of the billiard table and seized her wrists, pinning them behind her back. "Do you like to be tied, Cassandra?" he asked conversationally, watching her face.

"No. No, I don't."

He bent her over backwards until her head was almost touching the green baize of the table. She could smell the wine on his breath. "Have you ever tried it?"

She shook her head unthinkingly, but answered, "Yes, once. It frightened me, I didn't like it. Let me up, Colin."

He smiled at her with his lips, but his eyes were as cold as stones. After another moment he let go of her hands and stood back. "Perhaps you and I are better together as friends than lovers, my dear," he said softly.

She rubbed her bruised wrists and stared past him, struggling to mask her horror. "Yes," she said when she could speak. "Yes, I think we are."

A few seconds later the door opened and all three Lloyd sisters tumbled in, clamoring for billiard lessons. Cass excused herself and went upstairs to her room. Wade's last words had reassured her, but that night, as soon as Ellen left, she locked her door.

The next morning she rose early. After bathing and drinking a cup of chocolate, she went downstairs. As she'd hoped, no one was up yet except the servants. "May I have some tea in the library?" she asked one of them. That would establish her whereabouts for the next thirty minutes or so. While she waited for the tea, she prowled around the bookshelves, examining titles. Riordan's library was much better, she thought with a silly flutter of pride. Some of these volumes had never even been opened. More to the point, none seemed incriminating in any way—no *Layman's Guide to Regicide*, for example. She sighed with disappointment.

A maid came with a tray. She thanked her and waited until her footsteps died away, then went to the door. The hall was empty. On tiptoe, she scurried across it to the room directly opposite, opened the door, slipped through, and closed it silently behind her—then chided herself for not knocking first. What if Wade had been there, sitting at his desk? But he wasn't, thank God, and she leaned against the door, waiting for her heartbeat to return to normal.

The study was small; there would be little to search except the desk and an unlocked cabinet under the window. She set to work briskly, ignoring the dampness of her palms and the tight, airless feeling in her chest. She was taking an awful risk, but the opportunity was too good to miss. Last night Wade had admitted everything, but that was worthless as far as Mr. Quinn was concerned. He would want evidence, material evidence, and this was the first chance she'd had to look for it. She searched neatly and diligently, pausing every few minutes to listen for sounds outside. What she needed was a letter, a paper, even a cryptic note with an incriminating name on it.

But there was nothing. Nothing but bills, accounts, ledgers, and receipts, all related to the running of Ladymere. She found a bill for the services of a nurse-companion for Mrs. Wade in Bath. Mary, was her name. She felt a moment of compassion for the unknown Mary Wade. But there was nothing else.

She gazed around the room. There were no family portraits, no personal items that might have revealed something about the man who owned this house and occasionally lived here. A stag's head over the mantel told her he liked to shoot animals, and that was all.

She froze. Someone was coming. A man, from the sound of the footsteps. There was nowhere to hide, the room was too small! She went to the tiny space of wall behind the door and flattened her back against it. Her breath came shallowly while her heart hammered in her chest.

"Cassandra?"

It was Wade! He was in the library, looking for her! She heard a sound outside the door and stopped breathing altogether. She watched the knob turn before she shut her eyes in blank terror. She stood as still and silent as an upright corpse while the door opened. Seconds passed. The door closed. Not until she heard steps in the hall again did she open her eyes and discover the room was empty. Her knees started to knock against each other and she had to sit down.

Minutes later, she slipped unnoticed from the study and returned to the library. It occurred to her that she ought to have drunk some of the tea. When Wade found her a little later she was walking in the garden, pressing a camellia to her nose and reading *The Pilgrim's Progress.*

At noon the men played cricket and drank beer while the ladies watched, sipping lemonade. Then it was time for dinner. They were dining early today because their host had devised a special entertainment for the afternoon: a cockfight. One of the more loathsome of English pastimes, Cass had always thought, and made up her mind to contract a headache just before it started. She was seated between Wade and the indomitable Teddy again, and the meal was as heavy and interminable as yesterday's. Midway through there was a commotion outside. Laughter and raucous shouts sounded from the hall.

"It's Vaughn and MacLeaf, finally out of the mud at Stoke!" guessed Teddy. "Let's give 'em a real hazing."

All heads turned toward the door. Two grinning men appeared in it, stumbling, their arms around each other for support. No one greeted them, so Cass deduced it wasn't Vaughn and MacLeaf. She recognized them, though; she'd met them somewhere. Two disheveled ladies came up behind them, giggling and simpering, and all at once she knew who they were. Wally and Tom, Lord Digby-Holmes and Lord Seymour, and their two lights-o'-love. She wasn't sure these were the same two lights-o'-love she had met before, but the distinction hardly seemed important—certainly not to Wally and Tom. She was inexplicably glad to see them all, and was about to call out a greeting when the fifth member of their party staggered up, jostling the little knot in the doorway.

Riordan.

Cass's heart literally stopped. When it started again, it had to pump especially hard to compensate for the temporary standstill, and for a moment she was quite sure she was going to faint. She gazed at him across the silent room as every other person in it faded into invisibility and she was conscious of nothing but his well-loved face. He had a two-day beard and his black-and-silver hair was wild. He looked dirty and exhausted, but a private, fleeting light in his eyes warmed her to her bones. She'd never in her life seen anyone so beautiful.

Riordan put his arms around Wally and Tom and leaned against them, his head between theirs. "Good afternoon," he enunciated with a drunk's carefulness. Wally and Tom echoed the greeting, after which the whole trio lurched suddenly to the left. They regained their balance with difficulty while the two ladies behind them snickered and peered around their shoulders. "We happened to be in the neighborhood," Riordan went on, unperturbed, "and decided to pay our respects." He sent an exaggerated leer at Cass, then caught himself against the doorpost as one knee appeared to give way on him.

Wade stood up slowly. He wore a faint, philosophical smile. "Riordan," he said smoothly. "I don't believe I know your friends."

He introduced them with a flourish, only stumbling over the ladies' names—Cora and Tess, it turned out—and then wondered if there might be a morsel of bread and a drop of water for his crew of weary travelers. With a resigned shrug, Wade signaled for more food and more chairs. He went through the formality of naming all the other guests for the newcomers' benefit, and Riordan made a fatuous bow to each of them in turn. When the chairs arrived, he seized one from a startled waiter and plunked it down between Cass and Teddy Everton. He settled himself in it with a vulgar groan of satisfaction and put his arm around Cass's shoulders. She smelled like a garden and looked good enough to eat. He was angry with her for many reasons, but at the moment he couldn't recall what any of them were. He saw that she was pressing her lips together to keep from smiling. Before he could give it another second's thought, he kissed her.

This time Wade reacted. He stood up and leaned forward, pressing his hands against the edge of the table. "Listen here, Riordan," he said with more determination than anger. "You're in my home, and Miss Merlin is my guest. I'll thank you to keep your hands off her while you're here."

It wasn't the most gallant defense of her honor Cass had ever heard, but it seemed to cool Riordan off for the time being. He grinned sheepishly and muttered a sort of apology, something to do with not being able to help himself. It didn't cool Cass off, though; she still wanted to wrap her arms around him and never let go. She watched him reach for the glass of wine at his elbow and knock it over, staining the cloth a bright purple. She stole a quick glance at Wade. His eyes narrowed at her in return, as if to say, "Let's see how much of that he really drinks!" She felt a thrill of alarm. She had to speak to Riordan privately, warn him that Wade was suspicious, and that their glass-switching ploy wouldn't work here; but she couldn't see how to do it without Wade's noticing.

More food came, providing a momentary distraction. But Riordan was genuinely intent on satisfying his appetite now, and it would have taken more than a whispered word in his ear to get his attention. Cass watched him bite lustily into a leg of roasted turkey, his strong white teeth tearing the meat off in chunks, and she felt a lightness in her chest. At the opposite end of the table, Wally, Tom, and their lady friends were devouring their food with the same gusto, causing her to wonder when they'd last stopped for a meal.

Conversation gradually resumed as the high-spirited intruders began to be absorbed into the original company like old friends. After the meal, the drinking continued unabated and the noise level in the dining room grew deafening. Cass waited until Wade turned to speak to the viscount's companion, a lady named Miss Cluny, and then managed her first private word with Riordan.

"Wade is watching you," she told him, speaking just above a whisper. "He doesn't believe you're really drunk." She smiled politely, as if she'd just complimented him on his cravat, and turned away.

Afterward, she wondered if Wade could have heard. Almost before she'd finished speaking he stood up, glass in hand, and proposed a toast to the king.

Riordan looked at Wade; their eyes locked in silent challenge. "To the king!" the others responded, quaffing their drinks in cheerful obedience. Wade swallowed the contents of his glass deliberately, his eyes never leaving Riordan's. Cass gripped the edge of the tablecloth with nervous fingers and stared straight ahead.

"To the king." Riordan closed his eyes and downed the wine in four swallows, intent on not choking. It was his first drink in eleven months.

After that the toasts came rapidly—to the king, the queen, the Prince of Wales; to union with Ireland, the Catholic emancipation; to Cora and Tess. At each one Wade would fix Riordan with a cold, mocking eye and not take his gaze away until every drop in his glass was drained. Cass was transfixed with anxiety, but could think of nothing to do to stop it. When she reminded Wade of the promised cockfight, he waved his hand dismissively and said they would have it tomorrow; he didn't want to break up such a pleasant party.

Riordan knew he was getting drunk. The nice thing about it was that the drunker he got, the less he minded. What wonderful, friendly people they all were, and what amusing stories they told. He told some amusing stories himself, and they all laughed uproariously and slapped him on the back. This Everton fellow was an awfully good sort, too; he could do a first-rate impersonation of the prime minister. There were three sisters across the table —Lord or Lloyd, he thought their name was—

singing a madrigal in three parts. The wonderful
thing was that none of them could sing worth spit,
and that made him laugh. He slid down on his
backbone almost to the floor in hilarity, holding his
sides. When he finally recovered, he decided to
propose a toast himself.

"To the most beautiful woman in the world!" he
called out. "Cass Merlin." There were good-
natured "hear, hear's" and everybody drank. He
sat down and grinned at Cass. He could see she
wasn't having a good time.

She needed to relax. He told her so, with a heavy
arm draped across her shoulders and his nose
within inches of hers. She looked as if she was going
to cry. He was filled with a deep, uncomplicated
love that made him want to comfort her. He
touched her face with his fingers, not caring in the
least who saw, and then he kissed her. Oh, it was
good. No one tasted like Cass. Wade was blithering
about something, but he paid no heed. He pulled
her closer with one hand and put the other on her
thigh. God, he loved the feel of her. What were they
doing here with all these people, anyway? They
ought to be upstairs in one of Wade's fancy guest
rooms, rolling around in one of his big beds.

He felt a tightening hand on his shoulder and
looked up.

"I told you, Riordan, to keep away from
C'sandra, dammit," Wade was saying. He seemed
to be swaying on his feet, but Riordan thought it
could just as easily be his own vision. Cass groaned
something inaudible as he got up unsteadily from
his chair.

"Oh, yeah?" he asked eloquently. "What makes
you think you've got anymore right to 'er than I
have?"

"As I said before, this's my house and she's my
guest. That means hands off."

"Oh, yeah?"

Cass rested her forehead in one hand as the witless battle went on above her. A duel with pistols was proposed, then swords, then fists. Tom and Wally offered to be seconds. She might have been alarmed, but somehow she wasn't able to take any of it seriously; she could see the combatants and their seconds passing out before they got to the dueling ground.

"I've got an idea," piped up Teddy Everton. "Why don't you play cards for her? A nice civilized game of piquet. Then we can stop all the bickering and get back to business." He waved at the table, indicating that business meant drinking and eating.

Everyone thought this was a capital idea. Wade sent a servant for two packs of cards. "All right with you, Cass?" asked Riordan solicitously. She kept her head in her hand and didn't look at him. She felt stunned with embarrassment and disbelief and helpless amusement.

"But not to a hundred," Teddy complained. "That takes too long."

"One hand," suggested Wally. "Winner take all."

"All right with you, Cass?" No response. "I guess it's all right with her. Draw for deal."

Listlessly, Cass watched the cards fly past on the table in front of her as Wade dealt twelve each, two at a time. Everyone gathered around to watch. After drawing from the stock, Riordan scored for point and sequence, but Wade scored for triplets. Play began, with each man counting his score out loud after every trick. In minutes, the game was over.

Riordan won, twenty-eight to nineteen.

Grinning like a hyena, he accepted the gleeful congratulations of his friends. Wade folded his arms across his chest and grimaced manfully. Riordan toasted him, quite liking him at that moment. "To you, Colin, for taking it like a soldier!" Everybody drank.

"Well, Cass," he went on expansively, leaning back. "Let's go into Lancaster and get a room." This was greeted with enthusiasm by the listeners. Cass raised her eyes to him then, and he felt the first inkling that all wasn't well. "Eh? What d'you say?"

"What exactly do you think this hand of piquet means, Riordan?" she asked quietly.

The room went still. Damn it, he thought, trust a woman to put a damper on things. "It means you're mine, o' course," he said forcefully, and there was a masculine murmur of agreement around the table.

"I see. Does that mean I have no say in the decision?"

That flummoxed him. His wits were slow; he couldn't think of a speedy rejoinder. "Uh—"

"I assume you're thinking I'll come and live with you now," she went on relentlessly.

"Well, exactly, that's certainly—"

"I dare you to play another hand," she said, with a smile that ought to have warned him. "With me this time. If you win, I'll consent to be your mistress."

He agreed, with misgivings. Damnation, he'd already won her once, why did he—?

"What if he loses?" asked Teddy.

"Yeah, what if he loses?" echoed Tom.

Cass smiled again, and Riordan felt a cold premonition in the pit of his stomach. "If he loses, he has to marry me."

IX

EXCEPT FOR THE SURREPTITIOUS SCRAPING OF A PLATE
by a spellbound servant, there wasn't a sound in the
room. Everyone stared at Cass as if waiting for her
to laugh and admit she was joking. When it sank in
that she was dead serious, Wally let out a whoop,
and the tension broke. They all gathered around
again, joking and jostling and slapping Riordan on
the shoulders. He finally closed his mouth and tore
his eyes away from Cass's gray and unnervingly
sober gaze. He reached for his goblet with a sickly
smile, found it empty, and looked around for the
decanter in something bordering on panic. A laughing Viscount St. Aubyn filled his glass for him to the
brim, and he drank it down in one huge gulp,
spilling a lot down his neck. The wine was supposed to wet his throat and make speaking easier,
but when he said, "Draw for deal," it came out a
dry, palsied croak.

He drew an ace, Cass a nine. She cut, he dealt.

They were facing each other, their knees almost touching. He spread the remaining cards on the table in the shape of a fan and looked at his hand. His face blanched. Too many goddamn sevens and eights. He watched Cass arrange her cards calmly, expertly, her manner a study in total composure; only a certain tightness around the mouth suggested that something more than a few pounds was riding on the outcome of the game.

She discarded three cards and picked up an equal number from the stock. He did the same, and elected to leave the rest face down. All he accomplished from the pick was to replace his sevens and eights with tens.

"Four," Cass announced, to begin the calling.

"How much?"

"Forty-one."

"Equal." He let out a breath. Neither had scored for point.

"*Quatrieme*."

"We say 'Quart,'" he corrected, unreasonably irritated.

"Quart, then." She shrugged agreeably.

"Good," he conceded.

"I also have a tierce. Three aces."

He smiled. "Not good. Four tens. And three jacks."

She shrugged again. "I begin with seven."

"I begin with seventeen." He felt a little better.

She led with four hearts: ace, king, queen, and jack; after each trick she announced her score in a noncommittal tone. If she won the majority of tricks, seven or better, she would score ten, and Riordan began to hate and fear the light, uninflected sound of her voice. She led next with the ace, king, and queen of diamonds. Seven tricks. Ten points.

She led the seven of spades, and finally he won a

trick. He took two more, then led his jack of clubs. She aced it. She led the king of spades for the last trick, and won.

"Twenty-eight," she said, staring down at the pile of cards in front of her, lining up the edges with her long, slim fingers.

He blinked repeatedly and had to clear his throat. "Nineteen."

All hell erupted. Everyone moved toward them to shout congratulations or condolences, kissing, shaking hands, patting and slapping. The noise came to Cass's ears as if through a tunnel. Even her vision blurred. The only thing she saw clearly was the look of shock in Riordan's eyes. He stared as intently as if he'd never seen her before—or as if she were a madwoman holding a razor to his throat. Someone dragged him to his feet, someone else pulled her chair back and urged her to hers, and then they were all drinking a toast.

"To the bride and groom!" shouted Teddy Everton, raising his glass high.

Cass drained her wine numbly, welcoming the heat that spread through her a second later. Then she shuddered, watching from the corner of her eye as Riordan's hand shot out in another desperate grab for the decanter.

"Why don't we do it now?" Tom suggested when the uproar died down a little. He half-lay on the table, one elbow propped against a congealing platter of roast pork. "Leave now, I mean, for Gretna Green."

"Right-ho!" seconded Wally, pounding Riordan on the back. "If we left now, we could be there by morning. You'd be married before dinner!"

Rude shouts and laughter greeted this proposal. "I'll supply fresh horses and a coachman!" Wade chimed in. Cass looked at him in astonishment. He was definitely intoxicated—his face was red and

perspiring and he swayed a bit on his feet—but
there was a calculating glint in his bloodshot eyes
that outshone the drunkenness. What was his
game? she wondered distractedly, then understood.
Of course—he *wanted* her to marry Riordan; that
way he thought she could find out all his secrets.

The insistence that they leave now, tonight, grew
almost violent, and she was reminded of a pack of
hounds snapping at the backside of a hapless fox.
She hazarded a glance at Riordan. He was looking
at her again—not with shock now but with a kind
of reckless, swaggering challenge. She put on her
most insouciant expression, trying to match his in
carelessness. Their gazes held while he swallowed
yet another glass of claret and belched loudly. He
turned toward the waiting company. Cass's breath
caught at the top of her lungs.

"Whoever's going with us, let's get on the bloody
road."

New cries, more congratulations, as chairs were
pushed back and the party surged out of the dining
room into the hall. Riordan continued outside,
feeling an urgent need to relieve himself, and half a
dozen men followed him out. The ladies drifted
upstairs or into the drawing room. What was she
supposed to do now, Cass wondered—pack? She
started up the stairs uncertainly, noticing Wade
speaking to a couple of servants in the hall. She
stopped when he called out and then joined her,
taking her arm and leading her into an alcove off
the second floor hallway. The sun had almost set,
she saw through the window; the sky was a lumi-
nous strip of orchid over the dark trees of the park.

They leaned back on separate walls, facing each
other. She tried to replicate his conspiratorial grin.
"Well, well! This's a bit more than we bargained
for," he said, slurring his words only slightly. "You
sure you're game?"

"Oh, I'm game—only I doubt very much that there will really be a wedding, Colin."

"Don't be too sure—his honor's at stake now. Y'know, C'sandra, watching you tonight, I could almost believe you're really attracted to him."

"Attracted to Riordan? Don't be ridiculous."

"Maybe not consciously. But I remember the first time I saw you—he was kissing you and you were punching him in the jaw. Love an' hate. 'S a dang'rous combination." He tried to fold his arms across his middle, but they came unfolded immediately; she realized he was drunker than she'd thought.

She sent him a pitying glance. "I assure you, in this case there's no love. Only hate."

He smiled and raised his brows, unconvinced but unconcerned. She could not figure him out. "Well, it's too bad in a way if you do marry him, 'cause he'll wanna keep an eye on you, and we'll have to meet clandesh"—he giggled—"clandestinely."

She nodded, not certain if that was good or bad. Seeing him publicly had offered her a measure of protection against his strange advances, but now that safeguard would be gone. "True, but I'll be able to get much more information if I'm living in his house." She looked out the window again, watching two swallows soar past. This was the oddest conversation she'd ever had. She was playing too many roles at once, and sometimes she suspected Colin was playing one, too. For a second she tried to imagine herself marrying Riordan tomorrow morning. It was impossible.

She looked up to see a footman coming toward them along the hall, carrying her bag. "I had Ellen pack your things," Wade explained when she looked startled. "Well." He took her cold hands and grinned down at her. The wine had stained his teeth purple; she could see all the tiny lines around his eyes and mouth. "Have a wonderful wedding trip, Cass. I'll find a way to get in tush—in *touch* with you after you're back in London." He kissed her hands wetly, then raised his head to look at her mouth. She felt a stab of dread. But he only smiled a little regretfully and dropped her hands. Then he took her elbow and led her unsteadily back down the hall toward the staircase.

She could feel Riordan's eyes on her before she saw him. As she reached the last step, he pulled her out of Wade's grasp into his own and draped a possessive arm around her shoulders. She was dismayed when he lurched against her, knowing his drunkenness this time was unfeigned.

Enthusiasm for accompanying them overnight to Gretna Green had waned considerably; only Wally, Tom, and their lady friends had the heart for it now. But the others saw them off with undiminished eagerness. All the men kissed Cass; Teddy Everton kissed her for so long and with such fervor that Riordan finally grabbed his coat and pulled him off. Then they were bundled into the waiting post-chaise with cries of good will and farewell, and in no time at all the carriage was rolling down Ladymere's smooth, tree-lined avenue toward the highway.

A single candle in a glass box lit the roomy interior, casting shifting shadows as the coach rocked along. It was curiously quiet for a while as all six passengers adjusted to their surroundings and, as much as possible, to their circumstances. Cass and Riordan were given the rear seat to themselves; the others sat opposite, arms entwined, grinning stupidly. But soon Wally discovered the wooden crate on the floor with twelve bottles of Wade's best claret inside, and the party began all over again. It was decided that they should dispense with the bothersome formality of passing the bottle around while each took a sip. How much easier if everyone had his or her own bottle—and how much more *sanitary*, noted Cora in fastidious tones, the first words Cass had ever heard her utter. And so they sat, except for Cass each holding a bottle of wine, toasting and laughing and singing. The night wore on and the jokes grew bawdier, the caresses exchanged in the opposite seat more starkly intimate. Finally the singing gave way to yawning, then snoring, with someone rallying periodically to tell another joke, sing another song, or put another hand inside a bodice, before lapsing back into inebriate oblivion.

The candle guttered. Cass leaned an elbow against the window and peered across the dark seat at Riordan, huddled in his corner. She knew he wasn't sleeping because she was aware of every time he lifted his bottle to his lips. She also knew precisely how many mouthfuls of wine he swallowed on each occasion. It wasn't lost on her that he was drinking like a man trying to forget he was en route to the gallows. Now he had the wine bottle between his thighs, thrusting up at a lewd angle. She stared at it, unable to look away, and for a moment her vague and deliberately abstract mind-pictures of the wedding night, should this insane parody of a marriage actually occur, became graphically real. An uncomfortable warmth crept through her and her palms went damp. Then he reached for the bottle, releasing her gaze, and she went back to staring out the window.

Three times she opened her mouth to speak to him; three times she closed it again. What was there to say? *What are we doing here, Philip, how did this happen? Touch me, I'm so scared.*

Oh, why wouldn't he speak to her? She hated to see him like this; it tore her heart to shreds. She didn't know what it was that had made him stop

drinking all those months ago, but it must have
been something terrible. Now he was drinking
again, and in a way it was all her fault. No, it
wasn't, not really—but still, she couldn't shake a
feeling of responsibility. She wanted to take the
bottle from him and throw it out the window. What
would he do? Was he violent when he drank? She'd
seen no evidence of it so far. But she hadn't crossed
him yet, either.

Warring with her guilt was an equally powerful
sense of having been humiliated. Regardless of
what happened tomorrow, the position she was in
was degrading. She put her head in her hands and
squeezed her eyes shut, remembering the evening,
unable to think of something she could have done
to change the outcome. It had all seemed so unreal,
a night no one could take seriously. If she'd jumped
up and run from the room at the first hint that two
men were actually going to play cards for her, she'd
have betrayed her carefully crafted image of the
wild French hoyden. And she couldn't, she simply
could *not* have let him win her like a sackful of
guineas! She'd wanted to make the wager a little
more even, and at the same time take him down a
peg or two. She glanced at the dark, still, somehow
sinister form in the opposite corner. She'd succeeded with a vengeance. But to back out now
would only make things worse. If what Wade said
was true and Riordan was honor-bound to marry
her, refusing him would only add insult to injury—
and make them both look even more foolish than
they already did.

Rather than cry, she stared out the window,
watching the dark shapes of trees and hedges glide
past. There was a moon on her side, but for the
most part it refused to show itself through the thick
wisps of clouds. Sounds of snoring were irritating
at first, then restful as she grew accustomed to the

separate cadences. She propped her head on one
hand and let her eyes close. She imagined she was
in France, on an outing with her boarding school
classmates. To St. Cloud, perhaps, or Versailles, for
a picnic and then an overnight stay in a *pension*.
They'd laughed and sung songs and worn Mademoiselle to a frazzle, and now they were drowsy
and quiet, dropping off to sleep one by one. . . .

Riordan took a last shuddering swallow of wine
and backhanded the bottle out the window. There
was a quick, satisfying crunch from out of the
darkness. He smiled meaninglessly and wished he
had another to sail out after that one. Should he
open a new bottle? He beat on his stomach with
both hands; it sounded pretty full, not unlike a bass
drum. Maybe he'd had enough. Then again, maybe
not. He bent over the wooden crate at his feet. The
dark floor seemed to rush up toward his face as
the bottom dropped out of his stomach. He
straightened carefully and reconsidered.

He glanced at Cass. Sleeping. Good. At least now
she wasn't staring at him.

He stared at her. In the pale wash of moonlight
her skin was like some marble goddess's. She'd
looked like a goddess the night he met her. Aphrodite at the Clarion Club. A kiss in a garden for a
hundred-pound cast at hazard. He'd won that
night. Tonight he'd lost.

He leaned closer, peering, resting one long arm
on the back of the seat. Her parted lips shone like
wet silver as dappled shadows picked out the lovely
planes and hollows of her face. She was resting her
head in her hand, the fingers threading her inky
hair. He whispered her name, "Cass." Cassandra
Merlin. The hanged traitor's loose-living daughter.
The Honorable Philip Riordan's bride-to-be.

Elation and profound dread filled him equally.
Couldn't marry her. Couldn't. Too much to lose,

too many people expecting something else. He watched his hand go out to touch one errant lock of black hair. She sighed and he went still, the silky strands trapping his fingers. What he had to do was escape, leap quietly from the carriage now while they were all sleeping. He patted the fat purse in his pocket. Plenty of money. He'd be in London in two days.

'Course, Cass might be mad. Money—he'd give her money, and she'd get over it. Pretty soon things would be the way they were before. He'd keep at her until she gave in, became his mistress. He'd marry Claudia and become a great statesman. Oliver would be proud of him. Everything would be perfect. Perfect.

He took hold of the door handle. Bye, Cass. Her breathing was silent and even. Her shawl had slipped down one shoulder, exposing her upper arm in her gown to the elbow. She moved her hand to the space of seat between them, palm up, the sensitive fingers twitching.

He bent down on his forearms and laid his cheek on the inside of her wrist. Lightly, lightly. The fragile pulse beat against his skin with the softness of a bird's wing. His lips were nestled in her palm. He closed his eyes and breathed in her special scent. From out of nowhere came a swift, uncanny certainty that when she awoke and found him gone, she would weep.

He sat up carefully and stared straight ahead. In the seat opposite, Tess looked as if she'd fallen asleep trying to crawl inside Wally's waistcoat. Tom had his head back, mouth open, his snores like the last plaint of a dying bull. Cora sprawled limply across his lap, her face between his legs.

Riordan's head throbbed; his eyelids felt weighted. Outside, trees and hedges and prickly-looking bushes were speeding by at an alarming rate. Probably kill himself if he jumped now. Better wait. Cowardly to jump, anyway. He slumped back into his corner heavily. Tomorrow. He'd tell Cass he couldn't marry her tomorrow. Tell her straight out. She'd understand. Hell, she'd probably be relieved. His eyes closed on the sight of her glossy lashes resting like a crow's wings on her high, white cheekbones.

Cass woke up, confused, unable to remember falling asleep. It was still dark in the carriage, but outside the sky was lightening. She heard a guttural voice—the coachman's—and realized they were stopped at a toll booth. Then the coach jerked forward, rolling through a gate onto the single street of a sleepy-looking village. Something warned her that they had arrived.

The others slept on, huddled against each other in the opposite seat like a litter of puppies. Riordan slumped beside her on his spine, arms crossed, chin on his chest, breathing loudly. The carriage stopped again and she heard the thud of the driver's feet hitting the ground. Her heart jumped into her throat. They were here.

The door opened.

"Beggin' yer pardons, ladies and gents, but we're 'ere." Only Cass heard him, but she pretended not to. If the coachman went away now, it would be up to her to wake them all up—an appalling prospect. "I said we're 'ere!" he repeated, shaking Wally's arm roughly. "Whew!" he muttered to himself, "stinks like a gin mill in here." Then more loudly, "Gretna Green, folks, yer destination!" He shook Riordan's boot. "I'd like t' get this 'ere rig in the livery, yer lordships, so if you wouldn't mind—"

Finally they roused themselves, blinking stupidly, scratching and groaning and rubbing their faces. "Are we here?" Wally mumbled, hoisting himself out with surprising agility. On the ground, he gazed around at the quiet buildings, flexing his muscles, chafing his neck. "Lord, I've got to piss! Come on, Tom, let's see what's what."

Still in the carriage, Riordan clutched his head in both hands and ground his teeth, feeling as though two small men with pickaxes were gouging out his temples. He shuddered suddenly and felt a rolling sensation in his stomach. Sweat popped out on his forehead and his mouth started to water. Grabbing the doorframe, he hauled himself up and out of the carriage, and hit the ground at a run.

When Cass descended a moment later, he was leaning against the side of the building, his face a damp, fish-belly white, trying to stop shaking. "I've been poisoned," he rasped. "I'm dying." His red-veined eyes lit on the horse trough in front of him and he started toward it in a trance-like shuffle.

"Don't drink—" she started to warn him, but it was too late. He thrust his head into the blackish water and left it there, up to the shoulders, for so long she thought he was drowning. When he came up, sputtering and gasping, his black-and-silver hair was plastered back from his forehead and he looked like an otter.

"I wasn't *drinking* it," he said with weak reproach. He looked a little better; his cheeks under the three-day beard had a pinkish cast and his hands weren't shaking as much. They stared at each other. He resembled a Cheapside derelict on a particularly bad morning, and she looked like what she was—a woman who had sat up most of the night in a carriage, worrying. He'll call it off now, she thought. She wondered how he would phrase it.

"It's all set," Wally called out, coming toward them with Tess in tow, Tom and Cora behind.

All four looked obscenely chipper to Riordan. "For God's sake, don't shout."

"It's easy, there's nothing to it," Wally went on,

unheeding. "The tollkeeper does it, and we're the witnesses."

"The tollkeeper?" Riordan repeated stupidly.

"Or the blacksmith, but he's in Annan fixing a cart, so it's the tollkeeper."

The sun crept over the top of the roof opposite, sending shards of pain into his eyeballs. "The blacksmith?"

"Actually, anyone can do it, but it's usually the tollkeeper or the blacksmith, and we want this to be a traditional wedding, don't we?" He cackled and sent an elbow into Tess's ribs. "So, are we all ready?"

Then Riordan remembered. He was getting married this morning.

The pickaxes in his temples resumed pounding; he took an involuntary step backward and came up against the water trough. His knees buckled and he sat down heavily on the edge. His face went bloodless again and he stared up at Cass as if she were a specter of sudden and horrible death. He sent her a weak smile.

She turned her back on him, stood still for the space of a heartbeat, and started to walk away.

"Whoa, hold up, missie!" cried Wally, sensing his morning's sport was about to be spoiled. He made a grab for her arm and forcibly brought her back to the trough. "Hold on a blinkin' minute! No cold feet at this hour! Here, now—" He hauled Riordan up by the collar, took both their hands, and squeezed them together until their fingers entwined. He gave them a push to get them started, then walked behind them down the dusty street, talking all the while. "A wager's a wager, my friends. Twenty people watched it made and won— or in your case, Philip, lost—and now you're both bound to satisfy it. Your honor's on the line, you can't renege. I'm here to see you do your duty by each other. And by God, one day you'll thank me—"

Residents and shopkeepers began to appear in doorways and storefronts as the sun rose higher. Some stared, some nodded knowingly; strange young couples were commonplace in the little Scottish village on the border, their business there no mystery to the villagers.

Riordan heard none of Wally's words of encouragement. The urge to vomit was powerful. He fought it, concentrating on putting one foot in front of the other. Cass's hand in his felt as warm and welcoming as a dead bird's claw. His brain wasn't functioning; he couldn't put two consecutive thoughts together. He saw the tollkeeper's stone cottage ahead, and something inside him shuddered. It must have vibrated through his hand, because she turned her head sharply and looked at him. *Who are you*? he wanted to ask. She looked like a stranger. What was the expression in her wide gray eyes—challenge? Panic? He was too dimwitted to decipher it. He stopped and turned toward her, taking her other hand. "Cass," he mumbled, with no idea of what he was going to say next.

But Wally wanted no candid *tête-à-têtes* at this late stage, and hustled them forward with encouraging pats on the shoulders. "Now, now, can't keep the tollkeeper waiting."

"Wait a minute, damn it!" Riordan shook Wally off and they stopped again, within arm's length of the cottage. They all looked at him. Cass waited with a hurting, hollow fatalism, wishing now she'd taken the initiative; it would have softened the humiliation a little. But to her surprise, he didn't speak. Instead he ran his fingers through his wet hair a couple of times to comb it. He retied his wilted cravat and buttoned his waistcoat. Then he reached out with a shaky but gentle hand to push a wild strand of black hair away from her cheek and repin it on top of her head. For a second their gazes locked. She searched his face, but could not discover what he was thinking.

"Let's go, let's go," Wally urged, wary as a sheepdog.

And then, without touching, they were through the door and inside the cottage, and a bald man was waddling toward them, rubbing his hands.

"Top o' the morning! Name's Bean, George Bean. Let's see if I can guess which one's the lucky couple. Aha! Reckon it's this pasty-faced pair right here. Am I right? Whichever's whitest is the ones gettin' spliced, nine times outa ten. Not going to be sick on me, are you, girlie?"

Everyone looked at Cass. She was certainly pale enough to warrant the question. But she shook her head and straightened her spine, staring back at all of them with a sort of skittish valor. In that moment, Riordan knew he was going to marry her.

"Good. Now, first things first. The fee's four guineas."

"Four guineas!" Wally protested, and commenced to argue. Riordan pulled a handful of coins from his pocket and thrust them at Mr. Bean.

"Well, now," said the tollkeeper, pocketing the coins with a pleased smile, "appears like the groom's eager to begin. There ain't much to it, really. Most couples take hands about now. That's it. The groom goes first. All you say is, 'In front of these witnesses, we declare our wish to marry.' Got it? 'In front'—"

"I've got it." Riordan drew a deep breath, not knowing he was squeezing Cass's hand so hard she had to bite her lip. "In"—he had to clear his throat—"in front of these witnesses, we declare our wish to—marry." Afterward he listened to the echo of the words, his mouth open, eyes unfocused.

"That's it. Now the lady. See, you both have to say it."

Riordan looked down at Cass. She seemed far away, an image through the wrong end of a telescope. The tip of her tongue came out to moisten her lips. He heard a breath of air enter her lungs, watched her chest expand. "Before these witnesses." She stopped, and nobody breathed. "We declare our wish to marry."

Mr. Bean grinned. "Then you are!"

A second of silence while this was absorbed, then Wally and Tom were yelling, Cora and Tess were crying, and Cass and Riordan were staring at each other with equal parts amazement and horror.

"Kiss her! Kiss her, so we can!"

He did, with his eyes open, seeing his own shock reflected back at him in hers.

"Now, after you sign this here certificate, you'll want to stop at the Rose and Thorn for a nice wedding breakfast," Mr. Bean told them when the kissing and back-slapping were over. "Best little inn in town, and I don't say it because it's the only one, nor because my brother owns it. Ha ha!"

The dining facilities at the Rose and Thorn consisted of one huge table surrounded by wooden benches and chairs. Cass and Riordan were given the place of honor at one end, with their friends seated on either side. Wally proclaimed himself best man and set about ordering a lavish feast, for them as well as anyone else who happened by on this warm August morning. To Cass's silent chagrin, he took it upon himself to rent the "honeymoon cottage" for the newlyweds—a two-room house behind the inn, separated from it by a line of trees and a bridge over a useless but picturesque pond. He ordered champagne and invited strangers to join them, proposing toast after toast, seemingly unaffected by the prodigious amounts of food and wine he consumed. Everyone but Cass seemed to be bouncing back from the night before—even Riordan, who joined in the drinking and revelry just as though an hour ago he hadn't been sitting on the edge of a horse trough, trying not to be sick.

"To you, Cass," he said with a wide, reckless grin when no one was listening. "My beautiful new wife."

There was some sort of glint in his eye, but she couldn't tell if it was facetious or not. She could hardly look at him; her emotions were swerving back and forth between timid, trembling exultation and abject misery. She screwed up her courage and clinked glasses.

"To my husband," she said softly, trying the word out on her tongue. She watched his eyes darken and felt the same flushed, overheated sensation she'd had last night in the carriage. He leaned in and kissed her, not using his hands. After a moment her eyes closed and she sighed, giving herself up to it. But then six or seven people around the table began clapping and stomping their feet and calling out lewd encouragements. She shrank back, pink-faced.

The morning wore on and she grew more and more exhausted. She kissed so many strange men that she was dizzy from it. She drank a great deal of champagne but remained coldly, unrelentingly sober, as though the god of sobriety had put a curse on her. Riordan appeared to be drunk again, and grew increasingly amorous. Lust shone frankly in his bright-blue gaze; again and again she had to pull his hands away, mortified that he would touch her so intimately in public. She was drooping with fatigue, but would have accepted a painful, lingering death before she'd rise first and go outside to the "honeymoon cottage."

After what seemed like a hundred consecutive hours of enforced smiling and pretending, she looked up to see Riordan surge to his feet. Another toast, she thought, cringing—only this time he made her rise with him. He put an arm around her shoulders, as much to prop himself up as to bestow affection, and raised his glass in his other hand. "Ladies and gentlemen! If I may have your attention. My wife and I want to thank you all for being here, and for wishing us well as we begin our long, uncharted journey down life's, um, matrimonial— oh hell, I can't do it." He sagged against the table with a whoop of laughter, and soon everyone joined in. Cass didn't know whether to laugh or cry.

He regained a drunken sort of composure and began again. "What I mean to say is, I'm glad you're all here to join us in hoping this marriage is a long and happy one. As long and happy as my Uncle Hal's, in fact, God rest his soul. Uncle Hal had a saying, and I hope to be able to echo it someday: 'The happiest hours I've lived in my life were spent between the legs of my wife.'" He collapsed again in hilarity, beating the table with his fist. Cass whirled around, and he caught a glimpse of the back of her rigid, reddening neck before reaching out and grabbing a handful of her gown. He hauled her back unceremoniously and picked her up.

Pandemonium broke out around the table as he strode across the room toward the front door. Cass shut her ears to the whistles and catcalls and vulgar inducements, electing to bury her face in his neck. "Don't kill us," she ground out when he lurched sideways against the doorpost.

Bright sunshine hit them in the eyes with the force of a slap. A passerby, evidently a native, gave Riordan a wink and made a gesture whose meaning

Cass found easy to interpret, though she'd never seen it before. She'd been sure the others would follow them outside and accompany them all the way to the "honeymoon cottage," and her faith in prayer was restored when they did not. Then she was certain Riordan would slip on the rickety wooden bridge spanning the pond and tumble them both into its placid blue water, but providence smiled on her again. She suspected it would be for the last time today.

Miraculously, they arrived at the cottage unscathed. Cass had to open the door. Riordan stumbled through and kicked it closed with his boot. She swept the room with a glance, noting nothing except that it was clean and neat, then stiffened her arms and pushed back against his chest. "Put me down."

He obliged, puffing a little. She stepped away as he fell back against the door with a thud, grinning happily. They stood watching each other, eight feet apart, not speaking. Slowly Riordan's grin faded and a different light came into his eyes. Cass looked behind her to see how much farther she could back up before hitting the ludicrously wide, canopied bed. About three feet. But instead of pursuing her, he held out his hand. She hadn't expected that.

She took a couple of steps toward him and stopped. She gestured vaguely with one arm. "It's so—" What? Late? It wasn't, it was early afternoon. "I'm so—" Tired? True, but she didn't want to begin her marriage on that note. Her marriage! Lord God, she was *married*. To this wild man with a beard, who was coming toward her, grinning as if she were a piece of mutton and he hadn't eaten in days. "Wait!" He looked as if he meant to pick her up again, and this time she knew when he put her down it would be on the bed. "Wait!"

His delighted grin only widened. "I've been waiting for weeks, Cass. I don't have to wait anymore!" He drew her close with one arm around her waist, the other behind her neck, and kissed her lustily. His mustache tickled and his technique had lost all subtlety, but she found herself responding anyway because he felt so good and solid in her arms. His mouth was hot and eager, his hands urgent as they slid up and down her back and tangled in her hair. His hectic need excited her in spite of herself. She kissed him back thoughtlessly, opening her mouth to the fierce, sweet onslaught of his tongue. But Riordan's timing was hopelessly off; he took her reaction as a signal that she was ready for him to undress her and started fumbling at the buttons in the back of her dress.

"Oh, don't," she panted, pushing him away.

"Why? Oh, Cass, I want to."

"Don't you see? If we do this, if we—consummate this marriage, you'll lose your grounds for annulling it."

"Not consummate the marriage?" He said it as a boy might say, "Not have any Christmas?" Then he heard the part about the annulment. "*I'm* not having this marriage annulled!"

They stared, both taken aback by the vehemence of his announcement. He reached for her again and kissed her with a little more finesse, encouraged when she sighed into his mouth and put her hands in his hair. He told her how good she tasted, how much he loved to touch her, and she arched her back and let him nuzzle at the base of her throat. But even as her blood heated, a knot of fear began to tighten in her stomach, diluting the pleasure. They weren't in a carriage now or in front of a window, and what was happening wasn't going to stop with kisses. She began to tremble with trepidation instead of passion; and when he cupped her buttocks and tried to slide his hands between her thighs in back, she broke away again.

"What's wrong?" he asked in puzzlement. "Tell me what's wrong."

She told him. "You're drunk, and I've never done this before!"

He grinned at her and combed his hair with his fingers. "I'm not *that* drunk."

She waited for him to address the second half of her answer. He didn't, and she turned her back so he wouldn't see the misery and disappointment in her face. She took a quavery breath and looked up at the ceiling.

He went to her and touched her shoulders. She was stiff as a plank. "Honest, Cass," he told her softly, "I'm not that drunk. I was pretending for the others." He began a slow massage, intrigued by the way the sun irradiated individual strands of her glossy hair. There was magic in her skin for him; he couldn't keep his hands off it. He saw that the hairs on the back of her neck were golden, not black. He put his tongue out and touched their tickly softness. She shuddered deeply. At another time he'd have kept that up, even supplemented it with creative variations, but this wasn't Riordan's day for subtlety. He snaked his arms around her and squeezed her breasts while pressing his hardness against her bottom—and was amazed when she gasped in dismay, not desire, flinging away from him to the far side of the room.

"Cass! What is it? What's wrong?"

She kept her back to him. "I told you! I'm innocent and I'm frightened!"

He tried a laugh, hoping she'd laugh with him. It embarrassed him that she would say that now, lie to him at a time like this. And it was so unnecessary. He pushed his fingers through his hair again, wishing he hadn't drunk so much wine. The last thing he wanted to do was hurt her feelings. "Cass," he said gently, coming toward her. "Don't you know by now that I don't care if you are or not?" He put his hands on her hips and stroked her with his thumbs. "Sweetheart, it just doesn't matter."

Cass bowed her head. His disbelief cut as cruelly as a knife. He thought he was being kind, but it would have been more honest if he'd simply admitted that his expectations of a woman like her were, out of charity, low. No matter that he would find out the truth in a few minutes—or at least she hoped he would; she'd heard that a man could tell when it was a woman's first time. She wanted him to believe her *now*, before he had the evidence of his senses.

Riordan could see he was losing. He stared at all the tiny buttons down the back of her dress, saw the obdurate tautness in her neck and shoulder muscles. He felt unequal to the mental and physical dexterity the situation was fast requiring. He wanted their first time to be good, not weighted down with snarls and tangles and complexities he didn't even understand. He gritted his teeth, feeling frustration wash over him in a drowning wave.

Cass felt his hands slide slowly away. Guilt sliced through her like a chill, straight to the bone. She was ruining it for him, but she couldn't help it. She wanted him to see her for what she was, before he made love to her. She'd saved herself for him. She wanted him to understand the gift and savor it, not ignore it, not discover too late that she'd given it to him.

She heard him go to the bed and sit down. A boot hit the floor; another. She turned around slowly in disbelief. His coat and waistcoat were on the floor and he was engaged in unbuttoning his shirt. In gathering numbness, she watched him pull it over his shoulders and drop it on top of his other clothes. Her mind took note that he was beautiful, but she derived no pleasure from the thought. She had to turn away when he stood up to remove his stockings and breeches. Her arms went around herself in a frozen hug of protectiveness and she waited. He was her husband. He could do anything with her he wanted. Whatever happened, she vowed she wouldn't cry or ask him for—

"Don't go anywhere, will you, Cass?"

His voice was light and boyish. She felt a rush of air and realized he was passing behind her, moving toward the door. For three seconds she had an unencumbered view of his bare backside. She had to put her hands on her chest for fear her heart would punch its way through ribs and skin and plop out on the braided rug at her feet. Then he was through the door and gone.

She stared, flabbergasted, at the empty space he'd occupied. For a wild second she imagined him striding back to the inn and bursting in on his friends, stark naked. But he'd been carrying his breeches. Then she heard it, the mighty splash, and she clapped her hands to her open mouth to smother a giddy squeal of relief. She threw her head back and laughed. He'd jumped into the pond.

After the first shock, the water was like a revitalizing balm on his overheated flesh. Gradually his blood cooled and his heartbeat steadied. He stayed under as long as his lungs would allow, peering at green undulating things, savoring the sensuous chill of the water, thinking of Cass. When he came up, he turned and floated on his back. The azure sky was cloudless, the air soft. The lone duck that had paddled away in protest on his arrival lumbered cautiously down the bank and reentered the water, keeping its distance.

The cobwebs were clearing rapidly, but his need for his wife was only growing stronger. He felt the gentle lap of the water on his skin and it teased him with a memory of hers, soft and cool and inviting. The lilies on the bank smelled fresh, like her. He imagined her body enveloping him like the cool blue pond. He stood up and scrubbed himself clean for her with his hands. Here in the middle, the water came up to his ribcage. He flexed his toes, feeling the cold, squishy mud between them. Everything excited him. He felt as if his senses were snapping and sparking with life. He strode up the bank, shaking water from his hair like a dog. He dragged on his breeches and buttoned them, his eyes on the cottage.

Inside, Cass explored the two small rooms, bedroom and dressing room, with quick, restless steps. She opened her bags and passed her hands over her clothes without seeing them. She stared at the bed. Should she undress? Put on a nightgown? She couldn't stop moving, couldn't think. She decided to take off her shoes. At the mirror, she did a double-take. What a sight! She readjusted the pins in her hair to create a semblance of order, but her mind was elsewhere. There was nothing to be done about the twin spots of bright color on her cheeks, or the rapid tripping of her heart. She went to the door. Riordan was floating on his back. She turned away, breathless, flushing. She sat on the edge of the bed to calm herself. When at last she heard his step outside she sat up very straight, smoothing her skirt with one hand and clenching the other over her heart.

He entered quietly, testing the air. Water ran down his chest and stomach, his bare calves, and pooled at his feet. She couldn't stop staring. Half-naked, he seemed bigger to her than he ever had before. Without speaking, he went to the dressing room. In a few seconds he appeared in the doorway with a towel. He rubbed his hair and beard vigorously, watching her, then slung the towel over his shoulder.

"There's a door in back, did you see it?" she blurted. "It looks out over a meadow. It's pretty."

He lifted his brows. "Show me."

She couldn't tell if his interest was real or polite or amused, but she rose and went toward him, careful not to make contact as she sidled past into the dressing room. She pushed open a low door in the rear wall and went out. Riordan followed, ducking his head. They stood on a tiny porch, two steps up from a grassy yard. Beyond was a pasture, empty but for half a dozen spotted cows in the quiet distance. The porch contained one wooden, wide-armed chair, pushed back under the eaves of the cottage roof to keep it dry. For a few seconds they both thought of all the newly married lovers who had gazed out together across the humming field, or sat together in the chair, arms entwined, sharing their dreams. Cass came out to the spindly railing and turned around toward him, resting her palms lightly on top; Riordan leaned in the doorway. She'd never seen a grown man's feet before. She could hardly look away from the arrogant length of his, the bony toes, the elegant insteps.

"Do you like the country, Cass?"

She dragged her gaze up to his face. "Yes, I do. Very much."

"Good. I have a house in Surrey. I think you'll like it."

For some reason that shocked her, the thought of going to Riordan's country home as his wife. The reality of their marriage, she realized, hadn't even begun to sink in. She remembered what he'd said before. "Why—" She stopped. *Why don't you want our marriage annulled*? she'd started to ask, before her courage bolted.

"Why what?"

Courage returned, or foolhardiness. "Why did you marry me?"

He came toward her; she held her ground. He began to unpin her hair. Her heartbeat accelerated and her breath began to come in rapid, audible gasps. She thought he wouldn't speak, that his touch was her answer, but she was wrong.

"Because I wanted to."

Everything seemed to get brighter. She had to shut her eyes. She felt as if she were toppling over backwards and was grateful for the warm, steadying pressure of his hand behind her neck. His fingers combed her hair with whispery gentleness, stroking, lifting. He wrapped a shining lock around his forefinger and brought it to his lips. She wanted to touch him, but she couldn't move. "Look," he said unexpectedly. He turned her around, embracing her from behind.

"Oh . . ." Six cows were craning their mammoth noses over the worn stone wall that separated the yard from the pasture. Enchanted, Cass smiled as a dozen liquid brown eyes stared back at her with unblinking intensity.

"An audience," said Riordan. "What does it take to shock a cow, do you think?" He kissed the soft place behind her ear. She shivered, holding his hands still across her bodice. She felt his tongue on her ear, following the convoluted twists of bone and flesh, and opened her mouth in an involuntary gasp. "This doesn't seem to have much effect on them," he murmured.

"They must be eunuchs." She rested her head against him, loving the rich sound of his chuckle in her ear.

"Cows can't be eunuchs," he told her. One hand stole to the buttons at the back of her dress, and he had them open in a trice. "Mm, they like this. Look at the middle one, there."

She guessed he meant the one with the lop ears, but it was hard to concentrate on a cow's expression when he had her gown pulled down around her elbows and was lightly fingering the thin lace of her shift in front. Her body shook as if it were freezing. She took one of his hands and kissed the knuckles lingeringly. "You touched me once at Vauxhall, long ago, standing behind me like this. I thought I would die from the pleasure."

It was Riordan's turn to tremble. He turned her gently. The passion in her eyes slammed the breath from his lungs. His fingers traced her strong jaw underneath, trailed down to the pulse point in the hollow of her throat. "I remember. People everywhere, and all I wanted to do was hold you."

She put her hands to his face for a moment before pushing them into his hair, feeling the cool wetness between her fingers. There were droplets of water still on his beard. Standing on tiptoe, she leaned into him to capture them on the tip of her tongue. His arms tightened hard around her and he lifted her off the ground, holding her heart against his, feeling her heat. When he set her down and drew back, he saw where the wetness from his body had seeped through her shift, outlining her breasts. He put his hands under their gentle upcurves. Her lips parted; delicate pink color stained her cheeks. Watching her, he moved his fingers to her nipples and rubbed them softly through the sleek silk.

Her nostrils flared. Her hands came up to take his wrists. "I'm so glad, so glad," she murmured fiercely, staring up into his eyes, watching the expanding pupils turn them almost black. When he kissed her she strained against him and held onto his shoulders. His flesh felt cool and slick under her fingers, in contrast to the warm, rough texture of his tongue sliding across her lips, stroking and coaxing, sending cascades of pleasure through her.

"I want you so much," he whispered into her mouth, teasing her with little nips of his teeth. "So much, Cass. Is it all right?"

"Yes, yes." But she had to say it. "But you still don't believe me, do you?"

"I do. I do believe you."

But he didn't, and now it was so hard to care. She let him lift her and carry her inside, her face pressed lightly to the side of his neck, inhaling the wet, almost wild scent of him. He set her down beside the bed. His breath caught. She looked wanton to him with her gown tugged down in front, her arms bound to her sides in the sleeves. His need for her was becoming desperate, but he forced himself to go slowly. "You're so beautiful. Let me see you, Cass. I have to see you." Inch by inch, he pushed her dress down the rest of the way, past her hips to the floor. With a practiced ease that didn't escape her, he undid the laces of her petticoats and slid them down, too, leaving her in her shift. She was trembling. He took her hands and held them over his heart. "Are you afraid?"

She nodded.

"Should we stop?"

"Oh, no."

His smile of relief looked so heartfelt that she had to laugh, a light, giddy sound. He kissed her fingers one at a time, gazing intently at each one as if he'd never seen fingers before. "A ring," he said suddenly. "You haven't got a ring."

She shook her head dreamily. "Does it matter?"

"Not at this exact moment."

They kissed, their smiles colliding, fingers coming unclasped so they could touch each other. She pressed her hands to his back and felt the flexing of his muscles as he stroked her. She rubbed closer, enjoying the texture of his wet skin against her chest, her breasts. He kissed her slowly, deeply, until she was limp. She heard the sound of desire in her ears, like crashing waves. She was standing on tiptoe, arms tight around him, wanting to be closer, closer. Without stopping the kiss, he lifted her and laid her in the center of the bed, then sank down by her side.

He put a hand under one of her knees and brought it up, smoothing the hem of her shift back to the middle of her thigh. He kissed the top of her knee through her stocking, bit it softly, and then began to peel the white silk down, slowly, slowly, over her knee and down her long, smooth calf. She shifted restlessly and wet her lips. The sound of silk sliding against flesh made the blood rise in a hot flood to her cheeks. He smiled when she offered her other knee to him herself. But instead of attending to that stocking, he bent his head to the inner flesh of her thigh and placed a slow strand of open kisses, beginning at her knee and moving up until she stopped him with her fingers in his hair, gasping in fear and disbelief and all but unbearable excitement.

He raised his head, and his eyes were as black as a night sky. She looked at his mouth, her undoing, and shivered with dread and delight. "Shall I undress you first, or me, Cass?" he asked in an uneven whisper.

She tried to shrug, but her body wasn't obeying her mind. His hand rested lightly on her belly. He was waiting for an answer. "Don't make me choose," she blurted out, panicked. "I can't, I can't—"

"Shh." He pulled her up into his arms and held her, burying his face in her hair. Her heart beat wildly. She clutched his shoulders and hung on for dear life. "I only asked because I couldn't decide myself," he confessed, kissing the nape of her neck. He felt her laughter bubbling up and hugged her, wondering if he was in love. "Shall we do it together?"

She nodded. She was beyond shyness, but she couldn't keep from saying, "It's so *bright* in here."

He put his mouth to hers and whispered softly, so softly she understood the words more by feel than sound, "But I want to see you, Cass, I'm dying to see you. Don't be afraid. I would never hurt you, never. Let me, love, let me . . ."

She melted. He pressed her back down to the pillow and she took her folded hands away, letting him unlace her shift. "I never wear a corset," she began apologetically, staring over his shoulder.

"I know. It's one of the things I love about you."

Her skin felt chilled and charred at the same time; her breath came in painful gulps. He took one of her hands and placed it at his waist, and she remembered they were supposed to be undressing each other. But her fingers wouldn't work. He was intent on pulling her arms out of the sleeves of her chemise. He moved her motionless hand aside distractedly, pushed his breeches over his hips, and threw them on the floor. Immediately he returned to her shift, and before she knew it she was bare to the waist. She covered one hand with the other and brought them both to her breastbone in senseless shame.

Smiling, holding her gaze until the last second, he bent his head and kissed her tense knuckles. She felt his teeth next, then his warm tongue. She knew what he wanted. She obeyed because she wanted it, too. As she slowly dragged her hands away, her fingers grazed her own nipples. Her eyes opened wide. He growled low in his throat and pulled her wrists over her head. She had to have his weight on her, his hard chest against her breasts. Words of wanting tumbled from her lips, half-formed phrases that shocked and thrilled her. He said her name over and over like a chant until it was impossible for him to speak because he was kissing her so deeply. She was frantic for him, her body twisting, thrashing. The rough hair of his thigh teasing against her pelvis was an unendurable agony.

He kissed her hairline and her cheekbones, trailing his wet tongue down to her jaw, her throat. His body was as taut as a bowstring; he was shivering with the effort of restraint. A light sheen of perspiration skimmed his chest and neck; under the black hairs of his beard his face was flushed a hectic pink. He slid his hand down inside her shift and stroked the back of her bare thigh, her buttock. That she still had on any clothes at all seemed crazy to him all of a sudden. He pushed at the bunched-up cloth impatiently, and she kicked it down the rest of the way herself. Instantly his hand found her soft mound, his fingers sinking gently into the silky hairs, softly rubbing.

Her head went back. Eyes closed, teeth clenched, she tried not to call out, but it was useless. She couldn't catch her breath. Then his mouth circled her nipple and her cries turned to moans, her lips petulant, eyelashes fluttering. He was making her open her legs and his fingers were slippery and stroking and he was putting them inside her. Her thighs were clenching in some new way, at once defensive and urgently encouraging. He didn't know whether she was saying "No" or "Now," but he was past caring. Murmuring passion words in her ear, he parted her legs farther, farther, using his knees.

The first touch sent shudders of wanting through him. If he didn't slow down it would all be over. But he couldn't stop, couldn't wait, he needed to possess her. He took her mouth in a fervent kiss and sank into her. Her nails digging into his shoulders didn't warn him; his senses were concentrated elsewhere. She was hot and wet, but she was so tight, she felt like heated velvet. He thrust higher and heard her frightened gasp.

"Cass?" A sudden sick chill prickled across his skin. Oh no, oh no. Her stomach muscles under his were knotted and hard. He drew back to see her face, and froze. "Oh, Cass. Oh, love."

"It doesn't hurt, I like it." But her eyes were shut tight and tears glistened on the lashes.

He rested his forehead on her collarbone, his breath ragged. His only coherent thought was that Quinn would pay for this.

She shifted under him, pressing upward hopefully. "Do it," she whispered, "I want you to."

But he could only hold her. He felt as if his chest was burning. Remorse tasted like salt on the back of his tongue.

"It's all right." She stroked him softly with both hands, soothing him. "I'm perfectly all right. It was just for a second, and I think if you would continue—"

He raised his head and gazed down into her sweet, solemn face. "Don't, Cass," he said bitterly. "Don't forgive me so easily." His smile was tight and full of self-loathing. "You could hold this against me for years, for the rest of our lives."

She laughed softly. "Why ever would I want to do that?"

"You could, though. How many times did you try to tell me?"

"Not very many." She trailed her thumbs across his cheekbones. "It doesn't matter now. Do you think we could talk about it later?"

"Of course it matters. Cass, I never wanted to hurt you, I swear it. I'd rather hurt myself."

"Hush. It's enough. I've forgiven you whether you want me to or not. I only know of one thing you could do now that would be truly unforgivable."

"What?"

She smoothed the tense line between his brows and whispered. "Leave me like this, still wanting you so badly. Kiss me again, touch me the way you did before. Love me, Philip, make love to me. Make me yours."

His breath hissed through his teeth. He had something else to tell her, but she was offering him her mouth and he forgot it in the enveloping heat, forgot everything but the soft, exquisite feel of her lips and the taste of her tongue. He kissed her slowly, as if for the first time, and he meant it as a promise, a beginning. "Tell me if I hurt you." He was afraid to move. "Tell me, Cass."

"No, no, you don't hurt me." She was dying for him. There was no pain, only fullness and heat. She wrapped her legs around his and arched her back, bringing him closer, higher. The intimacy of this act took her breath away. He went slowly, slowly, watching her eyes. But it was too intense, she couldn't bear to let him see her. She pulled his head down and kissed him frantically. He breathed her name into her mouth in rhythm with his slow, steady strokes, over and over, feeling her tightness gathering.

"Philip, Philip!"

"Let it happen," he grated, helping her.

Her fingers gripped his arms and her mouth opened on the hard flesh of his shoulder. The pulsing convulsions that rocked her tore away the last remnants of his self-control. Even as he took her, fierce and wild, he knew this was no raw act of possession. What he gave her with such tender savagery was the essence of himself. Afterward she lay beneath him, limp and vanquished. But in his heart he knew, for good or ill, and for all time, he was hers.

X

THEY AWOKE AT THE SAME MOMENT, SHARING THE PIL-
low, blinking into each other's faces. Identical
expressions of confusion, recollection, and gladness strayed over soft gray and dark blue eyes in
unison. They might have been looking into mirrors.
Then the realization of what had woken them made
them smile, again in harmony. Through the open
window came the strains of a serenade, sincere but
profoundly unsteady.

"Our dear friends," Riordan murmured sleepily.

"Mmm." Cass rubbed her cheek against his
knuckles with drowsy pleasure.

"I suppose I'll have to go out and say something
to them."

"Mmm." She twined her fingers in his and
brought his hand to her lips. "But I don't want you
to go." She loved the lazy way the corners of his
mouth turned up when he smiled.

"But the sooner I do, the sooner I can come back

and make love to you."

Gray eyes darkened to slate. "In that case, what are you still doing here?"

He meant to give her a peck on the nose, but before he knew it he was wrapped up in her arms and legs, and kissing her as fervently as a soldier bidding his wife farewell before setting off to war. Laughing and breathless, they let each other go. She watched while he went to his portmanteau and drew out a jade-green dressing gown. Knotting the sash, he padded barefoot to the door, opened it—causing the serenade to break off in a sudden rising cheer—and closed it quickly behind him.

Cass stretched hugely, extending a limb into all four corners of the bed. She turned her face into the pillow and breathed the faint, fresh scent of her husband's hair. *Her husband.* Radiant, unexamined happiness washed over her in a dizzying gush. She sat up, unable to contain herself. Outside the voices were growing raucous again, and presently she could make out the words: "We want the bride! We want the bride!" She giggled and put her fingers to her lips, considering. Then she threw her legs over the side of the bed. If they wanted the bride that badly, they should have her.

She put on her old robe of worn apricot silk, wishing she had something finer. But then, she hadn't known six days ago when she'd set out from London that she would soon be a married lady. Consciously avoiding the mirror, she went to the door.

Riordan had planted himself sturdily in front like a sentinel; he glanced back in surprise when he heard the door open. A ragged hurrah went up from the small clump of well-wishers gathered in front of the cottage. Wally and Tess and Tom and Cora were

there, as well as half a dozen sympathetic revelers
drawn to the celebration by the powerful incentive
of free beer. It was almost dusk; the slanting sun on
the pond had turned it a bright gold. Birds called
across the evening sky, signaling the end of the day.
The air was as soft as a lover's breath.

The cheering died away to stunned silence.
Sleepy-looking and tousled, her skin flushed, Cass
smiled a sweet smile and slid her arms around her
husband's waist. Riordan didn't need their envy,
but it was an undeniable pleasure to know there
wasn't a man there who wouldn't have given a great
deal to be in his place. He smiled down at his bride.
She was the most desirable woman he'd ever
known, and particularly so at this moment. Her
lips were pink from his most recent kiss and there
was a dreamy look in her eyes. Her hair was loose
and hung around her shoulders like a dark cloud.
Her long white toes poked out, bare and vulnerable,
from under the hem of her robe. Squeezing her
close, he addressed himself to the crowd, hoping to
dispatch them quickly.

It worked. But then, he'd rarely been more
eloquent, not even on the floor of the Commons.
With a satisfied smile he watched them trail away,
full of mellowness and good will toward everyone,
over the bridge and back to the inn.

"Wally!" he called out, remembering. "I'll only
be a second, love." He kissed the top of her head
before walking out to meet his friend, who waited
for him beside the bridge.

Cass watched them speaking, unable to hear the
words, her eyes on her new husband. The sunset
was fiery on his skin, turning his face ruddy. The
color of his robe complemented his dark-blue eyes
so handsomely, she wondered if a woman had
given it to him. That brought a little stab of pain.

Followed by a slash of guilt. He'd given up so much in marrying her, and now he was doing a heroic job of making the best of a tragic situation.

She ought to have stopped the wedding. Oh, she knew it, she knew it. But she hadn't wanted to, she'd wanted him any way she could have him. All the nonsense about upholding his honor or sparing him embarrassment had only been an excuse. Selfish, selfish. But she loved him! Was it so wrong to reach out and take your heart's desire when it was handed to you?

She would make it up to him; she'd be the best wife any man ever had. She'd prove to him and all his friends that she was a decent woman, deserving of their respect. It would take time, perhaps, but she had limitless patience. And one day, if it killed her, Philip Riordan was going to fall in love with his wife.

He and Wally were shaking hands. Riordan looked grateful, she had time to think, before he turned and came toward her, ending her speculation on what that might signify.

They embraced as soon as the door closed.

"I missed you," Cass said, throwing away caution. "You were gone so long."

"I know. I thought they'd never leave."

"The way you spoke to them was wonderful." She rubbed her cheek against his chest softly. "What did you say to Wally?"

"I impressed upon him our urgent desire that he depart the neighborhood tomorrow morning. The earlier the better." He left out the part of the conversation in which he'd sincerely thanked his friend for his energy and persistence. If Wally had been surprised by that, Cass would be thunderstruck, and Riordan wasn't ready to share his new feelings with her just yet. In truth, he was terrified. That he'd married the traitor's daughter with the deplorable reputation was a shock. That he was falling in love with her was incredible. He needed time to get used to the idea. And cowardly or not, he wanted to understand better what her feelings were before he handed her his heart on a plate.

He pulled away to look at her. She was biting her lip. "What is it?"

She shrugged one shoulder in that totally French way she had. "So, you're anxious to be away. I only thought—"

"Not *us*, silly, them. I want *them* out of the way by tomorrow. Then I can have you all to myself."

"Oh!" She wrapped her arms around his neck, stood on tiptoe, and kissed him exuberantly.

He hugged her hard, deepening the kiss. "Do you like me at all, Cass?" he asked lightly, as if everything didn't depend on her answer. He kissed her eyes shut and ran his tongue along her lashes. "Do you think you can stand being married to me?"

The question made her want to cry. Her heart filled to bursting; she almost answered with her terrible truth. "It's not fair to ask such a question when you're kissing me this way," she parried breathlessly.

He smiled, moving back to her lips. "Why do you think I chose this moment to ask?"

"Answer a question for me," she said a moment later. "How will you explain to your friends that your wife won you in a card game?" She kept her tone airy to match his, but every nerve was taut.

Riordan knew the question wasn't idle. He didn't give a damn what his friends thought of him, but he already had a shrewd idea of what they were likely to think of her. "I'll tell them I never played a luckier hand," he whispered, nipping her earlobe and then salving it with his tongue.

Cass shivered with delicious pleasure. He backed her to the bed, slowly but steadily, kissing her all the while. Her knees struck the mattress and he tumbled her back, following her. She turned her head when his mouth came down again. It was difficult to keep up the conversation, but she wanted to know more. "And your family? What will you tell them? I suspect the Earl and Countess of Raine will be a teeny bit disappointed in your choice."

"Someday I'll tell you all about my family, and then you'll understand why their approval is a matter of monumental indifference to me." With one smooth, downward gesture he undid the sash of her dressing gown and spread it open. His eyes glittered with purpose, and she was fast losing her train of thought. "Cass, you have such beautiful breasts."

"And Quinn?" she gasped, clutching the coverlet, unwilling to let the subject drop but unable to concentrate on it. "Won't he disown you or something?"

"Probably. Or cane me. Oh Christ, you taste good." He moved to her other breast. His voice was a ragged murmur. "A little while ago I thought you'd had dozens of lovers, and I said I didn't care." He shifted so that he half-lay between her thighs, bent over her. "Forgive me, Cass, I'm such a fool. I've got no right to ask."

Her fingers were in his hair, holding his head where she wanted it. Her toes curled and uncurled, a few inches from the floor; she couldn't bear this much longer. "What?" she almost sobbed.

"How many men have touched you this way before me?" His tongue made excruciatingly slow circles around her nipple before his lips pulled gently, sending a sweet, aching arrow of wanting through her.

It might have been fun to tease him, but she was incapable of anything but the unadorned truth.

"No one," she panted. "Once Jacques Toussaint tried to—do this, through my gown, but his aunt came in and we—"

He stopped the rest with his mouth, laughing with relief, ashamed of himself but unspeakably happy. "Oh, sweet, sweet, Cass. How I adore you."

Her heart missed a beat or two. She couldn't help herself, she wrapped her bare legs around his hips. It felt so wanton and wonderful, soothing her calves back and forth over the silky material of his robe. His unmistakable reaction gave her a first taste of feminine power. Awed by her own boldness, she put a hand between them and untied his robe—not with his practiced skill, but with a shy enthusiasm of her own that charmed him utterly. Without thinking, she asked, "And how many women have done that to you? No!" She put her hand over his mouth. "I retract the question. Please don't answer."

He shrugged out of his robe and let it fall to the floor. By now there was a sizeable heap of clothing beside the bed. "The question's irrelevant," he told her as his fingers stroked her hip, her strong thigh, urging her legs farther apart. "A better one is how many will do it in the future." He slid both hands under her buttocks and lifted her. "The answer is one. Only one."

She gasped, her chin pointing to the ceiling. "Philip!" He withdrew slowly, returned, withdrew again. He was huge, he filled her completely. This was perfect. She brought his mouth down and kissed him, moving to his rhythm. For a few moments she enjoyed the illusion of control, even a suggestion of authority. But as the patient, merciless assault went on and on, her self-command floated off and disappeared, a forgotten cloud, leaving nothing but pure sensation. Never had she been more aware of her body, less able to think.

That was how he wanted her. Again and again he took her to the brink and held her there, the ruthless expert, savoring his power to drive her beyond endurance. She was weeping, almost mad from the pleasure and the wanting, and he wanted to keep her there forever. Using his body and his mouth, his whispered words, he made her wild. "Do you like this, Cass?" he murmured against her throat, holding himself away, not moving. Her answer was unintelligible. His dark-blue gaze pierced her, wouldn't let her look away. He teased her with a touch; she groaned in frenzied frustration, twisting. "Do you like it?" He wanted his answer. Another touch, light and tantalizing, meant to torment her.

But it was enough. Abruptly she burst free, with a low, rising moan that ended on a note of triumph, cheating him of the pleasure of releasing her. He felt the storm rage inside her until, like her, he was goaded past restraint. Shuddering, quaking, he started his own perilous fall. But he'd never dived from such a height before. "*Cass!*" he ground out, holding to her frantically. And with sweet, feminine graciousness, she cushioned his fall and saved him.

"How does it come about, wife, that you're not what you're reputed to be?"

Cass swung around from a dreamy contemplation of the black, star-filled sky and regarded her husband thoughtfully. She took a tiny sip of wine and replaced the glass on the rail behind her. "Perhaps that's a question you should ask Mr. Quinn."

"Oh, believe me, I shall." He slid down a little farther in the chair and steepled his fingers, resting his chin on top. "I suppose this means you never jumped naked into the fountain in the Tuileries while scores of young men looked on, clapping and cheering?"

Her eyes twinkled. "That's something you'll never know."

"Too bad. It was such a lovely fantasy." He sobered. "Why didn't you tell Oliver his conclusions about you were false?"

"I did, in the beginning. Not very forcefully, I suppose."

"Why not?"

She thought back to her first meeting with Quinn. "I think because I was proud. And hurt. My father had just died and I . . . didn't have much energy. My aunt had told me that my reputation in this country was in a shambles, and what Quinn said merely confirmed it." She shrugged, smiling a little, telling him it wasn't important.

Riordan remembered his last interview with Lady Sinclair. "But your aunt as good as told me your reputation was deserved. Doesn't *she* know better?"

"She did, before. But she really thought you and I were lovers. And Colin and I, too." It was the first time Wade's name had been mentioned between them since they'd left Ladymere. They both ignored it. "Anything else she might have said was for spite." She frowned. "When did you speak to her?"

"The day after you left." He got up and came toward her. "I'm not angry anymore, Cass, but when I found out you'd left without telling me or leaving any word, I wanted to—"

"But I *did*! I left a message with my aunt to send to you. Colin was in such a rush, there wasn't time for anything but a quick note. Aunt Beth said she'd send it to you by messenger."

"She lied. I almost had to drag it out of her." Literally, he recalled.

"I knew I should've left the note with Clara. Do you know, Philip, I truly think Aunt Beth hates me."

He saw the bewildered look clouding her eyes and took her in his arms, gazing over her head at the dark, silent pasture. "I'm glad you wrote to me, Cass. I couldn't stand the thought of you going off with him. Until I got to Ladymere, I didn't even know it was a house party; I thought it was only you and Wade."

She smiled, savoring the notion that for a little while he might have been jealous. Suddenly her smile faded and she pulled away. "Philip! Oh, my lord, I can't believe I forgot to tell you."

"Tell me what?"

"But we were never alone, and you were so drunk, and then afterward we—we were doing something else, and I didn't think of it. I feel like such an idiot—"

"What, Cass? What?"

"What Wade told me! Philip, he admitted everything!"

He took her by the arm and led her to the chair under the eaves. Putting her in it, he made her slow down and tell him all that Wade had said. Afterward he questioned her, patiently and thoroughly, until he knew the conversation by heart and there was nothing more to learn. Then he made her tell him everything that had happened over the weekend, moment by moment. He felt a prickly fear when she described nearly being caught searching Wade's study.

"Should I have told you sooner? I know I should have, but what could you have done, really? Written Quinn a letter, I suppose, but—"

"It's all right, love, don't worry about it. It's a fascinating piece of news, but there's nothing to be done immediately. When we're back in London will be soon enough to tell Oliver." He sat on the arm of her chair, bracing one hand against the back. "So it's to happen in November. Interesting. That coincides with the opening of Parliament. November fifth this year, I think."

"Does the king do it? Open Parliament, I mean."

"Yes, it's a ceremony. Every year the Members of the Commons are summoned before the throne in the House of Lords to hear the king's speech. The Gentleman Usher of the Black Rod knocks at the door to call us; to show our independence, it's part of the ritual to pretend not to hear him knock the first time."

They were silent, thinking.

"I don't think you should see Wade again," he said after a moment.

She looked up. "I don't see how I can stop. It's more important now than ever that I stay in contact with him. Now that he's finally taken me into his confidence, he'll tell me much, much more." Riordan said nothing, but his resolute expression didn't change. "You know, Philip, he's really not interested in me as a lover," she told him softly.

He laughed, incredulous. "My naive young wife, why would you think that?"

"Because we're not compatible."

"What does that mean?"

"We like different things."

"How do you know? You were never lovers."

"No. But—he likes—he wants to—"

She was embarrassed, and a sudden, sickening thought occurred to him. He lifted her hand, which had been resting on his knee, and held it. "Did Wade hurt you, Cass?"

She hesitated. "Yes. Once. It wasn't really too bad."

His fingers tightened reflexively. "Tell me."

She told.

He stood and put his hands behind his head, staring blindly at the night sky. He swore foully. "I remember that night. I *saw* him. I thought you were—" He broke off, cursing himself now.

Cass rose and put a light hand on the small of his back. "I should've told you before, perhaps. But we were both so angry with each other, and then I didn't think you'd care anyway. But it's over now."

He whirled around. "Did you really think I wouldn't care?" he demanded fiercely. "Did you, Cass?"

"Yes!" she cried, stung by his anger. "You were vile to me in those days, in case you don't remember! And I'd done nothing except what you wanted me to do, what Quinn was paying me for, and you treated me like some—prostitute!" Mortified, she felt tears spring to her eyes. She tried to turn away, but he held her shoulders and made her face him.

"Everything you say is true, I can't deny it."

"Then why were you so cold?" She had to swallow down the painful lump in her throat. "I couldn't understand it, because you'd been so nice to me before, but as soon as Wade came—"

"Don't you really know, Cass? I was jealous. I was sure you were Wade's lover and it made me furious. I'm so sorry. I hated myself for hurting you. I couldn't seem to stop." It was the closest he'd come to admitting how much he cared for her, and it frightened him. He lifted her chin. "But you've already forgiven me for misjudging you, remember? Think how cruel it would be to take it back now."

His forefinger traced the gentle outline of her lips, and she sent him a trembly smile. "I had forgiven; I just hadn't forgotten. Now I've done both."

He pulled her close. "Oh, sweet Cass, I don't deserve you."

"Perhaps you don't—because now I remember what we were doing when I forgave you. I think you're a smooth manipulator, Mr. Riordan."

"Indeed I am. Watch how smoothly I manipulate you into the bedroom, Mrs. Riordan."

"That's no test," she scoffed. She stood on tiptoe. He bent his head and she sank her teeth softly into his earlobe, a trick he'd taught her. "A real test is when you make me do something I'm not already longing to do." And she took his hand and led him into the bedroom.

"I love this room." Cass pulled the sheet up to cover herself and looked around. In truth, after more than fourteen hours inside it, she was just beginning to see the room. The open windows were covered in some gauzy homespun material that allowed light and privacy at the same time. The walls were white-washed, the roof thatched. Bright rugs covered the smooth wood floor. "Best of all I like this bed. It's so out of place—a brocade canopy in the middle of all this rusticity."

"Is that really what you like best about the bed?" Riordan asked in some consternation. He handed her her half-drunk glass of wine from the night table.

She took a judicious sip. "Maybe not entirely. The sheets are nice, too. And the colors in this coverlet—yeow!" Wine splashed on her fingers and stained the coverlet in question as Riordan made a grab for her under the sheet. She was ticklish under her arms, he'd recently discovered, particularly the right arm, and now it was one of his favorite points of attack. She was flat on her back, laughing and shrieking, holding the glass high in the air. His head dipped abruptly and he lapped at the tiny puddle of wine in the hollow of her throat. Her laughter turned to a contented hum, and he felt the delicate vibrations through his tongue.

"I thought you weren't supposed to be drinking wine," she murmured against his hair.

"I can if it touches your skin first. That purifies it."

She closed her eyes and sighed. Presently she asked, "Were you a—a serious drinker before, a—"

"A drunk? I suppose I was. At any rate, I certainly drank a great deal."

"What would happen if you drank the rest of the wine in this glass right now?"

He thought. "I have no idea. Given that, I think it's best that I don't."

"I've often wondered what happened that made you give it up," she said diffidently, asking but not asking.

He was quiet for a long time. At the moment she decided he wasn't going to answer, he rolled onto his back and put his hands behind his head. "It's not a very pretty story, Cass, but I'll tell you if you like."

She turned toward him, leaning on her elbow. "Only if you want to."

He smiled faintly and stared at the ceiling. Only if he wanted to. The last thing in the world he wanted to do was explain to Cass what a colossal mess he'd made of the first twenty-seven years of his life. Where should he begin? Last year? Ten years ago? Twenty?

"I didn't have what you would call a happy childhood. Not that that forgives or explains any-thing, but I thought you would want to have the whole sordid picture."

She recognized the dry, half-amused tone of his

voice but wasn't fooled by it. "Tell me what it was like," she said quietly.

"Our house was in Cornwall—still is, though I haven't seen it in years. My father inherited a great deal of wealth, so much that, try as he might, he hasn't spent it all even yet. I hardly ever saw him; when I did, he was usually drunk and abusive. My mother wasn't much in evidence either, but when she was she always seemed to be with a man who wasn't my father. I remember when I was six or seven, I was playing outside and I went into the little summer house we had on the grounds. She was there with a man, Lord somebody or other. I had no idea what they were doing, I just knew it was something I wasn't supposed to see."

He closed his eyes. "She was bare-breasted, her skirts up around her knees, straddling his lap. When she saw me she screamed. I ran. I just kept running and running—and nothing was ever said about it. Nothing at all. But she was so cold, and after that I saw even less of her. She treated me as if I were someone she barely knew—a neighbor's child. For years I thought it was my fault, something I'd done."

Cass knew his effort to sound matter-of-fact was hard-won. She squeezed her eyes shut, certain that if she cried he would stop.

"As for the others, my brother was a lout who liked beating me black and bloody better than anything else, and my sisters simply ignored me, as if I didn't exist—just absolute contempt."

"You were the youngest?"

"Yes." He put his hand in her hair and absently massaged her scalp. "I took to torturing my nannies, and later my tutors, as a way to get attention. I learned that the more trouble I caused the more people looked at me, really saw me. Of course, I was always having to escalate the mischief, to outdo myself. I think my family actually began to be afraid of me. That was exhilarating, in a way. But it made the isolation worse."

His voice changed and she looked up. "Then Oliver came. I was nine, so he must've been about thirty. But he seemed older, like some Old Testament prophet. Everything changed when he came. He wasn't shy in dealing out punishment, but that wasn't the way he controlled me. I'd had a hundred thrashings before I was eight; they meant nothing. Oliver gave me something no one ever had, and I guess it was self-respect. I know that sounds trite."

"No, it doesn't."

"He told me there was something fine in me, and I believed him. Probably because I was in awe of him and he seemed like the kind of man who only spoke profound truths. He said it was a horrible accident of birth that had set me down in the middle of a hive of Philistines—that was the way he talked—and I simply had to bide my time. He taught me my family wasn't worth so much pain. He said they were beneath me, that I was destined for higher things, and I had to wait out my sentence with them like an indentured servant. I know now that was claptrap, but at the time it was like gospel, a piece of good news that answered all the questions and made everything fit."

He rubbed his face with his hands and spoke through his fingers. "He established a daily routine, and that felt new and wonderful to me. Everything had been so chaotic before. I went from a hooligan to a model boy in about a month. All to please my tutor. To bring a smile to that thin, saintly face was like watching the sun come out. I lived for it. And of course I made him into my father. That was inevitable."

"And then?" she asked when he stopped.

"And then . . ." He went back to staring at the ceiling. "And then he went away. I walked into his room one day to show him a sonnet I'd written in Greek. He was packing."

"How old were you?"

"Fourteen. 'Going on a trip'?" I said. He'd gone to London before, sometimes for as long as a week. I always hated it when he left; I got ready for the bad news. 'No, Philip, I'm going away for good. I'm leaving tomorrow.' He said other things—he would miss me, he would write—but I couldn't hear any of it. I walked out without saying a word."

Cass put her lips on his forearm and stayed that way.

"I hid all night in the park, listening to the servants calling me, watching their lanterns through the trees. In the morning a coach pulled up in front of the house and Oliver came out, carrying his bags. I'd been waiting for him. I ran at him with a stick, a huge stick, high over my head. I could have killed him if I'd tried. Instead I smashed the bags out of his hands and then I started beating on the carriage wheels. The horses were terrified, rearing. A couple of footmen grabbed me, then the coachman, the butler. I wouldn't let go of the stick. They got me on the ground, and I was cursing and screaming and crying. When Oliver tried to speak, I only screamed louder. I didn't stop until the coach was out of sight."

Cass's arm stole around his waist but she kept her face buried against his side. Hot, scalding tears stung her throat; she wanted to weep for the child whose idol had first taught him to despise his family and then abandoned him to it. She felt his perspiration under her arm and heard his quick breathing, and knew he was reliving that day.

"There were a few letters from him after that," he resumed after a long time. "I never answered them and they soon stopped. I went back to my old ways with a vengeance, to spite him for leaving me. I wanted to forget every lesson he'd ever taught me about moderation and civility and restraint. Only now my vices were much more sophisticated. I'd tell you what they were, but I wouldn't want to shock your tender sensibilities."

She listened gravely and didn't return his cynical smile.

"After university and the obligatory tour of the Continent, I settled down to some serious degeneracy, using my father and my brother as guides. Gambling, whoring, drinking, every imaginable vanity; idiotic friends, women who were no better than—well, you see the picture. I told you it wasn't going to be pleasant."

"Were you ever happy, living that way?"

"No, I was miserable. But I was too stubborn to change. For one thing, I thought of it as my heritage. My destiny, almost. It was the way men in my family behaved. And for another, to straighten my life out would have been to give in to Oliver, and I was still too full of rage to allow that. I carried the anger with me for years, long after I knew it made no sense."

He fell silent. She ran the backs of her fingers up and down his ribs, wishing she knew something to say that would soothe him. "And then you met him again?" she prodded after a time.

He nodded. "In a tavern, no less. Needless to say, I was drunk. It was the middle of winter and he was wearing a cape with a hood. He looked like my image of St. Paul or another one of those humorless, unforgiving saints. He reprimanded me—with this sad, disappointed look in his eyes, as if I were ten years old again." He swallowed, remembering. "I felt such anger, Cass, and at the same time so much love."

"What did you do?"

"I told him to—" He laughed harshly. "I suggested he go away and leave me alone."

"But he didn't."

"No."

"What happened?"

"I'm not sure."

"I mean what happened after—"

"I know. I'm not sure. I was drinking heavily that night, more than usual, just to get his goat. The next thing I remember, I woke up in his house in Lincoln's Inn and it was morning. And I was covered with blood. Not mine."

She sat up, clutching the pillow to her chest. "Philip, my God!"

He stared straight ahead and spoke slowly and carefully, as though it were vital that she understand every word. "I had tried to kill a man. With a bottle. Oliver stopped it. I cut him, too. He gave the man's family money and made them agree to keep it quiet. The man didn't die, but it was close. Nothing more came of it."

"Oh, no, I don't believe it." She leaned over him, making him look at her. "You couldn't have done that, drunk or not. You *couldn't* have."

"I did. There's no question."

"You *didn't*."

He shook her off impatiently, sitting up and swinging his legs over the side of the bed. She sat back on her knees, cradling the pillow, staring at his rigid back. "You wanted to know what made me stop drinking and I've told you. Like it or not, that's what happened. Believe it."

She shook her head, not caring if she made him angry or not. "I will never, never accept that you tried to kill someone. I've seen you drunk and I've seen you sober, and I know it isn't in you to do such a thing."

He looked back at her. "Thank you for your faith, Cass, blind though it may be. It means more to me than you know."

"It's not faith, it's common sense." She shuffled toward him on her knees and wrapped her arms around his shoulders, ignoring his exasperated sigh. He could believe what he chose, and so would she. "So you felt grateful to Oliver for helping you out of your trouble and you changed your life. Is that it?"

This time he heard something in *her* voice, a faint note of skepticism that surprised and annoyed him. "Something like that. Only I wasn't fourteen years old anymore and I'd given up expecting him to walk on water. And I was shrewd enough to know it was no coincidence that we happened to meet shortly after some of my father's friends proposed that I try for a seat in the House of Commons."

"Do you mean that right from the beginning he—*recruited* you to work for him, be a spy for him?"

"That's one way to put it. I already had a perfect cover—the profligate drunkard I'd been before. The idea was to make contacts among radicals like Wade in the guise of a dissolute royalist, then disseminate misleading information while keeping my supposedly drunken ears open for news about the Revolution Society or the Friends of the Republic. It worked, up to a point, but we needed someone who could get closer."

"Me?"

"You." He took her hand. "I know you don't like Oliver, Cass. I don't really blame you, but I wish you could know him as I do. It sounds incredible, but after all these years he still sees something worth saving in me, and he wants me to be something fine."

"I don't see anything incredible in that."

He barely heard her. "No one knows me the way he does. And for all his faults, he's still the closest thing to a father I'll ever have."

"What are his faults?" she couldn't help asking.

"Single-mindedness. Loyalty to the Crown to the point of fanaticism."

Coldness, insensitivity, intolerance, she enumerated silently. Aloud she said, "You still love him, don't you?"

"Yes. He's like an anchor for me. His existence gives me a purpose."

The room was warm, but she felt a quick, uncomfortable chill on her forearms. She didn't want to talk about Quinn anymore. She moved back and pulled the covers up to her neck. "The sun's almost up. Come to bed."

He lay down beside her and took her in his arms. She snuggled close, enjoying the rough feel of his leg between hers. They exchanged a lazy kiss, knowing it wasn't leading to anything but sleep.

"I wish we'd known each other when we were children," she murmured.

"I don't know. I might've hurt you."

She yawned. "No, you wouldn't have. We'd have been best friends, done everything together. You'd have protected me and I'd have comforted you. And neither of us would ever have been lonely."

He almost said it then: *Cass, I'm so in love with you.* He closed his eyes and listened to her quiet breathing. They both fell asleep wondering what Quinn would do when he found out they were married.

They stayed at the Rose and Thorn for three days. They knew they'd incur the coarse ribbing of friends when it was discovered that they'd hardly stirred beyond the four walls of the bedroom during the entire honeymoon, but they didn't care. Sightseeing was the furthest thing from their minds. They were happiest in bed, and yet it wasn't only passion that kept them so contentedly quarantined. They never spoke of it, but each knew they'd snatched this intimate piece of time out of somber reality like thieves; they wanted to experience it whole, without distractions, aware that soon enough they'd have to pay the price for their larceny. So Hadrian's Wall went unexplored, the Solway Firth unseen. And still the three days disappeared as fast as water through cupped hands.

For Cass, they were the happiest days of her life. She'd never felt so cared for, so treasured. Not loved—not yet—but she didn't expect that. Only one thing marred her gladness. On the last night, Riordan wrote a letter to Claudia.

"Are you writing Quinn?" she asked, coming in from watching the moon rise over the pond. She laid a rose she'd just picked on the table beside him.

"No."

"Your parents?"

He shook his head.

She stopped asking, belatedly realizing it was none of her business. She went to stand in the doorway.

He looked up. "Do you remember the woman we met at the opera?"

She almost laughed, but she didn't really feel like it. Did she remember? "You mean Lady Claudia."

He nodded. "My marriage will come as a surprise to her," he said carefully. "I feel I owe her an explanation."

It took two tries to get the words out. "Are you in love with her?"

He pushed his chair back and went to her. "I thought I was," he said gently.

"Were you engaged?"

"No. But we . . ."

"Had an understanding?"

"Yes."

"I see." She felt swamped with misery. But as he held her, she made a decision to turn her back on all the sadness and consequences and second-guessing. She had him now, and his arms around her were solid and real; she wouldn't beg him to give her what he couldn't. This would be enough. For now.

Later, while Riordan sat outside on their front step to watch the moon, she passed by the table and saw his unfinished letter. She froze, too far away to read it, too close to miss it. She took a small, silent step nearer.

And breathed a deep sigh of relief. This letter wasn't to Claudia, it was to Wally. She scanned it idly, smiling. "Before life overtakes me again in all its myriad guises," he'd written, "I wanted to take the time to thank you again for your help. I shall always be grateful for your quick thinking and resourcefulness at a time when, it goes without saying, I was quite incapable of pulling off the stunt unassisted. Without you, who knows—" It broke off there. Cass tried not to feel piqued because he'd called their marriage a "stunt." People who read other people's mail deserved exactly what they got, she chided herself, and went outside to join her husband.

Too soon, it was time to leave. Riordan hired another fast post-chaise, but they stayed overnight at inns along the way, drawing out the journey as long as they could. As they neared London they laughed and spoke less, but touched more. Riding through Warwickshire, arms entwined, they watched green and yellow fields through the window and thought about what they'd done. Riordan

realized that all the dire consequences he'd feared
from an involvement with Cass seemed trivial to
him now. He had no idea what would happen next,
but he regretted nothing. Whenever he tried to
think about the future, all his mind conjured up
were images of Cass in his house—having a meal at
his table or pouring tea in the drawing room,
holding out her hands to the fire in the library. How
lovely it would be to see her clothes strewn about
on the furniture in his bedroom, her hairpins
littering the dresser. He'd walk into the room and
see her there, half-undressed, doing something to
her hair in front of the mirror. She sang off-key, he
now knew; he looked forward to hearing her soft,
absent-minded hum as she went from room to
room, engaged in her daily tasks.

He tightened his arms around her and she sighed.
"When will we reach London?" she asked, although
she knew.

"Tomorrow."

"So soon."

"I've been gone nearly ten days now. Oliver—
well, let's not talk about Oliver."

"No."

He tilted her chin up. "Do you know, Cass, I've
always wanted to make love with you in a carriage,
ever since the night we met. Do you remember?
You'd run away, and Oliver found you."

"And you were obnoxious—threatening to shoot
poor Freddy!"

He grinned. "But you *hit* me."

"You deserved it."

His hand caressed her breast slowly, coaxingly.
"But you liked what we did in the garden, didn't
you?" She only smiled. He began to open her dress,
thankful that this one buttoned in front. "I wanted
you so badly, Cass. I wanted you right there under
that tree."

"You thought I was the kind of woman who would let you."

"You would have let me, wouldn't you?"

Her head went back against the seat. "Only because I thought you were Colin."

"Liar." His hands inside her shift were skillful and sure.

"This is what you really married me for, isn't it?" she managed, trying to summon up some indignation.

"Let's say it was a healthy part of it." He bent his head. "What's wrong with that?" he murmured, kissing her soft peak.

She couldn't think of anything. Her eyes closed. "I'd like to know what some of the other parts were."

He moved to her other breast. "Well, there was this part. And this part—"

She broke away with a gasp and tried to push her skirts down. "Philip, stop, we can't *here*—"

"Why not?" He kissed her until she strained against him with a low groan. "There's a cave near Stratford," he whispered against her lips. "A little old man takes people through. Let's go there and get rid of the old man and make love in a cave. Standing up, with our clothes on. Let's, Cass. Say yes."

She said yes. But he took it as permission to finish what they were doing first, and she didn't correct him. It took much longer than expected. The next time they looked out the carriage window, they were miles past Stratford.

XI

WITH LONDON NO MORE THAN AN HOUR AWAY, THEY stopped. The inn at Watford was dirty and noisy, but they didn't care; they minded nothing that delayed the intrusion of harsh reality on their idyll. But morning came, as morning will, and then there was nothing to do but go home.

It had rained at dawn, but when their carriage pulled up in front of Riordan's house in Portman Square, sunshine was breaking through pewter-colored clouds and drying up the puddles. They took it as a good omen.

Walker greeted them in the foyer with shy pleasure. Before they could tell him their news, he congratulated them.

"How did you know, John?" asked Riordan, smiling and shaking hands.

"I expect the whole town knows about it by now, sir. Cards started coming in days ago. Look." He pointed to a silver tray on a table, covered with calling cards.

"Wally?" Cass guessed.

"Who else? We should have known."

"Lord Castleton has called twice, Lady Diana Sperry at least three—" Walker broke off, blushing, and stared at his feet.

Cass raised speculative eyebrows at Riordan, but he only winked and grinned at her. "Who else, who else?" he asked, unconcerned.

"Mr. and Mrs. Wylie, Mr. Eliot, Miss—ah, Chambers. There was a note from your brother; I put it on your desk with the rest of your mail. The gentlemen working on the bill to reduce capital offenses have been calling off and on all week. In fact, they're coming again this afternoon, on the chance that you'll be in. I haven't known what to tell them, you know, so—"

"Quite right, John. I suppose I'll have to see them today; I'm sponsoring the bloody bill, after all. Anything else?"

"Mr. Quinn has come every day to inquire."

Riordan's face was studiously impassive. "Has he?"

"He seems quite intent on seeing you."

"Yes, I'm sure."

"And there are several matters I'd like to discuss with you. At your leisure, of course, but one or two things really do need your attention."

"Yes, yes—but first I want to take Cass upstairs. Come on, love, you've never seen the bedroom. I'll be down in a few minutes, John."

Cass and Walker both colored and looked away from each other, smiling, and then Cass let Riordan pull her up the grand walnut staircase to the second floor. Now that it was to be hers, she took better notice of the house. "Are you very, very rich, Philip?" she inquired, eyeing the priceless-looking velvet and damask wall hangings, the gilded plasterwork of the twenty-foot ceilings, the rich Turkish carpets underfoot.

"I am, Cass. Isn't it wonderful? So much better than being poor, don't you think?" He felt supremely happy, holding his wife's hand and leading her down the hall to his bedroom.

"Your father must be incredibly wealthy; you're not even the oldest son."

"I don't live on his money, I live on my own. Investments, mostly. I've been lucky. I'll explain it all to you soon, so you'll know. Well, this is it." Suddenly he was nervous. "Do you like it? Is it too austere? You can change anything you want. We'll need another chest for your things, but there's plenty of room for it. This is the dressing room. My clothes don't half fill it, so—or you can have the whole dressing room and I'll take another; the little guest bedroom next door would do."

"I'd like to share this one with you, if that's all right. Oh, Philip, everything is beautiful!"

"Do you think so, Cass? Really?"

She turned back to the bedroom. The huge four-poster mahogany bed was covered in lush forest-green velvet. Wide sash windows were hung with matching velvet draperies in front and delicate white lace curtains behind. The walls were pale green, with ornate white plasterwork moldings high above. The furniture—a writing desk, night stands, chest of drawers, a small table—were of rich, hand-carved satinwood, masculine but elegant. Brightening the wood floor was a thick, patterned carpet of dark-green and light-blue wool. The fireplace was enormous; a bowl of fresh Michaelmas daisies sat on its carved marble mantelpiece, as if to welcome them.

Riordan plucked one and brought it to her. "Did you see the washstand? Look, Cass, it's fitted."

She buried her nose in the fresh-smelling flower, her brow puckered. "Fitted?"

"Water comes into the basin just by turning this knob. See?"

"Oh!" She clapped her hands. "I've heard of it but never seen one. Philip, how *grand*."

"Isn't it?" He looked around. "You'll need a dressing table, too. We can go shopping next week. For clothes, as well—you don't have nearly enough clothes. And you'll need a maid. I'm not sure any of the girls here will do, they're mostly—"

"May I have Clara?"

"Of course, whomever you want."

"She's a bit rough, I know, but I can't help liking her. She works hard."

"I like her, too. Have her, by all means. As for a housekeeper, I've never had one, but we can hire one if you want. Or not, it's entirely up to you." He turned to watch two footmen enter the room with their luggage. It reminded him of something else. "We'll go to Holborn to get the rest of your things this afternoon, if you like."

"But John said your committee is coming."

"Hang the committee, I can see them tomorrow."

She waited until the footmen had bowed themselves out. "Actually, I think it might be better if I went alone. I think it's going to be unpleasant."

"I know. That's why I want to be with you."

She took his hand. "Thank you, but I think it's best if I do it myself."

"Are you sure?"

"Positive. May I take the carriage?"

"Yes, of course. I'll tell Tripp."

They were standing in front of the cheval glass. They put their arms around each other and stood close, admiring their reflection. Husband and wife, they were both thinking.

"God, what a handsome couple!" Riordan gloated. "I think we should have a special dinner tonight, don't you? To celebrate our homecoming. Just us, no one else."

"It sounds perfect." Her smile wavered a trifle. "But soon, you know, we're going to have to go out into it. The world."

"Does that frighten you?"

She shook her head. "But I know what everyone will be saying and thinking. I should think it would frighten *you*."

He turned her to face him. "I could never be anything but proud of you, Cass. And no one's ever going to hurt you, I promise."

She wanted to tell him of her love so badly; the words were bubbling up like water from a spring. He traced her lips lightly with his finger, parting them, pushing in until he touched her teeth. He moved his finger in and out slowly, watching her eyes. She let her teeth glide gently over his nail and the fleshy part of his finger, then sucked it in with her lips. A servant came to the door, saw them, and retreated. They heard, but didn't move. He lowered his head to kiss her soft lips, still touching her mouth with his fingers. The kiss was excruciatingly erotic. He straightened slowly, almost undone when she passed her tongue over her lips in a quick circle. His stomach lurched; he saw knowledge darken her eyes. Her first blushing innocence was gone, but he felt no regret; she'd given it to him.

He stroked the long, sleek lock of hair that lay on her shoulder. "I have to go down now."

"Yes."

"Do you know how much I want to stay here with you?"

"Yes."

"Tonight."

She nodded.

They broke contact. In the doorway he turned, just to see her again. "I'm so glad you're here."

She closed her eyes and spoke from her heart. "I'm so glad you want me."

The leave-taking in Ely Place was as unpleasant as her worst imaginings had portended. Word of her marriage had preceded her here as well as in Mayfair, and Lady Sinclair wasn't taking the news well. She stood by while Cass packed her meager belongings, venomously eyeing each article as it went into the box.

"That scarf is mine."

"No, Aunt, I bought it in the Rue—"

"I lent it to you to wear to Catherine de Bourg's *soirée* last February. I remember precisely."

"Have it, then." She was careful to keep her face a blank.

"Don't you *dare* patronize me, Cassandra. I will not tolerate it!"

"I wasn't—"

"You may be married now to that arrogant libertine, but that doesn't mean you can come here and treat your family like hired servants. Don't forget who raised you, young lady, and who paid for the finest schools in Paris and gave you a life of absolute luxury!"

Cass hated fighting, but her mild temper was provoked. "My father paid for every bit of my schooling, Aunt Beth, and you know it! He sent money for my clothes and food, too, and it's common knowledge you turned a tidy little profit from that arrangement." She was throwing clothes into the box at random now, seething with pent-up resentment.

"Why, you ungrateful wretch!" cried her aunt,

red-faced. "You've brought nothing but shame to my brother's name, and now you have the gall to speak to me this way."

Cass's fingers curled around a handful of ribbons. She was blazingly angry. "If anyone besides my father has brought shame to the Merlin name, it's you!"

"Insolence! You're a viper in the bosom of this family."

She remembered a saying of Riordan's when he was pretending to be drunk. "Oh, bugger off," she said succinctly.

Aunt Beth went a deeper shade of purple. "Oh! The impudence! You vulgar little tramp! I hope that wastrel you've married passes on the disease of every whore he's been with! I should've thrown you out months ago, as soon as I learned you'd taken up with two lovers at once!"

Cass turned pale and drew in her breath. She wrenched the last drawer out of her bureau and emptied its contents into the box willy-nilly. "Two! Yes!" she shouted defiantly. "But at least I never slept with both of them at the same time!"

It was a wild shot, but it appeared to hit home. Lady Sinclair was so angry she danced in place and her teeth chattered. "Out! Get out! I want you out of this house this instant!"

"I'll leave when I've finished packing and not a minute sooner!" Cass shouted back, hands on her hips, all pretense of dignity gone. "You get out of my room!"

"I will not!"

Clara appeared in the door, her mouth a perfect O.

Cass pointed. "And I'm taking her with me!"

"Good! You deserve each other! The slattern and the slut!"

Cass slammed the lid down on the box and

bunched her small fists. "You are a mean, spiteful old woman. I hope I never see you again for the rest of my life." Her knees were shaking so badly, she wasn't sure she could walk. "Clara, will you help me with this box?"

"Yes, miss." There was a bright, excited gleam in the maid's eyes. She scurried in, easily lifted the heavy box, and went out.

"If I've forgotten anything, you can—"

"I'll throw it in the street!"

Cass bit back a truly vile epithet—another one of Riordan's. "Good-bye, Aunt Beth." She went past the older woman without looking at her and started down the stairs.

"It won't last," Lady Sinclair hurled after her, following. "You'll never keep him, he'll divorce you. It'll be easy, too—he's a Member of Parliament. That's who *grants* divorces, you know— Parliament! All his friends and cronies!" She stood in the front door while Tripp took the box from Clara and Cass watched, clenching her hands together. "But don't come here when he's through with you, Mrs. High-and-Mighty Philip Riordan. This house is closed to you!"

The door slammed and Cass jumped. The carefully impassive coachman helped her into the carriage. She sat, staring down at Clara, both of them wide-eyed and speechless. Cass had an urge to burst into tears, and another to laugh out loud for joy.

The maid found her voice first. "Was you serious, miss, about me comin' ter work fer you?"

"Oh, Clara, I'm sorry—I didn't even ask you first. Would you like to?"

"Ooh, yes, miss, would I ever!"

"Then come as soon as you can." She told her the address. "I can't say for sure, but I expect the wages will be better."

"I'd take *less* wages, miss, ter be shut of that

one." She jerked her chin toward the house. "Would tomorrow be too soon?"

"Tomorrow would be perfect. Good-bye, Clara."

"G'bye, miss. Thanks ever so much! An' give my regards ter yer new husband!"

Cass sat back in the coach and took deep, steadying breaths. In an amazingly short time, she felt better. The ugly, enraged sound of her aunt's voice faded a little with every passing mile. Even the air smelled sweeter the farther west she rode. A new chapter in her life was opening, and she had no inclination to mourn the closing of the old. She was on her way home to her husband, and she loved him.

She might even tell him, she thought with a sharp tingle of anticipation. She no longer felt guilty when she thought of the card game. It was *fate* that had brought them together, not alcohol or accident or manipulation. And he liked her, she knew he did. Not just physically, either, although he certainly liked her quite a good deal in that way. She hugged herself, shivering, thinking about tonight.

Besides loving him, she was terribly proud of him. He was ambitious, but not as much for himself as for others. She knew how he chafed at being forced to play the role of a self-involved sensualist. By rights he shouldn't be sponsoring this new bill to reform the penalties for capital crimes, but Mr. Quinn hadn't been able to hold him back. When he'd explained to her once that the law made no distinction between theft and murder and called for the hanging of a person convicted of any of a hundred and fifty-six crimes, his voice had rung with passion; she'd easily imagined him standing up in the Commons and urging his peers to take steps to correct a grievous wrong. "Nine out of ten criminals hanged in London are under twenty-one,

Cass, and children are given the same penalty as adults! We don't need a campaign against crime, we need one against ignorance and smugness and apathy!" It gave her a deep thrill of satisfaction to know Philip had the will and the power to make changes in the world, and she vowed she would help him in any way she could. Together, their lives were going to make a difference.

The carriage was moving slowly through the Strand. She opened her purse and counted out three pounds, ten pence. What could she buy him? The shop window she was passing displayed a frock coat of white drab with plate buttons. Much too dear, of course; besides, his taste was more conservative. Now the coach was stopped in front of a jewelry store. In the window she saw a gold watch with a chased case, diamond rings and stock buckles, a tortoise-shell snuff box mounted with silver. She sighed. Nothing there for three and a half pounds.

There was a bell hanging from a hook in the side wall of the coach. She took it down and rang it, holding it out the window. Tripp drove the horses to the curb, stopped, and jumped down.

"I'd like to get out and walk for a little," Cass told him.

"Very good, mum." He helped her to the sidewalk and tipped his hat.

"Will you wait for me here?"

"Yes, mum, as long as you like."

She sent him a grateful smile and plunged into the busy pedestrian traffic, intent on finding the perfect gift for her husband.

"And how would you like that engraved, sir?"

Riordan held the solid gold poesy ring in his fingers, smiling a little. "'*Tu et nul autre*,'" he told the jeweler. "And on the inside, 'P.R. & C.M., 28/8/92.'"

"Very good, sir. It'll be ready in about a week, I should think."

"A week! I need it sooner."

"How soon?"

He smiled again, hopefully. "Tonight?"

The jeweler threw up his hands. "Impossible!" They began to haggle, and Riordan didn't hear the opening and closing of the shop door. He broke off and turned when he felt a feather-light touch on his shoulder.

"Hello, Philip. A gift for your wife? I imagine there wasn't much time for that sort of thing before the wedding." Claudia held out her hands; he took them automatically. "When did you get back? Your letter came three days ago, but the news was old by then. Congratulations. I hope you'll be very happy."

Recovering slowly, he took her arm and led her toward the window, away from the proprietor's interested ears. Then he wasn't sure what to say. "You look beautiful, Claudia." It was true. "So the gossip reached you before my letter. I'm sorry. I wanted to tell you myself, but everything happened so quickly."

"Yes, so I gather."

He looked down. "You've every right to be angry."

"I'm not, though. Disappointed, but not angry."

"No? Your father and Lady Alice must be, though."

"They're confused. I told them you and I were only friends. Which is the truth, after all, isn't it?" Her smile was archly friendly, and he began to relax. "Now, tell me about you. Are you happy?

Can you make a good life with this Cassandra Merlin?"

"Frankly, Claudia, I have no idea. But I've married her, and I mean to try."

"Dear Philip." Impulsively she squeezed his hands and kissed him lightly on the lips. "I wish you luck."

He smiled with relief. "That means a great deal to me. You'll always be—" The words froze on his tongue and he went white. His grip on Claudia's hands tightened hurtfully.

She tried to follow his horrified gaze. The afternoon sun sent a slanting glare through the window, making her squint. "Philip, what's wrong?"

He stepped away from her with unflattering haste. "Good God. I've just seen my wife." Worse, she'd seen him. Mouthing a hasty excuse, he was through the door and out of sight before Claudia could say a word.

Claudia wasn't a malicious woman, but she was human; she couldn't resist a tiny, satisfied smile as she watched him go.

In vain Riordan searched the sidewalk in both directions for a yellow dress. There was one, up ahead, but the girl had brown hair. She must have gone into one of the shops to avoid him. The thought made him grind his teeth. Of all the foul, rotten luck—Cass had to catch him kissing Claudia in a shop window on the first day back from their honeymoon. She wasn't in the draper's, nor the milliner's, nor the silversmith's. He walked around the block twice, peering into every store window he passed. The thought struck that she might have gone home. He turned around and headed toward Mayfair, arms swinging, long legs striding briskly. He knew he could make her understand when he spoke to her; what he couldn't bear was the delay!

But when he arrived home twenty minutes later, Cass wasn't there.

Quinn was.

"Tell me it's not true."

"I can't."

Riordan had never seen his friend so upset. For once his steely control had deserted him; he clutched the top of his head as if to keep it on while he paced blindly between the desk and the library door. "You were drunk?"

"Yes."

"God!" He clapped his hands to his ears and kept pacing. He was dressed all in black, as if for a wake. His face was pale, his receding hair not perfectly clean. He seemed to have aged five years since Riordan last saw him.

"Can't you try to understand, Oliver? I was—"

Quinn whirled on him. "Understand what? That you allowed yourself to lose control to the point that you've married a woman who's no better than a—"

"Don't say it!" Riordan thundered violently, coming out of his chair. "It isn't true!" He reined in his temper with difficulty. "You were wrong about Cass, Oliver, and I want to know how it happened."

Quinn looked at him pityingly. "You're a fool."

"No. You were wrong. My wife was innocent when I married her."

"Innocent!" He threw back his head and feigned a hearty laugh. "Did you see the blood?"

Riordan took three steps toward him and stopped, clenching his fists. He seemed to see Quinn through a haze of black rage.

"Are you going to hit me again, Philip?" he snarled. "I've still got the scar from the last time." He pulled his shirt cuff back and held up his wrist.

Sickened, Riordan turned away and went to his desk. His hands shook.

A moment later, Quinn spoke more calmly. "It's done. Somehow we have to go on. And I must set aside my personal disappointment and concentrate on the higher purpose, which is to foil an assassin."

Riordan felt the words like razor cuts. He sat down heavily. "Cass is a good woman, Oliver. Please give her a chance. She's—"

"Did you hear what I said? We have more important things to consider. Now that King Louis has been arrested, we've—"

"*What?*"

Quinn looked at him in surprise, then disgust. "Are you telling me you didn't know?"

"No, we've been—" He gestured helplessly. "Tell me."

"Louis sought safety from an insurgent mob in the Assembly. The Swiss Guard who were supposed to be defending him were ordered to withdraw; many of them were shot while they were retiring. The Jacobins in the Assembly decreed that Louis be 'suspended' from office, and he and his family have been imprisoned in the Temple. Pitt's withdrawn our minister."

"My God. I didn't think it would come to this."

"The arrest has galvanized the revolutionary factions in France, and more importantly, here. It's a critical time, Philip. We urgently need new intelligence, and unfortunately Wade is still our best source."

"I have news of Wade. He admitted to Cass that he led the group who tried to murder King George."

"Is that all?"

"No. He told her the King is still their target and that the next attempt will occur in November."

"November." Quinn stared into space with narrowed eyes. "The new Parliament opens in November."

"Exactly."

"Two months. We've got to find out."

Riordan stood up; he knew what was coming. "I don't want her to see him again, Oliver." He flinched at the look on Quinn's face.

"Say that again. I must have misheard."

"Listen to me. He tried to hurt her. I asked you once if there was anything wrong with him where women are concerned and you said no. Your intelligence was wrong, Oliver, wrong *again*. I won't have her seeing him anymore."

Quinn controlled himself with a visible effort. "You're besotted, Philip. My intelligence was right on both scores. Someday you're going to realize that, and I pray it comes soon. As for her not seeing Wade, I can only think you've taken leave of your senses. It's crucial that we discover his plan, and you know it. Apparently he trusts her—we have no choice but to use her, however distasteful you may find it. But your feelings aren't important anymore. Something much bigger is at stake. We're talking about the monarch's life, Philip."

He kept speaking, but Riordan stopped listening. He couldn't argue with Quinn's logic, but the idea of Cass's seeing Wade again made him physically sick. With a flash of insight, he realized that she meant even more to him than Oliver's approval did.

He also knew Cass wouldn't see Wade if he didn't want her to. He cut Quinn off in the middle of a sentence. "Very well, I won't forbid her to see him. But it will be her decision. We'll ask her and she'll answer. Whatever she decides, Oliver, is how it will be."

Quinn sent him a twisted smile. Riordan was surprised when he merely said, "Agreed."

Tripp helped Cass down from the carriage at the same moment that another coach arrived in front of the house. From this one five men disembarked, and she correctly deduced they were Riordan's fellow committeemen come to discuss the reform bill. It made her feel proud that, although they were all older than her husband, he was their leader. She greeted them cordially on the front steps and led them inside, aware of their interested inspection.

Angry voices were immediately audible from the library. She was grateful when Walker appeared in the hall and took charge, shepherding the gentlemen out of earshot into the drawing room. She made her way toward the library, still holding the rolled sheet music she'd bought for Riordan from a ballad-seller in the street. The voices rose higher as she neared the door. With her hand on the knob, she heard Quinn shout, "Well, *think* about it, man! For God's sake! If you get her pregnant, the whole plan falls apart!"

White-faced, she opened the door, staring from one to the other. For a moment they both looked guilty, and she had a memory of Riordan's face an hour ago when she'd seen him in the shop with Claudia.

"Cass!" He came to her and took her hand.

"You have visitors, Philip," she said unsteadily. "In the drawing room. It's the men from your committee."

He swore, then put his arm around her. "Oliver, I'm sure you'll want to tell Cass how glad you are about our marriage."

The silence was palpable. Cass swallowed, waiting. She could sense a contest going on between the two men. At last Quinn made her a shallow bow and drew back his lips in a semblance of a smile. "I wish you . . . luck."

Riordan stiffened. "Is that all?"

Before Quinn could answer there was a knock at the door and Walker put his head in. "Sir, the men from the—"

"I'm coming!" Riordan looked down at Cass; he seemed to be trying to communicate something to her, but she wasn't able to read the expression in his eyes. She was startled when he kissed her on the mouth, hard, with Quinn watching. Then he let her go and walked out.

There was a minute of silence while she imagined what Quinn must be thinking. She remembered the words she'd overheard. Did it mean he didn't want them to—she blushed at the thought. She could think of nothing to say; small talk about her wedding trip scarcely seemed appropriate. Realizing that she still held Riordan's gift, she went to the windowseat and put it down beside his viola.

"Summer's over," she said finally, watching leaves zigzag down from the locust tree in the slight breeze.

"France's king and his family are in prison."

She turned with a sharp gasp.

"He's been suspended by the Assembly and locked in the Temple. He'll probably be tried for treason and executed."

"I can't believe it! The king! Marie Antoinette, too?" Quinn nodded. She shook her head, trying to absorb the news. "How will it affect events here?" she asked hesitantly, leaning against the wall with her hands behind her back.

"Englishmen don't like to see kings imprisoned. It'll stifle popular sentiment for a revolution here, which will make the radicals more desperate."

"Philip told you what Colin said?"

He nodded. "November. It's more important now than ever that you maintain contact with Wade, Miss Merlin."

"I understand. And—I agree with you. But Philip doesn't want me to see him again."

"And so?"

"And so—I'm afraid I'll have to abide by his wishes." She gazed at him steadily. "He's my husband, Mr. Quinn."

A look passed over his face so swiftly she couldn't identify it, though she was left with the odd impression that it was pity. He came toward her and stretched out his hand. "May we sit down?" Surprised, she let him lead her to one of the velvet-upholstered chairs facing Riordan's desk; he seated himself in the other beside her. For the first time since she'd known him, he looked uncomfortable. He spoke kindly. "I've known Philip for a very long time, Miss Merlin—"

"I know it's difficult for you to call me Mrs. Riordan. Why don't you call me Cass?"

A slow smile spread across his stern visage. "I thank you for that. I'll try to." He looked down at his hands. "Philip is a good man at heart," he began again, "as I'm sure I have no need to tell you. His childhood was miserable, though, and the influences of a despicable family aren't always so easy to shake off. Some men have to struggle against them all their lives."

"Philip is nothing like his family," she said defensively.

He smiled a sad smile. "I wish that were true, Cassandra. I wish it were true. I'm so sorry, my dear. I have something extremely unpleasant to tell you."

"I know about the man he's supposed to have tried to kill, Mr. Quinn. I must tell you I find that almost impossible to believe."

He nodded. "I know. It was so brutal, so—" He stopped, pained. "I often have to remind myself that it really happened."

He held out his arm and she gasped at the sight of the thick white scar extending from his wrist to the base of his thumb. "Oh, no. Oh my God." So it was true. She sat back in her chair, numb.

"But that isn't what I was going to tell you," he went on, speaking quietly. "In a way this is even worse." He looked away in apparent distress. "I don't know any words to use that won't hurt you."

"I'm sure it can't be that bad," she said, attempting a smile. But she felt a coldness seeping into her chest. She sat perfectly still, waiting. Outside, a cart passing in the street sounded shockingly loud.

Quinn looked at her, then away again. "Forgive me. I'll simply say it. The truth is, you and Philip aren't married. And he knows it."

Cass lost all color. She didn't know she'd stood up until she found herself on the other side of the room. "That's ridiculous," she got out, trying to laugh. "I don't believe you."

"I'm so sorry. But it's true, I swear it."

She pressed her hands to her midriff against rising nausea. "It isn't true. It's a lie."

Quinn was beside her, leaning toward her solicitously, seeming afraid to touch her. "I'm so terribly sorry."

"It's a lie!" She couldn't get past that, couldn't make her lips form any other words.

"The man who married you wasn't the tollkeeper, you see—wasn't a resident of the village. Philip's friend Wallace found him and paid him to do it. He was a peddler, passing through on his way to Carlisle. The marriage wasn't legal. My dear—!" He caught her before she slid to the floor and supported her in his arms, depositing her gently in the windowseat.

"I'm all right." She strained to sit up straight but kept slumping over against the wall. He held her ice-cold hands and chafed them. "It can't be true," she said weakly, "it mustn't be."

But even as she spoke there was a small, insistent voice inside that said it was. And she had always known it. Philip *wouldn't* have married her. The reason it had seemed like such a miracle was because it wasn't real. She remembered him shaking Wally's hand beside the bridge over the pond. He'd looked grateful, she recalled. Of course he hadn't married her. Of course.

"But we signed a paper!" she remembered suddenly. She wanted to throw off the heavy, dangerous fatalism that was engulfing her. "It would be proof."

Quinn shook his head in sympathy. "It won't mean anything. If it still exists."

Cass pulled her hands away and rose, refusing his help. She made her way to the garden door and leaned against it heavily. She was in too much pain to cry. She watched two squirrels in the locust tree chasing each other in circles. The late afternoon sun sent lovely angling shadows across the ivy on the high stone wall. She felt as if she were a prisoner who had been having a beautiful dream; Quinn had awakened her and her eyes were wide open now on the four walls of her cell.

Suddenly she whirled around and faced him. "It *can't* be true. I will not believe it. What could he imagine he would tell people afterward? That it was all a *joke*? It's despicable—he wouldn't do it!"

Quinn brought his folded hands to his chin and stared at her somberly. "I doubt he thought it through very carefully. Philip is a strongly sensual man. I've known him to go to great lengths to gratify his desires. But you're right, this passes all bounds. I imagine he thought you'd accept money and go away when it was over. I'm deeply ashamed of him, my dear. Deeply ashamed."

"You're saying he pretended to marry me so he could sleep with me?"

"I'm sure he has some true feelings for you—"

"And he expects to give me *money*? So that I'll go—" At last she choked on the words and couldn't speak again. Her emotions were in turmoil, veering back and forth between outrage and disbelief. "But I have nowhere to go," she whispered to herself.

Quinn heard. "Your aunt—?"

"No, that's not possible now." Then she was defiant again. "I don't believe you! Mr. Quinn, you're only telling me this so I'll go to Wade!"

He looked away as if embarrassed. "In a way you're right. If I didn't need you so desperately, I would never have intruded into Philip's private business. But I do. You're the only one who can help now, Cassandra. Wade is dedicated to overthrowing this monarchy. If your word were all we needed, we could stop now, but it isn't. He's very wealthy and he's the son of an earl. We must catch him all but in the act. And we can't do it without you." He went to her and took her hands again in what seemed a kindly grasp. "I know what a blow this is to you. If I'd known what would happen I'd never have introduced you to Philip in the beginning. You probably don't believe that, but it's true. But now it's too late, and I have no choice but to ask you to continue. For the king. For your country. To help put right the wrong your father tried to do."

"Wasn't his death enough?" Her heart was breaking; she could barely speak.

"I'm afraid not. I'm asking you to give more."

"And if I won't?"

He squeezed her icy fingers. "Then I lose. But so do you, I think. Cassandra, my poor child, he's not your husband."

She extricated her hands and stepped away from him. "I must speak to him."

"Yes, of course. But may I ask one favor?"

She shook her head unconsciously, but said, "What is it?"

"Don't tell him it was I who told you."

"Why?"

"Because it would put an end to our friendship. Philip means the world to me, Cassandra—I love him as though he were my own son. I believe he feels the same about me. We're so different, he and I, and yet we love each other. And we need each other."

Tears began to drift down her cheeks in helpless waves. "Why did you leave him, then?" she demanded thickly. "Why did you go away and leave him to his family?"

"I was summoned by the king, I had no choice! Do you think it didn't hurt me to leave him? I—" He turned away. "No, of course not. I'm the cold, impersonal spy, aren't I? I have no feelings, the sight of a sobbing, heartbroken boy means nothing to me—" He stopped again.

"I'm sorry," she ventured, holding her hot cheeks and dashing the tears away. "Forgive me, I don't know what to think, what to believe. I can't talk anymore."

"Wait! Please. Speak to Philip, do what you have to do. But know that Colin Wade's threat to the sovereign is very real. It's our responsibility now to set aside personal feelings if we can, no matter how strong or painful they are, and try to act in the best interests of our country. That's all I'm asking. Will you help?"

Standing in the doorway, pale and distraught, she answered, "I don't know."

On her way upstairs, she heard men's voices coming from the drawing room. Philip's was strong

and sure and persuasive, and the sound of it sent a
dart of agony through her. She reached his room—
their room—and went to his case, still unpacked,
on the bed. Where was the paper they'd signed,
their marriage certificate? She'd seen him pack it
the morning they'd left Gretna Green. It must be
here. "It won't mean anything, *if it still exists*,"
Quinn had said.

It wasn't there. That fact fell into her head like a
stone dropping down a bottomless cavern, sailing
soundlessly through darkness. The marriage certificate wasn't there.

She sat down in a chair next to the bureau and
clasped her hands on her knees. A maid entered
presently. "Shall I unpack for you, ma'am?"

Cass stared at her a full ten seconds before her
words sank in. She shook her head, staring intently.
The girl went away, bewildered.

There was no marriage certificate. Riordan had
shaken hands with Wally gratefully. And then she
remembered the letter. He'd called their marriage a
"stunt," and thanked Wally for "pulling it off." But
the tollkeeper, Mr. Bean, had seemed so experienced, so knowing. "Whichever's whitest is the
ones gettin' spliced, nine times outa ten." A peddler, Quinn said. Wally had paid him.

She thought of the way Riordan had laughed at
her the night she told him he'd have to marry her if
he wanted her. Then he'd gone to Claudia. She
hunched her shoulders in despair, seeing them the
way they'd looked this afternoon in the jewelry
shop. So handsome. So devoted. And she'd thought
they'd only kissed in friendship; after a little while
she hadn't even been upset.

She stood up, hugging herself. It was all true,
then. She looked around the room. "You can
change anything you want," Riordan had said. She
went to the fitted washstand between the windows.

Pink tea roses made a delicate pattern on the fine china of the basin. A faint scent of lavender wafted up from the fresh water inside the pitcher. She lifted the heavy bowl with both hands, her arm muscles flexing from the weight. Brought it up to chest height. Shoved it down and away, watching it shatter into watery fragments on the polished wood floor.

She went to the bed and picked up her purse. The little maid who'd come before stood gaping and motionless in the doorway, drawn by the sound of smashed porcelain; she had to push her aside to get out of the room. She went downstairs and out the front door without stopping.

"Miss—Mrs.—" Walker called after her tentatively.

She turned, standing on the sidewalk. "Tell Mr. Riordan good-bye, John."

"Yes, ma'am. Where are you going?" he thought to ask. "That is, if you—"

"I'm going to Beekman Place, to Mr. Wade's. I'll send for the rest of my things tomorrow." She watched his mouth drop open before she started up the street at a brisk pace. At the corner, she turned right and disappeared.

Quinn stood in the library window, watching her out of sight. His clasped hands hid the front of his face. He seemed to be praying.

XII

THE BRANDY LIT A TRAIL OF FIRE IN THE BACK OF HER throat and set off a small conflagration in her stomach, but Cass welcomed the burning numbness that followed. She had to pull herself together. Halfway through her teary story, she'd realized the Cass Merlin that Wade knew wouldn't care a fig whether her marriage was legitimate or not, except as it affected her access to Riordan's money. She'd be angry, maybe humiliated, but not hurt. Certainly her heart wouldn't be shattered.

She rose from the red brocade sofa in Wade's overstuffed, opulently furnished drawing room and began to pace in front of the unlit fireplace. "That bastard!" she cried. She was doing it for his benefit, but she found it wasn't that difficult after all to simulate fury. "He tricked me, Colin, and I'm going to make him pay!"

Wade crossed his yellow-stockinged legs and sat back against a satin pillow, smiling up at her lazily.

"He is a bastard, but we've always known that, haven't we, darling? And as much as you're going to hate it, I really think you should go back to him."

"Go *back*! I wouldn't give him the satisfaction, the slimy son of a—" She bit her lip; cursing wasn't really her style.

He chuckled softly. "Then how else are you going to make him pay? Besides, I need you in his house to find out things."

"What things?"

He wagged a finger at her. "Ah, ah, not yet; I told you I'm not ready to let you in on my plan."

Cass fought down an urge to scream. This was unbearable. Quinn wanted her to spy on Wade, Wade wanted her to spy on Riordan, and she was stuck, like a fly on a pin, precisely in the middle.

"Look on the bright side, my love. He'll have to give you lots and lots of money now to keep you quiet. It's no worse than being his mistress, and you get the added bonus of respectability. For a little while, anyway."

She tried to look as if this had cheered her. "Yes, but—I'd hoped to stay here with you for a few days, then look for a room somewhere. I'm just so angry with him, Colin."

"Find a room somewhere? Have you got money, then?"

"Yes, I've—" She stopped, remembering she couldn't tell him the source of her funds—Oliver Quinn. "I have a little, from my father. Not much."

"Really? I thought it was all confiscated."

"It was. He—gave it to me before he was arrested. Oh, Colin, can't I stay here? I wouldn't be in your way. You'd hardly even know I was here, I promise."

He watched her another moment, then unwrapped his legs and got up from the couch in his slow, drowsy way. He smiled in a manner she'd come to recognize and dread. "Do you really want to, Cass? Because if you did come, I'd want you in my way. I'd want it very much."

She started to say that perhaps he was right, perhaps she ought to leave after all, when he took her hands and drew them behind her back, holding them with one of his. With his other he pulled her chin up. She was repulsed by his wet lips and the predatory gleam in his reddish-brown eyes. It took all her self-control not to flinch when he kissed her. Then his hand drifted down and he began to squeeze her breasts, not quite hard enough to hurt but more than enough to frighten.

From somewhere in the house came a terrific pounding noise. Cass jerked her head away and stared in horror at the door to the hallway. She tried to pull free from Wade's strange embrace but he held her still, a tiny anticipatory smile on his lips.

Footsteps sounded. Riordan strode through the door and stopped, the butler dancing in distress around him.

"I beg your pardon, sir, I couldn't stop him—he wouldn't give his name and he refused to—"

"It's all right, Martin. Leave us. Well, Riordan, the very man we were speaking of. Won't you come in? I can offer you sherry or—"

"Let go of my wife or I'll kill you." Riordan's voice was chillingly matter-of-fact, but his face was a mask of black fury. Cass felt no fear, but Wade affected a laugh and dropped his arms quickly. Riordan held out a hand, his eyes never leaving Wade's. "Let's go, Cass."

She didn't move. "Go to hell."

He came closer. Wade put his hands in his pockets and took a noncombative step back. Cass remained motionless, arms at her sides. She watched Riordan's eyes shift from dark blue to black and felt a tiny ripple of danger.

"You can leave here on your feet or slung over my shoulder. It doesn't matter to me."

She tried a disdainful smile, but her trembling lips spoiled the effect. "I'm not afraid of you, and I'm not going with you. I'm staying here." She hoped he couldn't tell her knees were knocking against each other as she lifted her chin in defiance.

"Cassandra." Wade spoke quietly, reasonably. "I really think it would be better if you went."

She turned to him in shock. "But you said I could stay! You said you *wanted* me to stay."

Riordan growled like a goaded animal. As if sensing his danger, Wade took another step back. "But your husband wants you to go with him," he said placatingly, "and I'm afraid his wishes take precedence over mine."

She drew in a hissing breath. "My *husband*!"

"Indeed, my dear—he's your lord and master now, much as I wish it were otherwise. But a wager's a wager; and more important, a marriage is a marriage, however unorthodox the ceremony."

She closed her eyes, realizing she could expect no help from Wade. But she'd known that anyway. It suited his purpose to make her go with Riordan; he wanted the information he thought she could extract from him. Her hands clenched into fists. And Quinn wanted the information she could extract from Wade. She had as much control of her own life as a newborn baby! When was it going to matter what *she* wanted? She took a deep breath, summoning what little dignity she had left. "You won't let me stay, then?"

Wade shook his head, eyeing Riordan's snarling, almost feral countenance warily.

Her shoulders sagged. She shifted her gaze to

Riordan, taking note of the barely controlled violence in his posture. Ought she to be afraid of him? She supposed she would find out. "Then it seems I have no choice." She jerked back when his hand came up to take her arm. "But don't touch me," she warned in a voice full of loathing. "Don't you dare touch me." Bewilderment replaced the rage in his face for a split second. Their eyes met and clashed in silent combat until he lowered his arm slowly and stood back to let her pass. She sidled around, careful not to brush against him, as if the very thought of touching him disgusted her. "Good-bye, Colin," she murmured. She wanted to tell him she would see him soon, but something warned her not to push her luck.

"*Au revoir*, Cass," he drawled, sounding faintly amused, or pretending to. "I'll let Martin show the two of you out."

Outside, a storm was coming. The late afternoon air was a sickly yellow-green under black, rolling clouds, and there was a quality in the atmosphere of coiled violence. A gust of wind hit them before they'd gone a dozen paces, nearly knocking Cass over. Riordan reached out and tried to steady her. She pulled away instinctively and he cursed, but his words were lost on the hissing wind. She trudged along, head down, half-blinded by grit and cinders, until another blast literally blew her into a lamp post. Her hip bone throbbed; she muttered a curse of her own. She fought him when he tried to take hold of her again, batting his hands away, kicking out at his shins. He took her by the shoulders and shook her, hard. Then the rain came.

Huge, pelting drops that struck with the force of hurled eggs drenched them in seconds. He tried to drag her into a doorway for shelter, but she shoved him away. Bent nearly double, she waded into the wind and water, intent on nothing but forward movement. With the wanton violence of a squall at sea, the elements battered at her and blew her along, while inside another kind of storm raged.

At last the house loomed ahead. Her sodden skirts were heavy against her legs as she slogged up the steps. Riordan threw open the door and she hurried past him into the hall. The sudden quiet after the roar of the storm was uncanny. She kept going, heading for the staircase.

"Stop! Damn you, Cass, put one foot on that step and you'll regret it!"

His anger increased hers tenfold. She got two defiant steps up before his hands on her hips hauled her back and shoved her against the newell post without gentleness.

"What will you do, beat me?" she shouted, pushing the heavy, wet hair out of her eyes. "Or take a broken bottle to me, like you did to your friend Quinn?"

He went very still, his eyes as cold as shards of blue marble, and for the first time she felt truly afraid. He saw it and took his hands away. Water dripped steadily from his hair into his face. "I'm only going to say this once. Don't ever go near Wade again. Do you understand that? I don't want to hurt him, but I will. As for Claudia—" she made an inarticulate sound and tried to escape, but he reached for her again and held her still—"as for Claudia, I'm sorry you misinterpreted what you saw this afternoon. It was a kiss of friendship, nothing more. I would have explained that to you if you'd given me the chance and not gone running to Wade like a—" He stopped, visibly controlling himself.

Claudia! He thought she was mad about Claudia! It almost made her laugh. "Are you finished?"

"No! Claudia is my friend, damn it. I won't let your jealousy spoil that. I don't intend to avoid her, and I expect you to be civil to her when we meet, as we're bound to do."

For some reason this made her angrier than anything. "I'll do more than be civil, Philip, I'll be magnanimous. She can have you! Go to her, she's all yours! I can't stand the sight of either one of you!" She wrenched out of his grip and started up the stairs again. He was right behind her.

"Excuse me, sir. Cook asked if you and Mrs. Riordan are still planning to dine at seven o'clock."

The servant in the foyer sounded nervous. He jumped when the master turned on him with a barked "No! Get out!" and scurried down the hall the way he'd come.

Riordan caught Cass in the middle of the darkened upstairs hallway. "God damn it, you wait a minute! You're going to talk to me, here and now, and we're going to settle—"

"You shut up!" she threw back, incensed. "I'm not doing anything but leaving. Let go of my arm!"

"Leaving for where? Why?"

"Anywhere! Just so it's away from you! I have plenty of money, I'll take a room somewhere."

"Like hell you will. I forbid it. You're my wife!"

Tears sprang to her eyes. "Stop it! Liar!"

"What am I lying about? What?"

"You know! Take your hands off me or I'll start screaming and never stop! I can't bear to look at you!"

She jerked away again and plunged down the hall into their room. Someone had lit candles and thoughtfully turned down the bedspread. Her box wasn't unpacked yet, she saw with relief; she went to it and threw open the top. She heard him in the doorway but didn't look up. Where was the pink bodice she'd sewn the—there it was, at the bottom. Biting her lips, she ripped open the side seam and took out her money—eight hundred and thirty pounds, ten shillings.

She shook it in his face. "This is mine! I worked hard for every penny of it. Now I'm leaving and there's nothing you can do to stop me. I'll see Colin Wade anytime I want. I'll report to Quinn, not you. I don't ever want to see you again."

"Why?" He felt like tearing his hair.

"Because you're a liar and a cheat and a bastard! My God, Philip, how could you *do* it?" Oh lord, she was going to cry. She spun around and began to stuff the money into her purse. "Thank God I don't need you, Riordan," she muttered jerkily. "I can support myself perfectly well."

"You're not leaving."

"Like hell," she spat, mimicking him. She tried to step around him, but he moved when she did and she couldn't get by. "Will you get out of my way?"

He shook his head. "You're going nowhere." Before she could react, he snatched the purse from her fingers and withdrew the crumpled notes.

She let out a horrified shriek. "Don't you dare—Philip, stop!"

Holding his arms high so she couldn't reach, he tore the money in half, then again. Cass took three steps back and screamed. Tattered hundred-pound notes fluttered to the floor like confetti.

Stunned, she stared down at the scattered scraps of paper at her feet, then backed up to sit numbly on the edge of the bed. "My money," she whispered, holding her throat, staring at nothing. "All my money. Oh, God."

Riordan ignored the need to take her in his arms, knowing what she would do if he tried. He was nearly as shocked by the violence of his act as she, although he didn't regret it. He looked down at her bent head and pale, stricken face. He said her name quietly; she winced.

"Listen to me, Cass." His voice sounded raw and exhausted. "I don't understand what's wrong. But you can't leave. We have to work this out. Not tonight—too much has been said. You can have this room tonight; I'll sleep in the guest room next door." He closed his eyes against a sudden, graphic vision of the night he'd planned for them, her first in his home, and kept talking. "If it's what you want, I'll allow you to see Wade. You can pretend you're deceiving me and meet him from time to time. But carefully watched, and always in public places. And only for the purpose of exchanging information. As for us, as soon as we both calm down, we're—"

She shot to her feet. If contempt had a color, it was the shade of gray her eyes were now—the pale, cold, gleaming gray of granite after a winter rain. "There is no *us*," she spat, her lips curling over the word. "I will never sleep in this room. If you ever try to touch me again, I'll have you arrested." His angry snort brought two red spots to her cheeks. "As for Colin Wade, I'll see him wherever I want, as often as I want. Now, get out of my way."

He considered several alternatives, some violent, some not. Having the last word took on an abnormal importance. "I'm your husband; you'll do as I say." But when she pushed past him, he let her go.

In the doorway she turned. "You're not my husband and you can rot in hell." The last word meant a lot to her, too.

He heard her move down the hall to the guest room and slam the door. After that, there was silence.

The days that followed were the most miserable either of them had ever lived through. Cass literally couldn't bear to look at him, and the sight of her hostile, closed countenance dampened any interest Riordan had in putting things right between them. When he forced himself to try anyway, they always fought. "What the bloody hell have I *done*?" he thundered at her once after a strained and silent dinner. It didn't seem possible that merely kissing Claudia could have brought on this catastrophe. "Damn it, Cass, you're my wife!"

She stood up so fast her chair tipped over backwards and crashed to the floor. "Don't you call me that!" she cried, cheeks blazing. "How dare you? I'm living in your house, taking my meals here and sleeping in one of your beds. But don't you ever call this sham I'm forced to endure a marriage!"

After that, they spoke hardly at all.

She stayed in her room most of the time, reading or sewing or staring at the blue floral wallpaper. She wrote, too, in her journal, and began to look upon the activity as the one thing that was keeping her sane. Clara came, but there was little for her to do; her mistress hardly ever went out. She hardly ever ate, either, and the maid scolded her repeatedly until Cass lost patience and sent her away with harsh words. She saw Wade infrequently. Sometimes she went to his house unannounced and unescorted, deliberately to defy Riordan, and heedless of the bitter words that always came afterward. But usually she met him someplace neutral, a bench in Green Park or the back of a Fleet Street bookstore, with Clara never very far away, where she neither gave nor received any information of much use. Once, however, Wade hinted that the king wasn't his target anymore, to her utter consternation. If that were true, it meant they were back exactly where they'd started. But when she gave Riordan the news and told him she thought she ought to see Wade more frequently in order to learn the new object of his machinations, he only got angry and forbade it—as usual. Sometimes she wondered if she cared more about thwarting Wade than he did.

Riordan stayed away from the house as much as he could. He breakfasted in coffeehouses, where his friends gathered to talk and read the newspapers, and in the afternoons he met with his committees. At night he went to his club, where he plotted strategies and campaigns with his political cronies for the new term coming up in the House.

At home he went around in a baffled rage, snarling at the servants and staring fixedly at Cass when she made one of her rare appearances, searching for a clue to the dark mystery of why they were living like this. How had it happened? The magic days and nights after their wedding seemed to have happened to two other people. He didn't even recognize her anymore as the sweet, bewitching girl who had monopolized his thoughts and dreams for months. She was pale and thin, and she moved about the house like a wraith, disappearing swiftly when he surprised her in a room, or suffering his presence behind a frozen wall of silence that shut him out completely. He couldn't even make her yell at him anymore, and he would have preferred anything over this wan, speechless quiet. He listened every night in his room for a sound from her, only a few feet away beyond the wall. The rare creak of a floorboard or the rasp of a chair leg was ridiculously comforting after an hour or more of wondering if she was really there at all.

He could still remember why he'd married her, although his reasons no longer seemed relevant. A few months ago he'd thought his salvation lay with a woman like Claudia; he'd believed a life of the intellect was his noblest destiny, the surest means to effect the kinds of changes he wanted to bring about in the world. Then Cass came along and taught him that wasn't enough. He'd been subverting his nature to an idea, an abstraction. Because of her, he understood that passion was part of him, a good and necessary part, and that he needed her to make him whole. But in the end it was her courage, her willingness to sacrifice herself to a cause Claudia paid only lip service to that had made him love Cass, made him certain she was the woman for him, for his life.

But something had gone terribly wrong. Her enmity was so strong, he'd lost the heart to confront her. Or not yet, not yet. He could see she was in pain, but so was he. He needed to lick his wounds a little longer.

One night, sleepless as usual, Cass crept downstairs to the library to look for something to read. The light under Riordan's door was out, so she knew he was asleep and safely out of the way. She found the book she wanted by moonlight— Montesquieu's *De l'Esprit des Lois*—and reached up for it.

"Can't sleep either, Cass?"

She jumped a foot in the air and clutched the lapels of her robe as if a mad rapist had leapt out at her from a dark alley.

Riordan had to laugh. "I'm sorry, I thought you saw me."

She ought to have seen him—he was sitting behind his desk with his bare feet resting on top of it, wearing his dressing gown. She held her book to her bosom and stared at him owlishly, not speaking.

"I've been thinking of what you told me about Wade and wondering who he has in mind to eliminate these days. I was thinking it might be Pitt."

"Pitt!" she scoffed, taken unawares and forgetting she wasn't speaking to him unless absolutely necessary. "Why Pitt? He's the essence of neutrality. Except for Fox and his crowd, he's the best friend France has in England."

A slow smile spread across his face. "You have been studying, haven't you? Soon you'll be giving me lessons in politics."

She blushed, trying to ignore the pleasure his words gave her. She didn't care two straws for his opinion, she reminded herself. "One thing I have learned," she said stiffly, "is that there were enough injustices committed during the *ancien régime* to justify this Revolution."

"Is that a fact? Such as what, I wonder." This was the longest conversation they'd had in days. He kept his voice mild, his posture unaggressive.

"Such as what? Such as the corrupt and bungling administration of laws, justice, and taxes. Such as the idle luxury of the nobility and the priests while the peasants were taxed, tithed, conscripted, and starved. Such as the fact that the aristocracy had all the privileges and did nothing to earn them, and that the Estates General hadn't been convened since 1614." She drew a breath. "I can go on."

How beautiful she looked, standing so straight and tall in her old robe, the white of her nightgown showing beneath the hem. Her hair was down and soft-looking around her shoulders. He found himself wondering if her feet were cold; if they were, he wanted to warm them for her. "You've no sympathy at all, then, for the aristocrats who've been driven from their homes, all their possessions confiscated? They say the Comte de Vieuville shines shoes in the Place d'Erlanger and the Comtesse de Virieu darns stockings on the pavements, like some street vendor on the Pont-Neuf."

"Yes, but it's the *émigrés* who've brought on the reprisals against the ones who stayed. The *émigrés*

are no better than traitors when they call on
foreigners to declare war on their own country."

He raised his brows. "But do the scapegoats
deserve to die? Batches of them, trundled down the
Rue Saint-Honoré in their tumbrils to the guillotine?"

"Colin says it's wrong to watch the Revolution
merely through the narrow window of the guillotine."

Riordan's face darkened. "Does he? What does
he think of watching it through the window of a
spontaneous bloodbath?"

"What do you mean?" She pulled her robe more
tightly about her.

"Early this month, Cass, the mob—your harmless crowd of drapers and soap-makers—killed
eleven hundred men, women, and children. The
gutters were piled with mutilated corpses, and no
one tried to stop them. It began as an attack on a
group of priests and ended with the murder of all
the prisoners in Paris. Only four hundred were even
political prisoners; the rest were common criminals, pulled out of their cells and cold-bloodedly
massacred."

Cass was shuddering, her shoulders hunched. "I
don't believe you. It's impossible. Colin says—"

"The hell with what Colin says!" His feet
slammed to the floor and he stood up. "Ask *Colin*
how the Princesse de Lamballe was murdered. Her
crime was that she supervised the queen's household. She was stabbed to death on the corner of the
Rue des Ballets. They sawed her head off with a
knife and tore out her heart and genitals. One brave
revolutionary put her head on the end of a pike,
another ran her heart through with his saber, and a
third made himself a mustache from her pubic
hair." Cass had turned her back. He couldn't make
himself stop. "Then four men harnessed them-

selves to the body and set off for the Temple to show the severed head to the queen."

"Stop it, stop!" She put her hands over her ears and squeezed her eyes shut, every muscle tensed, desperately trying to block out the lurid picture his words painted. Suddenly he was behind her; she felt his gentle touch on her back, and a long tremor went through her. Minutes passed. As soon as she could speak normally, she said, "Please take your hands off me."

His fingers on her shoulders tightened. He drew a ragged breath. "I'm sorry, Cass. But I don't seem to be able to go on like this."

She went rigid, still staring at the blank wall in front of her. "Then let me go."

"I can't. I wish I could." An endless silent moment, and then his hands fell away.

She could feel her heart thudding in her chest. She reached out to the wall with one stiff arm, like a blind woman. Without letting go, she negotiated the space between Riordan and the door, careful not to touch him. Her bare feet were silent on the hall floor, and then the staircase.

Riordan picked up the brandy decanter from the table beside him and poured some into a small glass. The first sip was like a bitter explosion in his mouth, but the second tasted almost mellow. How quickly the body adjusts to its poisons, he mused. Calmly, cold-bloodedly, he considered getting drunk. It didn't matter much to him one way or the other. He set the glass down without finishing it and after a moment he left the room, following his wife upstairs to bed.

XIII

CLARA STOOD BACK, HANDS ON HIPS, SURVEYING HER mistress's reflection in the dressing table mirror. "Lord, miss, if you ain't as pretty as a bloomin' picture. I never saw a dress like that in my life. Never knew I had such a hand at ladies' hair, either. Now if you'd only use that rouge like I told you, yer beauty would be raverging."

Cass's lips quivered with the ghost of a smile, but she shook her head. "I don't want it, Clara. You've put too much powder on me already." She picked up the cotton daub and began to blot it under her eyes.

"Lord, there she goes, after I just got them blue circles hid! Why can't you leave well enough alone? I had you all perfect, and now yer ruinin' it. I swear, I don't know why I bother."

Cass stared blankly into the mirror, the smile fading, and mentally echoed Clara's sentiment. She'd never prepared so carefully for an evening

she looked forward to with less eagerness. But she'd
been bathed, dressed, brushed, powdered, and per-
fumed within an inch of her life, and despite her
half-hysterical vow to Riordan that she wasn't
going, it appeared that she was.

What could he possibly be thinking of? she
wondered yet again, absently pulling at one of
Clara's careful but artless-looking curls at the back
of her neck. What was in his mind that he would
flaunt this obscene joke of a marriage before a
hundred of his friends and family at a reception in
a hired room at Almack's? And what did he propose to tell them when this was all over—that she
had *died*? Did he really imagine she would disappear that thoroughly, that—conveniently? She shut
her eyes, feeling the familiar burn of tears in the
back of her throat. Well, perhaps she would. She
was so tired, so very tired, and yet it seemed she
never slept. She wept at nothing these days, and in
the mornings she could scarcely think of a reason to
get out of bed. She found it physically painful to be
in Riordan's company, and she couldn't say two
words to him without wanting to cry or scream.
When he'd told her of this ludicrous "wedding
reception," she'd been too aghast at first to utter a
sound. Then she'd found her voice and told him he
was mad, that the only way she'd attend would be
in her coffin.

But he'd won again. He'd simply carried on with
his plans as if she'd consented, and in the end it was
her own inertia that had beaten her. She hadn't the
strength to fight him anymore. Her pride had been
trampled so thoroughly already that another public
humiliation hardly seemed to matter.

"Leave us alone for a minute, will you, Clara?"

Her hand tightened around her white gloves; she
hadn't heard him enter. She turned, affecting a

nonchalant attitude. He'd never come into her room before. He made it seem smaller. She took in his plain blue coat of fine, light wool and his closely fitted gray breeches, acknowledging with dry-mouthed reluctance that she still found him the handsomest of men. His unpowdered hair was brushed straight back from his high, intelligent forehead. He'd just shaved; his cheeks glowed a healthy pink. Her eyes flickered over his long, handsome legs, observing the elegantly casual way he held himself, and came to rest on his dark-blue, frankly admiring gaze. She colored and looked away.

"You look like some exotic white bird," he said quietly, his voice a caress. "You have the most beautiful neck, the loveliest skin—"

"Please! Please, don't."

He gave a short, harsh laugh and came closer. "No, of course not. It would never do to tell my wife she's beautiful. I don't know what got into me." He reached for her hand, but she jerked it away without thinking. He went still, his face as impassive as a wood carving. "I have something I would like to give you. Would you please stand?"

Flushing again, she rose and turned her body toward him, though she kept her face averted.

"Relax, Cass, I don't intend to stab you." He reached into the inside pocket of his coat and pulled out an object. She looked down into his open palm and saw a locket on a gold chain. "This was my grandmother's. She left it to me, to give to my wife."

Cass's eyes swam. "Don't do this to me, I'm begging you—"

But he carried the two ends of the chain around her neck and fastened them in back, hardening his lips in determination. The metal was still warm from his body. She breathed softly and suffered his touch as he settled the locket in the cleft between her breasts with his fingers.

"She took out the miniatures of her and my grandfather so they could be buried with her. She said to put new portraits of my wife and me inside. That's what I intend to do."

"Why, Philip? Why are you doing this?"

He placed the palms of his hands on her bare chest and held them there. "Your heart is beating so fast." Spellbound, he watched the blood beneath her skin gradually suffuse her neck, her cheeks. "Do you know how much I want you? I think I'm dying for you. I want to take you here, Cass, now, in your bed."

Her flesh was burning, every nerve in her body tingling. She had to wet her lips before she could speak. "Then it would be rape."

He shook his head. "I think not." Both hands moved softly down to cover her breasts, making the slippery sound of flesh on silk, and his eyes darkened. He whispered. "I don't think so."

Out of the chaos in her brain she seized on her only defense. "Colin came into my room once at Ladymere, like this. While I was dressing. He gave me a gift, too. It was a p-piece of the Bastille." She looked over her shoulder, as if it might be on the bureau. "I still have it, you might—"

His choked curse cut her off. Breathing hard, Riordan dropped his arms and stepped back. He knew she invoked Wade's name to infuriate him; what galled him was that it always worked.

"Are you ready?" he asked in a voice he could hardly recognize. She nodded once. "Good. We wouldn't want our guests to arrive before we do. But I have something to tell you first, Cass, and I want you to listen closely. You've spent your last night in this room. From now on you'll sleep with

me in our bed, our room. Don't shake your head—
you'll do it."

"No!"

"Yes. I want my wife. And by God, I'm going to
have her."

She was stiff-lipped with fear and agitation and
something else. "You're a lying son of a bitch,
Philip Riordan—"

"We don't have time for that, love." He took her
rigid arm and urged her to the door. His sorrowful
smile was patently false. "I'm afraid we won't have
time for it later, either. Clara?" he called to the
maid, who was loitering in the hall by the stairs.
"Bring Cass's coat, will you? And whatever else she
needs." The maid passed them with an uncertain
smile, eyeing her mistress's face.

"I think you'll like my cousin Edward," he told
her as he led her down the steps, his hand lightly
supporting her elbow. "He's the only decent member of the family, really, aside from me. My brother
George will try to compromise you, I shouldn't
wonder. Both of my sisters have decided to snub
you, at least for the time being, which I assure you
is a great blessing. And my father can't come—he's
ill—but you'll have the dubious honor of meeting
my mother." He continued to chat amiably about
the people she would meet and how she could
expect them to treat her, but she heard none of it.
The focus of her anxiety had shifted. She no longer
dreaded her wedding reception. She dreaded what
would come after it.

They stood side by side inside the door to the
spacious, candlelit assembly room, holding hands
as if they liked each other, greeting guest after guest
until Cass began to see people as vaguely smiling,
featureless blurs. Her own smile felt painted on.
She could hardly breathe in the unaccustomed

corset the seamstress insisted she must wear with this dress. "To *poosh* up za *boosum*, madame, is *necessary*, yes?" Yes, if the object was to push it into her throat, she thought wanly, smiling and offering her hand to yet another curious, frankly staring arrival. In another mood, she might have been amused by some of the greetings she received. Everyone knew her unique history and the circumstances of her so-called marriage, and their resultant self-consciousness made for some interesting first lines. But in general she was treated with more courtesy and respect than she would have dreamt possible, and she knew it was because of Riordan's exalted position in the world. Money and power could purchase respectability for anyone, it seemed —even her. But she wondered more than once as she stood there, holding Riordan's arm and saying grateful, appropriate things to his friends, what they would do if she suddenly called them all to attention and announced the truth. She didn't think even his influence would be strong enough to secure respectability for either of them after that.

Then why didn't she do it? It wasn't for lack of courage. And it wasn't because she feared the disapprobation of these people. With a sick shudder she realized it was because she wanted to protect him. Because she still loved him. Deeply, with every cell in her body and with her whole soul. She was overcome with self-loathing; the only thought that gave her any consolation at all was that she'd never gotten the chance to tell him.

"Philip, *darling.*"

Riordan was brushing cheeks with a small, delicately-boned lady of middle age or better. Even before he introduced her, Cass guessed she was his mother because of her eyes, large and dark blue like his. She had a girlish, bird-like manner at odds with her age, which she took pains to disguise by the liberal use of face powder and cosmetics. Unbidden, an image came to Cass's mind of a little boy in a summer house, surprising this woman and her lover in the act of love. What would it be like for a boy to have a promiscuous mother? she found herself wondering. She couldn't really imagine it. She supposed it might cheapen sex for him, perhaps make him wary of women when he became a man. She stared at Riordan speculatively.

He'd introduced his mother as Lady Millicent. "But you must call me Millie, I suppose; everyone does. I absolutely forbid you to call me Mother."

"I wouldn't dream of it," murmured Cass.

"Oh, how silly of me, Roddy." She took the arm of the gentleman standing beside her. "Cassandra, this is Roderick McPhee. Roddy, my charming new daughter, and I don't think you know my son Philip." Lady Millicent's escort was a handsomely dressed, dashing-looking fellow a year or two younger than Riordan. The two men shook hands without noticeable warmth.

"How's Father?" asked Riordan blandly.

Only a slight flaring of the nostrils revealed that Lady Millicent found the question tactless. "Not very well, I'm afraid; but I'll tell you all about that later. So! It's really true, my youngest child is married?"

"As you see." He drew Cass's cold hand to his lips, putting a tender kiss on her knuckles.

"I'm delighted for you, of course, but I must confess to a teeny bit of surprise. I'd thought you and that lovely Harvellyn girl would—ah, but one never knows, does one? And who's to say an impulsive marriage hasn't as good a chance for success as one more carefully considered?" No one answered. "Well, I'm sure I wish you a long life of perfect happiness together." Her ladyship's attention seemed to wander as she spied friends across the way. "Oh, dear, there's never any time to talk at these large affairs, is there? But we'll all be seeing one another tomorrow at George's, won't we? Just the family, how lovely. Ta!" And she sailed away.

Smiling tightly, Riordan watched his mother depart on the arm of her youthful escort. "What I love about Mother is her warmth," he said, lowering a cynical eyebrow at Cass. "Don't you feel welcomed into the bosom of the family now, darling? And you'll be enjoying that same graciousness and cordiality from all of them, I assure you."

She kept silent. Inwardly she was trying to understand how he could stand there and tell such a monstrous lie to his own mother, straight-faced, however much he disliked her.

"Come, love, you have to speak to me sometime. What will people think?" He put his fingers lightly on her jaw and tilted her face up. The expression of hopeless disappointment clouding her gray eyes made him clench his jaws and quell the urge to shout at her. But there was no time to say more; other guests were arriving and they must greet them together.

His brother George, Viscount Lanham, resembled him hardly at all, thought Cass, except perhaps around the mouth; but no, Riordan's was strong and sensual, she amended after a moment's inspection, and George's was merely sensual. Fulfilling Riordan's prediction, George kissed her and put his hands on her at every opportunity—which wasn't very often because Riordan made a point of keeping her anchored to his side. He got her away from his brother as soon as he decently could, on the excuse that he must officially open the festivities by leading her through the first *contredanse*.

"I don't want to dance with you," she told him as he guided her out on the floor—the first words she'd spoken to him directly in many minutes.

"Nevertheless, you will," he retorted, annoyed. The music and the dance began. "Would it be too much to ask you to smile occasionally, my love?" he asked in a quiet, deceptively pleasant tone as he led her down a double line of admiring ladies and gentlemen. "You've proven you have no conversation; are you out to show you've a disposition to match?"

She pressed her lips together, disdaining to answer.

"No, really, darling, I know meeting my family has been a bit of a shock, but your eloquence this evening leaves a great deal to be desired. Are you feeling all right?"

Forcing an amiable smile, she said softly but succinctly, "Go to hell."

He made a low bow to her curtsy. "Ah, my sweet, how I adore the sound of your voice. What we need to work on now is the message." He took her hand and held it high, leading her in a stately pivot. "Some men prefer quiet wives, I'm told, but I'm not one of them. I do, however, want one who doesn't curse at me."

"I'm not your wife."

He pressed the small of her back with a light hand and grinned down at her. "Not lately, that's true. But after tonight you will be again. Careful, darling." He held her elbow when she missed a step.

She couldn't even pretend to smile now. "You couldn't possibly—" The intricacies of the dance separated them at that moment. She glared across at his smug, insufferable countenance and contemplated bolting. He would catch her before she went three feet, but at least she'd succeed in embarrassing him.

As if reading her thoughts, he reclaimed her a few beats before the music required it and took her hand in a stronger grasp. "Couldn't possibly what, my angel?"

She gritted her teeth. "What kind of a man would want a woman who despises him?" she ground out in a harsh whisper.

"The kind who's tired of waiting, I expect." His own smile was beginning to wane.

"I have no intention of allowing you to touch me, tonight or any other night."

"Then I'll have to take what's mine without your permission."

"I'm not yours!"

The dance had ended a few seconds before; they bowed and curtsied hastily and stalked off the floor more like duelists than newlyweds, though he still held her hand.

"Cassie! Lord, if you ain't a sight! Give us a kiss."

"Oh, Freddy!" She threw herself into her cousin's open arms with heartfelt affection, her eyes misting. "Oh, my, I'm so glad to see you."

"Faith, I'm glad to see you, too! I wouldn't have missed this for anything. Hullo, Philip, congratulations and all that." The two men shook hands, Riordan a bit grimly.

"How've you been, Freddy?" asked Cass. "I haven't seen you in ages."

"I'm tip-top, as usual, and Cassie, I've got the most smashing news. I'm to be married, too!"

"No!"

"She said yes last night—I haven't even told Mother. I'd have brought her along tonight, but she's come down with a chill. Hope it ain't related to saying yes! Ha ha!"

"Oh, Freddy, that's marvelous. I'm so happy for you. Is it Ellen Van Rijn?"

"Yes, and she's a peach of a girl, Cassie, I know

you'll love her. But isn't it wonderful, both of us getting married? Who'd have thought it last spring in Paris, eh?"

She said something inaudible.

"But say, you haven't heard the rest. Guess who else is about to tie the knot?"

"Who?"

"Mother."

"No! To whom?"

"Fellow named Edward Frane. Ugly blighter, but rich as Croesus. You knew him, didn't you?"

She could only nod with her mouth open. As angry and out of patience with Aunt Beth as she was, she wouldn't have wished Edward Frane on her. Still, the arrangement had a certain symmetry. She sincerely hoped they would make each other happy, but she wouldn't have staked much on it in a wager. The irony wasn't lost on her that she'd once refused Edward Frane in a fit of indignation because he'd asked her to be his mistress, and yet that was exactly what she had become to Philip Riordan.

Freddy led her in the next dance, Riordan's brother George in the one after that. Then came a succession of partners, some of whom she knew and some she didn't. She began to feel ill, but since dancing was preferable to speaking she never said no. Always she could feel Riordan's eyes on her, though she scrupulously avoided looking his way. She was aware that he was drinking, not pretending to drink, though so far it seemed to be with moderation. Once, when they were together, she said, "I see you're drinking again," keeping her tone flat and unweighted.

"Would you rather I didn't?"

"It's perfectly immaterial to me one way or the other."

He stared into his wine. "Curious. It's immaterial to me, too." And he put the glass down.

A little later, when the musicians paused, he claimed her from her latest partner and led her to an alcove where Lady Helena Strong sat ensconced, sipping ratafia with two other matronly guardians of the door to the *haut monde*. Lady Helena spoke to Cass with only a trifle more civility than she had in the eyeglass shop two months ago. After a bit of stiff chit-chat, Riordan asked pointedly about Walter, Lady Helena's son, which brought a bright flush of color to her cheeks—inexplicable to Cass until she recalled that he'd once lent the Strongs a great deal of money to conceal Walter's unseemly theft from the family business.

"Oh, by the way," he continued with scarcely a pause. "The invitation to your *fête champêtre* arrived. Thank you so much. We're delighted to accept, aren't we, Cass? A weekend in Oxfordshire sounds just the thing before the winter term begins."

Lady Helena looked as if she'd swallowed half a dozen sharp stones. She made a swift and valiant recovery, though, and expressed pleasure that they could attend in halting but determined accents. When Riordan took her hand and kissed it, no one but Cass saw the solemn wink he flashed her ladyship in farewell.

"I take it we were not invited to the *fête champêtre*?" Cass whispered as they made their way toward the dining room.

"Not until now," he confirmed, smiling and nodding to friends as they went.

"Why did you do it, force it on her like that? It was practically blackmail."

"Because as odious as she is and as intolerable as her house party will certainly be, she and her friends hold the key to your entrée into the highest social circles in London, Cass. Quite frankly, we can't do without her."

Cass stopped walking and faced him in astonishment. "But what difference does it make? I won't be around long enough for it to matter anyway!"

He still held her hand; he squeezed it until she blanched. "What the hell is that supposed to mean?" he demanded, his face reddening.

For once it was she who remembered there were people all around. "You're hurting me," she said quietly, looking away.

His hold gentled but he didn't release her. "I asked you a question."

"To which you know the answer very well."

"I know nothing except that you are the damnedest woman I've ever known!"

"Let me go, Philip. People are watching us."

"Are they? Then we ought to give them something to see."

She hissed at him. "Stop it, stop, don't you—"

Too late. He pulled her against him and cut off her objections with his mouth. "Kiss me back," he murmured against her lips, holding the back of her neck. She tried to shake her head. "Kiss me, Cass, or I'll put my hands on your behind." A muffled gasp of outrage. "Very well—" But before he could slide his hand from her waist to her buttocks, she put her arms around his neck and pressed against him.

"You bastard . . ."

Taking advantage of her ill-judged decision to speak, he sleeked his warm tongue into her mouth and tasted her, feeling the tremors that shuddered through her as he did so. For another full second she tried to stifle her reaction. Then she gave up. Nothing had ever felt so right as his mouth on hers, his hands pressing her against his long, hard body. Their eyes were closed, their senses engrossed; they didn't hear the scattering of good-natured applause until the kiss was over. Riordan held her a moment longer before turning toward their small audience with an expression that seemed to say, Who *are* these people? Cass blushed to the roots of her hair and would have fled in shame and despair if he hadn't been holding onto her with an iron grip.

"I think they liked that, don't you, darling? Shall we do it again?" He pressed his lips to her hairline.

"I'm going to kill you," she muttered in perfect seriousness.

He chuckled and guided her into the dining room, where a sumptuous midnight supper had been laid out on long tables. Feeling better than he had in weeks, he kept his arm around her waist and made her sample delicacies from his fingers until she told him, in complete truth, that if he did it again she was going to be sick on his shirtfront. After that he allowed more space between his offerings, though he kept her hand.

How the next hour passed, Cass was never afterward able to recall; it went by in a dark, buzzing fog as her mind locked in morbid anticipation on what would happen later tonight and her body teetered on the brink of exhaustion. She must have spoken, eaten, drunk wine, moved about, but to her it seemed as if she were locked in a small black room with no one and nothing but her own nightmarish thoughts. The worst was that she'd told Riordan, more clearly than words ever could, that she still wanted him. No, no, that wasn't the worst—the worst was that in a little while she would give herself to him, freely and without coercion, and then her defeat would be total. The thing she had sought to avoid at all costs, becoming his mistress, would be a *fait accompli.*

When she'd told him once that making love with

him would be "wrong," she hadn't been being coy.
It wasn't religion and it wasn't social disapproval
and it certainly wasn't parental guidance that had
formed the basis of Cass's sexual morality. It was
her own hard-fought conviction that people who
loved each other had the responsibility to postpone
their physical union until they'd made vows of
commitment to each other in marriage. That conviction hadn't stopped her from almost giving in to
him more than once, before their charade of a
marriage, only to have her heart's desire thwarted
by some timely, or untimely, interruption. And
therein lay the source of her anguish: Despite her
best efforts, the strongest utilization of her will,
Philip Riordan could make her do anything he
wanted. The soul-shriveling part of it was that she
would have to take money from him when this was
all over—she'd have no choice, she had to live—
and then there would only be one word for what she
would have become. Whore.

Or so it seemed to Cass's fevered reasoning as she
went through the motions of social civility with his
friends, some of whom had become hers, dancing
and laughing and sparring in conversation, while a
shrill whirring in her ears increased and a sense of
unreality encroached on her perceptions. Her skin
began to seem too sensitive to touch; people and
objects began to look backlit, unfamiliar. She saw
herself as if from some distance away, swirling
among a colorful crowd of dancers, endlessly
changing partners. And then slowly, so gradually
she wasn't aware of it until it was too late to be
frightened, it all began to fade away, until at last
there was nothing but a pinprick of light far away
and a faint humming sound. And then there was
nothing at all.

From across the room Riordan saw his wife falter

in the dance, missing an intricate connection with her partner. Frozen motionless, he watched her take a tentative sideways step, one arm outflung, frowning a little, her eyes half-closed. He dropped his punch cup and was halfway to her before he heard it shatter on the floor. He had no sensation of running, only of movement, and no idea he was shouting her name. His only thought was that he must catch her before she fell.

He was too late. Like a heap of bedclothes, she seemed to fold in on herself, her arms and legs boneless. Her head struck the floor last, with a sharp *crack*.

Kneeling beside her, hands shaking, he straightened her crooked limbs, unaware of the oaths and startled gasps of the crowd gathering around him. He held her neck and explored the back of her head with feather-light fingertips, not daring to breathe. A swelling behind her right ear, but no blood. Gradually he became aware that people were urging him to lift her, offering to help him. He waved away assistance and lifted her himself, feeling a painful catch in his heart at how light she was. A man was telling him to follow. He did, blindly, down a hallway to an office of sorts, with a desk, chairs, a divan. The man said something about "Mrs. Willis's room" and waved toward the divan. He laid Cass down and croaked out, "Get a doctor!" before crouching beside her.

Her skin was clammy and cold and sheened with perspiration. Her face was absolutely without color. He kept saying her name, holding her hands in a tight clench, trying to warm them. When he realized her breathing was shallow and erratic, he pulled her dress down and lifted her, frantically pulling on the laces of her corset in back. When he laid her back down she took a deep, shuddering breath, her eyelashes fluttering. But she remained unconscious, and after that he could think of nothing to do but hold her.

A doctor came. Helpless, he watched him examine her pupils, her pulse, her heart, the back of her head. Through it all he remained in a cocoon of misery, hearing the reassurances of his friends like the buzzing of insects in another room. He was urged to go into the hall for a few minutes and he went, numbly, half-conscious that the doctor must be examining her in some intimate way he wasn't allowed to see. When the minutes stretched too long, he went to the door and brought his fist back, but at that moment it opened and the doctor told him to come in.

Cass had her eyes closed, but her color was better; she looked asleep, not unconscious. He bent over her and touched her cheek with the backs of his fingers, then straightened. "How is she? Is she going to be all right?" When the doctor nodded, he closed his eyes and privately uttered his first prayer in many, many years.

The doctor, whose name was Mason, spoke softly; he had to go closer to hear him. "Your wife fainted, Mr. Riordan; I imagine she was unconscious before her head hit the floor. In that, she was very lucky—the skull was not broken, though the brain is concussed. She knows her name, however, and where she lives; none of her limbs is paralyzed."

"Dear God." He felt relieved, but chilled to the bone.

"Apart from all that, she doesn't seem to be in very good health. Has she been ill recently?"

"No." He was shaking his head positively, then stopped. He went rigid. "Has she?"

"Well, I couldn't say for sure, but she seems weak, perhaps even undernourished, and definitely below her normal weight. My first thought was that she was pregnant, but I've examined her and she is not."

Riordan leaned all his weight against the door.

"I say, she's going to be all right, you know," Dr. Mason assured him, patting his arm in a bracing way. "All she needs is a good rest and plenty of wholesome food. And of course she should be kept quiet for the next several days, no activity or upsets, that sort of thing. I'll look in on her in the morning."

"Can she be moved? May I take her home?"

The doctor looked thoughtful. "Ye-es, I should think so, if it's not far—"

"It's not."

"—and proper care is exercised. You want to avoid a lot of jolting, is the thing, which would certainly be painful and perhaps even dangerous. Can you manage that, do you think?"

"Yes, I can manage that."

A little while later, Riordan carried Cass home in his arms.

She awoke completely towards dawn, though she'd been swimming in and out of a hazy consciousness for hours. In the light of a single candle at the bedside, she made out that she was in Riordan's room, in his bed, and that he was sitting beside her with his back to her, his head in his hands. She thought he might be dozing, he was so still. Events of the evening came back to her in short picture-bursts. She knew she was ill, but she couldn't quite recall the chain of events that had brought her to this moment. Was it the next day? How had she gotten home? She had a memory of being carried . . . but no, that was preposterous, it must be a hallucination. She raised a tentative hand to her forehead. Her vision wasn't perfect; she was seeing things through a cloud of little black dots.

Her head felt like a hollow glass bowl and ached in the oddest way.

She must have made a sound or a movement; Riordan swiveled around to look at her. She thought he looked strange in the candlelight, whiter than usual, and haggard. He whispered her name as a question. She had to run her tongue over her teeth before she could speak, her mouth was so dry. "What happened?" Then he did a curious thing. He took her hands in both of his and pressed her knuckles against his forehead hard, just for a second. When he looked up, his eyes were fierce.

"Most wives just say they have a headache," he murmured, his tone a failed attempt at lightness. "Must you always go to such extremes?"

She peered at him, uncomprehending.

He cleared his throat and blinked something out of his eyes. "Do you remember fainting?"

She started to shake her head, then reconsidered. "No."

"You fell and hit your head on the floor. You were unconscious for a while, then you were sleeping."

"Last night?"

"Yes. At the reception. Do you remember now?"

"Maybe," she said after a moment's thought, then gave it up. "May I have some water?"

He reached for the glass on the bedside table. With his arm behind her neck, he supported her while she took a few swallows, but he could see the movement pained her. "How do you feel? Head hurt?" She gave a noncommittal hum, and immediately he knew she was one of those sick people who never complain. "The doctor's coming in a few hours. He says you're going to be fine." Her eyelids were drooping; she was falling asleep again. "Cass?"

"Mmm?"

"You scared the hell out of me."

Her eyes closed. "Serves you right," she murmured on a tired sigh, and slept.

When the doctor examined her again, he merely confirmed what he'd said the night before—she'd injured her head, wasn't in any danger, and needed rest and quiet. Nevertheless, Riordan kept up an almost constant vigil for the next few days, leaving her only to sleep for a couple of hours in her old room next door, and always instructing Clara to come and wake him if there was any change at all. After two days, Cass's headache faded away, a little of her appetite returned, and she was afflicted with nothing more serious than a profound fatigue. She slept large chunks of the day away and was, perversely, much more awake at night. Riordan liked to come into the room and find her with her knees drawn up, a book on her lap, reading by candlelight. She'd pull her glasses to the end of her nose and look up at him, and she would look so wifely to him, so beautiful. Sometimes she even wore a nightcap, and he would experience a queer feeling in his chest, at once hungry and protective. As much as he could, he kept his hands off her. But when he adjusted her pillows or straightened the sheet for her, it was almost more than he could stand and sometimes he had to touch her—lightly, fleetingly. After, they would both look way, pretending it had been an accident, never speaking of it.

Their conversation was quiet, calm, designed to keep her tranquil. Yet it wasn't bland; if anything, it recalled the days before Wade, when they'd enjoyed reading and talking, and simply taken pleasure in each other's company. For Cass it was a time to put aside bitter thoughts and allow herself to heal, in body and as much in mind as possible. Nothing had been solved, everything was waiting down the hall or around the corner, a little out of sight. But it was peaceful here in the eye of the storm, and she was permitting herself to enjoy it a little longer.

One evening about a week after the accident, following a solitary meal in the dining room, Riordan climbed the stairs to her room with a slow, measured tread. His tap at the door brought Clara into the hall. "She's awake, all right. Talkin' about gettin' up tomorrow, too. Appears like she's gettin' restless. That's a good sign, ain't it?"

He didn't know. He sent Clara away and went in.

She was reading the *Gentleman's Quarterly*, and she sent him her usual reserved smile in greeting. He startled her by sitting beside her on the bed instead of taking his customary chair. She shifted to give him more room and put her paper down.

"How are you feeling tonight?"

"Much better, thank you."

It was her standard answer; he no longer set any store by it. He was quiet for a while, fiddling with the coverlet between them. "Cass," he said presently, then paused again.

His tentativeness was unusual; she looked at him curiously. All at once she knew what he wanted to say. A mistress was one thing, but a pathetic invalid was another. He was tired of coddling her and he was going to send her away. An arctic coldness crept through her, along with the stunning realization that she didn't want to go. As bad as things were between them, not seeing him at all would be a thousand times worse. She turned her face away and focused her body and mind on one thing: not crying.

"I know our marriage was a bit unconventional," he was saying, still hesitant, "and we didn't start out with some of the advantages other couples begin their lives together with." He forced a little laugh. "Like a few minutes to think it over beforehand."

Her head came around and she looked at him in amazement. "What are you talking about?"

"I'm trying to say I want us to make it work, Cass. It was good before, you can't deny that." An instinct for self-preservation kept him from saying exactly how good he thought it had been. "But something's gone wrong, and for the life of me I can't figure out what it is."

She couldn't believe her ears; she'd thought they were long past this. "You must be mad," she breathed. "Or you must think I am."

His lips tightened, but he kept his tone calm and conciliatory. "Perhaps so, but I still want us to try to start over." He brought something out of his pocket and reached for her hand, holding it firmly when she tried to pull away. It was a ring. He didn't put it on her finger, but opened her hand and pressed it into her palm. "I was buying this for you that day you saw me with Claudia in the shop. Our kiss was innocent, Cass, I swear it. Take this for your wedding ring and let's begin again."

The heavy gold seemed to burn in her hand. *Tu et nul autre*, she read. *You and no other*. She put the ring down between them carefully. "Philip, is this a joke? Take it back, please, I don't want it. Your hypocrisy takes my breath away."

There was nothing but stunned silence while she kept her eyes on the ring, not able to look at him. It goaded her into saying more. "I told you once I wouldn't be your mistress. Now I find I have no choice. I suppose I should kill myself, to avoid what a better woman would call a fate worse than death, but I haven't the courage. I only ask one favor, that you stop calling this squalid thing between us a marriage. For God's sake, lie to your family and friends, but at least be honest with me!"

His shock and anger were warring with bewilderment. He took her shoulders, bore her down to the pillow, and brought his face close to hers. "We *are* married! I'm your husband! Are you saying you don't think we're married?"

"I know we're not!"

"We are!"

"Liar! The tollkeeper wasn't the tollkeeper, he didn't live in the town! Damn you, I know everything! Now let me go!"

"No! What are you talking about? Cass! Cass, for God's sake—" He controlled himself with an effort and released her, but kept her pinned down by his closeness. His mind was a jumble. "Tell me how you got this notion into your head. Who told you such a thing?"

Her lips curled. "What difference does it make? I know. And I'm not telling you who told me."

He sat up. "Wade!"

She smiled unpleasantly.

No, not Wade, she'd been angry before that, gone to Wade *after* she'd been told this lie. Who, then? He tried to recall the afternoon. Oliver was the only one he knew for certain she'd spoken to, but that was impossible. He disapproved of her, certainly, but he would never do anything like this. Who, then? Someone she'd met in Oxford Street that day? Wally, for a joke? Her aunt! Freddy! He couldn't think straight.

He took hold of her again and gave her a little shake. "Whoever told you this was lying, Cass. We *are* married."

She pushed him away. "Where is our marriage certificate, then?" She wouldn't cry. Oh, she had hoped never to have this humiliating quarrel!

His brows went up. "I thought it went the way of the wash basin. Didn't you destroy it?" She shook her head pityingly. "Well, *I* didn't do anything with it!" Her expression made it plain she didn't believe him. "Damn it, Cass, we're married! Who told you we weren't? Tell me!"

Silence.

"How can I defend myself if I don't know who's attacked me?"

Stubborn silence.

"Whoever it is, he, she—they're *lying*. Why won't you believe me? This person is a *snake*, Cass. I'm telling you the truth! Besides, how could I have done anything so devious? Don't you remember the condition I was in? I could hardly say my own name, much less—"

"No, but your friend Wally could. The two of you probably arranged it beforehand, before we left Colin's in the coach. Philip, I can't stand this conversation—"

"*Wally*? Well, Christ, Cass, all you have to do is ask him and he'll tell you that's not true! He's—"

"Oh, I'm sure of that! He would hardly admit it, would he?"

Muttering something vile, he stood up and began pacing back and forth between the bed and the fireplace. Suddenly he stopped. "We signed something else there, remember? A paper they kept. They'll still have it, it's the permanent record."

"Philip, there's no such thing."

"We'll go and look! As soon as you're well! We'll go and—" He broke off, remembering. "I can't go." She laughed a bitter laugh and he strode toward her, stifling a string of curses. "The opening of Parliament is a little over three weeks away, my dear wife. You may think I'm nothing but a bounder, that I spend all my time deceiving women, but the fact is I'm sponsoring a bill this session which will save a great many lives if I can get it passed. It's what I've been working on all summer, and there's still an incredible amount of work to be done—committee meetings, constituents' meetings, strategy sessions with the men who support me. Damn it all, Cass, I cannot go to Scotland this month!"

"No, I can see that," she said mildly. "But then, I never asked you to."

With a fearful oath, he turned around and started pacing again. She watched him from beneath her lashes, berating herself for actually having seen, at least for a few seconds, a glimmer of hope at the end of the dark, wretched cave she felt herself to be in.

Presently he stopped again, struck by another idea. "Walker! We'll send John! You trust *him*, don't you, Cass? He could go, I could send him tomorrow. It would take about a week, there and back, if the weather's fine. He could get an affidavit from the damn tollkeeper, get a copy of the record." He went to her and sat down on the edge of the bed, taking her unwilling hands. "Would that satisfy you? I can't think what else to do. If you can, tell me and I'll do it."

His sincerity almost undid her. All she wanted in the world was to believe him. The very intensity of her desire for it warned her of the danger. He'd called Quinn a snake, but was it reasonable that his oldest and best friend would try to destroy his legitimate marriage? She didn't think so. She had no experience of treachery that vicious, and could not credit its existence.

Still, what harm would it do to send Walker?

She pulled her hands away and folded them in her lap. "I do trust John," she said slowly, "even though he's your employee. I don't think he would do anything dishonorable. But—"

"But you have no trouble believing *I* would!" He

was blazingly angry, but at the same time a vast, golden relief was rising in him. The mystery was solved. Cass had made an enormous blunder because she'd been lied to. She hated him because she'd been misled. Their marriage wasn't over—it was only beginning! He felt like shaking the truth into her so they could stop wasting time. Instead he had to go through this stupid business of sending Walker to Gretna Green. "You know, love," he told her, "when this is resolved and you see what a colossal idiot you've been, you're going to owe me a very large apology."

"I doubt that."

A slow smile changed his face. "And I've just thought of the perfect way for you to show your contrition."

She frowned, ignoring this. "As I was saying, I do trust John. But even if I agreed that you should send him, don't you need him here? Now more than ever? From what you've just told me—"

"Of course I need him here. I'm offering to send him anyway. What do you say?"

She looked away, thinking, fingertips resting lightly on her lips. Again the possibility that he was telling the truth tempted and beckoned behind the corners of her mind, but she shied away in superstitious fear of the bright, shimmering joy such thoughts summoned. "But how would you tell him?" she fretted. "What would you say?"

"I'd tell him the truth. I know it's awkward, but there's nothing for it, he'd have to know. But he's the soul of discretion, Cass, I can assure you it would go no further."

She closed her eyes a moment. "All right. Send him." She tried to sound cool and businesslike. "But I must tell you, I expect very little from this."

"Do you, love?" he asked softly. "How did you become so cynical, I wonder." He reached out to touch her cheek, but she turned her face away. He settled for a lock of hair that lay across her breast and rubbed its sleek, dusky softness between his fingers. His anger had dissipated like summer storm clouds. "I expect a miracle from this. I expect to get my wife back."

She felt his warm hand faintly brushing her collarbone. Her heart was beating too fast, her body responding to the vibrations in his voice. "If John Walker returns with the proof of our marriage, Philip," she said as steadily as she could, "I will apologize to you in any way you choose. But until then, I would prefer it if you didn't touch me."

He traced a path down her throat with two fingers, to the top of her nightgown. "Oh, love," he whispered. "Be sure of that before you say it. Because I'll do my best to oblige you, and I wouldn't want you to regret it later. Tomorrow, or the next day. Or now." His fingers slipped just inside the top of her gown and caressed her with slow, deliberate skill.

It would have taken so little to give in to him, so little, and she wanted him so very much. "I'm quite sure," she said in a breathy falsetto that made him smile.

"What about a kiss, then," he coaxed. "To seal our agreement to send John."

"I hardly think that's necessary."

"I think it is. I think it's vital." He ran his forefinger along her bottom lip with light, gentle urgency, leaning close. "Kiss me, Cass. You know you want to."

She took a deep breath through her nose. "Perhaps I do, but you always—do more after that, and then I can't—"

"I won't this time. I promise. Just a kiss." Her lips were an inch away; he could feel her soft breath

on his face. He decided not to wait for her answer.
But just as their lips met she whispered yes, and her
willingness sent a shock wave of wanting through
him. He meant to be gentle, to be true to his word,
but he couldn't stop himself from tasting her with
his tongue while his hand pulled the sheet away
from her breast and caressed her through her
nightgown.

"No, Philip, you said—"

"I know, but this is part of it. It all goes together."

Specious reasoning, the working part of Cass's
brain noted. Her hand lay on top of his, useless,
permissive, maybe subtly encouraging. How could
anything so lovely be wrong? And she'd missed him
so terribly, this was like being allowed into the
sunshine after a bitter cold winter. He was touching
her lower now, along her ribs and belly, trailing fire
everywhere, still kissing her deeply.

"I want to give you so much pleasure," he
breathed into her mouth. "I'm dying to be inside
you again. I want to hear you say my name, Cass."

She was shaking uncontrollably, her fingers
clenching and unclenching on his arms. Somehow
she managed to turn her face away. "You have to
stop," she told him on something close to a sob.
"You said you would."

He put his cheek next to hers and discovered she
was weeping. "I'm sorry, love." He drew a long,
shuddering breath. "But it doesn't make sense to
me not to love you."

It didn't make sense to her, either. She lay still,
waiting for her racing heart to calm, savoring the
warmth and rightness of his body against her as
long as she could. When he drew away, he took the
best part of her with him, and she knew it would be
that way always.

"Will you keep the ring, Cass? You don't have to

wear it," he hurried on when she started to shake her head. "Just keep it. Anywhere. Under the bed, if you like. Will you?"

She hesitated. Then, "Yes, all right."

They gazed at each other, he smiling, she holding back. He found the ring on the bed. He closed her fingers around it, kissed them, and stood up. "Walker's still downstairs. I want to catch him before he goes home." He put his hands in his pockets and rocked a little on his heels. He looked cocky. "One week, Cass. You've wronged me terribly, you know. Your apology will have to be very heartfelt, very moving. Very *long*, too, and drawn out. It might take—"

"Good night, Philip."

He chuckled gleefully, anticipating her capitulation. "Good night, my dearest wife. Don't forget— one week." He grinned again and was gone.

She stared at the closed door, brushing her fingers across a faint, irrepressible smile. One week.

XIV

THE WEEK PASSED WITH EXCRUCIATING SLOWNESS—FOR Riordan because he knew what would happen when it was over, for Cass because she didn't. She suffered his teasing, near-constant attempts to seduce her with an increasingly light heart, and his contagious happiness tempted her to hope again. Luckily, his work kept him out a good deal of the time, attending meetings and endlessly talking to his cronies in his political clubs about the bill he would sponsor and other parliamentary business; otherwise his persistence would surely have worn down her defenses before the week was out.

She was up and about now, eating and sleeping well, feeling almost like her old self. But except for one new friend, a woman named Jennie Willoughby, Cass saw no one and remained at home. Their social life was deliberately quiet, all but curtailed, while they waited for Walker's return. Riordan's mother went back to Cornwall without seeing them again, and his brother paid no call. Cass wondered if he felt slighted, but couldn't summon any regret for his family's coldness on her own behalf. She liked them as little as he, and felt content to be ignored by them indefinitely. Lady Helena's "*fête champêtre*" took place without them, to their immense relief; anyway, it was the invitation that was important, Riordan assured her, not one's attendance at the bloody thing. Aunt Beth sent a stiff note inviting them to her engagement party; Cass sent a stiff note back, declining. She knew she could end the rift between them with a word, but she didn't care to, at least not yet. The things Lady Sinclair had called her at their last meeting were still perfectly fresh in her mind; if they were to become cordial again, she would always suspect her aunt's motives.

She read a great deal to make the time go faster. She also renewed another pastime she'd begun a few months ago, a secret one even Riordan didn't know about, which gave her hours of pleasure and contentment: writing. She wrote essays, mostly, about London life from a woman's viewpoint, but also stories and even a poem or two. Her proudest achievement was a letter to the *London Gazette* about the need for a reduction of the number of capital crimes—not coincidentally the subject of Riordan's bill. She wrote it under the name "C. Lindsay," Lindsay being her mother's maiden name. To her astonishment, two days after she sent it, it appeared in print.

That evening, one of the rare nights when Riordan had the leisure to stay at home, he and Cass sat in their separate chairs before the fire in the library. A light rain pattered outside, imbuing the room with a warm and cosy feeling. Riordan got up to stir the fire, then to poke his head out the French doors and test the air. The smell of wet leaves wafted in, moldy and pungent. Neither spoke, but both wondered if the rain were slowing Walker down. Today was the sixth day.

He came back to his chair and unfolded his evening paper. Cass tried to pretend she was engrossed in her book but kept stealing glances at him, waiting on pins and needles for him to turn to the editorials, as he always did. At last he came to the page. She watched his expression with covert intensity.

"Hm," he said once. And "Ha!" a little later.

"What is it?" she asked, all innocence.

He kept reading. "Well, now."

"Something interesting?"

"Mmm."

She was almost squirming with impatience.

Finally he looked up. "Yes, as a matter of fact. Here's an editorial that sums up the argument I intend to make to the House in two weeks, Cass. It's as though this Lindsay fellow took the words out of my mouth."

She shivered with excitement, bursting to tell him.

"Listen to this. 'In a country that prides itself on being the most civilized in Europe, the carnage reaped on the scaffold every year in the name of justice or criminal deterrence is a national disgrace. Thinking men must wonder whether it be justice or bloodthirstiness that sentences a boy caught stealing a sausage and a man caught murdering his wife to the same brutal end.' Good, eh?"

"I wrote it."

"That's exactly what I'm going to tell them, too. That ought to make the blighters sit up and take their hands out from under their arses."

"I wrote it," she said a little louder. He peered at her, frowning. She took off her glasses, folded them, put them in her lap, and looked at him.

"You what?"

"I wrote that editorial." She was amazed at how calm she sounded. "I sent it in on Wednesday. I never expected them to print it."

"Cass! You wrote this?"

She nodded, pursing her lips, struggling to look modest.

Riordan stared down at the paper, then back up at Cass. "Good lord, woman." He held his hand across to her. "Come over here. Come!" She came. He took hold of her wrists, gazing up at her in astonishment.

"Are you angry?" she asked worriedly.

"Angry!" He pulled her, unresisting, onto his lap and wrapped his arms around her. "Lord God Almighty," he marveled softly, "what have we wrought here?" He was looking at her as though he'd never seen her before, and she blushed like a schoolgirl who'd won first prize in the essay contest. "I'd better take care my constituents don't read this—I'd hate to lose my seat to my wife in the next by-election!"

She beamed like a sun god. "You really like it?"

"Like it? Cass, I think it's splendid. I'm so proud of you."

Pure delight filled her to overflowing. "My father was a journalist, did you know?" He nodded, smiling. "For this, I did a little reading, but most of it came from just listening to you and writing it down."

He was charmed by her self-effacement. "I had no idea I was so eloquent."

"You are. Very eloquent." Suddenly she was shy, and she didn't know where to put her hands. "I've written some other things, too. Would you like to see them sometime?" But then her nerve failed. "Oh, but they're nothing, really, just silly drivel, you wouldn't care to—"

"I want to see them very much. Everything you do interests me, everything you think. You're the most fascinating woman I've ever known."

Her heart contracted. She had no reply, could only look into his penetrating blue stare and feel her control trickling away like water down a window. The newspaper slid from her lap to the floor, unnoticed. Finally she thought of something to say. "You're trying to seduce me again."

His mouth curved in a slow smile. "There, you see how astute you are? But I meant every word." He ran a finger down the side of her neck very softly, watching her color change. "Lord, Cass, your ears are almost transparent, they're so delicate," he told her wonderingly, apropos of nothing.

"You said you wouldn't do this. This is . . . exactly what you said you wouldn't do."

"Did I say that?" He moved the wide palm of his hand up and down her backbone in a lingering, hypnotic rhythm, and she nodded slowly to the same cadence. "When?" He lifted her hair and let it fall in an ebony cascade down the back of her neck.

She rested one hand on his shoulder. "That night."

"That night you were in bed?"

"Yes."

"And I kissed you?"

It came out a sigh. "Yes."

"Like this?" His thumb and forefinger on her earlobe exerted the minutest pressure, no pressure at all, but her head moved surely toward his and their lips touched in a whisper of a kiss. In seconds it changed, flared hot and bright like oil on a wood fire as their arms tightened around each other. Their tongues met in the slow dance of love, and Cass knew with a helpless, hopeless shudder that she no longer cared whether he was her husband or not. He was her love, her life, and this was happening now.

"Philip. Philip."

He twisted sideways and bent her back until her head was against the chair arm, leaving him with a hand free to caress her bodice, her abdomen, her sleek thigh. All the while his mouth never left hers but claimed it again and again, his warm tongue flashing, deep and seeking, as if to the core of her. She made no attempt to stop him when he slipped his middle finger inside her gown, between her breasts, and eased it against the plump flesh on either side with slow, seductive strokes.

If Riordan had ever wondered about the strength of his will power under cruel and unusual conditions, all doubts were laid to rest that night when he didn't lift his wife up, lay her before the warm hearth, and take her with all the overwrought passion in his body. But because he loved her not only with his body but with his heart and his mind, he only held her and caressed her, taking a bit of comfort in the certain knowledge that she would let him if he asked, that indeed, at that moment she'd have done anything he wanted. But he'd made a promise and he would honor it, even though neither of them could remember now why she'd asked for it or why he was keeping it.

"Who told you we aren't married?" he whispered against her lips, unashamedly taking advantage of her helplessness in order to pry out the information he wanted.

Not fair! thought Cass. Her body ached from wanting him. No fair forcing her to think at a time like this. Instead of answering, she bit his lips softly, then his invading tongue, with a sure instinct for how to distract him.

He squeezed his eyes shut and prayed for control,

uncertain who was supposed to be seducing whom.
"Who told you?" he persisted, gently shaking her.
"Tell me."

"I can't. Not yet." At last she managed to put her
fingers on his mouth, holding him away, while
sanity made a gradual and unwelcomed trip back.
"Please don't ask me. If John Walker comes home
with good news, I will tell you, I promise." She felt
she owed Quinn that much. But if he was lying,
then Riordan would need to know what sort of man
his best friend was, to protect himself. "Now let me
up, Philip. You must."

He almost obeyed, but then he didn't. He liked
her in this position too much. He kissed her
instead, while he told her, in explicit detail, what
she would have to do to redeem herself when
Walker got home.

The next day Cass had a visitor. George, Viscount Lanham, said he'd come to see his brother,
but he didn't seem at all incommoded when she
told him Riordan was out and wouldn't return until
evening. Cass hadn't seen George since that night
at Almack's. She wanted to be friends, even though
George's interest in her didn't strike her as brotherly and the liberties he took—the hand-holding that
went on too long, the kisses that ought to have been
on the cheek but were invariably on the lips—
made her want very much to keep him at arm's
length. She ordered tea and cakes and sat him down
a good distance away from her in the drawing
room, then set about inquiring politely as to how he
did, how his family was, and what he thought of all
this rain.

She studied him while he answered, impressed
again by how little he and his brother resembled
each other. Then an alarming thought struck—
what if they'd had different fathers? She dismissed

it immediately, ashamed of herself for such a wicked speculation, but the notion returned with perverse frequency as the conversation went on. After all, it wasn't so very unlikely, was it, considering the things Riordan had told her about his mother? Still, it was unworthy of her, thought Cass, and even if it were true, what did it matter? It had absolutely nothing to do with anything now. It was idle and petty and malicious, and with an act of will she cast the unbecoming thought from her mind once and for all.

The viscount slouched in the middle of the sofa across from her, his legs spread wide in an aggressive and somehow suggestive posture, it seemed to her; was it his way of flirting? If so, it wasn't successful. Even apart from his crudeness, his body had no appeal for her, though she knew there were many who would call him a handsome man. She found herself comparing his coarse, big-boned toughness to Riordan's hard but elegant strength, only to discover there really was no comparison at all. And all at once she felt a fierce, physical longing for Philip. She missed him. She wanted him. Oh, she wanted him! She bent her mind to the task of paying attention to what his brother was saying.

They found they had a mutual friend in Wally, Lord Digby-Holmes, who shared a bench with the viscount in the House of Lords. Wally seemed to have shared the highlights of Cass's elopement with his lordship. "Faith, I wish I'd been along for *that* wedding," George exclaimed, folding his arms across his chest and winking at her in what seemed to Cass a most offensive manner. "Heard you were all drunk as magpies. What a sight it must've been, the six of you waking up in that carriage the next day! They say Philip was so sick he couldn't walk. Eh? But he did the right thing—a wager's a wager, after all." He seemed to recall his manners. "But faith, he's a lucky man, by God! Couldn't have done any better if he'd tried, which is what I tell everybody who says otherwise."

This appeared to be intended as a compliment, so Cass murmured something faintly grateful.

"Now what really would've been funny is if Wally and Tom had married those two whores at the same time!" He struck his knee with his hand and roared with laughter, spilling tea on the sofa cushion.

Cass flushed. At least he hadn't said "those *other* two whores," though she suspected the thought wasn't far from his mind. "Tell me about your family," she suggested with icy calm. "What was Philip like as a child?"

"Philip? Oh, he was a terror, a real bad 'un. Hasn't he told you? Drove us all mad when he was a boy. Had a devil in him, it seemed like."

"But you were so much older. No doubt you could put him in his place easily enough." She said it in an even tone, but her eyes were cold; she was remembering what Riordan had said about the kind of brother George had been. She realized that no matter how long she knew him, no matter how fond she might grow of him, she would never forgive George for that adolescent brutality.

"Oh, I could and I did," he admitted without remorse, "and for his own good. And believe me, he needed it. Not that knocking him about helped much, him being such a persistent little bastard. Never let up with his tricks and his tantrums and his evil tongue. Until that sanctimonious schoolmaster came, he gave us all fits."

"Mr. Quinn, you mean?"

"Quinn. Now there's a weasly beggar if there ever was one. I never understood what Philip saw in him—*sees* in him, for I hear they're still friends." He shook his head in bewilderment, and for once

Cass was in sympathy with him. "Me, I couldn't stand him. Looked like a scarecrow and talked like God. Gave me the jitters. Seemed like he wanted to have power over people, possess 'em almost, and I wasn't having any of it. Philip got taken in by him, though, for a time."

"Taken in? How do you mean?"

"Like he'd put a spell on him or something. But then the blighter went away, and Philip went back to his old self. Only then he was even worse." He stroked his chin, and there was a speculative glint in his eye. "I could tell you some things about Philip that would make your hair stand on end. I remember once—"

Cass stood abruptly. "You know, I believe I'd rather you didn't." She went to the fireplace and pretended to stir the coals in the grate. "Why do you think Mr. Quinn wanted to 'possess' people?" she asked, partly because she wanted to know, partly to get him off the subject of Philip's scandalous behavior, the details of which she was not anxious to learn.

George stood up too and went to lounge beside her at the mantel. "Couldn't say. Some people are like that," he philosophized. "Makes 'em feel important. But that wasn't the schoolmaster's worst quirk, to my mind."

"No?"

"No." He sidled closer. "If you ask me, he had a thing about women. Didn't like 'em." He held up one hand, palm out, to disclaim, "Oh, I'm not saying he liked men better, or boys, or anything of that sort—farthest thing from my mind. He didn't like what men and women *do* together, if you get what I mean." He raised his thick brows and leered at her.

"I think I take your meaning," Cass said coolly, moving an unobtrusive step back.

The viscount lowered his voice to a new, intimate note. "Remember once when I was about seventeen. We had this new chambermaid, name of Hettie. She was a year or two older than me, and nearly as randy. But it's a randy age, isn't it? For a boy, at any rate. What would you be, now, eighteen? Nineteen?"

"Really, it—"

"No matter. So anyway, one day Hettie and I were together in the library, getting to know each other better. Oh hell," he grinned, apparently deciding to abandon all pretense of delicacy, "we were on the couch, is what we were, going at it. Well, sorry, but you're a married lady, and we're family now, aren't we?" He took her red-faced speechlessness for acknowledgement and went on. "So—who walks in on us in all our glory but the schoolmaster? Lord God, you ought to've seen him. Went off his hinges, right before our eyes. His face turned so purple, veins popping everywhere, we thought his head was going to explode. I feared for the girl's safety, I truly did. And swear? I never heard such swear words in all my life. Not vulgar, mind you; more like out of the Bible, Old Testament curses or some such thing. It was as if God himself had found us there, and was sending us straight to hell for our sins. I'm telling you, the man was definitely *non compos* for a few minutes."

"Who was?"

Relief washed over Cass in a rush. She hurried across the room toward Riordan, who was leaning in the doorway, and took hold of his arm. "Philip, I'm so glad you're home," she said with quiet fervor.

"Are you, love?" He wasn't sure what had provoked this uncommonly cordial greeting, but he knew he'd be a fool not to take advantage of it. Before she could slip away, he put both arms around her and kissed her on the mouth. It was a thorough and, except for ending much too soon, a satisfying kiss, especially since Cass didn't pull back or even seem embarrassed despite his brother's keen, if slightly sullen, observation. "So who was *non compos*?" he asked again when it was over, turning toward George but keeping an arm around Cass's shoulders.

When George didn't speak, she answered. "We happened to be talking about Mr. Quinn," she said lightly. "Your brother was . . . reminiscing about old times."

"Ah," smiled Riordan. "Old times. Those giddy, halcyon days of our youth, eh, George? Nothing but warm memories for me; how about you?"

The viscount returned his brother's look of sardonic amusement in kind, and at last Cass caught a subtle, fleeting resemblance between them. "I'll talk to you another time, Philip," George said abruptly. "I've got to go."

"So soon?" Riordan's regret didn't sound very convincing. He and Cass followed George out of the drawing room, down the hall to the front door. The two men shook hands; and this time when George kissed Cass, it was on the cheek.

The door closed behind him. Riordan turned Cass in his arms and tried to steal another kiss. But with George gone, she felt safe again. No, she thought, "safe" was too strong a word; she felt *comfortable* now. Sidestepping Riordan neatly, she started up the stairs.

He watched her go with a decidedly wistful look. "George didn't do anything, did he, Cass?" he thought to ask when she was halfway up the steps. "You know what I mean."

She knew what he meant. "No, of course not. He just talks."

"What did he talk about?"

She turned back with an arch smile, her hand on the railing. "You, mostly. I learned some interesting things about you today, Mr. Riordan."

"Did you? Don't believe half of 'em."

"If I believed half of them, I'd run screaming in fright from the house this very minute."

"If you knew what was in my mind this very minute, you might do it anyway."

"Really? Is it so very terrifying, then?"

"Depends on how you look at it." He took a step toward her. "Shall I tell you what it is?"

She walked up a step backwards. "I think not."

He came closer. "Sure?"

She went back another step. "Positive."

"I think you'd find it interesting." He was moving quickly now.

"Doubtless, but—Philip, no!" He made a run for her and she bolted away up the stairs, shrieking with panicky laughter.

He stopped three-quarters of the way up the staircase and listened to the sound of her running footsteps in the hall, the slamming of her door. He sagged against the handrail, chuckling softly. But soon his smile faded, turned into a scowl. This couldn't go on much longer. Where, oh where the bloody hell was Walker?

Riordan pressed down too hard on his pen and suddenly the paper under his hand blossomed with bright splotches of black ink. He muttered a curse and threw the quill across his desk. It was stupid to worry, a waste of time and energy, and he had half a dozen more important things to do. True, all true, and yet he couldn't get past this futile, obsessive awareness that right now, at this moment, Cass was with Wade.

He'd argued against it, done everything but tell

her not to go, sheepishly conscious all the while that he was being unreasonable. Oliver had been the reasonable one, pointing out in his pedantic way that they would be meeting in a public street, Clara in tow, with one of his nameless, faceless agents observing them all the time. He'd known he hadn't a logical leg to stand on, but the idea of Wade going anywhere near his wife made his blood boil. Still, he couldn't contradict Quinn when he'd argued that not only was this the first time Wade had ever written to ask for a meeting with Cass— since their marriage it had always been she who initiated their *tête-à-têtes*—but that time was growing short. Only four days remained before the king was formally to open the new Parliament, and if they were ever to learn Wade's plan the time was now.

Goddamn bloody logical, incontrovertible arguments. But what if the son of a bitch touched her? What if he drew her into some secluded spot on the street and put his hands on her?

He stood up from his desk—he'd long since given up pretending he was writing a paper on the need to reduce Civil List revenues—and prowled around his library restlessly. He knew he was being an idiot, letting outlandish possibilities eat away at him, behaving like some half-mad old woman, but he couldn't help it. There was something wrong with Wade, and he didn't want Cass near him. And he didn't care if the security of the whole bloody English constitutional monarchy depended on it.

He gave the globe in its stand a fierce swipe and sent it spinning, letting the rotating sphere brush against his palm until it wobbled to a stop. When he lifted his hand, he saw beneath it the boot-shaped representation of Italy. Italy. He wanted to go there again, with Cass this time. As wasted and dissolute as his Continental tour had been seven years ago, he'd truly loved Italy. But not until now had he known anyone he wanted to share it with.

He sat down heavily on the edge of his desk and thought of all the clothes in the wardrobe upstairs that he'd bought for her and she wouldn't wear. He wanted to see her in them. Clothes he'd picked out because he'd thought they complemented her fragile coloring. Clothes she wouldn't touch, because she didn't believe they were married.

Bloody hell! Where was she? She'd left at ten o'clock this morning and it was almost noon now. Plenty of time for that bleeding pastel fop to tell her whatever he had to tell her. He didn't even care what he had to tell her; all he wanted was his wife back. It seemed incredible to him, as he swung one foot loudly and damagingly against the delicate rosewood desk leg, that he'd never told Cass he loved her. He would tell her today, if she would ever get herself the hell home.

And where was Walker? Eight days he'd been gone now, the longest, most frustrating eight days Riordan had ever lived through, a purgatory he wouldn't wish on anyone. And the worst of it was, he feared he was through waiting. If Walker didn't come today, he doubted he could continue the erotic game he'd begun a week ago with Cass— touching incessantly, playing at seduction, deliberately arousing her while not allowing himself to succumb. It was knowing he wouldn't have to force her, would hardly even have to persuade, that made it so hard. He wanted to respect her scruples, yet he knew they were built on sand. She *was* his wife. He only hoped he had the strength to keep from shouting it in her face before he started kissing her and pulling off her clothes.

He heard sounds from the front of the house and

stood up. After a moment there were footsteps in the hall. Hers. And then she was there.

He took one look at her face and went to her, reaching for her cold hands. "Are you all right? Did he hurt you?"

"Hurt me? No, of course not." She looked at him in surprise. "Oh, but Philip, what he said—I can still hardly believe it!"

"Come here and tell me." He led her over to the windowseat and sat down beside her, keeping her hands. "Tell me."

She told. On the fifth of November the king was to be murdered. Shot down by men from the Strangers' Gallery—she didn't know who or how many, but Wade wasn't to be among them—while he addressed both Houses of Parliament in the Lords' Chamber.

"I wish you could've seen his face! I think he's mad, Philip. He said there'll be anarchy afterward, blood in the streets. The government will topple, and at last I'll have my revenge on you and all the others like you." She shivered, then colored slightly. "I—had told him before that you're—arrogant and insufferable."

He grinned and raised his brows. "Did you, love?"

"Yes, I thought it would make him more sympathetic. More willing to tell me things. I told him you said hanging was exactly what my father deserved."

"Poor Cass. That was a good lie," he murmured softly, touching her cheek with fleeting fingers. Then he turned brisk. "I'll have to let Oliver know immediately. But first, tell me again everything he said, as exactly as you can remember it. And everything you said to him."

She complied, thoughtfully and carefully, and when she finished he went to his desk to compose his message to Quinn. She left him and went upstairs. It was the middle of the day, but she ordered a bath anyway. Being with Wade had made her feel dirty.

It was while she was seated at her dressing table afterward, putting her own hair up—Clara had the afternoon off—that she heard a perfunctory knock, saw the door open and Riordan stride toward her. He was grinning broadly, his eyes were dancing, and he looked as if he'd swallowed a canary.

"What?" she asked, smiling back involuntarily. "What is it?"

"He's here."

"Who?" But then she knew. "Walker!"

"Walker. I told him to get something to eat and we'd meet him in the library." He rested his hands on her shoulders and grinned down at her in the mirror. "Hurry, Cass. Aren't you ready yet?"

"Stop *leering* at me." Her heart was pounding in her chest and she could see that she was flushing. "No, I'm not quite ready." Her fingers trembled, and it took twice as long as usual to pin her hair up in the loose chignon she was wearing these days. At last she stood up and faced him. "Now I'm ready." She smiled a slow smile. "I've been ready for a long time," she murmured huskily, leering a little herself and deliberately letting her breasts brush his arm as she sidled past him. Two could play this game.

He growled low and made a grab for her hand, all but pulling her out of the room. Neither spoke or looked at the other as they moved down the hall and then the staircase, but they had never been more aware of each other, and never so much of the same mind.

Walker was there ahead of them. Cass went to him and gave him her hand, noticing how worn out he looked. "Such a long trip you've had," she told him quietly. "Thank you, John."

He ducked his head and murmured something unintelligible, not looking at her. It wasn't like him to be so uncomfortable with her. Her heart stopped and she felt a chilly flutter of premonition.

"Did they feed you?" asked Riordan, clapping him on the back heartily, oblivious to undertones. "Let me fetch you a drink. Brandy? Claret?"

"No, nothing, thank you. I don't care for anything at all." The secretary ran a hand through his fair, disheveled hair and shifted his weight from foot to foot.

Cass found a chair and sat down, clutching her knees with white-knuckled fingers.

"Well, tell us the news!" Riordan rubbed his palms together, gleefully expectant, coming to stand beside Cass. She looked up at him strangely, he thought, not returning his smile. He gave her shoulder a reassuring squeeze and then put his hands in his pockets, legs spread, waiting for the good news.

"Sir, I'm terribly sorry," Walker mumbled almost inaudibly.

"Sorry? What about?"

"I'm afraid they have no record of the marriage."

"What? That's impossible."

Cass's eyes closed. She went chalk-white and sank against the back of her chair. *I knew it*, she thought numbly; *I knew it*.

"No, sir, they don't. And in addition, the toll-keeper said he wasn't there on the twenty-eighth, not—not in the town at all. He recollected in particular that he was in Annan that day, burying his mother."

"That's a God damn lie!" Riordan exploded, moving toward him menacingly.

Walker cringed but held his ground. "I went through the records, sir, all they had. There were no nuptuals between Riordan and Merlin on the twenty-eighth, or any other day, and I went back as far as June and as recently as September." His shoulders hunched in desperation. "It just wasn't there. It wasn't."

There was a long, exquisitely painful silence. Cass broke it. "Thank you, John, for all your trouble." Her voice sounded unnaturally high, almost disembodied. Somehow she got to her feet. "Why don't you go home now? You must be very tired."

Walker looked at his employer. He was staring into space, confounded, floored, incapable of speaking. After another lengthy pause, the secretary turned and walked out of the room.

Cass knew only one thing, that she could not bear a confrontation. The pain was less severe already. It was as if all of her had burned up in a flash fire, and nothing was left but ashes. The important thing was to hold on to this numbness. She skirted around the still form of Riordan and moved toward the door without a sound.

"Wait!"

She stopped.

"This is insane, Cass. I can't understand what's happening. Look at me." She did. The sight of her face made him want to bellow out his fury and bewilderment and smash his fists against the walls. "Cass," he whispered. "I'm in love with you."

Tears overflowed immediately, flooding her cheeks. She swallowed over and over. Finally she got it out. "Then you should have married me."

She turned to flee and he lunged for her, grabbing her arm. "Damn you!" he shouted, baring his teeth, his fingers biting into her flesh. "Why can't you trust me?" He shook her hard. "Why?"

She couldn't answer, could hear nothing but her brain's fevered admonishment, *Get away, get away*! She wrenched out of his grip and flung away from him. He stared after her through the empty door, listening to the final sound of her footsteps on the stairs.

Then he had an idea.

XV

CASS TOOK A LAST LOOK AROUND THE ROOM. HIS ROOM, which she would never share with him now. The few belongings she was taking were packed in a small bandbox lying open on the bed. The clothes he'd bought her still hung in the wardrobe; books and writing materials he'd given her lay in a neat stack on the bureau. She would take none of them. So there was nothing else. She went to the box and closed it.

But with her hand on the handle, she paused. There was one other thing. Not to take, but to leave. She reached up to untie the thin blue ribbon at the back of her neck, and slid the ring off it into her palm. He'd said she needn't wear it but she had, secretly, next to her heart. Her eyes went helplessly to the inscription—"You and no other." Her throat tightened. She'd thought it impossible that she could cry a single new tear, and yet here came more.

She moved to the bureau and set the ring down with a clink of finality. Raising her head, she saw a watery reflection of herself in the glass: a pale young woman with grieving eyes. What a cunning disguise the body made for the soul, she mused; no one looking at her in a casual way could tell that inside there was almost nothing left, only empty, echoing space. Before the swollen ache in her chest could paralyze her, she went to the bed, picked up her box, and walked out of the room.

Riordan's valet was coming toward her in the hall. "Is Mr. Riordan still here, Beal?"

"No, madam, he went out about an hour ago and hasn't come back."

"Oh, I see. Thank you." She had to turn away before he could see the fresh gush of tears— whether of relief or regret she wasn't sure. But no, this was better; it *was*. Nothing needed to be said between them now, and if she saw him again she would undoubtedly cry in front of him. This way she could take a snippet of dignity with her.

She'd taken two steps down the staircase when the front door opened and Riordan entered. She froze. He was whistling. He stood in the foyer, stripping off his gloves, looking energetic and purposeful. And *whistling*. What was left of her heart broke in half. He looked up and saw her then, so there was nothing to do but come down the rest of the way.

"Hello, Cass." He noticed her box. "Going somewhere?"

"Yes. I'm going away."

He saw her red-rimmed eyes and turned grave. "Are you? Where?"

"I'm not sure." Her voice gave her away, she knew; it was thick from weeping.

"Have you any money?"

She focused her solemn gray gaze on him and said nothing.

"No, of course not," he said, half-smiling. "I tore it up. I apologize for that."

She drew herself up, a spark of anger beginning to flicker beneath the ashes. "I'm going to ask Mr. Quinn for an advance," she said stiffly, "on the money he's promised to pay me when Wade is caught."

"Oh, don't do that. Come in the library, I'll give you some money." He started down the hall. "Come!" he called over his shoulder.

She stood stock-still. Hurt and confusion and fury battled inside her. Confusion prevailed. She put her box down and followed him.

He was pulling notes out of the back of a drawer in his desk. "This is all I've got in the house at the moment." He counted it quickly. "About three hundred pounds. I'll owe you the rest, all right?"

She swallowed and nodded, putting out her hand.

"But there's a condition."

She snatched her hand back. This was more like it. "What condition?"

"You must give me two hours of your time."

She flushed scarlet and backed away.

"Oh, no, you misunderstand, I didn't mean—" He paused to laugh. "But what an enchanting idea," he murmured on an intimate note, causing new color to stain her cheeks. "I meant, two hours *outside* the house. In full view of the public eye, both of us conducting ourselves with perfect propriety. Well, me, anyway; I can't speak for you, can I?"

"What are you talking about?"

"I'm talking about you and me taking a walk, Cass. I want to show you something. Will you come?"

She frowned with suspicion. "A walk?"

"A walk."

"And then you'll give me the money, and . . . let me go?"

"Yes, if it's what you want."

"It's what I want." She paused again. For the life of her, she couldn't think of anything she had to lose. "Very well. I'll go with you."

"Good!"

By the time they'd crossed Oxford Street and Piccadilly, passed the Queen's Palace, and skirted the southern edge of St. James's Park, Cass had a fair idea where they were heading. But why in the world he wanted to take her to Westminster, and presumably to the particular House of Parliament there in which he spent his working days, she couldn't guess. And she refused to ask. He spoke little, to match her mood, but he wasn't at all gloomy; she sensed, in fact, a definite cheerfulness bubbling beneath his quiet surface. He swung a walking stick between his fingers with unmistakable jauntiness, while calling out lighthearted greetings to his acquaintances along the way. In the blackness of Cass's mind, it seemed the cause of his high spirits could be but one thing: her imminent departure. She sank deeper into her private misery and spoke not a word.

"Welcome to the venerable rabbit warren," he announced with a wave of his hand, breaking in on her profitless thoughts. She looked around. They were crossing Old Palace Yard, opposite the Abbey, where buildings ancient and new seemed to grow out of each other like barnacles. "Warren" was an apt description, she decided, for shops, law courts, coffee houses, government offices, and even private homes coexisted here on intimate, overcrowded terms, clustered around the nucleus of Westminster

Hall. Over it all hovered a dark-smelling, unsanitary dampness. It was anything but grand, and seemed a great deal more medieval than modern, yet there was vigor in the diversity and energy in the chaos. Riordan's tone and manner were consciously modest, even deprecating, but there was a flush of pride in his face; glancing about, she had a glimmer of an idea why.

"Walter Raleigh lost his head right . . . here," he told her, pointing to the ground at their feet, while she tried to ignore the hand he held at the small of her back. "Milton was married over there, in St. Margaret's. Oliver Cromwell's head sat on the roof of the Hall for twenty-three years. Sir Thomas More was tried there, and the Earl of Essex, and Guy Fawkes. That's the House of Lords, Cass, in the Chamber of Requests. And this—this is the Commons."

She regarded with surprise the modest, three-story stone building with leaded windows and a slate roof. "It looks like a church," she observed. Perhaps if she pretended she was on a guided tour with a stranger, she could get through this.

"It is. Or it was, St. Stephen's Chapel. It was deconsecrated in 1557, and it's been the House of Commons ever since. Come on, let's go inside. I want to show you—" He stopped, his eyes on the figure of a stoop-shouldered gentleman coming down from the stone portico. The man saw them in the same moment. He squinted, then raised his arm in a sort of greeting.

"That you, Philip Riordan? I've got a bone to pick with you!"

Cass was astonished when Riordan halted in his tracks like a schoolboy caught in a prank. But he took hold of her arm and marched bravely toward the older gentleman, as if preparing to take his punishment.

"Good afternoon, sir. What a pleasure to—"

"Don't 'good afternoon' me. What's this reform nonsense I hear you're planning to introduce this term, before I can even get my coat off?" The speaker was past sixty, a heavy-set individual in a scratch wig and round spectacles, with a deeply lined, profoundly weary countenance. "I'll oppose you, my boy," he warned, stabbing at Riordan's lapel with a stubby finger. "You can count on it."

"I expected that, sir—"

"What do you mean, taking up time with fluff like this? We'll be at war with France inside the year if I have my way, and that's a damn sight more important than whether a horse thief hangs or goes to jail."

Riordan grinned. "You're quite right, but I'll wager we can find time for both."

"We'll see about that. Who's this, then, your new wife?" He touched his hat, and his care-worn face softened.

"Yes, sir, this is Mrs. Riordan. Cass, I'd like you to meet Mr. Burke."

Extending a hand, Cass had to retrieve her fallen jaw. *The* Mr. Burke? Edmund Burke? But this man was so old! "I'm honored to make your acquaintance," she said earnestly. "I'm a great admirer of your work."

Mr. Burke looked skeptical.

"It's true," Riordan assured him. "She's read almost everything you've written." His eyes twinkled. "In all candor, sir, she likes you better than I do."

The great statesman lowered his brows in a fierce scowl. "Then you've married well, you young rake, and much beyond what you deserve. Let's hope some of her good sense rubs off on you." He turned back to Cass. "I don't envy you, madam. Keep an eye on this scoundrel. The only admirable qualities

I've noticed in him are a keen mind, absolute integrity, and the ability to get along with anybody. A dangerous start." He touched his hat again. "Good day to you both. And good luck."

It was Riordan's turn to close his mouth. He stared at the portly, retreating back of Edmund Burke in utter stillness, repeating the great man's parting words in his head, committing them to memory. After a moment he looked down at Cass, unable to conceal his elation. "Lord, Cass, did you hear him? He—"

"He likes you," she finished, trying not to smile.

"Why shouldn't he?" There was no reason why Riordan's pleasure should please her, but it did.

"Because! My reputation's a shambles, I come to the sessions pretending I'm drunk, I—"

"Perhaps he's been told how matters really stand," she suggested quietly. "Isn't he the leader of his branch of the Whigs?"

"Yes, but—" He stopped, considering. "It's possible, I suppose. After all, Pitt knows, and some of the other ministers as well." He paused again; his face was a study.

"It would mean a lot to you, wouldn't it? To be known for what you are by the man you respect so much?"

He smiled into her eyes, loving her dearly at that moment. He wanted to kiss her, but of course she wouldn't let him. But there would be time for that later. "Yes, it would," he said simply, and took her arm.

But she didn't move. "I think there must be two men inside you, Philip," she told him, her voice bleak. "One of them is noble and generous and upright. But the other is a liar and a hypocrite. I'm sorry we ever met."

He shook his head slowly, without anger. It wasn't only he she didn't trust, he realized, it was herself. She hadn't enough confidence in her own worth to believe he loved her, that he could have married her. It was a melancholy insight. "After you change your mind about me, Cass," he said with quiet determination, "I'm going to make you change your mind about yourself. That's a promise."

But first things first. Without waiting for her to answer, he put his hand on her elbow and hurried her up the steps, through the arched portico, and into the House.

The cloakroom was the old church cloisters. Red tapes dangled from the coat hangers lining the walls—so the Members could hang up their swords before going into the Chamber to debate, he explained. Much less bloody that way. "But we always keep our hats on, Cass. Can't imagine why, but it's a tradition. Spurs, too, if we like. And you can't arrest us, we're immune. Speak ill of us and we'll have *you* arrested, for breach of privilege." He nodded to a porter standing by the door, then led her through another passageway to a high-ceilinged, medium-sized room. "And this is the dark and comfortless Lobby. When a vote's taken on a bill, we don't raise our hands or shout out. We walk out here if we're for it, and the Speaker counts us. It's called a division. Come on, this way." He pulled her through a short hallway to another door and threw it open. "The Chamber," he announced proudly.

His enthusiasm was touching; in spite of all he'd done, she couldn't bring herself to hurt his feelings. "Very nice," she said politely, marveling at how small it was, more cozy than grand, not at all what she'd expected. It was even paneled. More than ever it looked like a church, of the Reformed variety.

"That's the Speaker's Chair," he said, pointing to

a plain, straight-backed chair on a raised dais. It faced two large groups of benches separated by a green carpet. "I sit here, on the Whig side." He dropped her hand and walked toward the back of the Chamber. "Here!" He was so far away he almost had to shout. "The important Members sit in front!" He came toward her again, smiling. "Strangers sit up there." He pointed to a three-sided gallery above their heads. "A Stranger, of course, is anybody who's not a Member. Burke sits here, on the Treasury bench since he broke with Fox and the other Whigs."

"Will he really oppose your bill?" she asked, worried in spite of herself. But what she really wanted to ask was, *Philip, what are we doing here*?

"Oh, yes. That was a foregone conclusion. 'Reform' isn't a word in Burke's vocabulary."

"Then why do you like him so much? Wade hates him."

"Yes, I imagine he does. Burke's his worst enemy. He hates the Revolution for the same reason he hates reform—they both upset the traditions of the past." He dropped down in Burke's seat on the Treasury bench. "Why do I like him? Because his mind is brilliant, he's as honest as he is stubborn, and he'd die before he'd compromise his principles. And he's the most extraordinary speaker. Or rather, he used to be. Now they call him the 'dinner bell of the House.'"

"Why?"

"Because as soon as he rises to speak, everyone leaves." He chuckled fondly. "Well, he goes *on* so. You have to remember, many of the M.P.'s are only simple farmers or merchants—they haven't the patience for his convoluted arguments and flights of fancy. And he's getting on in years—he gets weary and out of sorts, and then he can't seem to bring his speeches to an end. Ah, but you should've heard him a few years ago, Cass. There was never anyone like him."

"And yet Colin doesn't see him as harmless, I don't think. He really despises him."

"His power is in his writing now. When he lost the support of the Whigs, he went over their heads to the people. It's mostly because of him that public opinion is turning away from France these days."

He stood up. She was afraid it was time to leave, that for some reason he'd wanted her to see all this before he let her go, but now the tour was over. "How many Members are there?" she asked. She was stalling, she realized glumly, and despised herself for it.

"About six hundred and fifty."

"So many! Surely they can't all fit in here."

"No, only about half show up at any one time. It's always been that way."

"How does it work? What do you do?"

"We debate. The Speaker calls on the Honorable Gentleman from Muddleton-on-Sea. He rises. He begins to speak—extemporaneously, of course; any man caught with notes is hooted out of the Chamber. All the other Members are either absent, asleep, talking out loud, or hurling letters back and forth to each other. It's the most extraordinary thing, Cass, you would hardly credit it. If he's a dull speaker, poor fellow, he's interrupted by jeering so loud you can't hear a word he says. But if he's good, the whole Chamber listens in absolute silence. Junior Members soon learn that they won't be governing Great Britain single-handedly after all. Some go into a long sulk after their maiden speech and don't say another word for years. Others set out to learn the game."

"Like you," she guessed. "That's what you've done."

"What I'm *doing*. It's a long process, but worth

the effort. Because although I'm not governing Great Britain, this House of Commons is."

She smiled. "And I thought it was the king."

"No, we only let him think so." He took out his pocket watch. "Well, love. Let's go, shall we? It's getting late, and I have one more thing to show you."

She felt a weakening in the knees at his thoughtless endearment. The pain of leaving was almost too much to be borne. All at once, it struck her that she didn't have to bear it. She could choose to stay with him. Who would care? Who would know the truth except her, and him, and John Walker? He was waiting, his hand outstretched. She shuddered as the vista of a life with Riordan—or as much of one as he cared to give her—spread before her mind's eye and she balanced on the brink of capitulation. But at the last second she drew back.

"Philip," she said tensely, "what are we doing? Why did you bring me here? Please, this is—difficult for me. Mayn't we go home now?"

He came close, but didn't touch her. His face was extraordinarily tender, his eyes seeming to see to the bottom of her soul. "You promised me two hours," he said gently. "It's almost over. Believe me, sweet Cass, I want to go home as much as you." He put his hand out again. "I don't ask you to trust me. Just to come with me."

She hesitated, then slipped her hand in his.

Out of the Chamber they went, through a different dim passageway, down a winding stairway of damp stone, and along another series of narrow halls, until at last they came to a studded double door. She looked at him inquiringly; his expression was odd and unreadable. He held the door open for her. She went past, took three steps, and stopped. By the light of a hundred votive candles, she saw that this time she was in a real church.

"What is it?" she faltered, whispering.

"The Lower Chapel. It's only used by Members nowadays, for weddings and christenings." He cleared his throat and stood in front of her. "I thought it would be a good place for us to get married."

No, he couldn't do it without touching her. He reached for her lifeless hands and took a deep breath. "Will you marry me again, Cass? I love you with all my heart." He pulled her closer, taking her stunned silence for indecision. "Marry me and let's get old together. You'll be the most beautiful little old lady."

Still she didn't speak, but neither did she protest when he wound his arms around her and rested his forehead against hers. "I'm so in love with you," he murmured, brushing her nose with his lips. "I'm a good catch, Cass—even Burke says I'm an honest man. And there's a group of men in Buckinghamshire who've invited me to stand for the next election from their district. As strange as it seems, it looks like I'm a man on the rise. Are you going to say yes? I don't mind getting down on my knees if it'll help."

He touched the tears on her face softly with his fingers. "I love you," he said into her shining eyes. "I'll never stop loving you, even when I'm a shriveled up old goat of a man." He dropped his voice. "I'll always be after you, too, because I'll only get more virile the older I get. You won't be able to keep—"

"Oh! Philip!" She flung her arms around him and buried her face in his shirt. "Oh! Oh!" was all she could seem to say.

"Does that mean yes?" he laughed, embracing her, lifting her off the floor, and then immediately loosening his hold for fear of breaking her ribs.

"Yes! Oh, yes, yes, yes. Oh, Philip!"

"It's a good thing I'm the one in this family who gets paid for being eloquent," he grinned, then kissed her with all his pent-up passion. "Do you love me, Cass?"

"I do, I do love you. I love you, Philip, I've always loved you." She was giddy with happiness. It was as if a dam had burst inside, and the long-submerged words of love were spilling from her lips in an irrepressible cascade. "Shall we really marry, then? Here?"

"Here, as soon as I can speak to the canon and arrange it. I spent half the afternoon trying to find him, but he wasn't available."

"Will it be soon?"

"It will if I have anything to say about it. Because we won't really be marrying, we'll be solemnizing new vows, so there'll be no need to wait for the banns. I don't see why it can't be done right away."

Solemnizing new vows. She hooked her arms around his neck and hugged him. "You mean this time we won't just 'declare our wish to marry'?"

He didn't return her teasing smile. "You are my wife, Cass. You were before and you are now. Do you believe me?"

"I'm not sure," she murmured, wetting her lips. "Maybe you'd better show me."

He made a sound in his throat, part hum, part growl. "Why, you cheeky wench. And in the Members' Chapel, too."

She felt cheeky. "What better place to have a Member than in his chapel?" she asked, pressing herself against him, loving the way his eyes widened in amusement and answering desire. He brought her even closer and kissed her with the slow, sensual urgency that always undid her, then walked her two steps backward until he had her pressed against the thick oak door. She loosened her arms around his neck enough to give him room

to touch her but not enough to break the kiss. Her
breasts changed shape in his palms. His tongue
filled her mouth; her head went back and she let
him nibble and taste while one of his hands restlessly stroked her stomach. When he pushed himself against her and murmured something starkly
suggestive in her ear, she knew it was only his
weight pressing against her that was keeping her
upright.

She also realized how close they were to committing a sacrilegious act. She pulled away with a
heroic surge of will and whispered against his
throat, "I've thought of a better place." Riordan
was breathing hard, and unable to remember what
this related to until she finished, "In the Member's
bed."

"Ahh," he said on a shuddering sigh, "the Member's bed. Yes. The very thing." But he looked
around reluctantly. "Still, these pews couldn't be as
hard as they look. If we—"

"Philip!"

He chuckled. "Tell me you love me before we
go," he urged. "I don't think I heard right before."

She brought his head down and put her lips to his
ear. "I love you," she said distinctly, then repeated
it for good measure, in a sibilant whisper, her teeth
nipping his earlobe.

He shivered involuntarily. "Oh, Cass. Are you
going to get it."

The mixture of threat and promise excited her
unbearably. Without another word, they took each
other's hands and left the chapel, intent now on
nothing but the deadly serious business of getting
home fast. Walking was out of the question. They
found a hackney near the park and flung themselves into it like escaping criminals. Riordan
called out the address to the driver imperiously and
promised him an extra crown if he could make it in

under a quarter of an hour. Inside the coach, they collapsed with laughter, amused at their own eagerness.

Twelve minutes later, the coachman pulled up before Riordan's residence in Portman Square and waited for his fares to alight. Nothing happened. Swells, he thought; must be waitin' fer me to open the blinkin' door. He got down with only a low-key grumble, though; a crown, after all, was a crown. But when he jerked open the door and looked inside, the lady gave a kind of shriek and the gent snatched his hand out from under her skirts and they both turned beet red. Which just went to show, swells weren't no different from common folk. Well, *some* different, he grinned, pocketing the bright new guinea the swell tossed him. "It's all right, we're engaged," said the gent, and the two men exchanged broad winks.

"Engaged!" cried Cass, once they were in the house.

"Just a little joke, my sweet."

He was grinning like a fool and she had to laugh at him. "Some joke—oh!" He picked her up with a flourish and kissed her while her mouth was still open. Her pique flew away; her only concern now was whether they would make it to the bedroom or consummate their union in the middle of the stairs. The passing of a maid in the hall settled that, but she had to frown a stern warning at him to prevent him from calling out another cheerful impropriety such as he had to the coachman.

Before the door closed they started to undress each other. But it wasn't efficient; their hands kept getting in each other's way, fumbling at buttons and fasteners. They made an unspoken agreement to take their own clothes off, and accomplished it in rapt silence, eyes locked, with great economy of movement.

Naked, they embraced. At the first touch Cass was ready; she wanted to feel him inside, now, without preliminaries. But he'd taught her a better way, and she ground her teeth and prepared to endure the agonizing pleasure of waiting. For once they didn't talk. She shivered under the touch of his hands on her arms, her shoulder blades, her spine, stroking and pressing, as if relearning what her skin felt like. His chest hair had always delighted her, so soft and sleek; it grew downward so neatly, she'd wondered once if he combed it.

She let her hands drift down his diaphragm to touch the hard muscles of his belly, and brushed the intriguing trail of hair below his navel with the backs of her fingers. He was erect and ready, but seemingly in no hurry. He cupped her breasts and lifted them, watching her face, stroking the nipples with his fingertips. Her mouth opened on a soft sigh. He bent his head, she thought to kiss her, but instead his lips found her hard little peak and devoured it. She put her fingers in his hair and held on for dear life, moaning and murmuring his name, feeling sparks shooting through her. How strange and wonderful, she thought when he went down on one knee and began to tongue her navel. He held her steady with his hands on her buttocks, kissing and sucking her, and then he told her to open her legs.

She stopped staring blindly at the ceiling and looked down. He couldn't have said that. But no—she hadn't misheard, because he repeated it.

"Philip, I—"

He raised his head, and his eyes were as black as onyx. "I want to kiss you here, Cass." His hand cupped her pubic mound. "Open your legs for me."

"But—this isn't—"

"Yes, it is. It's good and natural, and I promise you'll like it."

Well, he was her husband and his word was law. After another second's pause, and with a Gallic shrug that under other circumstances would have made him laugh, she slid her feet a few inches apart.

It wasn't really kissing, she discovered quickly. It was more like—oh God, it was like heaven on earth. "Philip! I don't think I can stand this!"

He rose, lifting her in the same movement, and carried her to the bed. He laid her on her back and sat beside her. His mouth was wet, a fact which embarrassed and fascinated her. Before she could think of resisting, he parted her legs, pushing her knee up, and bent his head to her again. At first she jumped, and jumped again, because the place he was nibbling with his lips was so sensitive. But soon they both learned what she could tolerate. Her head fell back against the pillow. Sensations she'd never experienced, never even suspected, bombarded her in a gentle, remorseless assault of pleasure until she cried out softly, begging him to stop.

He stopped.

"No, don't—I didn't mean it!"

His throaty laugh coaxed a sheepish snicker out of her, but then her breath caught as he obeyed her latest command and went back to what he'd been doing. Her stomach muscles were knotted, knees flexed, hands and toes clenching the coverlet. There was nothing in the universe but her body and his mouth. Her head thrashed from side to side, but otherwise she held perfectly still. Her insides were liquifying, the hot tide of need rising fast. She thought he said "Now," but if he was giving permission it was too late. The explosion came an instant before, fragmenting her and propelling the pieces into space. For unknown seconds she ceased to exist. As she came back to earth, there was another concussion, then another, but they were gentler and full of sweet release.

She reclaimed herself gradually, becoming aware of her posture—wanton in the extreme—and of Riordan's head resting warmly on her thigh. She reached for his hand and cradled it on her belly, stroking it, feeling her own fingers on her skin. She'd never felt so alive, and yet so utterly strengthless. Love overflowed in her heart, but the energy to tell him so was hard to summon. She took a tremulous breath and sighed, "You were right, I liked it."

Although he could appreciate it, Riordan wasn't sharing her mellow feeling at that moment. His body felt like a drawn bow, and the arrow in it as well. He knew a thoughtful lover should give his partner time to recover, even revive, but he'd reached the outer edge of his endurance. He sat up on his knees, slid the pillow out from under her head, and put it beneath her hips. He smiled into her widening eyes and drew her legs up, hooking them over his shoulders, stroking their silky softness from knees to groin. "This is natural, too," he felt called upon to explain. Holding her steady, he drove slowly into the velvety softness of her.

She cried out.

He pulled back. "Am I hurting you?"

"Oh God, no. It's so deep!"

He eased into her again gently, watching her face. She was so beautiful, and she was in love with him. He could have climaxed then, but he made himself hold still deep within her while she adjusted to his fullness. His fingers went unerringly to her secret places, and he felt her quicken to life around him as he caressed her.

"Oh, it's good, it's good," she whispered. Blood pounded in her extremities; her abdominal muscles

were taut and quivering, craving new relief already.
Where was the lassitude of a minute ago? This was
all she wanted, all she needed now—Philip throbbing inside her, loving her, filling her with this
acute and perfect pleasure.

He had to move, he couldn't hold back. He
gripped her hips and lifted her higher, thrusting to
the hilt, using his powerful thighs to piston her. He
winced at the pleasurable pain of her fingernails
biting into his knees. He felt like a cocked gun,
ready to explode. Oh Christ, he couldn't wait for
her, it was impossible—but then he saw her back
arch before she let out a cry that could have been of
rapture or the purest torture. Immediately he un-
leashed himself, grinding his teeth and pulling her
thighs hard against his middle, not even hearing the
long, raw groan that tore from his throat in the
intense ecstacy of the moment.

Afterward they lay sprawled in each other's arms,
replete, too drained even to speak. When a little
energy returned, he rolled her on top, enjoying the
solid feel of her full weight on him. Cass put her
fingers on his chest and rested her chin on her
wrists. "Let's do it again," she suggested with a
straight face, then snorted with laughter at his
expression.

They kissed, holding each other, murmuring
wild, tender compliments. To lie together and say
"I love you," without fear of being used or of
sounding foolish, was an addictive joy they hadn't
even known they were missing. So they said it over
and over, in all the ways they could think of, and
then they told each other how miserable they'd
been apart.

"Would you really have left me, Cass?" he asked,
holding her, as shadows slipped unnoticed over the
bed and the room took on the cool lemon bright-
ness of the autumn afternoon.

"I thought I would. I was going to. But then . . . then I had second thoughts."

"When?"

"In the Commons. When you were sitting in Burke's seat. You were so . . . I don't know."

"What?"

She thought. "You seemed the antithesis of the kind of man who would trick a woman into thinking she'd married him." She stroked his stomach, her head on his shoulder. "Was that why you took me there?"

He was smiling. *Antithesis*, he thought. She used bigger words now than he did. "No. I wanted you to see the Chamber and know that part of me, but I'm not really sure why. I didn't think it would change your mind about anything."

"I love that part of you. I'm so proud of you, Philip." She made slow circles around his navel with her fingernail, watching his abdomen rise and fall with each breath. "Will you really stand for election from Buckinghamshire?"

"Perhaps."

"Much more glory there than in St. Clawes, I expect."

"St. *Chawes*," he corrected, his mouth twitching. Her skin felt like watered silk. When she soothed her sleek thigh back and forth over his hairy one, he could hear the faint, raspy sound of it. "If you'd left me, I'd have brought you back, you know. I'd have torn your money up again, Cass, and again anytime you had any, so you'd have to stay with me."

She put her lips on the pulse in his throat. "No, you wouldn't. You'd have let me go, and we'd both have been wretched."

He considered. "Possibly," he conceded. "I'm sorry I did that—tore up your money. I couldn't think of anything else to do to keep you from leaving."

"Never mind. What I regret is not telling you what was wrong sooner. But I felt so humiliated, I couldn't bring myself to speak the words. I thought you'd made a joke of me. I'm so proud, Philip. I thought talking about it would give you even more to laugh at me for, so I kept it inside. It was wrong of me—I should've shouted it out that day you dragged me back from Colin's. It would've saved so much time."

"You were hurt. I don't blame you. How you must have hated me."

"Never. Never that, not even at the lowest point. I always loved you."

Now was no time for tears, yet both of them felt like weeping. Instead they kissed, softly, experiencing the bittersweetness of the past together and then letting it go.

After a time Riordan shifted so they were facing each other, lying on their sides, his hand in the hollow of her waist. "Who told you we weren't married?"

She'd known it was coming. Even so, she couldn't bring herself to say the name. "He's as close to a father as I'll ever have," he'd once told her. How could she destroy something so precious to him by uttering one word? She was incapable of it. Perhaps it was cowardly, but she decided to give Quinn the opportunity to tell Philip himself. If he would not, then it would be her responsibility, and she would do it. But it would be so much easier for Philip if the news came from Quinn first. Perhaps he had an explanation for what he'd done. She couldn't imagine, couldn't conceive of a motive that would justify the pain they'd both endured because of his lie, but she conceded the possibility that there might be one.

"I will tell you after we're married," she said

lightly. He frowned and started to speak. "Again," she added hastily.

He rose up on one elbow. "You still don't believe me!"

"It's not that, I—"

"You're protecting this person until you're absolutely sure I'm not lying! Isn't that it?"

"No! I *do* believe you. I wouldn't be here with you if I didn't!" Well, she reflected, that might or might not be true; she would think about it later.

"Then tell me who it is."

"Listen to me, Philip." She sat up and faced him. "It's better if this person—oh, *damn* it! If I tell you *why* I won't tell you, you'll know who it is! Please, can't you trust me? It won't be for long, I promise. And I swear I will tell you when we're married, unless the person—" She broke off in frustration. How she hated this secret! "Trust me," she said again. "I do believe you. And I love you with all my heart. But don't let's talk about it anymore. I couldn't bear it if we fought today!"

He reached out and pulled her back into his arms. "All right, Cass, I won't ask you now. God knows, I don't want to fight, either." And as he began to kiss her, his need to know the liar's name receded and another, stronger need took its place. But even while passion flared between them again and again during the long afternoon and night, the troubling truth nagged at the back of his mind that someone had tried to hurt them, to drive them apart. And for as long as Cass didn't trust him enough to tell him who it was, their enemy was winning.

XVI

FOUR DAYS PASSED. THE HOUSE RANG WITH THEIR laughter, and the servants went about their duties smiling for the first time in weeks. If this was living in sin, Cass no longer cared. She'd read a phrase once in a novel—"in thrall." That was how she felt now—in thrall to her husband. As for Riordan, he joked that between making love and sleeping to regain his strength, he was getting nothing done, and he with a bill to introduce in one week. It was the honeymoon all over again, with an important difference—they were both in love and no longer afraid to say it.

Only Cass's continued refusal to name the one who had lied marred their perfect happiness. Once he understood that she would not relent regardless of the pressure he exerted, Riordan stopped asking her. Still, it was never far from their minds. She sent Quinn a terse note explaining her terms—tell Riordan the truth before they were married or she would do it for him—but so far there was no reply.

The date of their second wedding ceremony was still in doubt. Reverend West wasn't able to see the situation from Riordan's viewpoint and insisted that without proof of a first marriage, they would have to begin from the beginning, with the banns duly announced and a conventional ceremony. Riordan was in the process of going over his head to the Bishop of London, and the matter was under negotiation. To have a standard ceremony would, of course, announce to the world that the first one hadn't been legal. He wanted to protect Cass from that if he could; she'd suffered enough from scandal and gossip in her short life. The damage to his own career concerned him hardly at all. If they had to marry again as if for the first time, he would do it gladly. Whatever it took, he wanted the misunderstandings of the past behind them.

The morning of the fifth of November arrived. Cass sat at the foot of the bed in their room, hugging the post, still in her nightgown, and watched while her husband finished dressing. He had put on a white shirt and cravat, black breeches, and a black waistcoat; his black coat hung on the back of a chair. He'd sent his valet away so they could be alone a few minutes before it was time for him to leave. She watched as he brushed the thick, gleaming black-and-silver hair back from his forehead, flexing his knees a bit to see the top of his head in the cheval glass. He wasn't a vain man; he peered critically at his reflection once, flicked imaginary lint from his shoulders, and turned around. The toilette was over.

"You look wonderful," Cass exclaimed, guileless as always with him. "What a lucky wife I am!"

She looked tousled and beautiful and heartbreakingly young. He crossed to her in three strides and pulled her into his arms. They stood that way for a long moment, she listening to his heart beat, he inhaling the scent of her hair.

Cass was the first to break away. She knew it was hopeless, but she gathered her courage and asked him anyway. "Philip."

"What, my love?"

"Please—please don't go. I can't bear it that you'll be in danger."

He reassured her, as she'd known he would. "I won't be in any danger, foolish girl. After the gallery fills, everyone will be detained and searched for weapons. The king won't go anywhere near the House of Lords today. There'll be no shooting, sweetheart, only a bloodless arrest."

"I know, but—"

"Wade will be arrested immediately afterward, and the would-be assassins will be prevailed upon to implicate him."

She shivered, thinking of her father. "Prevailed upon," she knew, was as often as not a euphemism for tortured.

He hugged her, knowing exactly where her thoughts had led. But neither of them spoke Patrick Merlin's name, and presently she raised her head again to look at him.

"But what if Wade's changed the plan?" she fretted. "Quinn was right, Philip—I should have seen him again."

"No," he said firmly. "You will never see him again. That part of our lives is finished, Cass. After today, we both start over."

Their eyes held, dark blue on solemn gray. "I love you so much," she whispered. She stood on tiptoe and kissed him.

His arms tightened around her almost painfully, and then he let her go. "Don't worry. I love you. I'll be back in a few hours."

And he was gone.

Cass spent the morning in the library, trying to read. It was raining. After a few pages, she would get up and look out the window. When that palled, she wandered around from room to room, staring out new windows, until there wasn't a vantage in the house from which she hadn't watched the gray, silent drops thud grimly to earth.

He was late. "A few hours" turned into six. She gave up all pretense of reading and devoted herself to worrying. At four o'clock she went upstairs to their room and lay across the bed. She knew it was foolish to let herself get this overwrought; the chances of anything happening to him were miniscule, all but nonexistent. Logic and love trod separate paths, though, and rarely converged. She rolled herself up in a ball of worry and, after another half-hour of misery, fell into a restless sleep.

She awoke to his kiss, light as a snowflake on her cheekbone. Without thought, she threw her arms around his neck and held on. Her fervor told him what she'd been through this day better than words could have. He stretched out beside her and kissed her gently until her grip on him relaxed. The room was awash with dim, watery light. A gust of wind hurled a quick wave of rain at the window. She held him and kissed his lips with grave urgency and told him again that she loved him. Only then did she ask, "What happened?"

"Nothing. Nothing happened."

She sat up. He put his hands behind his head and blinked up at her. For the first time she saw the grimness around his mouth and eyes. "Tell me," she said quietly.

He drew a tired breath. "Everything went smoothly. The Members of both houses were assembled in the Lords' Chamber, waiting for the king's entrance. The Strangers' Gallery was full, you couldn't have wedged in another soul. The guards had instructed everyone to give up any arms they might be carrying before they entered the gallery, and they'd even collected a sword or two. But most people denied having anything."

"And then?"

"At the moment the king would have come in, the gallery was surrounded and everyone in it was ordered into the lobby. There was a lot of confusion, but no one got out. Then each man was searched. It took most of the afternoon."

"And?"

"And there wasn't a weapon among them. Not a pistol, not a penknife, not a hatpin. Nothing."

"Oh, no." She sat back on her heels. The implication began to dawn on her. "Oh, this is awful. This means—"

"We're back where we started." He tried a smile to lighten the bleakness of his tone, but it wasn't successful.

Cass put her hand inside his unbuttoned waistcoat and stroked his ribs in sympathy. After a while she said, "I wonder what will happen now. Will Quinn want you to keep playing your part?" He shook his head slowly, meaning he didn't know. "He'll want me to see Wade, though," she guessed. "We can be sure of that."

"Doubtless, but you won't do it. You'll write him a note, expressing surprise that no attempt was made on the king's life today and wondering what he plans next. But I meant what I said this morning, Cass—you've seen Wade for the last time."

The news didn't sadden her. They listened to a cart clatter down the sodden cobblestones in front of the house and watched the light in the window fade from gray to umber. A little later she sank down beside him and took him in her arms.

Charles Willoughby paused with his hand on the knob of his front door. "I don't know why you two have to go so soon, you're breaking up the whole party. Are you sure you can't stay?"

"Yes, do," echoed his wife. "It's not so very late."

Cass and Riordan smiled at each other and then at their hosts. Before either could reply, William Leffing-Stoke—who bore the unfortunate but inevitable nickname of Laughingstock—spoke up for them. "You forget, Charles, they're newlyweds. Nine o'clock *is* late to them, unless they're at home alone." Everyone laughed. The party spilled out onto the Willoughbys' front porch: Charles and his wife Jennie, Riordan and Cass, Leffing-Stoke, Horace and Jane Thibault, Nigel Drumm, and Michael Cramer. The men were all members of Riordan's committee, and tonight they were celebrating the extraordinary success of his speech this afternoon in the House, introducing their reform bill.

Riordan stood behind Cass with his arms around her, not bothering to dispute his friend's explanation for their early departure. The night was unusually mild and the conversation dragged on, as conversation will at leave-taking time. Finally the men began to shake hands, the women to embrace. Cass had met Jennie Willoughby several times before and liked her enormously. She was older, thirty or so, but she was high-spirited, irreverent, and unfailingly kind. Even more, she seemed to have a genuine interest in taking Cass under her more experienced wing and helping her down the complicated, pitfall-strewn path to becoming a good parliamentary wife. Jennie was her first real woman friend since leaving Paris, and Cass treasured her for it.

"I'm having a tea next week, Cassie, probably Thursday. Can you come? Jane's coming," Jennie said, laying a hand on her other friend's arm. "I'll make sure to invite a few women you don't know, so you can meet some new people."

"You're so kind," Cass said sincerely, squeezing her hand. "I'd love to come."

Later, as they walked home arm-in-arm, she told Riordan about the invitation, marveling at how kind people were.

"And why shouldn't they be kind to you?" he demanded.

"Oh . . . you know."

"Because of your father?"

"That, and my reputation, the way we married, Wade—everything. My life's a scandal, Philip!"

"It might have been once, but not anymore. From now on you and I are going to be so respectable, we'll bore 'em all to tears."

She leaned against him as they walked along, her head on his shoulder. "That ought to sound boring to *me*, but it doesn't. Not in the least."

"Nor to me."

She smiled, and didn't have to look up to know that he was smiling, too. "Philip, I'm so proud of you tonight, I'm bursting. If only I could have been in the House!" He'd downplayed the possibility of any danger, but still hadn't allowed her to come to hear his speech. "Will you give it all over again when we get home, just to me?"

He threw his head back and laughed, imagining it. "If only my audience were half as sympathetic as you, love."

"Charles Willoughby said they *were* that sympathetic. He said you could have heard a feather fall after you started speaking."

"A gross exaggeration," he demurred modestly.

"And Mr. Drumm said they interrupted to

shout, 'Hear him! Hear him!' at least half a dozen times."

He grinned down at her. "They did. I must admit, it was very cheering."

"Now even if Mr. Quinn wants you to resume your old role, I should think after today it would be impossible. No one will believe it anymore."

"I'm not sure of that. I was very good at playing the rogue, you know; quite a natural talent."

"Yes, but you're even better at this. Oh, Philip, I'm so excited for you!"

He laughed and hugged her, lifting her off the ground.

It was almost ten when they got home—not because it was a long walk but because they stopped so many times under streetlamps to kiss.

Walker was lurking in the hall, waiting for them.

"Good lord, John, would you go home? Do you know what time it is?"

The secretary smiled. "I'll go in a little while, if you don't mind; I've been doing some work on the rebuttal for the end of the week. Sir?"

"Yes?"

"Mr. Quinn is waiting to see you. He's been here at least an hour. In the drawing room."

Cass stood still. So, he was here. The burden of her troublesome secret was about to be lifted. She was glad, but concern for Riordan swiftly overshadowed the relief. How hurt he was going to be! He sent her an apologetic smile and began to tell her he'd join her upstairs soon, but she cut him off by hugging him hard, heedless that Walker stood nearby, and kissing him full on the lips. Then she lifted her skirts and ran upstairs.

Bemused but smiling, Riordan went down the hall to the drawing room.

"I hear things went well for you today," Quinn began, once they were seated at opposite ends of the sofa. A servant had kindled a new fire in the fireplace and replenished the visitor's glass of barley water before bowing himself out and leaving the two men alone.

"Very well, we think. The bill has a good chance of passage. Of course, Burke hasn't sunk his teeth into it yet."

"And do you really imagine your eloquence is any match for Edmund Burke?"

Riordan raised his brows. "Not my eloquence, perhaps. But I think I've got justice on my side, not to mention logic."

The older man's laugh was tinged with scorn. "I've never known the House to be swayed overmuch by those two commodities."

"You're cynical."

"Perhaps. But don't get your hopes up, Philip. Reform is a long, slow process; it can't be accomplished overnight by ambitious youths."

"Youths?" He smiled faintly. Oliver seemed to be trying to be disagreeable. "Why don't we stop beating around the bush? We're not talking about reform, we're talking about me. More precisely, what you want from me."

Quinn set his glass down. "You promised me two years, Philip. It's only been one."

Thank God, they were finally going to talk about it. "It's been fourteen, almost fifteen months," he corrected. He eyed Quinn steadily. "Oliver, I can't give you the rest."

"Can't?"

"Very well—won't. Everything's different now. I'm very sorry."

Quinn's face was unreadable. "You've changed, Philip."

"God, I hope so."

He didn't return Riordan's wry smile. "This is because you're married, isn't it?"

"Cass is part of it. A big part." It was surprisingly easy to admit it. "But the rest has to do with finally knowing what I want to do with my life, how I can best serve the country. And it's not by pretending to be drunk and reporting to you the unguarded conversations I overhear. Christ, Oliver, I'm almost thirty years old! I can make a better contribution in other ways, I'm sure of it. Can't you see that?"

"You're very full of yourself tonight, aren't you? Flushed with success from one well-received speech—"

"It's a bit more than that," he interrupted coolly.

Quinn stood up. His limbs were rigid, his pale face gone pink. Riordan realized all at once that he was furious. "Perhaps, but I wonder what all the reforms in the world will avail us," he almost shouted, "if the forces of chaos prevail and our sovereign is murdered!" He made a visible effort to keep his voice down.

"Damn it, Philip, I need you. And I need your wife. Can't *you* understand that? Wade outsmarted us! We've got to find out what he's thinking now, what his plans are. It's absolutely vital!"

"Are you seriously suggesting I let Cass see him again?"

"She has to, she's the only—"

"It's out of the question! No!" He was on his feet, too. "Wade knows he was betrayed—"

"Yes, but he doesn't know it was she. Probably a dozen people knew of the plan."

"What if you're wrong? What if he told no one but her, to test her? And now you're suggesting I send her back to him? I won't do it. That's final, Oliver, it's my last word."

There was a knock at the door. "Yes!" called Riordan angrily, thinking it was another servant, but it was Walker.

"Sorry, sir, but a messenger just brought this. He's waiting for a reply."

"At this hour?" He took the envelope Walker held out. An eerie feeling of *déjà vu* came over him as he read his own name in the well-known handwriting of Lady Claudia Harvellyn. He opened it and read.

> "Chawton Hall, Somerset
> "8 November 1792

"My dearest Philip,

"Forgive me. If there were anyone else I would not trouble you, but there's no one. My father is dead. Not his heart—a coach accident, yesterday. Grandmother is gravely injured, expected to die soon. I am hurt, but well enough to write this. Oh, my friend, can you come?"

The next part was scratched out, but under the ink he could read, "Forgive me, if there were anyone else"—She must have realized she'd written that already. It was signed simply "Claudia."

He looked up. "My God."

Quinn said, "What is it?"

"It's Claudia. A coach accident in Somerset. Her family's dead—dying. She's hurt."

"I'm so terribly sorry, Philip."

He went to the small writing desk in an alcove, opened it, and penned a hasty note. He took it to Walker, saying, "Give this to the messenger, and give him some money."

Walker went out.

"Are you going to her?" asked Quinn.

"I have to." He paced between the fireplace and the door, thinking out loud. "The budget debate will take up the next three days. This is Monday. Burke and the others won't begin the rebuttal on our bill until Friday at the earliest. I can be back by then. I'll leave early in the morning." He stopped speaking and stared off into space, thinking about Lord Winston Harvellyn and Lady Alice, his mother. Kind, gracious people, the English aristocracy's finest. He would miss them both very much.

"What will you tell your wife?"

"What do you mean? I'll tell her—" He halted, remembering, and colored a little. "You mean, because it's Claudia."

"Well, yes. I should think that might be a bit touchy. None of my business, of course." There was a pause. "Why don't you tell her you're going to Cornwall to visit your father? If it's awkward about Claudia, I mean. He's ill, isn't he?"

"Yes . . . not seriously, I don't think." He put his hands in his pockets. "Damn it, Oliver. I don't want to lie to her."

"Ah," said Quinn. "Well, then."

"On the other hand . . ." He hesitated. "Oh hell, I don't know what I'll do."

"Whatever you think best, of course. Well." Quinn came toward him, his arm outstretched. "It's late, I must go." They shook hands.

"Oliver, if you feel I've let you down, I deeply regret it," Riordan said quietly. "I know what I promised, and I think you know how much your respect means to me. But I honestly believe I can do more for the country—*and* the monarchy—in this new life than I could ever have hoped to in the old."

Quinn's manner was unexpectedly sanguine. "No doubt you're right. It'll take some readjustment on my part, that's all. I'm getting old; such things take longer nowadays."

"Nonsense, you'll never be old." Riordan patted his friend's shoulder warmly, the closest either of them ever came to physical affection with each other.

At the door, Quinn said, as if on an impulse, "Would you like me to look in on Cassandra while you're gone? To make sure she's all right?"

Riordan was surprised, and deeply touched. "I'd like that very much. Thank you, Oliver. You know, I want so much for you and Cass to be friends."

Quinn didn't speak. He only smiled.

Upstairs, Riordan pushed open the bedroom door and went in. The bed was turned down; Cass's dress lay across a chair, her shoes and stockings on the floor beside it. Soft voices came from the dressing room. He went to the open door and stood, unnoticed, watching Clara brush his wife's hair. She was in her nightgown and wrapper. She saw him then, and for a long moment they gazed at each other's reflections in the glass.

Clara glanced between them. She raised knowing eyebrows, put the brush down, and went out without a word.

Cass examined his face anxiously. Something was on his mind, but he didn't seem distraught or upset. Had Quinn not told him after all? "Is he gone?" she asked tentatively.

"Yes."

"Did you . . . quarrel?"

"No, no." He picked up the brush and began to stroke her sleek, silky hair, watching her eyes close. After a while he abandoned the brush and used his hands, lifting the heavy mass from the back of her neck and letting it tumble through his fingers, a rich, inky black. A feast for his senses. He rested his hands on her shoulders, caressing her collarbone.

"Is anything wrong?"

"Yes, actually. It's . . ." He looked into her grave, concerned face. She was so precious to him. He thought of the time when they were fighting, when he thought he'd lost her. He took a breath. "It's my father."

"Your father?"

"He's more ill than I thought. I've just received word." He could hardly get the words out. Now he wished he'd told her the truth. Too late.

"Oh, Philip. I'm so sorry." She turned around and embraced him.

He held her head against his chest. "I have to go to Cornwall tomorrow."

"It's that bad? Shall I come with you?"

He swallowed and closed his eyes. "No. Thank you. I'll go on horseback and return on Friday."

"Friday? Oh, the debate."

"I don't really think he's in any danger, Cass. Please don't worry, will you? I'll just . . . see him and come right back."

She squeezed him tightly. "I'll miss you."

He buried his face in her hair, holding her, then brought her to her feet. "I'll miss you," he said fiercely. He opened her robe and pushed it back over her shoulders, watching in the mirror behind her as it fluttered to the floor. Then he took handfuls of her nightgown and slowly raised it over her knees, her thighs, her buttocks.

Cass watched his eyes turn opaque, still focused on her reflection. She put her hands on his face and pulled his mouth down. "Show me how much you'll miss me."

He did.

Cass leaned back against the carriage seat and closed her eyes, pleasantly exhausted after an afternoon of shopping and socializing. She'd joined the subscription library in Mayfair as well, and the haughty matrons who frequented it had welcomed her like visiting royalty. She'd felt almost, but not quite, like a fraud. She *was* a nice person, after all, and she was getting smarter all the time. If they liked her now solely because she was Mrs. Philip Riordan, that didn't mean that someday they wouldn't like her for herself. Armed with patience and a healthy measure of indifference, she had the leisure to wait for as long as it took.

Her hand went out to one of the wrapped parcels at her side. Her extravagance still shocked her. But she'd wanted something splendid to give Philip when he returned. It was a cloak of fine downy wool, black, lined with gray fox. Conservative but elegant, the shopkeeper assured her, and she knew it suited him perfectly. She could hardly wait to give it to him.

Two whole days before he returned! What would she do with herself? At first, as extraordinary as it seemed, she hadn't missed him at all; indeed, she'd very nearly welcomed his leaving. Since that day in the Members' Chapel when he'd asked her to marry him again, she'd existed in a state of near-total happiness, and the longer it went on the more it frightened her. Sustained joy like this wasn't natural, or so her experience had taught her. Riordan's absence would restore some needed balance, she reasoned, and return her to a more normal state of mind. She needed time to think, to put into perspective the events of the last few weeks, so that by the time he returned she might have discovered a way to extend the term of this precious, but surely temporary, euphoria.

But she hadn't found a way, and now all she wanted was for him to come home. What seemed unnatural now was living without him. She didn't want to ponder the miracle of their reconciliation anymore; she wanted to *see* him.

Two more days! How would she occupy her time? Jennie Willoughby had invited her to a card party tomorrow night, and that would be pleasant, of course. And she could always read, and work on her new article. She was tentatively calling it "Women and Revolution." This one would definitely be under her pseudonym; even Philip didn't know she was writing it.

She recalled a conversation with him one night last week as they lay in bed, reading. She'd interrupted him, as was her habit when something puzzled her or caught her fancy. And as was *his* unfailing habit, he'd put his book down and given her his complete attention.

"Philip, it says here that all men are created equal; no man has a natural authority over his fellow man . . . so on and so on and so on—" her finger skipped down the page—"conventions form the basis of authority among men; to renounce liberty is to renounce being a *man*; *man* consults his reason before listening to his inclinations . . . and so on and so forth. Darling, I was just wondering. Why is it that in all these political books I've been reading, they never, ever utter the word *women*? *Never*. Why?"

He'd frowned, considering it. A moment passed. Finally he answered. "It's included." And he turned a page and went back to his book.

She looked at him in silence. "Oh," she said, and after another minute went back to hers, not quite satisfied.

The carriage was slowing down, entering the solid, unpretentious respectability of Portman Square. She quite liked her new house, with its elegant stone facade, the gracefully arched entranceway.

A man was ascending the shallow front steps to the door. She didn't have to see his face to recognize him; she knew too well that gaunt body, the jerky, loose-limbed movements. It was Quinn.

Tripp helped her down and took her packages while Quinn waited for her on the top step. She went toward him steadily, head high, nothing in her look or manner betraying her deep unwillingness to see him. "Mr. Quinn," she greeted him, but didn't extend her hand. "Will you come in? Philip's out of town, but—"

"Yes, I know. It's you I've come to see."

The words gave her a quick chill, but she moved past him calmly enough and gave her coat to a servant in the foyer. Quinn wore none, not even a hat, though the day was freezing. She decided against taking him into the library; she wanted the formality of the drawing room for this meeting. She suspected neither of them wanted tea, but she ordered it anyway, then asked him to have a seat. She remained standing. He'd come to see her, he'd said, but evidently he wasn't going to speak first. He was watching her, his pale, other-worldly face expressionless, waiting for her to begin.

"Did you receive my note?" she asked finally. "I sent it to you more than a week ago."

"I got it."

There was a pause. So he was going to make it as difficult as possible. "Why haven't you told Philip, then?" she blurted out.

"Told him what?"

"The truth!" Her anger hit the surface with unexpected force, taking her by surprise. She heard the note of fury in her tone and took several deep breaths to calm herself. She would accomplish nothing by screaming at him.

"Mr. Quinn," she began again. "The last time you and I spoke alone, you told me something about my husband I now know to have been . . . not the truth. The best possible interpretation I can put on it is that you made a mistake. That seems incredible, but I shrink from the only other explanation that comes to mind—that you deliberately lied to me so that I would leave Philip and go to Wade."

Quinn crossed his long shanks and leaned back. "I still want you to go to Wade."

She stared. "But do you deny that you lied?"

"Yes, I deny it," he answered readily.

"But—we're to be *married*! Married *again*, I should say!"

"Do you think so?" He clasped one bony knee in both hands. "I wouldn't count on it. In betting parlance, that would not be a sure thing." He reached into his jacket pocket. "This is, however."

"What is it?" She looked with distaste at the envelope he put on the sofa beside him.

"Money. The other thousand pounds you were promised after the assignment was completed. I'm willing to give it to you now if you'll return to Wade."

Cass couldn't quite summon a laugh, though one certainly seemed called for now. "You must be completely out of your mind. Philip would kill me if I saw Wade, for one thing, and for—"

"Tell me, Cassandra, are *you* afraid of Wade?"

"I—" She paused, uncertain of the answer. "It doesn't matter whether I am or not, I'm not going to see him. My God, I can't believe you would offer me money! Philip is my *husband*, and he—"

"And you have no need of money, that being the case," he finished with a snide smile.

The anger came bubbling up again, and this time it wouldn't be suppressed. "I'm through protecting you!" she cried. "I intend to tell Philip everything I know about you as soon as he comes home. I don't care anymore about your so-called friendship, and I suspect you've never cared about it either. I think you used me, and you've used my husband, and you'd use anyone in the world if you thought they could help you get what you want! Did you steal our marriage certificate, Mr. Quinn? Did you bribe the tollkeeper to say he hadn't married us?"

She went closer, unafraid, her eyes flashing fire. "Philip never tried to kill anyone, did he? Admit it! You told him that so he'd feel obligated to you and do what you asked. You're a vicious manipulator. You took a boy's innocent adulation and used it for your own ends. You tried to make Philip believe he was a violent, alcoholic lout who would try to kill a man in a drunken rage and then turn on his best friend. How did you really get that scar, I wonder? I'll wager Philip had nothing to do with it!"

She was shaking with emotion, on the verge of weeping. There was a tap at the door and she turned away to hide her face. The maid put the tea tray down, curtsied, and went away. When Cass turned back, Quinn was calmly pouring tea.

"Sugar?" When she didn't respond, he dropped in a teaspoonful, shrugging, then poured himself a cup. He took a few audible sips before setting the cup down and looking at her.

"I've never liked you, Miss Merlin," he said matter-of-factly, "and I've done a rather poor job of pretending I did. But what I told you about Philip was the simple truth: he did not marry you. I'll go a step further. If he *ever* marries you, I'll add another thousand pounds to your fee."

"I want you to leave now." She could barely contain herself.

"I'm not ready to leave." He stood up and came toward her. She saw the dislike in his eyes, undisguised at last, and resisted taking a step backward. "Listen to me, girl. Wade is a dangerous man, but he means you no harm. You have to go back to him and find out what he intends. Listen to me!" He grabbed her arm when she started to move away and held it in a hard, painful grip. "Time is running out. He's booked passage on a boat to France in two days. Whatever is to happen will be soon, and *we must stop it*. Is that clear to you?" He took her by the shoulders and shook her, peering into her eyes with feverish intensity. "This is more important than your jealousies and stupid quarrels! This is the King of England! Do you—"

"Stop it! Let me go!" She shoved him off violently and stumbled to the door. "If you don't leave this minute, I'll call the servants and have you thrown out. I mean it." She was trembling, breathing hard, her knees shaking.

His manner changed. He lowered his voice. "I'm sorry, I was too harsh. Forgive me for frightening you."

"I'm not frightened. I want you to go."

"In a moment. I want to leave you with one more thought." He picked up the envelope and brought it to her, forcing it into her hand, squeezing her fingers around it. "Philip told you he was going to visit his poor, ailing father, didn't he?" he asked, his face close to hers. She could smell the peculiar essence of his breath. "He didn't. He lied to you again. He went to see Claudia Harvellyn, in Somerset. Her country estate at Wellington."

"Liar." She tried to pull away, but couldn't.

"He's in love with her. He always has been. The baser side of his character conceived a physical passion for you, Cassandra, and he—"

"Let me *go*!"

"He pretended to marry you so he could have you. He's almost through with you now, but not quite. I know this because he told me."

"Bastard!"

"Since you don't believe me, I suggest you ask the servants. Ask Tripp where he took him in the carriage yesterday—to meet the coach going to Wellington, not Launceton. Ask John Walker where his employer went. Ask Beal—"

With a final jerk, she wrenched her hand out of his paralyzing grip and fell back against the door. Unable to speak, she pulled it open and stood aside, holding onto the knob for support.

Quinn's face was full of contempt. He pulled something else from his pocket. "Here's the letter he wrote her. Never mind how I got it." Cass shrank back as if from a poisonous reptile. "You don't want it? I'll tell you what it says. 'My dearest Claudia. I will be with you as soon as I possibly can, tomorrow afternoon at the latest. All my love, Philip.' It's dated Monday night. You still don't want it? I'll put it here on the table."

"Get out," she tried to say, but the words were inaudible.

"Find out what Wade intends, Miss Merlin. It's all you can do now to redeem your miserable life. Send word either to me or to Philip as soon as you learn anything. Then take the money and get out of London."

He went past her, down the hall, and out the front door.

XVII

A GARGOYLE FOR A DOOR KNOCKER. HOW FITTING, thought Cass, reaching up to the hideous, half-human face and letting it fall against the brass plate underneath. The sound was loud and unpleasant. She closed her eyes, waiting, thinking of nothing, and in a moment Wade's butler opened the door.

"Mrs. Riordan, how nice to see you." He stepped back to let her enter.

"Is Mr. Wade at home, Martin?"

"He is, madam, but he's entertaining visitors at the moment. Business associates, I believe. Would you care to wait in the drawing room? It shouldn't be much longer now."

His amiable formality allowed her to relax a little; what, after all, could happen to her in such staid, conventional surroundings? She followed Martin into the drawing room, and a moment later he brought her a glass of sherry and some biscuits.

It was eleven o'clock in the morning, but she sipped the sherry gratefully. For courage. ·

She heard masculine voices raised, coming from the direction of Wade's study. She went to the doorway and listened intently. But she could make out none of the words and dared not go any closer; the study was at the far end of the hall and she would easily be noticed by any passing servant.

As little as she wanted to see him, she wished Wade would come, and knew it was because she was afraid to be alone, afraid to think. She'd done enough of that last night. Her eyes burned from weeping and her head was fuzzy from sleeplessness. There was a physical pain in the center of her chest. She pressed her fist against it for relief, but there was no relief.

She went to the window and gazed out at the dreary day, tracing the trails of raindrops on the glass with her finger. *Philip, Philip*! It was a near-constant chant on the edges of her mind. *Why did you do it*? *How could you hurt me this much*? She put her face in her hands, swallowing to keep the tears back. If only she could hate him! This time her humiliation was total, but the pain she felt was even stronger than the anger. And the worst was not knowing why. What had she ever done to deserve cruelty like this? What contempt he must feel for her! But why, *why*? As excruciating as it would be, she needed to ask him. When this dangerous game with Wade was finally played out, she would return and confront him. Powerless as she was, she would not let him go completely free.

But what was she doing here? *I'm here because I want to be*, she told herself, beginning to pace between the door and the windows. But was it true? What if this was only a childish, self-destructive impulse, a craven attempt to make Philip sorry?

She recalled her state of mind at Ladymere all those months ago, when she had longed to do something gloriously heroic so that he would admire her—no, so that he would love her more than he did Claudia. Was that what this was all about? Was it?

No, she didn't think so. She'd been a child then. She was anything but a child now. Wade frightened her, but she was here. If Riordan hadn't forbidden it, she'd have come before now, regardless of the danger. Why? Because she believed in the importance of the job Quinn had hired her to do, and because they'd made a bargain and she needed to keep her word. The fact that Riordan didn't want her now only made things easier. Clearer. Now she had no attachments, no one to hurt, and no one to worry about her. She would "redeem her miserable life," as Quinn phrased it. She'd grown to revere the institution of the English monarchy as she'd read and listened and learned; she had no wish to be a martyr, but she was willing to take this risk, on her own, to try to preserve it. However murky her other motives might be, this one was true and real.

But was she really going to be able to do it? Or was Quinn's faith in her ability to uncover Wade's plans only a fanatic's delusion? She couldn't think straight, couldn't feel anything but pain; how was she supposed to outwit an assassin? She sipped more sherry and tried to clear her mind. But behind everything, weighing her down like clods of earth on a coffin, was the knowledge that regardless of what words she found the courage to say to Riordan, in a matter of days she would never see him again. That made everything else in her life, including this last-minute try at foiling Wade, seem as cold as dead ashes.

She heard the study door open, and the men's

voices came to her clearly. She moved a few steps to see down the hall, but kept away from the door. Besides Wade, she recognized two of the half-dozen gentlemen standing in the foyer: Ian Thorn, whom Riordan already knew to be one of Wade's henchmen, and Mr. Sherwood, the silent, older man she'd met at the house party in Lancashire. So he *was* one of them. She listened carefully, but their conversation was unremarkable; whatever secrets there were to tell had been told already. At that moment the butler said something in Wade's ear and he looked up. Cass was in shadow, but she had the feeling he was staring directly at her. Something in his face caused her to feel the first faint tremor of panic.

The men left—gradually, she thought, as though not wanting to vacate the house in a group. Wade strolled down the hall toward her in his unhurried way. A part of her noted the elegant combination of his plum velvet jacket and dove-gray waistcoat. He stopped at the door and stood for a long moment without speaking. She could think of nothing to say to break the odd silence; the expression on his face was disturbing but indecipherable.

"I'm sorry if my coming here is a bother to you, Colin," she finally managed, "but I didn't know where else to go. I've left Philip for good. You told me once I could stay with you. I'm hoping you'll let me now."

He came closer, still without greeting her, watching her in a peculiar, measuring way. "Why did you leave him?" he asked suddenly. "What did he do?"

"He—" It wouldn't do to say he'd broken her heart. "He beat me. When he was drunk. I'm never going back to him."

Something flashed across his features. He put his hands on her upper arms and kneaded them, bringing her closer. There was a brief, excited flicker in his cinnamon-colored eyes. "How did he do it? With his hands? A strap?"

Appalled, she pulled out of his obsessive grip. "I don't want to talk about it. It was horrible!"

"Of course," he said quickly, his voice softening, his face assuming the proper attitude of sympathy. "And now you're here, asking to stay with me. But are you quite sure it's what you really want, Cassandra?"

She knew what he was asking. It was the moment she'd been dreading. Up to now it had always been possible to back away, pretend she didn't understand the arrangement and leave before things went too far. But not anymore. Staying with Wade would mean sleeping with him—it would be folly to pretend otherwise. If she was going to do it, it would be because she chose to do it. That was important to her. She couldn't bear to think Riordan's brutality had thrust her into a situation she couldn't control, or that she would be so passive as to allow this thing to happen to her without any exertion of her own will. She made her decision quickly, before her fear could cripple her.

"Yes, Colin, I'm quite sure."

He smiled with his lips. "Then of course you may stay. I wouldn't want you anywhere else."

She shuddered involuntarily. There was silence again until she recalled herself enough to say, "But—perhaps it's an awkward time for you?"

"Awkward? In what way?"

"I couldn't help noticing the men you were meeting with just now. I wondered if they might be part of your . . . organization." She waited for him to speak, but he didn't. "And then I thought perhaps you were planning something important, since the . . . thing we spoke of before never . . .

never happened." Oh, why wouldn't he say something? She feared she was giving herself away while he only watched and waited.

"And you wondered what happened that day in Parliament, did you?" he asked finally, pleasantly. "I got your note, by the way. I thought it too dangerous to reply."

"Oh, I see." She didn't know exactly what he meant, but kept talking. "I did wonder what had happened, yes, after what you'd told me. But I assumed something had gone wrong and you were being cautious, waiting for another time. And then when all those people were arrested and no— assassin was among them, I thought someone must have found out the plan and told the authorities."

She swallowed, feeling herself flush. She'd never been a very good liar; it didn't help to think that her life might depend on being one now. "You don't have to tell me anything," she rushed on, "if you think it unwise. I'm not really asking you to—I only came because I had nowhere else to go, and you were kind to me before."

"Kind? Is that what you thought it was, kindness? My dear, I'd have sworn we understood each other better than that." He surrounded her throat with one hand, squeezing the sensitive cords playfully, hurtfully. She held perfectly still and didn't breathe. He kissed her hard, his lips closed, eyes wide open, still holding her by the throat. "I'm so glad you've come," he whispered. "And I want to tell you all about the plan. I want you to know everything."

Why didn't the words bring any thrill of triumph? She'd always thought his face cruel, and never more so than now. His eyes were glittering with suppressed excitement. She knew with deep certainty that he was going to hurt her, that the price she would pay for his revelations would be very dear. She prayed for courage while he caressed her, murmuring in her ear, "But come upstairs with me first. There's something I've always wanted to do with you. Then I'll tell you everything. Will you come?"

"Yes," she whispered, but hardly any sound came out.

"And you want to come, don't you? You want me to touch you. Say it."

"I—" She shut her eyes and drew a shallow breath. "I want you to touch me."

He kissed her again, smiling his ice-cold smile. Then, with his arm around her shoulders, he led her out of the room.

"The master told me t' come see if you needed anything, mum." The maid stared discreetly at the pale young woman who was sitting at the edge of the bed, buttoning her shift with shaky fingers. She had to repeat herself before the lady looked up and noticed her. "Can I get you anything at all, mum? Some tea?"

"Some tea," Cass murmured, but she wasn't ordering it so much as saying the words out loud to make sense of them.

"Yes, some nice hot tea. Would you like some?"

Cass put her hands to her temples and tried to think. "No . . . my dress," she said finally, pointing to where it lay on the floor. "It's—I've torn it. Can you—" She couldn't seem to think of the simplest words.

"Yes, mum, I can sew it for you." The maid bent and retrieved the wrinkled gown. She had a sweet face. She kept it poker-straight, but Cass looked away to avoid her eyes. "Will there be anything else, then?"

"No. Yes—Could I have a pen and some paper?"

"Why, yes, mum."

"Thank you." Unable to return the maid's smile, she only watched her curtsy and walk from the room.

Presently she got up from the bed, stiffly, and crossed to the mirror over the bureau. With a mixture of curiosity and revulsion, she stared at her image. She was as pale as a wax figure, but otherwise she looked much the same as she always looked. Only one bruise showed, a purplish, spreading stain on her throat where he'd pressed his thumb. Her eyes were flat-gray and expressionless; the horror didn't show, either. She felt a humming, tingling numbness; it began in her blood and beat into her limbs and her brain, a fragile shield, a membrane as thin as an insect's wing between herself and hysteria.

She put her hands on the edge of the bureau and straightened her shoulders painfully, closing her eyes to the sight of her own face. If she looked at it any longer, she might drive herself mad. She turned away and stared around the room, taking better note of its overstuffed, almost feminine opulence than she had when he'd first led her into it. There were trunks and boxes everywhere, proof that he was going away. Suddenly her knees were shaking; she had to sit down. She moved aside half a dozen pink pillows and lowered herself onto a purple satin settee. For a moment she rested with her head in her hands, but then she sat up straight. She had to get hold of herself.

It could have been worse. He hadn't raped her, after all—though not for lack of trying. It might have been better if he had. Then he wouldn't have been so angry, wouldn't have had the leisure to think of so many ways to make her pay for his failure. At least she hadn't had to pretend to enjoy it. She'd quickly realized that he didn't want her excited, he wanted her frightened. So that part had been easy.

Without warning, a sob rose from some deep place inside, and before she could think of controlling it she was weeping without restraint. She'd hated the numbness, but this was even worse. This pain was too intense, as if with each hiccuping cry her heart were being wrenched from her chest. She fell to her side and let the choking, corrosive sobs overwhelm her.

Gradually she quieted. The peace of exhaustion was a blessing. The realization came slowly that she had not lost her mind; she was not going to lurch into hysteria. She was herself. She had survived.

And she knew what she knew. There was nothing left now but to tell Quinn. Then it would be over.

There was a tap at the door and the maid came in again. Cass took the writing materials from her without a word and she curtsied herself out, smiling her friendly smile.

Wade had a small writing desk set in the wall between the windows. She opened it and sat down. For a moment she considered whether she ought to direct her letter to Quinn or to Riordan. The former, she decided. Apart from the pain and awkwardness of addressing any words at all to Philip, what she had to convey was urgent; a tragedy might occur if she sent her note to him and he ended up dallying in Somerset with Claudia past Friday. She daubed the pen in the inkwell and began to write.

"Dear Mr. Quinn:

"The king is to be murdered on Saturday as he rides with his hunting party to Windsor. As the road turns south outside of Eton, four men dressed as monks will offer to bless him. But they will set upon him and try to kill him. I do not know the names of the men; all are ready to give up their lives for their cause. Colin is their leader. He plans to sail for Calais tomorrow night, and believes I am going with him.

"Our business is finished now. I have your money and you have my information. In a few days I will leave London, as you advised.

Cassandra Merlin."

There, it was done. If she could talk Wade into letting her leave the house on the pretext of some errand, there would be no need to send this letter. But of course she couldn't leave that to chance; she would try to enlist the maid's help now, before he returned. She'd seemed kind; it was likely she would take money in exchange for handing a note to a messenger and saying nothing of it to her employer. After that, Cass could worry about getting away from here. The important thing was to get the information to Quinn. What time was it now? Two or three in the afternoon, she thought. She must act quickly. She folded the letter and addressed it.

There was a soft knock at the door.

Surely it was the maid. All the same, she put the note inside the front of her shift and stood away from the desk. "Come in."

It was Wade.

He closed the door behind him and strolled toward her, his movements as languid as always. His eyes flickered over her half-clad figure with cold contempt, and in a flash she remembered all the things he'd done to her, the things he'd made her do. Would he try again? With ice-calm certainty she knew that if he did, one of them would be dead when it was over.

"Feeling better, my love?"

"No." She'd told him she felt nauseated before he'd finally given up and left her alone. It wasn't a lie then, and it wasn't now. He smiled slightly at her response. "Colin, I left the house so quickly, I didn't bring anything with me. I'd like to go back and get my clothes."

"Would you? What for?" His smile widened at her blank look. "You won't be needing any here. Oh—I told the maid to throw your gown away. You won't be needing that, either."

"You what?"

He laughed outright. "Close your mouth, Cassandra, you look foolish."

"Colin, what are you talking about? Of course I'll need my clothes." She felt a prickle of horror, but managed to speak calmly, as if taking his words for a joke.

"No, not really. Not after tonight. By the way, love, what were you writing?"

She felt the blood draining from her face. "I wasn't writing anyth—Oh, you mean the paper the maid brought? I th-thought I might write a note to my aunt, to let her know where I've gone."

"Your aunt? Oh, that's not very good," he admonished, shaking his head with mock sternness. "You should've said your cousin, perhaps, or a friend. Much more believable." He came closer. "Where's the letter?"

"Letter? What do you mean?"

"Let's see, it's not on the *desk*," he said archly, moving a few articles around, "not anywhere in *sight*," scanning the room. He smiled again. "Why, Cass, it must be on *you*!"

She backed away, her hands out to hold him off. "Colin, don't. I have no letter, I swear. You're frightening me, please—no!"

He made a grab for her hair and pulled her head back, using his other hand to rip open the front of her chemise. The folded letter fell to the floor. Then he pushed her hard in the chest with the flat of his hand, sending her back against the bedpost with a violent crack. "Sit down on the bed and don't move," he snarled.

She obeyed, trembling, holding the back of her head with one hand and the torn halves of her shift with the other. The truth was dawning on her and a well of terror was opening at her feet.

He stooped to pick up the note and opened it with a flourish. " 'Dear Mr. Quinn,' " he began, mocking her in a high, exaggeratedly feminine voice. " 'The king is to be murdered on Saturday as he rides with his hunting party to Windsor.' Oh, very good. Splendid, in fact." He read the rest to himself. "I like this part—'In a few days I will leave London, *as you advised*.' A nice touch, that. It's bound to inspire a world of guilt in the poor fellow after you're dead. Women are so skillful at inducing guilt; I think it's one of your special gifts."

"You knew all along," she whispered. She was having trouble making her tongue work. She gauged the distance between herself and the door, and despaired.

"All along," he agreed cheerfully. "Did you think it was coincidence that I appeared that first night at the Clarion Club? By no means. I did it just to make Riordan squirm." He grinned at her, enjoying her fear. "Our first meeting in the park was more contrived than you thought, too. You really threw yourself into it, didn't you, darling? I quite admired you when you fell off your horse."

"What are you going to do?" She looked behind him frantically. Would it do any good to start screaming?

"You mean about you? I'm afraid I'm going to have to punish you. You've been so deceitful, Cassandra, completely untrustworthy. I don't believe you've ever told me the whole truth about anything." He backed up to the wardrobe without taking his eyes from her and pulled down a dressing gown of salmon-colored silk. In one violent motion he ripped out the long cord around the waist and came toward her, twisting it in his hands. He laughed at her expression. "Oh, I'm not going to strangle you, Cass. Not yet. Be a love and hold out your hands. No? You won't help me?"

She opened her mouth to scream. She saw the flash of his fisted hand an instant before it smashed against her temple, and she was unconscious before her head hit the mattress behind her.

She awoke to the sound of her own muffled groan and a sharp throbbing in her skull. Almost worse was the stiffness in her upper arms, which were stretched over her head as she lay face-down on Wade's bed. She raised her head groggily and saw that her wrists were tied to one of the bedposts at the bottom of the bed. The rest of her was free. She sat up slowly on her elbows, dizzy and nauseated, feeling the blood beat painfully in her temples. She dragged her legs to the side of the bed, dropped them over, and sagged against the bedpost.

He knew. Her brain was sluggish and unfocused, but a score of unsolved mysteries were answered now. She understood why he'd treated her so roughly that first evening when he'd brought her home to her aunt's house, and again on other occasions. He'd known he could do anything he wanted, and she would endure it because she had to. It was what she was being paid for. For him it had all been a sadistic game, and it wasn't over yet.

He must have known Philip would follow her to Ladymere, too. He'd gotten him drunk on purpose, she realized—though surely he couldn't have foreseen the bizarre consequences of that. They'd all been Wade's puppets—Riordan, Quinn, herself. Instead of thwarting an assassin, they'd been aiding him.

But *how* had he known? At the Clarion Club when she'd first met Philip—no one but Quinn had known he would impersonate Wade that night for her benefit! She pressed her fists to her aching forehead and tried to think. Did it mean Quinn was a traitor? She couldn't believe it; it was too preposterous.

It didn't matter much, either. Unless she could escape, the King of England would be murdered in two days, and she probably much sooner. Her numbed fingers couldn't untie a bow, much less the vicious knots Wade had pulled against her wrists. His bedroom was at the center of the house and its windows faced the alley, not the street. Calling for outside help would be futile. But what about inside help? She stood up.

"Help me! Help! Somebody help me!" She took a deep breath and screamed as loud as she could.

Within seconds, the door opened and the maid burst in.

"Help me!" Cass cried breathlessly. "Untie my hands! Wade—" She halted on a gasp, shrinking back against the post as the young, fresh-faced maid raised a poker over her head and waved it threateningly.

"He says t' hit you with this if you make a sound! Shut your mouth unless you want me t' bash in your brains! Do you hear?" Cass nodded, horrified, and the maid lowered the poker. They were both breathing hard and staring wild-eyed at each other. "I'll do it, too, don't think I won't! I've done it before!"

"Please," Cass tried again, more softly, fear making her lips stiff. "For the love of God, I'm begging you—he's going to kill me! If you'll help me, I'll give you money. I've got a thousand pounds, you can have all of it. Only help me—"

"A thousand pounds?" said Wade from the door. "My, Quinn was more generous than I expected. Too bad you won't be able to enjoy it. Thank you, Annie, you did very well. Go back into the hall now and wait."

The maid actually blushed with pleasure, curtsied to her master, and retreated, carrying her poker.

Wade came closer to examine the knots around her wrists, and she had to struggle not to cringe away from him. He put his hand inside the gaping folds of her shift and fondled her insultingly. She strained away but couldn't escape. "What a great cow you are," he said, his lips curling in an ugly snarl. "I despise you, you know. All of you."

And in that moment she understood at last that he meant women. No wonder he'd never pressed her to become his mistress, nor even seriously tried to seduce her. He was incapable of it. The only way he could enjoy her at all was by hurting her. Another piece of the puzzle fell into place.

"You'll be glad to know, Cass, that your note to Quinn has been handed to a messenger, and even now it's winging its way to his depressing little flat in Lincoln's Inn. If he's at home, he should have it within the hour."

She stared. "You *sent* it?"

"Oh, indeed I did. I read it again, darling, and I really must compliment you on that brave, fatalistic tone. Very effective, I must say."

"But why? *Why* did you send it?"

"You really can't guess? I thought you were more astute, I did, indeed."

Suddenly she knew. "Because it's not true," she breathed. "Oh, my God."

He touched the tip of her nose waggishly. "Excellent! Smart girl! No, it's not true, not a word of it.

But it'll certainly occupy the time and attention of a lot of people while the true plot goes forward. Can you guess who's really going to die, my love? No? Think. You've become such an intellectual lately, surely it'll come to you. If not our dimwitted monarch, then who? Who's the Revolution's worst enemy in England?"

He watched her expectantly, then threw his head back and laughed. "I believe she's got it!" he crowed. "I knew you were a clever girl!" He put his hand under her jaw and squeezed it hard, bringing her face close to his. "But there's one more detail I'll wager you haven't guessed. It's a surprise, and I've been saving it for you until this moment." He stepped back. "Come in now," he called over his shoulder.

Her eyes flew to the open door. A moment passed, and Wade began to look annoyed. At last a man appeared in the doorway. Cass had to blink to believe her own vision. "John?" she croaked. "Is it you?"

It was Walker, Riordan's secretary. Her shy friend, the man she'd always thought had a crush on her. He looked away, embarrassed perhaps by her near-nakedness, and didn't speak.

"Say something, John, don't be rude," Wade teased.

Walker glanced at him, then back at Cass. "I'm . . . sorry."

Her voice was a desperate whisper. "John, are you helping him? Oh God, it's not possible!"

He dropped his gaze and stared at the floor between them.

Wade went to him then and crooked a casual arm over his shoulder. "Now, this I never expected," he said silkily, his face close to Walker's. Cass watched them in sick fascination. "You're sorry for her, aren't you? I believe you actually like her. Do you want her? There's time before we have to leave." Walker colored and tried to move away, but Wade held him still. "It's all right, my feelings aren't hurt. I would like to watch, though." He put his hand behind Walker's neck and massaged him slowly. His voice dropped intimately. "What do you say?"

"No! No."

"Well, that's definite enough," Wade chuckled. He kept stroking the younger man's neck. "Tell Cassandra about your special talent, John. I'll bet she thinks all you do is Riordan's drudge work. Tell her what a ready hand you are with a pistol. Especially at close range, indoors, with no distractions."

"What are you going to do?" Cass breathed, horrified, when Walker didn't speak.

Finally he looked at her. "I'm going to kill Edmund Burke."

There was a look in his eyes she'd never seen before, a bright, hard purposefulness that was all the more frightening because it was perfectly sane. She held his gaze, searching for a way to connect, to make contact. "John, you can't. Think! This is murder, cold-blooded and cruel. He's an old man, a decent man—"

"He's the enemy!" Walker interrupted hotly. "If it weren't for him the English would have sided with the French patriots long before now. It's his lies and slanders that have brought our countries to the brink of war!"

His savage tone told her further argument would be a waste of breath. She hardly recognized the soft-spoken, retiring secretary she'd known in this grim, violently committed revolutionary. So he had been the leak. She tried to absorb it, but it was almost impossible to believe. Still, his presence was the proof. She remembered the day he'd given her Burke's *Reflections on the Revolution in France* in Riordan's library, with instructions from his employer to read it. How ironic the situation must have seemed to him.

She knew it was hopeless, but she tried again. "Please listen to me. Killing Burke now won't accomplish anything. He's already done his work, it's too late to change popular opinion. If anything, you'll make a martyr of him and only do harm to your cause. Oh, John, listen to me! It's insane to think this can—"

"You're wrong. Burke's working on a new diatribe now. Riordan's got a copy of it and I've read it. He calls the Jacobins atheists, murderers, and barbarians. For men like us he advocates exile and death. He's a cancer! He has to be silenced! He's—"

"And tomorrow he will be," Wade interjected smoothly. "As he rises to attack your dear husband's reform bill, darling. As Riordan's clerk, John will be an inconspicuous nobody in the venerable Chamber; he'll be able to get as close to Burke as he likes."

Cass was aghast. "But they'll catch you, John! You'll never get away!"

"Not at all," Wade insisted, "we have an excellent plan for—"

But Walker interrupted him firmly. "That may well be true. But you see, I'm willing to take the risk."

Cass rested her head against the post she was tied to and fought back tears of desperation. What could she say to him, what could she do? He was determined to go through with this regardless of the consequences, and she could think of no other arguments that would sway him. She watched as

Wade ran his thumb across Walker's lips, and for a second she thought they would kiss. Naive as she was, it was finally obvious even to her that they were lovers.

"Doesn't it bother you," she burst out recklessly, "that you're taking all the risks while he sails safely away to France?"

Wade's eyes gleamed with malice, but Walker only shook his head as if he pitied her. "Good-bye, Miss Merlin. I'm sorry you came here today."

He was leaving. Panic engulfed her. "Wait, don't go! John, please—oh please, help me!" The pleading note in her voice appalled her, but she couldn't help it.

He wouldn't look at her. He stood with his back to her in the doorway and said, "I told you. I'm very sorry." And he went out.

"I'll be with you in a moment," Wade called after him, then moved toward her. "I wish I could stay and chat, love, but you'll appreciate that this is a busy, busy day for me. Moving, you know; such a bore. Still, I'll see you in an hour or so, I promise. I have one more tiny little surprise. To see what it is, you'll have to go down to the cellar with me. Too bad you aren't dressed more warmly, isn't it? Ah, well, you won't be there long enough for it to matter. This surprise will be over very quickly."

She jerked away when he tried to kiss her. "Bastard!" she spat. For once her hatred was even stronger than her fear of him. "Animal! Rot in hell, you murdering son of a bitch! You may kill me, but you'll never get away with murdering Edmund Burke. They'll track you down and catch you, and then they'll hang you! You'll never—"

"Oh, Cass, you guessed!" he interrupted with mock dismay. "Now the surprise is ruined. How did you know?"

"Know what?"

"Why, that I'm going to hang you! My, you *are* a clever girl." This time when he kissed her she didn't react at all. "'Bye for now, darling, I *must* run. Oh, and be as quiet as a little mouse, won't you? *Entre nous*, I think Annie would as soon bash your head in with that poker as not. Ta!"

XVIII

RIORDAN BROUGHT HIS FIST BACK AND HAMMERED IT AS hard as he could against the scarred oak door. His breath came fast from taking the steep steps to Quinn's flat three at a time. The exertion and the pain in his knuckles eased his need to do violence, but did nothing to dampen his rage. When the door didn't open soon enough, he kicked it savagely with his riding boot. He still wore his spurs; they made a delicate, jingling counterpoint to the harsh sound of hard leather smiting wood.

"What's the meaning of—Philip! For heaven's sake—"

Riordan shouldered past him without a word and slammed the door shut.

"This is a surprise," Quinn said after a second's hesitation. "I didn't expect you back until tomorrow." He was in his shirt and waistcoat; the remains of a grim-looking meal lay on a table pulled close to the meager fire.

"I'll bet you didn't."

"How is poor Claudia?"

"Recovering." Riordan spoke through his teeth. His fury was reined in but obvious. That Quinn was ignoring it only made him angrier.

"I'm glad to hear it. Sit down, won't you? Will you have some—"

"Enough!" Riordan slashed the air with his hand, then dug into his pocket and drew out a wrinkled piece of paper. "I want to know what this means. Take it. Read it!" Quinn took the note. When he didn't read it out loud, Riordan read it for him, his voice vibrating with furious accusation. "'Quinn told me everything. I will never forgive you. Cass.'" He grabbed the letter back and crumpled it in his fist. "Explain it, Oliver! I'm waiting!"

Quinn ran a long-fingered hand through his thinning hair. "Oh dear," he said with sincere-sounding regret, "this is most distressing; no wonder you're upset. And it's my fault, I admit it. When I was visiting with Cassandra yesterday—you recall I asked if I might look in on her?—I, ah, accidentally let it slip that you were in Somerset, not Cornwall. It was purely a slip of the tongue, but she caught it immediately. After that it seemed better to tell her the whole truth. I'm so sorry, Philip. Does this note mean she's left home? I must say, I'm surprised. I never thought she'd—"

"Stop it! You're lying!"

Quinn's thin nostrils flared. "I've apologized for my carelessness. I will not be insulted."

"That won't work this time," Riordan snarled. He pulled something else from his pocket. "Recognize this? It's the note I sent Claudia by messenger. How do you suppose Cass got it?"

"I haven't the slightest idea. What are you implying?" But his pale face had gone paler and his tone was unconvincing.

Riordan's temper exploded. "You gave it to her!" he roared. "It was you, wasn't it? *You're* the one who told Cass we weren't married! Admit it, damn you!"

"I have no idea what you're talking about. Calm yourself, this isn't like you. I would hate to see you revert back to the kind of—"

Riordan's vicious growl cut him off as he came at him, but at that moment someone knocked at the door. Scarcely able to hide his relief, Quinn went past him and opened it.

It was a young man in a dirty coat. "Got a message for a Mr. Quinn, from Beekman Place," he announced. "You him?"

Quinn took the note. "Yes, I'm—"

"Who gave it to you?" Riordan cut in, shoving Quinn aside violently.

"A girl," answered the messenger, backing up.

"What girl? What did she look like?"

The young man blanched. "Pretty, young—"

"Black hair?" Riordan thundered.

"No—yellow!"

"I'm having the house watched," Quinn said quickly when Riordan turned on him. The messenger saw his chance to escape, and ran. "I tell you, Philip, I have a girl inside the house. This is from her!"

"You're lying. Give me that."

"No."

"Give it to me!"

Quinn turned away, but Riordan spun him around by the shoulder and grabbed the note out of his hand. For a moment they were both shocked by his violence. Seeing the look on Riordan's face, Quinn stopped sputtering and took a step back.

Riordan recognized the handwriting immediately and his body froze. Oh Jesus, he thought. Oh Christ Almighty. With numb, nerveless fingers, he

opened the letter and read. When he finished, he
looked up at Quinn, and there was murder in his
eyes. "You bastard," he said in a rabid whisper.
"You sent her to him, didn't you?"

Quinn shook his head over and over, swallowing.
"I didn't, she did it on her own."

"Read it, you lying son of a bitch."

"Philip, listen—"

"Read it!" He forced it into his hand.

Quinn read. Suddenly his face relaxed. "At last,"
he breathed softly. He looked up. "This is it, Philip.
Finally. We have him now. He won't—"

Riordan seized him by the shirt and slammed
him against the near wall. "I don't care about
Wade!" he roared. "I should kill you for this! But
you're not worth it. But I'll do it anyway if Cass is
hurt!" His voice lowered; his eyes narrowed malev-
olently. "You never cared a damn about me, did
you? It was an act from the beginning. All those
years I idolized you, prayed that you'd come back,
you never thought of me once. You wouldn't even
have remembered my name if you hadn't thought
of a way to use me!"

"That's not true." Quinn's voice shook. "I always wanted what was best for you."

"You're a liar. You don't know how to tell the
truth."

"I admit I thought your marriage was a mistake,
but—"

"So you destroyed it."

"I thought you'd come to your senses soon and
realize she was beneath you. Philip, she's impure,
she's not the woman for you, don't you see?
Claudia was supposed to be your wife, she was—"

"What the hell are you talking about?" Riordan's
face was ugly; his grip tightened viciously. "What
did you think would happen if you succeeded? Did
you think she would disappear into thin air?"

"She had money. She was going to leave the country!"

He bared his teeth in a savage snarl and shook Quinn like a dog. "Who do you think you are? God? This is my life! You thought you had a damned puppet, didn't you? A lapdog for the king and his ministers, someone you could rely on in Parliament to always do the right thing. You even had my wife picked out for me!" Quinn didn't deny it. "You'll have to tell your employers the truth soon, Oliver, because they're in for a rude surprise. Tell them that because of your arrogance and stupidity they've lost their pawn." He shook him again. "It doesn't matter anymore what you did to me, my friend, but you're going to pay for hurting Cass. I swear it." He shoved him hard against the wall and released him, then headed for the door.

"Wait! You can't go there. Stop, you'll ruin everything!"

Riordan turned around in disbelief. "What?"

"If you go there now, Wade will only call off the plan again! We'll be back where we started!"

Riordan almost laughed. "Do you think I care about that? He's got Cass, you son of a bitch. He's a murderer and he's got my wife!" He started again for the door.

"Stop."

Something in his voice made Riordan pause with his hand on the knob. He turned around slowly. He flinched, but wasn't really surprised to see the pistol in Quinn's hand, leveled at his midsection. Something inside him shifted painfully; something hardened; something was lost.

"You can't go now. She'll be all right. We'll arrest him tomorrow when he tries to board his ship. I'm sorry, Philip, but it has to be this way. She'll be all right."

Oddly, he felt no fear, and noted with interest the

veiled panic in Oliver's face. "I'm going to her, my old friend. You'll have to kill me to stop me." Without hesitation, he began to walk toward Quinn.

Quinn held the gun higher, taking aim. "I'll shoot, I swear I will. Don't come any closer!"

Riordan never slowed his pace. "Shoot."

Quinn's gun hand was shaking, his face perspiring. "I'll have to! Don't make me!"

"Do it, then." He stopped a foot away, the gun inches from his chest. He could hear the jerky sound of Quinn's breathing, see the sweat beading under his nose. Very slowly he put out his hand and surrounded the cold barrel with his fingers. He gave a tug.

Quinn let go.

His face collapsed. "Damn you, Philip, he'll get away. We've lost him again."

"I thought that was all you cared about," Riordan breathed, suddenly feeling weak in the knees. "Why didn't you pull the trigger?"

For a long time Quinn didn't answer. Color returned slowly to his bleak, bony features. "Perhaps I'm not altogether the monster you think I am," he said with shaky dignity, straightening his shoulders. "I said I'd always wanted what was best for you. Among all the lies, that at least was true."

"Maybe. Or maybe it's only that your cowardice is even stronger than your fanaticism." He held out the pistol, and Quinn's eyes flickered in surprise. "Here. Take it, I have my own." He patted his waistcoat. "Put your coat on, you're coming with me."

"What?"

"There may be trouble getting Cass out. I need you, and there's no one else. But I want to see you in front of me this time, not behind. It makes me feel safer."

"Philip—"

"Your coat, Oliver. Get moving."

Quinn remained motionless a few more seconds. Something in Riordan's face must have told him that to refuse would be dangerous. He put his pistol in the waistband of his breeches and went to get his jacket.

"Cold, darling? Not much longer, I promise. Let me tighten this a bit here, like so. There. How's that?"

It wasn't the cold that made Cass tremble, though the damp stone cellar was almost freezing. Splinters from the rough wooden wine cask she was kneeling on cut into her shins, but she didn't feel them. She was past feeling anything now except despair.

"This is fitting, don't you think? First the father is hanged for a traitor, and now the daughter follows him for the same crime—and in the same manner. For you, of course, a guillotine would have been more appropriate, but I didn't have time to make one. They're not as straightforward as you might think, by the way. One has to do all sorts of tedious calculations with balance and distance and who knows what, or they simply don't work. Or not at first, I should say. One must try and try again, and it really gets quite gruesome. This will be ever so much better, I promise. What was that, darling? Did you speak?"

The top of the empty cask on which she knelt came almost to his shoulders. She had to look down to see him, but the noose he'd knotted around her neck was already so tight, she could scarcely turn her head. He'd slung the rope across a beam directly above her and secured the slack to a wooden post to her right. Now he gave the taut line a playful tug, making her rise up even higher on her knees to keep from choking. With her hands bound behind her back, she had no way to keep her balance; if she toppled off the wine cask, she would choke to death in seconds.

"I invited John to come and watch, you know, but he declined. Odd, isn't it? He has no qualms about shooting Mr. Burke, but he can't bring himself to witness the simple execution of a traitor."

"Colin," she got out. If she arched her back and craned her neck high, she found she could speak. "Please. Tell me. Why did you betray my father?"

"Who told you that? Quinn," he guessed, when she couldn't answer. "He's a liar—he must've said that to get you to help him. I liked Patrick, actually. He and I wanted the same things. I was sorry when they hanged him."

She tried to absorb this, but new thoughts were already crowding her mind. "Colin," she said again, trying not to whimper.

"Yes?"

"What will you do with my body?"

He came around to face her, his look of malicious whimsy deserting him for a moment.

"I'd like to be b-buried"—she had to swallow to keep talking—"with my father. Please. Don't just —throw me away."

"Bloody hell," she thought he muttered.

There was something else she wanted to tell him, but she couldn't remember what it was. She tried to clear her head. It was important to her that she die consciously, not in a thoughtless, panicked daze. But she was so frightened. Would her neck break when her weight snapped the rope tight? Would there be terrible pain, or only a gradual blackening and then nothing? She prayed for the strength to be brave, whatever happened. And she wished she had her clothes. She hated being half-naked in front of

Wade when she died. Frivolous, perhaps, at this dire hour, but she felt it strongly.

She remembered what she wanted to tell him. "Colin," she choked out. "I forgive you." The words made her cry, she wasn't sure why. It was time to pray for the forgiveness of her own sins, but her mind was too full of chaos. Wade had gone behind her again. She heard him curse her and then give another savage pull on the rope. Her head jerked up and her breath caught in her lungs. Would it be now? Was this the last second? Was this?

But no—he was beside her again. "Listen to me, bitch," he snarled, "I don't need your forgiveness. I'm your executioner. I'm ending your life because you committed crimes against the Revolution." Suddenly his voice lightened. "You've given me an idea, though. I had planned to leave your corpse right here, but now I think I'll dump it on Riordan's doorstep." He smiled at her choked-off gasp, then laughed. "Best would be in his bed, where you've spent so many happy hours of late, but I haven't time now for the kind of ingenuity that would require. If only you'd come a few days earlier, darling, John could have helped me arrange it."

"Please," she whispered, "for the love of God—"

"Shut up! Yes, the bed would've been ideal, but the doorstep will do perfectly well. He'll find your carcass there tomorrow morning when he returns from visiting his lady friend in Somerset."

Through clenched teeth, her low moan of desolation filled the silence between them. She only stopped when, past a blur of tears, she saw him go behind her again. Now, she thought. It's now. She took one last breath. Oh, dear God—

From over her head came a loud but muffled noise. Of what? The walls and ceiling were so thick,

it was impossible to tell. Could it have been a shot?
Fresh sweat broke out all over her. The possibility
of rescue multiplied her terror a hundredfold. Now
there was scuffling, perhaps running footsteps.
Wade came around her slowly, listening as intently
as she; in each hand he held a cocked pistol.

"No one can get in the house," he said aloud,
although to himself. "It's impossible."

But the footsteps were louder now. Cass's bloodshot eyes strained on the cellar door at the top of
the curving stone steps twenty feet away. All at once
a heavy crash sounded as the door slammed open
against the plastered wall. Wade went down on one
knee and took aim with both pistols.

But the first man on the stairs was John Walker.
His hands were behind his back. Quinn had one
arm around his neck and the barrel of a gun in his
mouth.

Wade lowered his arms. He jumped up suddenly
and darted back to Cass's wine cask, raising his
booted foot high and resting it on the rim. She felt
the cask wobble under her and closed her eyes.
When she opened them, Riordan was coming down
the steps behind Quinn.

He halted when he saw her and went dead white.
Her heart stopped beating. She could see her own
shock and horror reflected in his eyes. He leaned
against the wall at the bottom of the steps, never
taking his eyes from her, a pistol in his hand, and a
chaotic mixture of hope and new terror pulsed
through her.

"Don't come any closer or I'll kick this cask out
from under her! Back off!"

"Move away from her, Wade," Quinn shouted
back, "or I'll shoot this man!" He was fifteen feet
from Wade. He'd taken the gun out of Walker's
mouth and put it to his temple.

For eternity, no one moved or spoke. Riordan

stood as if paralyzed, watching the indecision in Wade's face, the pistols pointed at him and Quinn, the boot on the edge of the cask.

"Drop your guns, both of you, or she's dead!" Wade yelled again. He flexed his knee a fraction and the cask wobbled a second time. Cass couldn't control a gasp of panic.

But that horror paled when she saw Riordan toss away his pistol and walk slowly toward her, arms at his sides.

"Philip, no!" she tried to shout, but it came out an incoherent croak.

"Get away from her, Wade," he said softly, moving steadily.

She screamed when Wade's gun fired. But instead of Riordan, it was Walker who crumpled to the floor, leaving Quinn standing alone. Wade was wild-eyed, his remaining pistol moving back and forth between the two men on their feet in front of him, his foot still poised on the rim of the cask.

Cass saw it in Riordan's eyes the second before he made his move, and groaned low in her throat in abject terror. With a hoarse shout, he sprang. Wade's gun hand whipped around toward him and there was another explosion.

Riordan dropped to his knees, holding his bloody shirtfront.

Cass screamed again, but the sound turned into a grotesque gurgle as Wade shoved hard at the cask and she toppled off into darkness. The roaring in her ears was so loud, she didn't hear the firing of the final shot. Before the rising blood blackened her vision, she saw Riordan pitch forward, one hand clutching his chest, the other stretched out to her, his face contorted in agony. Her last thought was that it was no consolation at all to know they were dying together.

XIX

SHE WASN'T DEAD. UNLESS SHE WAS IN HELL, SHE couldn't hurt this badly and be dead. Her head felt as if an explosion had gone off inside, leaving nothing in its aching shell but worthless debris. There was shooting pain down the length of her spine whenever she moved any limb. Her hands and feet were numb, her stomach persistently nauseated. Worst of all was her throat. It was sheer agony to swallow, and speaking was out of the question. It was as if she'd been strangled, as if someone had tied a—

She opened her eyes wide; only the pain in her back prevented her from sitting straight up. She remembered.

Part of it, anyway. The very last part, as the blackness in her head had thickened and she'd thought she had ceased to exist. But unless she was mistaken, above her head was Colin Wade's ceiling, and she was lying in his bed. Had everything been a dream? The tears spilling down her cheeks when she tried to swallow told her it had not. And then a new version of the blackness descended, and she slipped back under it.

The next time she surfaced, someone was holding a cup to her lips and trying to make her drink. Unthinkable. Somehow she made her arms work enough to bat the cup and the woman's hands away—she thought it was a woman—before it was time to sleep again.

Blackness and pain. Light and pain. Blackness again, with its constant companion. Now it was food they were torturing her with. She wanted to cry out her fury and frustration, but making even a tiny sound was excruciating. Please, please, leave me alone! she pleaded silently, using all her feeble strength to fight them off and finally achieving success, of a sort. The blackness returned.

But now a dream was trying to penetrate it, trying to pull away the kindly shroud that curtained her from reality. Her silent screams were futile; she could not wake up. Time after time she had to relive the agony in Philip's face as the bullet struck him and blood spread out across his chest like a blossoming poppy. She was drowning in her tears, breaking apart inside from unbearable pain, but the dream wouldn't stop.

And then a miracle. Someone was shaking her by the shoulders, speaking shrilly in her ear, and at last the awful image receded and she swam up into the light.

"Miss Merlin. Miss Merlin!" Two round blue eyes peered down at her anxiously. "Are you awake now? I'm Dora; Mr. Quinn hired me to look after you. Are you awake?"

Cass nodded, and was surprised when the movement caused only a flickering spike of pain down her spine.

"Then let me run and get Mr. Quinn before he leaves—he was just here to see you, but you were sleeping."

The woman named Dora scurried away, out of the line of her vision; vaguely she heard her diminishing footsteps along the hall and then on the stairs. She was going to get Quinn. Cass's mind tried to absorb what that meant while she waited, gazing vacantly around the room. She lifted her hands and looked at them. Her wrists were chafed from being tied, but there was hardly any discomfort now when she moved her arms. She tried her legs, bending her knees tentatively. A shooting pain, nothing more. She wasn't paralyzed.

But it was difficult to care. She was alive and Philip was dead, and she wanted it to be the other way around.

Did she have to stay awake for Quinn? She was too exhausted even to cry, and she was unspeakably grateful for this fatigue that was keeping anguish at bay. But there he was, gliding toward her silently across the carpet. He looked tired. He was dressed all in black. She wished she could sit up; lying flat on her back in front of him made her feel helpless. But she had no strength to move.

He drew up a chair and sat down close to the bed. "Thank God you're awake. We've been very worried about you, Cassandra," he said in grave, priestly tones.

She wondered who "we" might be, but asked instead, "What day is it?" Her voice came out a whisper, like a dry wind blowing across dead leaves.

"Sunday."

Sunday. She found it faintly interesting that she'd been sleeping for three days.

There might have been a long pause before he spoke, or there might not; she couldn't tell. "You're a very lucky lady, you know. Two things saved your life—the rope was already pulled so tight, there wasn't enough slack to snap the bone in your neck, and your body weight was insufficient to cause you to strangle before I could get to you, lift you, and cut the rope."

She blinked at him feebly. "You saved my life?"

He raised his brows and his lips pulled apart in what she imagined he intended for a smile.

"Then I'm grateful." With an effort, she stretched her hand toward him; but he either didn't see it or pretended not to, and she let it fall to the coverlet, empty. "Is Colin dead?" she asked presently.

"Yes. Walker, too—by Wade's hand." His face grew even more solemn. "I sincerely thought you would be in no danger, Cassandra, and I apologize most sincerely for my error. But thanks to you, the king is no longer in any peril, and we—"

"It wasn't the king he was planning to kill," she whispered, on the brink of exhaustion. If only he would go away. "Walker was going to shoot Edmund Burke in Parliament. On Friday. The letter I sent you about the king was a trick. He told me afterward it was to be Burke."

Quinn's black eyes were huge. He sat back in his chair and stared at her, his mouth open, his arms hanging down at his sides. "Burke!" he managed to say finally. "Yes. Yes, it makes sense. Good lord. Walker was going to do it? He'd have been cut to ribbons, but of course, by then it would've been too late. Good lord," he said again. He leaned toward her, his eyes gleaming with intensity. "Cassandra, you saved Burke's life!"

She shrugged and looked away.

"I still can't believe it! I can't wait to tell Philip —he'll be even more grateful to you than if you'd saved the king," he chuckled, rubbing his hands.

"Quite frankly, Philip hasn't much affection for the monarch." His smile faded. "My dear, are you ill? You're so pale, shall I—"

"He's alive?" she choked out, straining toward him, her face bloodless and drawn. "Philip is alive?"

Quinn looked disconcerted. "Yes, of course he's alive." He seized her arms and tried to ease her back down to the pillow. "Good heavens, I thought you knew! He was wounded badly, but he's recovering." He paused. "Claudia's taking care of him in her home and he's improving every day—oh, my dear. I beg your pardon." He lapsed into silence.

Cass covered her face with her hands to muffle a sob of joy, while her heart broke into a hundred new pieces. He's alive! She thanked God over and over, but couldn't stop the tears that spilled past her fingers and made a hellish burning in her throat. In her fevered brain she heard a low, cultured voice reading to him, saw slim white hands soothing him. She pressed her palms to her heart, but the pain was intolerable. But he's alive! she sang to herself, and it brightened the edges of her darkness.

Quinn spoke quietly. "He wanted me to tell you how grateful he is, how much he appreciates all you've done. He asked me to tell you good-bye. And to give you this."

She reached out blindly for the envelope he was holding toward her. A glance inside told her it was money. Her hand dropped to her side and her eyes closed. She swallowed down fresh tears. "I'm so tired," she rasped hoarsely. "Please—"

"Yes, of course. Forgive me." He got to his feet. "Dora's here to look after you; she'll get you anything you need. Your belongings are here, Philip had them—" He stopped, cleared his throat. "The doctor will be in again in a day or two. He says you need rest, but he expects you to recover fully in about a week. You were very, very lucky, my dear, although I daresay it doesn't seem that way now. But the spirit will revive as the body heals, I promise you."

She tried to smile, but couldn't manage it. For a second she thought he was going to touch her, pat her arm or squeeze her hand reassuringly; but in the end he only made a formal little bow and left the room.

Three days later, he returned. He was gratified to see her looking so much better, he said; did she feel well enough to travel? She told him she did, as an ice-cold wave seemed to break over her heart and she anticipated his next words. Would she like him to book passage for her on a ship leaving in four days for America?

A long moment passed. And then she said yes.

This time he did touch her, a fleeting brush of his fingertips on her shoulder. She'd never known him to be so gentle. "Leave everything to me," he said quietly. "I'll take care of all the arrangements. You can leave directly from here. Dora will do your packing for you. All you have to do is concentrate on getting strong."

She lay still for a little longer after he left, then reached for the bell-rope at the bedside. In a moment Dora came in.

"Yes, miss?"

"I'd like a proper bath today," she said in her hoarse croak. "Will you press my high-necked green gown with the white petticoats? And after that I'll need you to help me with my hair."

"Yes, miss," said Dora, round-eyed. "Are you sure you should be getting up so soon, miss?"

"Very sure," Cass said grimly, throwing back the covers.

* * *

The butler answered her knock almost immediately.

"Is Mr. Riordan here?"

His brows lifted a fraction in swiftly veiled surprise. "No, madam."

"Is—may I speak to Lady Claudia, then?"

"Whom shall I say is calling?"

"Miss Merlin."

"If you will wait here for one moment."

It seemed less than a moment before he was back, begging her to follow him and leading her down an elegantly appointed hallway to an even more elegant drawing room. Claudia's home was everything she'd known it would be, she noted with a sinking feeling. But Philip wasn't here, and that at least was a mercy. She cursed her own cowardice.

It was a moment before she saw Claudia, stretched out on the sofa before the massive marble fireplace, wearing a dressing gown, a blanket covering her lower body. A bandaged foot protruded from the bottom of the blanket and rested on a satin pillow. She was still beautiful, but undeniably ill; whatever angry or unpleasant words Cass might have said to her died on her lips unspoken.

If Cass was surprised to see her in this condition, Claudia was looking at her as if she were a ghost. Swallowing her nervousness, she walked straight over to her. "I'm sorry to disturb you," she said huskily, "but I didn't know you were ill. I only wanted to ask you a question."

Claudia still stared. Finally she recovered enough to cry, "Philip said you were dead!"

Cass flinched as if she'd struck her. Tears threatened, but scathing anger saved her from that humiliation. "It seems he exaggerated," she bit out. "Where is he? Is he here?"

"Here! No, of course not. He's at home."

So, he was well enough to ta'ṣ care of himself

now. She wasn't sure if she was glad or sorry. "I see. Then I won't trouble you any longer."

"Cas—Mrs. Riordan, are you all right?"

"I'm not Mrs. Riordan," she snapped. He hadn't even told her that, so she was innocent of Philip's treachery. Her feelings toward Claudia ought to have softened, but they didn't. "I'm perfectly well, thank you. Good afternoon."

And she left Lady Claudia as she'd found her, staring at her with her mouth open.

It felt strange to knock at the door she was accustomed to walking freely in and out of. She waited, resisting the need to lean against the doorpost; only an hour out of bed, and already she was exhausted. A man she'd never seen before opened the door. Walker's replacement? "I'd like to see Mr. Riordan," she told him.

"I'm sorry, miss, but he's not receiving visitors; Mr. Riordan is ill."

"I'm aware that he's ill," she said tightly. "I want to see him anyway."

"I'm sorry, that's impossible."

The man was big enough to fill the doorway, and he was not going to let her in. Frustration made her grind her teeth. "I have no card, but if you take my name up, I think he will see me." She thought no such thing; in fact, there was an excellent chance he would refuse to see her. But she knew she had to try.

"Very well, miss," the man conceded impassively. "Whom shall I say?"

She told him her name, detecting no flicker of recognition in his face.

"Very good. Would you care to wait in the hall?"

"How kind," she murmured, struggling to keep sarcasm out of her tone. She went inside, and immediately sank down on the armchair in the foyer while the butler, or whatever he was, ascended the staircase and passed out of sight. She rested her head on the back of the chair and closed her eyes as fatigue swamped her. She almost hoped he wouldn't see her. She lacked the physical and emotional strength for a confrontation now. Oh, Quinn was right, she should have gone directly away, not subjected herself to this! It couldn't possibly be anything but painful. But Riordan didn't deserve such passive self-exile from her. That he was telling people his "wife" was dead proved he expected her to accept her banishment docilely, but she was not going to disappear so conveniently for him. Not quite yet.

She heard loud, quick footsteps coming along the upstairs hallway. In a moment she recognized Beal, Riordan's valet, coming down the steps, wearing the same expression on his face she'd recently seen on Claudia's.

"Mrs. Riordan!" he exclaimed, staring, shocked. "We thought you were dead!"

The bitterness rising in her throat stung like acid, but she managed a tight smile for Beal's benefit. "Not quite," she grated. "Is Mr. Riordan well enough to have a visitor, do you think?"

"Why, of course! He's sleeping, but he—why, he'll be—"

"Surprised," she finished grimly. "Then I'll go up. It's all right, I still remember the way." She left him standing in the hall, staring after her in amazement.

She might have seemed cool and collected to Beal, but she was trembling with nervousness as she walked down the dim hallway toward Riordan's bedroom. To survive the next few minutes, she needed to concentrate on the kind of man he'd proven himself to be. Liar. Hypocrite. Seducer. She paused with her hand on the knob to gather

her wits, and to drive out of her mind the demoralizing realization that despite all that, she was still in love with him. She pushed the door open soundlessly and went in.

The room was dark; the only illumination came from the fire in the grate and two candles burning at the bedside. She stood listening to the silence and feeling the pounding of her heart. As her eyes adjusted to the dimness, she saw that he was asleep. A cowardly voice inside her reminded her that it wasn't too late to leave. She shook it off and moved purposefully toward the bed.

She folded her hands under her chin. A slow frown marred her features. Why, he was so thin! She could see the sharp, elegant bones in his face under the day-old stubble of beard. His black-and-silver hair had been brushed back from his forehead, and his face was paler than the white pillows piled around him. His nightshirt was unbuttoned to the waist; under it a thick white bandage was wrapped around his chest. One hand rested on his stomach, the other at his side. His eyelids flickered once, as if he were dreaming.

Cass bit her knuckles, hard, but it didn't stop the fierce, helpless rush of love. Speaking her mind to him seemed suddenly pointless. She hated herself far more than she hated him. "*Damn you*," she whispered, and turned to go.

A flash of something gold on the bedside table stopped her. Her hand trembled as she reached for it. Her ring. The warmth of it in her hand went straight to her heart. *You and no other*. She swallowed painfully and dashed away treacherous tears. Why had he kept it? It slipped from her fingers as she tried to put it back, and landed on the table with a soft clatter. She stood perfectly still.

Riordan opened his eyes and looked at her.

Instead of reacting, he only rubbed his hand over

his eyes in an oddly weary gesture and dropped his arm back to the sheet. He looked up again, and this time he frowned at her. And blinked. Shook his head and rubbed his eyes again. He pushed himself up a little on his elbows. He cleared his throat; his voice was tentative, almost amused. "Cass?"

"Hello, Philip. I came to say good-bye." She took a step back and clasped her hands at her waist so he couldn't see them shaking. She was ridiculously aware of how low and raspy her voice sounded. "I didn't realize you were so ill—if I had, I wouldn't have come."

He sat up a little higher, though the movement seemed to pain him. "Cass?" he repeated.

She'd thought he couldn't go any whiter, but he did. She began to feel concern, but hid it behind angry words. "It seems you told so many people I'm dead, you've begun to believe it yourself!"

Riordan drew in his breath sharply and his eyes burned with a fierce light. "Cass!" he whispered, and threw back the covers.

The vulnerable sight of his bare legs under his nightshirt caused her to feel a dangerous softening. She suppressed it. But when she realized he meant to get up, she rushed toward him and gently pushed him back down.

He clutched at her arms and wouldn't let go, staring at her as if he'd been struck by lightning. "Oh God, tell me I'm not dreaming," he breathed. "I've seen you so many times. Is this real, Cass?" He put his hands on her face and tried to draw her down to him, but she took his wrists and pulled away. She hoped she knew better by now than to let him touch her.

"It's real," she said tersely, backing away again. "Stop it, Philip. Don't!" But he wouldn't stop. He threw the covers off again and tried to stand. "Oh!" she cried, exasperated, and went back to him. "You shouldn't do this! Will you lie down? No, stop it—"

But he had his arms around her and was holding her tight between his knees, sitting on the edge of the bed, trying to look at her and bury his face in her hair at the same time. "Hold still, Cass," he grunted, "you'll hurt me." And finally she stopped squirming.

"Damn you," she almost sobbed, standing stiffly, but unable to keep her arms from going around his shoulders.

"Wait, now. Wait. Don't curse me, love."

"I curse you to hell forever, Philip Riordan." Her whole body was shuddering. She breathed in the smell of his hair, his clean flesh, mortified that he could feel her tears now on his own cheek.

"Cass, Cass," he crooned hoarsely, "I think I understand what's happened. Just let me hold you." His heart was so full, he couldn't explain it to her yet. He closed his eyes and cupped her thin shoulder blades in his hands, pressing her against him as hard as the wound in his chest would allow. He could feel the long, shuddering tremors running through her body. He gentled his hold and pulled back to look at her; the pain in her eyes went straight to his heart. "I love you so dearly," he whispered.

She sighed and turned her face away. "No more lies, Philip. I'm begging you."

He slid his fingers into her hair and made her look at him. He had to ask. "Did Wade hurt you?"

She shut her eyes tight. "Yes," she murmured brokenly. "But he didn't rape me. He tried, but he couldn't." She couldn't tell him more. She opened her eyes. As strange as it seemed, the look on his face made her want to comfort him. Her fingers fluttered to his cheek in a helpless, fleeting caress.

"Listen to me," he ground out through his teeth.

"Quinn told me you were dead. I saw you hanging."
He couldn't repress a shudder of revulsion at the
memory. Softly he unbuttoned the high neck of her
gown and folded the cloth away from her throat.
The sight of the scarred, abraded flesh brought
tears to his eyes. "Oh, sweet Cass."

She blinked to clear her vision. Was he crying for
her? The worst pain of all was the pain of hoping.
Numbness was better. And yet he'd said . . .

"Quinn told you?" she quavered. "Quinn—"

"Told me you died. And I wanted to die, too."

"But—he told me you said good-bye. He said
you were staying with Claudia. He gave me money
from you and said I was to go away!"

He made an anguished sound and pulled her
close again. "It was all a lie. Oh Christ, I thought
you were dead." He slid his hand between them
and pressed it against her heart.

It was racing, and her mind with it. "Philip," she
breathed, beginning to weep again, "then it *was* all
a lie? Are we truly married?" He kissed her where
his hand had been, then raised his head. He didn't
have to answer; she saw the truth shining in his
eyes. "My love. Oh, my love. Forgive me, I should
have believed you."

He touched his fingers to her lips, parting them
softly, and then he kissed her. They were both
shaking. He held her breasts, feeling her breath
tremble in and out of his mouth. "Yes, you should
have believed me," he murmured, watching her
eyes darken as he kissed her and kissed her.

Cass's fingers clenched on his forearms. "But he
showed me your letter," she cried, remembering.
"You called Claudia 'my dearest,' and you signed
it, 'all my love.' And then you went to her." She
pulled back. "Didn't you?"

He sighed. "Yes, but—"

Suddenly she put her fingers on his lips. "I don't care. Don't explain. It doesn't matter, as long as you love me."

His mouth quirked; he wondered how long she would sustain that attitude. "I *will* explain it, because it's important for you to understand, but not right now. Now I only want to hold you." They rested against each other, touching, softly stroking, listening to the miracle of their breathing. Cass put her lips on his forehead and closed her eyes, her hands pressed lightly against his back. He trailed sweet, open-mouthed kisses on her skin, brushing her hair aside with his lips, murmuring against her neck. "Can we lie down, sweetheart?" he asked presently. "I haven't sat up this long in a week."

"Oh!" She almost jumped away. "Are you hurt very badly, Philip? I thought *you* were dead, before Quinn told me. I saw you fall, and then—" She couldn't continue.

"No, no," he assured her, taking her hand, "I just bled a lot. The doctor said Wade's gun must not have been loaded right." He waved his hand, dismissing the subject. "Aren't you going to lie down with me? You're sick, too, you know." He grinned, almost cackled, as he thought about how they would recover together, side by side in their big bed. "But take some clothes off first, Cass. You'll be—too hot like that."

"You're a shameless seducer and you always have been." With tears still shining on her cheeks, she couldn't stop smiling. She tucked him in on his side, then stood with her hands on her hips. "If I take my clothes off, do you promise to behave?"

"No," he answered promptly. "But since I can hardly stand up, you won't be in much danger. Worse luck."

She hesitated a second longer, then began to

undress. She flushed a bright crimson under his burning stare, and by the time she got down to her chemise her nerve failed.

"Oh, don't stop," he said huskily, the humor in his eyes not completely able to hide the pleading.

She watched him, her lips parted, her color coming and going with every breath, and pulled her shift over her head. She scampered around to her side of the bed and jumped under the covers, showing him only a blinding white streak of moving skin.

He put his arms around her and drew her close. "Was that you or a flash of lightning I just saw running across the room?"

She giggled, snuggling closer. "I'm so happy," she sighed tremulously. Resting a light arm across his stomach, she could feel the strong thud of his pulse, though it might've been hers. It didn't matter. The wind blew, rattling the windows. Winter would come soon. She'd always hated it, but now she welcomed it, looked forward to it. To be with Philip when it was cold, when it was snowing, raining, blowing—or when it was warm, hot, balmy, sultry—She shivered in ecstatic anticipation of everything that lay ahead for them.

"What?" he asked, his lips on her temple.

She shrugged helplessly. "I'm so *happy*," she said again, though now the word seemed pitifully inadequate. She could feel him smiling. They lay together for a long time without saying a word, in acute and perfect peace, and it was as if their bodies and spirits healed more in those moments than they had in all the long days in their lonely, separate beds.

"Philip," Cass said at last.

"What, my love."

Her rusty voice was tentative. "I know Oliver has hurt us terribly—you especially, because he was your friend and you cared for him and trusted him. I don't know why he did what he did. It was unbelievably cruel, and selfish, and arrogant. He caused so much pain, so much unhappiness—I know all that, and yet—all the same, he saved my life. He didn't have to do it, he could so easily have let me die. But he didn't. For that, at least, I can't hate him."

"No," he said, stroking her cheek, "nor can I. In a way I feel sorry for him. The impulses that drive him aren't normal. Somewhere in my mind I knew that, but I ignored it. I called him single-minded, but I think I always knew it was more than that, even as a child. In some ways what happened was as much my fault as his, because I refused to see him as he really is."

"No, Philip, you weren't—"

"It's true, Cass. I needed him to be perfect. My mentor. My father."

"Perhaps he needed you to be his son, as well. Someone he could control. Your brother said he needs to possess people. Philip, I'm convinced you never hurt Oliver, or anyone else. I can't tell you how he got that scar on his wrist, but I know you didn't give it to him. I *know* it. And he used your guilt to make you help him."

Riordan lay very still, thinking. Gradually something dark and heavy inside him seemed to lift and shimmer for an instant in bright light, then disintegrate in a shower of sparks, leaving him free. "I love you, Cass," he whispered.

"I love you." She caressed his throat with soft, soothing fingers. "And do you know, Philip, in spite of everything, I think Oliver loves you, too."

"Yes," he said sadly, "I believe he does. But he'll pay for what he's done, I promise you. It's ironic, but I have more power now than he does—and partly because of him. And I can make him pay."

He felt her shiver and tightened his hold. "Don't think about him. He can't touch us anymore. The only thing that matters now is kissing you. Now, right now." He did, tenderly. "Do you know what a miracle this is, Cass? I thought you were dead." He shook her a little, wanting her to understand the enormity of it. "And here you are in my arms, in our bed. It's as if *I've* died and come back to life."

"I love you, Philip. I'll always, always love you." She closed her eyes and kissed him back, propped up on her elbow, leaning over him but careful not to touch his bandaged chest. Soon they were both breathing hard. His restless hands on her bare skin under the covers were making her moan. They pulled away at the same moment. "Darling," she gasped, "I want to make love with you so much. So much. But we can't do this, we have to stop. You know we do."

"Do we?" He ran his hands through his hair and paused to let his heart slow. She was so good for him; she was better than medicine.

"I knew I shouldn't have taken my clothes off."

"No, you *should* have taken your clothes off. That was the best part."

"Yes, but we should read or something. Or ring the bell and have some food sent up. Are you hungry?"

"I'm starving. I'm dying of hunger." He turned toward her, but she dodged his descending lips.

"I'm serious," she laughed. "If we don't stop, you'll hurt yourself."

"I wouldn't if you'd hold still."

There was merit in that. He saw acquiescence in her eyes and moved in again. She held still for as long as she could stand it. "Oh God," she groaned, clutching at him much harder than one ought to clutch at a sick man. "We can't! How can we?"

He kissed her again, then pulled his mouth away

just far enough to make himself intelligible. "There's something I never told you about the Commons."

She blinked dazedly. "The Commons?"

"To become a Member, a man has to demonstrate resourcefulness, inventiveness, and a willingness to meet terrible obstacles head-on." She tried to see his face, but he held her steady. "Cutting right to the point, I have an idea. Would you like to hear it?"

She nodded slowly.

He put his hands in her hair and murmured two explanatory sentences in her ear.

She pulled away and stared at him. "God, I love this country," she breathed, awed.

Two months later Philip and Cassandra Riordan stood before the Bishop of London in the Lower Chapel of St. Stephen's in Westminster. In front of a hundred of their closest friends, they exchanged vows of love, obedience, honor, and fidelity. A collective sigh of satisfaction rose from the wedding guests when the unconventional ceremony was over, for the bond of devotion between the bride and groom was shiningly obvious even to the dullest among them. Still, some thought the post-nuptial kiss was more enthusiastic than need be, and went on a bit long for perfect seemliness.

Sir Wallace Digby-Holmes elbowed his companion in the ribs—Mary, was it? Or Maria?—and sent her a wide leer. He took a proprietary interest in the goings-on. He'd smarted a bit at first over not being chosen best man again, but now he was taking it philosophically. After all, Edmund Burke was a great and famous statesman; you couldn't really fault Riordan, a rising star in the Whig party now, for picking him over his humble self. Then too, Burke was vaguely rumored to be in the groom's debt for something or other, no one knew quite what. Something heroic, people said, and that pretty wife of Riordan's was supposed to be in on it, too. It sounded like wild gossip to Wally. The last time he'd seen the happy couple, they hadn't been able to keep their hands off each other, and today things looked pretty much the same. Apart from anything else, he didn't see how they'd have had *time* to be heroic.

Conspicuous by his absence was Oliver Quinn, once the groom's closest friend. Word had it there was a rift between the two men now. At any rate, the king's faithful servant was toiling for his sovereign in the Indian colonies these days. Some place called Chandragupmatawan, where the heat was so intense, at noon you could fry a piece of meat on a rock. In the shade. Or so it was said.

The bride's matron of honor was her dear friend, Jennie Willoughby. Her cousin Freddy and his new wife sat in the front pew, nodding and smiling. Even her aunt, who was no longer Lady Sinclair but plain Mrs. Edward Frane now, and who sat beside her new spouse in the next row back, seemed moved by the ceremony. Either that or, if one believed the wagging of vicious tongues, she was weeping because her niece's husband was so much richer than her own.

Clara, the bride's maid, and Beal, the groom's valet, sat together in a back pew. "Well," sniffed Clara, wiping her eyes with Beal's handkerchief, "that's done, i'n't it? Don't she look a sight, though? I'm the one told 'er ter wear 'er hair up like that," she couldn't refrain from confiding.

"Oh, yes, lovely," said Beal, who was admiring the cut of his master's blue velvet coat, which he'd pressed himself this morning. When Clara gave him back his handkerchief, he captured her hand and held it quite boldly, though continuing to stare

straight ahead. "What'll you gamble, Mistress
Clara, that there's a new addition to the Riordan
household before the year's out?" he murmured
insinuatingly, giving her hand a squeeze and her
middle a wee nudge with his elbow.

"Ooh, la, I ain't a wagerin' woman, Mr. Beal,"
answered the maid with a becoming blush. She
turned her face from him as if to admire the crowd,
but really to hide a smile. She could take Mr. Beal's
side of *that* wager without so much as a blink, she
could, and lay him heavy odds on it to boot. For her
mistress had told her this very morning, with that
lovely gay laugh of hers that could make a day-old
corpse sit up and grin, that she was already two
months gone.

ATTENTION PREFERRED CUSTOMERS!

SPECIAL TOLL-FREE NUMBER
1-800-481-9191

**Call Monday through Friday
12 noon to 10 p.m.
Eastern Time**

*Get a free catalogue;
Order books using your Visa,
MasterCard, or Discover;
Join the book club!*

Leisure
Books

LOVE
SPELL